DIVINE APPOINTMENTS

DIVINE APPOINTMENTS

Susan Maria Lotto

Copyright © 2006 by Susan Maria Lotto.

Library of Congress Control Number:		2005902925
ISBN:	Hardcover	1-4134-9168-5
	Softcover	1-4134-9167-7

All rights reserved. No part of this book may be reproduced or transmitted in any form or by any means, electronic or mechanical, including photocopying, recording, or by any information storage and retrieval system, without permission in writing from the copyright owner.

This is a work of fiction. Names, characters, places and incidents either are the product of the author's imagination or are used fictitiously, and any resemblance to any actual persons, living or dead, events, or locales is entirely coincidental.

This book was printed in the United States of America.

To order additional copies of this book, contact:
Xlibris Corporation
1-888-795-4274
www.Xlibris.com
Orders@Xlibris.com

28544

For the sick and suffering . . .

ONE NIGHT, A man had a dream. He dreamed he was along the beach with the LORD. Across the sky flashed scenes from his life. For each scene, he noticed two sets of footprints in the sand; one belonged to him and the other to the LORD.

When the last scene of his life flashed before him, he looked back at the footprints in the sand. He noticed that many times along the path of his life there were only one set of footprints. He also noticed that it happened at the very lowest and saddest times in his life. This really bothered him and he questioned the LORD about it, "LORD, you said that once I decided to follow you, you'd walk with me all the way. But I have noticed that during the most troublesome times in my life, there is only one set of footprints. I don't understand why, when I needed you the most you would leave me." The LORD replied, "My precious, precious child, I love you and I would never leave you. During your times of trial and suffering, when you see only one set of footprints, it was then that I carried you."

From Footprints
By Margaret Fishback Powers

ACKNOWLEDGMENTS

IN MUCH THE same way that "*it takes a whole village to raise one child*," it took a large support network to help bring this novel to fruition. More importantly, it took the nurturance and guidance of my own personal "star angels" who helped me through my growth process, and in doing so, enabled me to complete this book.

I wish to thank the early contributors to my intellectual and clinical development: Dr. Paul Florin, Dr. Art Swanson, Dr. Sharon Maxwell, and Dr. Kirkland Vaughans. The ripple effect of your instruction and supervision has touched hundreds of lives.

I would also like to acknowledge the many "special" co-workers and administrators of the various mental health, chemical dependency, and foster care agencies in which I have been employed over the past two decades: Ms. Brenda Hart, Ms. Jean Williams, Ms. Lynette Brown, Ms. Teresa Ukattah, Ms. Gayle Crick and the multitude of dedicated employees at Family Support Services Unlimited, Inc.; Mr. David Jablons and Ms. Catherine MacRae of The Institute for Community Living; Mr. "B" Addison and Mr. Steve Hunt of The Alpha School for Progressive Living; Mr. Alan Blumenson of The Children's Village; Ms. Sandra Dizengoff of Canarsie High School; Mr. Martin Robinson, and all of the other devoted residential and group home child care workers with whom I have worked side by side. You treated clients as they should be treated—like human beings who are worthy of dignity and respect. The applause for your efforts echoes throughout the heavens.

My deepest appreciation to those who filled in the gaps when my fund of historical facts was porous: Ms. Sabrina Bryan, Ms. Patricia Sarles, and Mr. M. Karl Leeds.

I also want to thank those who graciously offered me technical support: My sister, Linda Lotto, Mr. Lawrence Neuman, Mr. Arthur Goldstein, Ms. Nellie Vogelsohn, and Leah Panzer.

True friends come far and few between. I consider myself blessed. Thank you to my loving friends, Sabrina, Mamie, Cheri, Kimberly, and Dexter, for being you.

Tambien, muchas gracias a mis amigos de La Republica Dominicana: Monica, Judy, Frito, Omar, Mundo y la familia.

Five years ago, when my soul was crippled, the Lord sent one of his "star angels" to an Al-Anon meeting to give me crutches until I was able to walk on my own again. God Bless You Holly.

The strength of a great woman is measured by her wisdom, patience, virtue, capacity to nurture, and the ability to love all of God's children as if they were her own. My sincere gratitude goes to you Jubae, "my second mother," for always being there. You are truly one of this world's unique blessings.

Troy, if the Author of Creation decides to have me draw my last breath tomorrow, or in another hundred years, thoughts of you will be amongst the few that linger in my mind in my last dying hour. I am eternally grateful that I had the opportunity to experience a love that was *"like the color blue."*

A heartfelt thanks to my Aunt Jean whose exuding kindness never ceases to amaze me.

Without a doubt, I was blessed with two "star angels" shortly after my birth. A special thanks to my parents for teaching me to believe in the goodness of the human heart. You watched over me, you let me go, and never doubted my ability to succeed. I am the product of your faith and love.

A final thanks to my Higher Power for listening to my prayers and trusting in me to deliver his message to the world in its divinely appointed time.

WHEN I WAS little I thought that each of us had star angels above in the vast velvety darkness, twinkling and tinkering about so bright, carefully watching over us as the nighttime dangers lurked about, chancing to prey upon a lost vulnerable soul whose angel had momentarily carelessly looked away. As I grew older and observed the multitude of evil that infiltrates the lives of many living in Glory, Glory Hallelujah America's many inner-city dwellings, I adapted my original naive notions. Bearing witness to our industrial cities' frequent starless nights, I figured that the reason why so much malevolence pierced our inner city contingency was because our angels simply could not see us. I used to believe that the world was a just and semi-good place. And then I grew up . . .

CHAPTER ONE

IT IS 1998 NOW and I just turned twenty-eight years old. I was born on June 13 in 1970 as our world left the crazy, political sixties, anticipating a respite in the freshly, but haphazardly, carved-out seventies. Don't know what happened in other parts, but the seventies, and then the eighties, wreaked havoc, spiritual demise, hatred, and a hell of a lot of pain where I came from in New York City. Same as I heard it did in Detroit, Watts LA., Chicago, and the ghettoes of sun-drenched Miami. I was born in the infamous Women's House of Detention at Riker's Island in Queens, New York. Due to my eighteen-year-old mother's acquired passion for heroin, and the consequential tenacious hold that it had on her infirmed, convulsing body after having only been recently incarcerated and therefore without her drug of choice for four days, I was born prematurely, unexpectedly if you will, and very, very addicted. Although Mama never spoke much of my initial entrance into this world, nor of our fortuitous bonding, I learned through randomly overheard conversations with her street comrades, and subsequent subjection to bits and pieces of psychosocial material while in the grips of different social service agencies, that I was born in the middle of the night in a dank cement cell amidst her drug-starved tremors and agony. The way I heard Mama tell it once before, lighting up a casual joint with one of her welfare hotel associates was, "Yeah, I was fucking shaking so bad that my water broke. And there she was before I had the chance to scream for help from any of 'dem stupid police' . . . Did it better myself anyway. 'Dem ol' police wudda just fucked everything up." "Ain't that right?" was my mother's associate's reply. "Hell yeah, damn this here's some good shit, huh?"

Like I said, I don't know too much about my first few days of life, but I heard that when it was all said and done, and Mama had completed her business by herself, she hollered for somebody to take her newborn, drug-addicted daughter from her so she could be left alone with her monkey on her back. I was told that New York City had long before made accommodations for unfortunate birthing situations such as mine. The powers above transported me to some New Age social reformation—a prison nursery. I believe I was left in relative close proximity to my mother for two to three weeks for "bonding purposes," and then transported to my first foster home experience. An incipient welfare recipient in the making. I don't know exactly how much bonding transpired between me and my mother during those first few weeks of life. In addition to the prison's iron-clad rules concerning appropriate visiting hours for mother-child bonding, I would imagine that Mama was more invested in severing all ties with her monkey than interested in forming new attachments with the likes of the quavering, agitated me. But she must have spent some time forming an elusive early bond because it was during one of those initial contacts that she said that she stopped feeling sick long enough to look into my beseeching, pain-stricken eyes to decide upon naming me Victoria. Mama said that she once learned that the name stood for strength, victory, and power—all the qualities that she lacked, but hoped like hell would somehow find their way into my tormented, but yet searching eyes.

Well, maybe now is a good time to explain why I am writing this. It sure ain't because of any underlying literary creative genius that's patiently waiting to enfold some artistic masterpiece. Oh yes, of that you can be sure. Who but the life-starved Jerry Springer watching housewives with cheating husbands and rug rat kids would be interested in somebody else's misery anyhow? Now, let me set the record straight before I go any further. I am writing my autobiography, aka tragedy, solely because I was directed to do so by my relentless, but beloved NA sponsor who has finally reached her peak of frustration with my apparent inability to smoothly, or even "unsmoothly," proceed through the requisite twelve steps of my almost daily Narcotics Anonymous fellowshipping. In other words, my growth seemingly came to a dead halt—*bleep*. While I had no trouble at all admitting that I was a die-hard drug addict with its typical accompaniment of "dysfunctional" asocial and amoral life patterns, I simply came to an abrupt stop—dead end—when I had to start talking and believing in all that mess about a higher spiritual power greater than myself, etc., etc. Now I figure that if I want to stay clean I had better be honest with myself in all facets of my recovery process, and in my concerted effort at honesty, I can't talk any mess about this higher power business, and then analyze myself within the context of this unique spiritual relationship, with my present Victoria-centered, rather atheist convictions. In one of my sponsor's far and few between exasperated outbursts, she said, "Well, how the hell do you think you got to where you are now anyway?" I sheepishly responded, "By myself." Now don't get me wrong. I don't hold anybody at fault for believing in the heavens and all of that holy stuff if it benefits them. To each his own. But as far as I'm concerned, I believe I've done real good for myself, by myself. I'm coming up on my first year clean, and that in and of itself is one hell of an accomplishment, bigger than two mountains that are laid atop of one another, if you ask me. In addition, I work a legal job, support myself without the begrudging assistance of my long-lost friend, Mr. Welfare, recently took some courses at a community college, and still try to increase my educational knowledge on a regular basis by looking up such things as vocabulary words when I don't know them. I also don't have any unwanted babies that I unthinkingly brought into this crazy world without the appropriate emotional equipment to care for them. (I guess the last personal achievement don't count for too much though since part of the reason I don't have any miniature Victorias running around yet is also due to a miscarriage during my teens and two abortions during my twenties. Don't really want to put a feather in my hat that doesn't go there.)

Anyway, as I was saying before I rudely interrupted myself, my NA sponsor finally exhausted herself of all possible rationales, pleas, and threats to get me to believe in a higher spiritual power. She made me read that parable "Footprints" so many times that I can recite it verbatim, upon command. You know, the one that talks about the guy on the beach who, after triumphantly surviving all of life's trials and tribulations, realizes that God carried him through the acme points of all of his times of suffering. Now it's a nice inspirational paragraph and all, but ain't no spirit but the spirit of Victoria ever carry me through anything, unless of course, you want to talk about those E.M.S. folk who carried me twice to the hospital emergency room. The first time was when I was stabbed in my side when some goddamned fool was actually stupid enough to believe that I was someone who had something worth robbing when I was almost twenty. What the hell would I have given him except some foul-smelling, semen-blotched-up holey drawers, if I was even wearing any. The second time was when I was so high on some bad crack, I'd have wished for that same fool to come by again to stab me up some more. But this time, not carelessly missing any vital organs, so we could have all been rest assured that I'd be out of my misery once and for all. Anyway, not trying to sound selfish or supercilious or nothing, but I think I'm a modest enough type of person to admit if I ever bid acquaintance with any benevolent spirit type. Nope, I believe I did it by myself—to the top. But I trust my sponsor and this NA thing enough to follow through on any seemingly logical or beneficial task that they put before me. You see, my NA sponsor believes that somehow, after retracing the haggard, torturous steps of my life, I'll understand that like the guy in "Footprints," a higher spiritual being carried me all the way. I think she's crazy, and we may be witnessing one of the more fine and subtle cerebral dysfunctions resulting from her past polydrug addictions, but what the hell. I promised to stay clean, no matter what. This must be one of the "whats."

OK, now that we are all crystal clear about the truthful origins of this paper-and-pen journey, let me make some apologies from the get-go before we get into the less censured autobiographical ying yang. My first apology is for my tendency to jump around a lot—take you all around the block before I finally get back to the business of my original point, if I hopefully haven't forgotten it as yet. That, I'm sure, will happen often too. But you see, although it was never officially diagnosed by any of the university-learned, experientially endowed professionals who were hired to figure out what exactly made me tick, and stay afloat or submerged in dysfunction, depending on how you looked at it, I believe I've always had a touch of that Zeitgeist syndrome Attention-Deficit/Hyperactivity Disorder (ADHD). But, no matter how schooled you are, people, particularly disinterested and uncaring people, will see what they are looking for—what's most simple. Since, as I am told, only one out of four children with ADHD are girls, there obviously weren't too many preconceived notions associating me with ADHD and those other little boys with ants in their pants that were born with a positive "toxicology." God only knows how they diagnosed me—probably with just plain simple craziness, if there is such an official diagnosis.

You see, I just did it—flew right off of my original point through a garden variety of similar and dissimilar others. Anyway, my mind generally works like that, always has, and probably always will. Sorry.

My second apology is for my inclination to abruptly and mercilessly switch up on you with my writing style as if the real author of this is "The Two Faces of Victoria." In other words, we could be going along oh so smoothly, and I'll successfully be trying out some of my newfound vocabulary and grammar, and then whammo, I'll jump right into my familiar vulgar street lingo with you like we were all chilling in the fucking hood. This will especially happen when I get emotional. I think it's the same thing that happens to most Puerto Ricans I know. They could be talking English just as nice and fine as any other American, but let them get excited or passionate about something, and they revert back to their Spanish just as fast as the bill collectors come on the first day of the month and pre-adolescent boys come the first time they're near their "shorties" and even think about having sex. I think it has something to do with our first language—our most familiar form of communication that we will undoubtedly revert back to when our emotions have been pricked to the point of bringing our more tender selves to the surface. That point at which intellect, and everything else, flies right out the goddamned window. Such is the case with me. Not that I will spew forth in Spanish. I only know a few words in Spanish despite my Dominican extraction. What I mean is that when boxed into the four walls of the emotional space of my past or present, guarded by the emotional defense police that resists entry from any unwanted intellectual intruders, I will quickly alter my communication patterns by donning familiar verbal garb. To those of you who find it offensive, my sincerest apologies are extended.

Thirdly, I apologize to each and every one of the characters that you are about to meet, most of whom are dead or at least incarcerated for life in penal institutions or in their own man-made, irreversibly destroyed, hellish souls, for all of my participation in wrongdoings toward them, and equal ignorant acceptance of their wrongdoings toward me, as we blindly, but yet propelled by greedy, prejudiced, and equally ignorant specters of civilizations from our pasts, grappled with our existence in the land of the brave and supposedly free. I apologize for not getting to know them better, and therefore for being unable to allow the full intensity of their inner life forces to shine through in this composition, before their souls were impenitently encrusted over by their individual hardships, doused dreams, traumas, and insurmountable pain. One of the things that I have learned through NA and my concomitant willingness to open my eyes, remove any motes of egocentric dust from my lashes, and perceive all walks of society with a purer heart, is that we all have a story to tell, of equal importance and magnanimity. Nobody is perfect, and given what we have, we generally all try to do the best we can. The times, places, and characters may change, but the themes are unfortunately, and fortunately, perennial and eternal. I apologize for not having stumbled upon this truth sooner, thereby perhaps having had more timely opportunity to sprinkle some of this simplistic essence on to those people who walked behind, in front of, and at times, side by side me during my youth. Those miscreant, misunderstood, memorable creatures that dwelled in the projects, welfare hotels, burnt-out cars and buildings, and porous, tin-can shanty shacks from around the new and third world countries of this planet, that made their mark on me, on our communities, but never really had the opportunity to explain themselves. Maybe if I would have known then what I know now, it would have made an iota of difference. Maybe it wouldn't have. Maybe it would have been nice to try and wait around to see. Maybe there's still time. Maybe there's hope.

For all of this I apologize. Yes, I am truly sorry for everyone who never had a star angel observing and watching over them, not even but for one moment in their entire lives.

My ultimate apology is extended to my mother, deceased now from an AIDS-related illness for about twelve years—another frail, ill-fated individual who, without ever having experienced the watchful nurturance of her own star angel, attempted to give me mine, by placing the last of her hopes and dreams into a name while looking into the eyes of her newly born, helpless infant in a prison nursery twenty-eight years ago. Victoria—meaning strength, victory, and power. Mama, I'm sorry that you never had the opportunity to try and wait around to see.

CHAPTER TWO

I cried because I had no shoes. Then I met a man who had no feet.
—Steven Wright

WHEW! I JUST did it—just banged out that first chapter, now didn't I? Didn't show it to my sponsor yet, but I bet she'll be mighty proud, although perhaps somewhat disappointed that I haven't come any closer to being spiritually awakened than before stirring up any of this business from my past. Yeah, yeah, I know, upward and onward, valiant soldier.

OK, so where were we? Oh yeah, we were just getting to the part where I was released from jail for the very first time and likewise had managed to successfully kick my first drug habit. A point, as you will see, that was unfortunately not a point of no return. On hell, they say that the apple never falls very far from the tree. I think it falls even less far from its initial seedling experiences. It's almost prophetic.

So what happened next? Let's see. Well, Mama stayed at the Women's House for about sixteen months in total. That incarceration was due to her slapping the mess out of some foreign store owner who tried to stop her from stealing sweet cakes from his corner grocery store. When New York's finest came on the scene, she was hollering and cussing like usual, pockets full of sweet cakes, swollen belly full of me, had the man backed up against his own store counter with her pointed twitching finger inches away from his face, high as hell, with another incriminating bag of dope stuffed in her otherwise empty change purse in her worn coat pocket. And then, had the nerve to turn and start up on the police. Yep, that was my mama, if you caught her on a good day. Just like I heard "dem ol'" Harlem preacher boys say—all fire and brimstone. Anyway, that little stunt landed her in the Women's House of Detention, and me, in the first of my multiple experiences with New York City's progressive foster care system. Perhaps, though, it was a good thing, Mama being arrested like that just days before my delivery. Maybe this is a prime example of how fate sometimes works in strange and mysterious ways. Lord knows I could have as easily been born in some alley. Or worse yet, with one of Mama's horrific drug-addicted cronies from the male species in the nearby vicinity, whose deflated conscience could have easily allowed him to discard me in some abandoned lot or garbage pail as soon as Mama turned her head, blinked her eyes, breathed too deeply, or nodded out into a narcotic-induced flight from consciousness. Picture that. Me, perched on some putrid, maggoty nest of garbage, with flies and roaches picking at my skin. While I, feverish and convulsing, and too young and undifferentiated in my neo-natal stage of development to have acquired any recognition of normalcy, would have somehow arrived at the sagacious conclusion that I would have been better off dead. So, in comparison to all of my infant peers whose addicted mamas did not end up incarcerated and were instead laid out to rest on a man-made mountain of artificial and organic decay by some emotional zombie, I guess I was pretty lucky. Blessed, if it will make my sponsor happy. But what the hell kind of luck is that?

I remember I once came across a same-age foster girl in one of my many foster homes when I was about nine years old. She told me her name was Ann and that I was very lucky. Ann asked me whether my mama had ever beaten me. I flatly told her no. She then told me that I was lucky. I didn't feel too lucky, and since her matter-of-fact identification of me as lucky began to prickle my every nerve, I proceeded to defend myself by generating a list of all of Mama's transgressions, one by one, as if they were permanently etched in my lifetime memories' chronicles. All of them, with one significant exception—she had never beaten me. Hence, I began, "Mama often left me alone, placed me in the temporary care of losers, drug addicts, alcoholics, thugs, whores, sociopaths, mental patients who weren't hospitalized but should have been, and with practically any other wretched soul from the bowels of humanity who could not conjure up the presence of mind to say 'no' quick enough when she asked them to mind me for just a minute." I continued, "Mama unknowingly starved me at times, kept company with the dirtiest, meanest men from every borough in NYC who used to mercilessly beat her and me, couldn't and didn't do shit when I was fucking child molested, made it virtually impossible for me to get a consistent education, placed me in more schools and inhumane living conditions than you got hair on your head, and never thought of me once when she carried on like a fool, cussing up a storm or beating somebody upside their head. And you call me lucky, humph." "Yep, just like I said," replied my temporary foster sister, "You sure is lucky." With that I peevishly marched away, turning her words over in my mind, trying to figure out if she was crazy or whether I had somehow missed something in my daily lessons about life. After mulling it over in my mind for about fifteen minutes, I finally determined that she was insane—

so insane, that I'd be happy to give her my monthly appointments with the agency psychiatrist as a small token of my sympathy, and decided that I was not going to waste one more tidbit of time cogitating over such nonsense.

Luck was supposed to mean that you hit the number or lottery for lots of money. It should not come down to two pre-pubescent girls disputing over which of their young lives contained the least of all evils. The latter was not luck, but insanity in motion.

Now looking back, who knows? When I was twenty-three and some change, was freshly released from one of NYC's Department of Correction's Secured Drug Rehabilitation Programs, and was finally "wanting to want" to do some serious thinking about turning my life around, breaking the cycle so to speak, I encountered a pretty, but very skinny, white woman in a psychiatric clinic that I needed to attend in order to obtain a psychiatric clearance for permanent residence at the halfway house in Staten Island in which I was residing. Our paths crossed. Her appointment was for 3 PM. Mine was for 3:30 PM. Upon leaving the clinic, I had just missed my bus. Her inconsiderate male friend had "dissed" her by not showing up. So, we made the best out of a bad situation, said "Fuck it," and headed for McDonalds for a late lunch. I ordered the number 1 Big Mac Value Meal. She ordered plain tea because she, as I shortly thereafter discovered, was a recovering anorexic and very, very thin. And from the looks of things, it seemed that she wanted to stay like that. Clueless about eating disorders prior to our encounter, I thoughtlessly chomped away on my Big Mac and large order of fries. She, while looking away from the food on our table, briefly summarized the disease of anorexia, its formidable hold on many well-to-do, educated white folk from rather plush suburban communities with unrelenting rigid and controlling parents, and the subsequent slow, unconscious suicidal deterioration of its victims' physical and emotional beings. All I could say was "Well, goddamn, ain't that something, well goddamn." Even when she queried me about my past and my reasons for being involved with the psychiatric clinic, my mind remained stuck on the foreign waters of pain from different shores, and all I could say was "Well goddamn, ain't that something." Staring at me wide-eyed now, the extra skinny woman must have figured that I was crazy and in frequent need of psychiatric assistance due to an ongoing flagrant psychosis. Nonetheless, all I could do was repeatedly murmur, "Well, goddamn" in breathy whispers until I finally pushed my remaining fries aside, grabbed my drink, and stumbled out into the street, mumbling "Well, goddamn" all the way back to the halfway house.

Life's lessons sometimes come in small and big doses. This was an extra large one deceptively wrapped in a very skinny package. What had crystallized vividly in my mind was that pain, like people, comes in all different forms, shapes, colors, and sizes. It is sometimes blatant, it is sometimes subtle. But it is always more easily alleviated when we lend an attentive ear, offer a helping hand to its present victims who could have just as easily been ourselves, or probably were at a different time, in a different place, in a different form.

Well, in case you were anxiously waiting to bear witness to a prime example of what I was referring to in my first apology—meaning my inclination to take you for waltzes around the block—you must have just been pleasantly relieved, or even fluttering with excitement. I mean there you were, expecting to hear about my neonatal foster-care experiences, and instead we end up in the land of luck at McDonalds with white ladies who starve themselves by their own hand, and then, once again, in the ever-flowing murky waters of pain. Sorry, but perhaps this time my slip was unconsciously purposeful—if you can understand that—as opposed to being completely unintentional, as it is guaranteed to be in the future.

I simply don't recall a thing from my first year and a half of life. Plus, Mama, nor any of her cohorts, was around to tell me about it later. I plainly don't believe folk who talk about possessing vivid memories of their first few months of life, including their birthing. I mean, experiencing withdrawal symptoms at age day 1, being in a jailhouse makeshift nursery, and then being passed from stranger to stranger for the first eighteen months of life, seems like a pretty memorable package of experiences if you ask me. And I don't remember shit. So, like I said, I truly don't get what those folk with the grand memories are talking about. Probably just making it all up.

The only sacred detail that I can offer you is that during the middle of January, when I was about six months old, I was brought to my second foster home on an emergency transfer basis. I once overheard one of my childhood social workers tell somebody the story on the phone when Mama, five years later, went and got herself arrested again for stealing soap and bread out of a bodega, and I, like usual, was awaiting another foster home placement. Anyway, in the case of my second foster home placement, I honestly don't believe that its emergency nature was directly related to anything that happened to me. I believe the entire lot of us—four kids in all—were abruptly removed from the home when our foster mother burnt the three-year-old little boy's heels to teach him to stop running out of the apartment whenever she would beat him. I don't remember his, what must have been, deafening and bone-chilling screams, but since hearing about it, I've always imagined.

My second foster home placement must have been uneventful. I remained there without being removed again for an entire year until Mama was released from Riker's Island and situated in some form of "adequate housing" for mother and child. Hence, at eighteen months old, I began living my life with Mama, and our bonding process picked up from where it had left off the last time.

CHAPTER THREE

I'll always love my mama . . .
—The Intruders

MAMA WAS NOT an inherently bad person. She was simply a hollow soul by the time I got around to knowing her. Oh, I know I do my share of badmouthing her on occasion. It just seems easier and simpler to point the finger in another direction at times, especially when explaining a completely macabre situation. Definitely simpler than pointing at oneself. But Mama, like many other accursed, despairing people I know, was doomed before she was ever conceived, forget born. She did the best she could with what she had, which was virtually nothing.

During the period that the human race has basically reserved for joyful, carefree play, unconditional love, guidance and affection, and a day-by-day enfolding of exciting, inspiring, and mysterious new learning experiences, my mama was resolutely schooled in one life area only—daily survival skills. For her entire life, that was Mama's only objective, plan, and hope—to survive each day, one day at a time, and still be physically alive by nightfall. This was her only skill, and all she knew and cared about. For this reason I always knew she loved me, albeit in a peculiar kind of way, because she, as any mother animal does with its young, attempted to pass on to me her only mastered skill the best way she knew how—through modeling, observation, practice, and repetition. And for that, I loved her back.

Mama's major problem was drugs, and Mama always used drugs. Lots of them, in every variety, and with every possible method of getting them into her body. There wasn't one new trick or concept you could have taught Mama about drugs, except one—how to stop using them. However, by the time I came around, she didn't want to. Unlike me, Mama wasn't born addicted. She might have been born small and unhealthy due to her own mother's early adolescent age at the time of her birth—thirteen, to be exact—and destitute living conditions, but she surely wasn't born with any chemicals in her system. That came shortly after. I guess the fact that Mama always did drugs with such fervor throughout my entire life, it just seemed like she did them forever. But she didn't. Mama probably started at about the age of nine or ten.

Unfortunately, Mama was just one of those people who couldn't afford to use drugs. Not ever. You know how some people can eat enough for an entire hog family and still stay slender as a rail, while others look at chocolate cake and put on pounds. Or how other people can smoke two packs of cigarettes a day until their skin shrivels up, hair falls out, and spinal chords bend from old age, and can still puff away until the cows come home, while others smoke one pack a day for five years and drop dead from lung cancer. Well, it always seemed to me it was a similar situation with Mama—Mama being the one to blow up like a balloon or develop lung cancer in a day. Like it was in her genetic constitution or something—chromosomes lined up to form the message in huge bold italics. JUST SAY NO! But Mama didn't say no. I guess we'll never know what would have happened if she did.

So drugs became Mama's first love, her deity, linked with her survival instinct. Somehow the two interfaced. But in the end, the drugs won out.

Mama used drugs everywhere—in our far and few between apartment situations, in the shelters and welfare hotels where it was forbidden, in the streets, in prison, and in drug rehabilitation centers when she was court-mandated to attend them on an in-patient basis. Once, while high off some free-based cocaine, Mama bragged to me that she was the youngest client at her first few drug rehab programs, and the first one to figure out how to sneak drugs into the facility. That was Mama—to know her was to love her. Usually.

Mama was born in an impoverished, squalid community of tin can and grass huts in the Dominican Republic in 1952. Her mama, who was Haitian and thirteen years old at the time, became impregnated by a white Christian missionary from the United States who raped her and forbade her to tell, less it hinder his godly status and reputation, of course. My grandmother, along with her parents and older brother, was one of many cases of Haitian folk who had somehow managed to surreptitiously cross over the Haitian border into the Dominican Republic in search of a better life without getting caught. We were always a resourceful, although reprobate, family. Anyway, shortly after crossing the border, my grandmother's father took off. Abandoned his entire family. Typical. So, my starving great grandmother and her two pre-pubescent children slithered into the outer perimeter area of a poverty-stricken skeletal Dominican village and fortunately were not asked to leave. Every night, all three managed to force themselves into the remnants of a straw shack that someone had abandoned, or more than likely, condemned. I was told that the shack was about the size of a big doghouse, only more porous. By day, the family of three helped tend the sugar cane fields in exchange for food scraps. After living this life for approximately six months, my great grandmother took ill, laid herself down amidst the flies and rubbish on top of the dirt, and died two days later. I have no details to provide with regard to who, with what, where, or how she was buried.

A kind and generous, but also extremely poor Dominican woman, who lived more toward the center of the shack community, took pity on my grandmother and took her into her slightly larger abode, which at least had rags stuffed in the roof's holes. My grand uncle remained by himself in the straw doghouse.

The years passed. Everything was going along just fine. Until one day, along came the missionaries, filled with God-fearing law, knowledge, and morality, just bursting to impart some of their sanctimonious ways on to the ignorant, underprivileged, seemingly barbaric hicks of my grandmother's perishable village. One of them kept one eye on the Bible, and his other, on thirteen-year-old grandma.

One day, as dusk approached and my grandmother was finishing her work in the fields, her brother told her to take a short walk with the preacher man down the dusty road. She went, and my grand uncle went back to his doghouse lodging to lie down to rest, with two extra pesos to rub together in his pocket. The missionary raped my grandmother about ten minutes later, and sent her back to her hut with nothing but his admonitions.

So, you see, from my mother's blood, I received a mulatto heritage—half black from my Haitian grandmother and half white from my American grandfather. But my mother was born on top of Dominican soil, which makes me legally half-Dominican. (I am clueless with regard to my father's identity. However, given my complexion, we've always surmised that he was black.)

Mama never spoke too often of her childhood spent growing up in the Dominican Republic. In fact, Mama never spoke much at all, except to make perfunctory statements or directives to facilitate coexistence. She definitely did not sit around talking about her feelings or telling stories about her past. And when she did, her eyes did most of the talking.

Before I continue, let me describe Mama for you so we'll all feel more familiar with one another. (We'll get into my physical attributes later.) Mama was of average height and weight, although carrying a disproportionate amount of body weight in her hips, upper thighs, and behind. Mama's hair, which tended to be dry and wiry, but not quite kinky, was of the color that you typically only find in folk of mixed races. It was a fawny kind of sandy color, gilded with streaks of paling gold and cinnamon. Her skin, which by the time I got around to knowing her, was the color of very light coffee, flawed by a disorderly arrangement of scars, crescents, and discolorations from her collection of life's mementos. Barring the blemishes, Mama's face, much like her body posture, was best described as average. She had high cheekbones, but a small enough nose and thin enough lips, to soften the intensity of their prominence. It was her eyes that were Mama's most mesmerizing feature. Eyes, that if you dared stare into long enough, bore right into your soul and made you feel the discomfort of many a generation, somewhere deep down in the pit of your stomach. Without the finishing touch of her eyes, unless, of course, Mama was engaged in one of her typical rowdy bellicose outbursts, she could have rightfully been described as one of those women who could have passed down the street without anybody bothering to give a second glance. But not with those eyes. Her eyes were captivating. Embraced by long black, inky lashes, Mama's eyes were big, bold, and hazel, emblazoned by strokes of amber and a light shade of emerald. Indeed, it appeared as if Mama's eyes contained jewels of the most exotic nature. And the angrier she became, the more those jewels blazed, radiating with such intensity that most folk just backed down fearing that their skin would be scorched by her glare alone. Yes, looking back now, I believed it was Mama's eyes, and her accompanying forceful stare, that kept many human forces of evil at bay. When she was not pained or angry, and her eyes were not identical to those of the angel of the bottomless pit, they were dazzling, sexy, captivating, and simply beautiful—although they primarily magnetized a demonic assortment of men.

As I was saying before I rudely interrupted myself again, Mama never generated a hell of a lot of information about her life in the third world Caribbean. In fact, I had no clue she retained any Spanish communication skills at all. (Stupid me, until her knowledge of Spanish was unexpectedly demonstrated to me, I had always taken it for granted that her mama had communicated with her in Haitian-Creole. But, now I realize that my grandmother, who was literally already living on the edge of the Dominican settlement, probably had to do everything in her power to "acculturate" into the Dominican community as quickly as she could. The survival instinct must filter through our genes.) I learned that Mama understood Spanish one evening when I was approximately nine years old. We were in the back of a small corner grocery store in the Bronx, about ready to purchase some Heinekens, and Frosted Flakes for my dinner, when three Puerto Rican men in their twenties entered the store. With the exception of the three Latino men, the store's owner and all of its patrons, were black. Mama's ears subtly pricked up as two of the men rattled away with one another as they passed us by. As soon as they were about to turn the aisle's corner, Mama quickly flung the cereal and beer on top of the canned juices, pinched me on the arm as hard as she could, eyes looking like they were on flame, and quickly propelled me out of the store. Once outside in the musky night air, Mama hauled ass to the inner vestibule of an adjacent building. Just as I was about to question her, I heard it—pop-pop. Then I saw the three men flee into an awaiting car across the street and drive off in the direction of the Grand Concourse. That's how I learned Mama still understood Spanish.

I learned Mama could talk in Spanish approximately three years later when we were ejected from a welfare hotel for the zillionth time. This time we were at the hotel on 116th Street in Far Rockaway, which I liked because of the close proximity to the beach, but did not like because it felt like we were at the end of the world. Mama was caught getting high in the bathroom, although she had been warned about using drugs on the hotel's premises once before. Besides, the hotel "administration" was already wary of her other clandestine illicit behaviors. Namely, sex for money and/or drugs. Anyway, we were ejected and in search of other available modest accommodations. Hence, one day while trying our luck back in Harlem in terms of rummaging about for rooming, Mama ran into one of her street chums—an emaciated, balding, Panamanian woman who looked like she had put too many spikes in her arm—who eagerly told Mama about a very cheap two-room basement apartment right off of Manhattan Avenue in Spanish Harlem. She told Mama that the small building's manager/ superintendent, who lived on the premises, was an ancient dilapidated alcoholic who, if he liked her, would take her in immediately and never bother her again. In fact, my mother's toothpick, skinny friend assured her that if she threw him a bottle at the end of every week, he'd be sure to keep an eye out, "If you know what I mean." It sounded like a match made in heaven. Too good to be true. But there was one teeny-weeny problem. Even I, in my meager twelve-year-old wisdom knew that. A small problem, but yet powerful enough to drown the entire suggestion—hook, line, and sinker. That's why, once again, I stood with my mouth agape when we started heading over toward the Spanish side of Harlem where the Puerto Ricans and Dominicans lived. I was so taken off guard that my feet remained firmly planted in place, as if they had sprung roots into the concrete. Probably still be standing there, except Mama turned around, hand on hip, eyes beginning to glitter, and said, "Victoria, what you waiting on, standing there all froze up. You better hurry the fuck up on. We've got an apartment to see about." I started to open my mouth to respond, but then thinking about it twice, clamped it down shut. Granted, Mama was a little off in certain ways, a true-to-definition nut case in others, but she sure as hell wasn't stupid. If Mama thought we had a fair chance of getting this apartment, then I guessed the fair chance was there to be had, because my mama never gambled with assumptions. But had I not witnessed Mama starting off in the direction of Spanish Harlem, I would have made the intelligent guess that our chances of getting this apartment were slim to none. You see, at least in those days, people preferred to stay with their own kind. It was just easier and safer that way. I don't believe it's a human natural instinct to be like that—so clannish—but I believe we've been forcibly segregated for so long, it's rather become conditioned into our pattern of relating. Anyway, in the early 80's in Harlem USA, the Puerto Ricans lived with the Puerto Ricans, the blacks lived with the blacks, and the West Indians began to form their own salient groupings. That meant that Spanish Harlem was for the Latinos, and not for me and Mama's black asses.

When we arrived in front of the four-story building, the superintendent was outside, slightly tilting to one side, jabbering away in fluent Spanish with two other Latinos. And my mama, who never ceased to amaze me, God rest the dead and bless her soul, seized my hand and strutted right up to them Spanish folk, and started spewing forth in Spanish. Her "Dominicana" spirit had been temporarily reawakened.

We got the apartment, and like the moribund Panamanian woman had forewarned, the superintendent never bothered Mama again. In fact, we stayed in that basement apartment longer than in any other apartment ever—almost three years. But, just to be on the safe side, shortly after moving in, Mama initiated this good-natured ruse to guarantee our continued welcome. From the corner of our avenue to our apartment door, as well as inside the corner bodega, Mama only spoke Spanish, while I, dumbly nodded my head up and down and occasionally blurted out, "Si, si."

While potentially useful bits and pieces of skills, lessons, and experiences were obviously engraved in Mama's running stream of life's remembrances, she rarely spoke of her childhood, and when directly queried, would typically avoid providing specific details or any mention of associated sentiments, as if the actual act of conjuring up her past would be an unbearably painful experience. Mama, who, by the time I reached school age, had become so seemingly oblivious and impenetrable to the guileful tendrils of pain, actually winced, as if she had accidentally bit down on to some caustic substance, every time she was queried about her early years in the Dominican Republic or of her subsequent migration to the United States. A very subtle, practically imperceptible, flinching of her shoulder muscles, was similarly observed whenever a plane passed by overhead. Once, when we had a relatively decent housing situation that was in very close proximity to La Guardia Airport, I noticed a fat, lone tear cascade down Mama's face as she sat, as if in a trance, when a particularly loud jet rumbled through the sky. Despite the improvement over our general living conditions, we moved out of the apartment two days later.

With the exception of my knowledge of vague, inconsequential, and personally meaningless details about Mama's past, such as "It sure was hot there—hot as fucking Africa," I finally learned the more complete package of Mama's life in the Caribbean with its accompaniment of pale joys, vicissitudinous sufferings, and precocious exposure to the incisive truths about the more dark and cruel side of human nature. The lesson came about one day when Mama observed through our apartment window the tail end of a pre-pubescent, boisterous, verbal dispute between me and a younger, somewhat smaller, and definitely uglier, pitch-black Jamaican girl who had recently moved into the building around the corner. I was in the midst of calling her all kinds of "banana boat, blood clot black spots," telling her "to go on the fuck back to where she came from," when I heard Mama call me to come upstairs. I was rather surprised when I heard Mama's voice projecting out into the street in all directions, primarily because she typically left me alone to tend to "my own business," but also because it was already sunset on a balmy summer night and I figured she was setting about her business to go out into the streets for the evening. When I went upstairs, Mama was looking at me, almost sideward and very strangely, as if in a deja-vu type of reverie, but she wasn't high. Not on any chemical substances anyway. She eventually returned to a more alert state of consciousness and gestured to me as if to ask, "What's up?" Still adapting to the strangeness of this unprecedented questioning experience with my mother, I shrugged my shoulders and briefly summarized how I was avenging a fight from the previous day in which my victim's older sister had pulled out a handful of my hair before I accomplished to blacken her eye, draw blood from her lip, and pummel her plump body on to the sidewalk. Mama said, "You shoulda' kicked that bitch up the pussy too—now sit down, I want to talk to you." On that evening, way past the sky transforming into an inky blackness, the moon and its extension of stars lazily embedding themselves into the blanket of darkness, the young children carrying their sweaty, dirty bodies into airless, cramped, and often morose apartments, and the assortment of bums, addicts, and human scapegoats finding solace in some hallway, basement, or alleyway with their chemical substances of choice, Mama explained to me the origin of that one lone, fat tear, and the gallons of others that she was too emotionally deflated and frightened to shed. The small gaps in her vignette of her first seven years of life were filled in four years later from her death bed after I begged her to let me into her heart, even if but only for a few hours, so that I could share one precious, invaluable memory of her life before she died.

Mama began . . .

Mama said we Americans wouldn't know poverty, real poverty, if it took off its hat on a street corner, shook our hands, and slapped us dead up in our spoiled little faces. Mama said our children's wants and needs were usually trivial in comparison to the daily cries for food scraps and shelter of our sisters and brothers from far away lands. And Mama swore that we were clueless with regard to the secret of self-possessed happiness. She felt our futile search for inner tranquility and spiritual joy was buried, and then misdirected, on to fallacious and superficial paths by ignorant powers of being many, many years ago. Unfortunately, years of oppression, pain, and ignorance had turned our existence here on earth into the old doleful adage—life's a bitch, and then you die.

Don't ask me how, but Mama always believed in the Lord, his kingdom, and all of the Biblical teachings—except for one. She believed that it was not when the first man plucked the apple off the tree in the Garden of Eden, but when the next man came along and pulled off a second apple, began to compare his apple to the first, started to belittle the first man for his "different" apple, and then set about to construct a status hierarchy of men and apples, that our real problems began.

Mama remembered her childhood in the Dominican Republic as being a time period in which she often had a starving, empty belly, rank squalor up to her knees, no bathroom facilities, no electricity, no familiarity with any indices of formal educational systems, about two, maybe three articles of clothing to wear over her body each year, and a ridiculously cramped shelter made from multiple combinations of rags, straw, cardboard, and pieces of aluminum. But life was simple and she didn't recall ever being unhappy. Her mother's love for her was indubitable, and regardless of their pitifully small rations of food at night, and worn, ill-fitting, mismatched clothing, when she looked up into her mother's eyes, her heart and soul were filled with an ineffable peace and wholeness. Mama and most of her people did not have any timepieces or calendars, but they understood the significance of the rising and setting of the sun, and they understood the passing of seasons and years. And they were extremely gifted in the areas of patience, nature, tolerance, gratitude, community, and survival.

According to Mama, she generally frolicked about with the other Dominican children on the fringes of the sugarcane fields under the hot sun and mindful eyes of a few elderly women while her mama and the rest of the community tended to the fields. Afterwards, they bathed and, as needed, washed their clothes in a nearby stream, ate, and then rested under the shade of familiar trees. Such natural events as rain and intense heat were taken in stride, casually and easily, without complaint, and in the virtual absence of irritated sentiments. People made love, delivered babies, argued, laughed, and passed through their daily routines with a similar quality of simplicity, smoothness, and emotional levity. People often took ill and died young. The life transition was also perceived, and undergone, in a wieldy, uncomplicated manner.

Mama had two favorite memories. The first was of those evenings during which the family with the old, weathered, battery-run radio would play the static-filled merengue music in front of their shack, and in so doing, invited the entire community to join them to a night of dancing, singing, knee-slapping, hand-clapping, and socializing. Mama described how she would sleepily slap her hand down on her thigh to the beat of the music while lazily lying sprawled on top of her mama's lap. Mama's second favorite, and quite vivid, memory involved receiving the one and only tangible gift that she ever received from her mama—a used rag doll with a marred plastic head displaying the blonde, blue-eyed face of a Caucasian girl-child.

The story goes that when Mama was about five years old, which would have placed her mama somewhere around eighteen, an older Dominican man saw grandma while visiting his family on his day off from work at the rum factory. He must have liked what he saw because after that first Sunday, he came around on a lot more Sundays—some Saturday nights too—to pass some time with grandma and occasionally take a stroll in the fields with her at night, way after my mama was asleep. It was during one of these visits that the Dominican man brought grandma the rag doll as a token of his affection. According to my mama, although grandma swore he bought it, my mama believes he must have found it along the roadside—a toy that some rich tourist kid discarded so she could holler for a bigger and better one. I guess we'll never know the truth about that.

Anyway, when Mama woke up the next morning, she found grandma sitting there grinning a wide, toothy smile, arms stretched out to present her with her first real toy. Somehow, before Mama had awoken, grandma had even found a glossy purple ribbon to tie around the doll's neck—just to make it all official like, you know. Well, if my mama wasn't just as tickled and jubilant as a child could be, laughing and squealing with delight, convinced that this was the very best and sunniest day of her entire life. The way Mama told it you could not convince her that there was a more perfect doll anywhere on the planet. No, my mama had found her joy—signed, sealed, and delivered within the essence of a used ragged doll, as well as in the understanding that it was symbolic of her mama's unmitigated love and devotion. Hence, she named it Felicita—meaning "little, happy one" in Spanish—to represent the presiding emotion in both the donor and the recipient of this significant, although unfortunately portentous, gift.

Mama simply adored Felicita. She clutched her against her thin, little bosom when she slept at night, took her to play in the sugarcane fields, set her upon a rock to keep her company while she bathed in the stream, and coddled her while eating her sparse meals. As time passed, she eventually succumbed to the imploring request of the other little children, allowing them to play with Felicita by talking to her and stroking her, as long as she remained in an extremely close and safe proximity. Mama and Felicita were, from the very first day they met, best of friends, and attached at the hip. Only on one occasion, when grandma pulled a switch off of a tree and beat Mama's bear mischievous behind for sneaking a few peaks at some grown-ups doing the nasty, did Mama release her hold on Felicita and turn her to face in another direction so she would not be directly privy to her moments of shame and humiliation. Although, as all best friends eventually do, Mama shared with Felicita the details about her chafed, smarting bottom before she closed her eyes to go to sleep that night.

Overall, Mama was happy, and what was more important, she recognized it. (If you're happy and you know it, clap your hands . . .) That was, up until one day when Mama was approaching her seventh birthday and it became obvious that grandma had taken very ill. Grandma was about twenty, and up until then, while always pathetically skinny, had generally managed to maintain good health. But now, her typically slender, petite body frame was appearing increasingly gaunt, languished, and flaccid. Grandma had constant diarrhea, a limited ability to prevent herself from regurgitating any form of nourishment she swallowed, and a body temperature that unpredictably vacillated from being flushed with fever to trembling from unexplained chills in the middle of sunny eighty-five-degree temperatures. Mama also said that grandma had a wracking, phlegmy cough that abruptly surfaced from the deepest chambers of her respiratory system and exhausted her from its unrelenting, raging grip on her infirmed body. Mama was scared, but not nearly as frightened as grandma who realized that her death would eventuate in the demise of her daughter as well. Grandma knew that while she was once upon a time and long ago accepted into the Dominican community, at least as accepted as was possible for an illegal Haitian alien to be, there was absolutely nobody who would assume responsibility for her child. Nobody. Even if there was an isolated bleeding heart in the crowd, people in those days were entrenched in their own poverty, in the inextricable hopelessness of their own daily existences, and in that of their children's. They could not afford to squander one morsel of generosity in a stranger's direction, less they would find the inexorable bony finger of death pointed in their own direction. Grandma was quite aware that it was considered an auspicious blessed event to live a long healthy life in a settlement in the backwoods of the impoverished third-world country in which she resided; and given the shadow of the shade of the frown that passed over the medicine woman's brow when she consulted with her about her symptoms, grandma was equally well aware that she was not one of the chosen blessed few. Grandma knew that she was dying, and while she could perhaps handle her own pending physical death, she did not have the endurance to withstand the anguish of leaving her daughter behind to a similar fate. While grandma was beside herself with worry and concern, Mama's emotions ran the gamut from fear to sadness, from despair to neutrality. Perhaps it was because of the innocence of her young age, or perhaps it was a foreboding of Mama's uncanny ability to ward off any uncomfortable emotion with denial, but Mama managed, albeit with the occasional intrusion of unwanted fret and gnawing grief, to continue going about her childhood business, while grandma went about her business of dying. Although behaving as if unaware, Mama's future appeared very bleak until one day . . .

While resting in the shade of a tree with a cool rag thrown across her forehead, grandma looked up, and though initially believing that the fever had caused her to become completely unhinged and prone toward hallucinations, she realized that what she saw before her was not a mirage at all, but instead a circuitous response to her incessant prayers about saving her daughter's life. The missionaries had returned, and Mama's father was in the lead, stirring up the dust as he trudged up the road. And then, as if under easy sail, carried from the heavens and effortlessly placed into her clouded thoughts by the most propitiate and beloved of seraphs, grandma got an idea.

That night, way after the rest of the community consoled their exhausted bodies with sleep, grandma quietly slithered out of Mama's embrace and crept out the door, propelled by a fiery passion, straight down the makeshift dirt path to the straw doghouse-looking hut in which her brother continued to reside. She stuck her twig-like arm into an aperture on the side of a lopsided wall, and shook the sleep from her estranged brother firmly, not permitting him to give her his back and shrug her off until morning. When grandma's brother dragged himself from out of his shelter, stood erect, and swallowed saliva to moisten his desiccated throat, he looked at his invigorated next of kin curiously with one eye, while continuing to rub the sleep from the other with his loosely clenched fist. Grandma immediately gripped him stiffly beneath the elbow and led him to sit down in the moon-illuminated darkness on top of some paralyzed stumps. With a voice as forceful and potent as the goddess of war, grandma informed her brother that since it was initially his selfish greed and egocentricity that indirectly resulted in Mama's conception, he was going to atone for his venomous sins by playing the lead part in a ruse that would hopefully guarantee Mama a more fulfilling and fortunate life. In many ways, grandma made her brother an offer he could not refuse. Now I'm not trying to suggest that grandma held any physical or monetary threats over her brother's head. She had about as much actual clout and power as a cow about ready to enter a slaughterhouse. But she had three omnipotent pieces of artillery in her favor. She was armed with righteous convictions—fighting for what, beyond a shadow of doubt, was rightfully due to her and her offspring. She was fighting with an emotional energy that was fueled by a loyal and effervescent love for that which was created and fashioned within her own body. And she was fighting her brother, her own flesh and blood, who had acted out of desperation with the unthinking mind of a starving, angry, and needy adolescent boy, orphaned at fourteen years old, and destined to live the remaining years of his life burrowed into a wretched facsimile of a straw doghouse on the fringes of an impoverished Dominican community, of which he would never became a proper member. He, without question, had been in pain and had missed his mama too.

I've come to learn that guilt is a powerful emotion. It compels us to respond in the strangest of ways. Some of us spend a lifetime denying its presence—one of our more silly endeavors. Once guilt wraps its stalwart talons around our hearts, it's there to stay, for better or for worse, in sickness and in health, regardless of our feeble attempts at denial and impassivity. Ironically though, it's just when we acknowledge the presence of our guilt, and perhaps pass a comment about its notorious, unbeatable grip, that it hesitantly, almost imperceptibly, loosens its hold and eases its way out of our lives. Grandma, with all of her best intentions and Mama's well-being in mind, reached into the reservoir of human spirituality that night and plucked the right chords to persuade her brother to acknowledge his repressed guilt's presence. And in doing so, set off a chain of events that were critical in molding Mama and my future destinies.

On a day that appeared like any other, my grandma's brother approached Mama's father while he was perusing his Bible in solitude. As directed to do by grandma, he flatly informed the God-fearing status-conscious missionary that he had reneged on their secret pact of many years, in that he had spread the truth about the sordid details surrounding his niece's conception to many a willing and eager-to-listen Dominican ear within the community. Energized by the gradual waning of his own guilt, as well as by grandma's forceful words, his own renewed sense of righteousness, and the missionary's seeming weakening demeanor, grandma's brother threatened that unless Mama's father acknowledged paternity by immediately taking Mama back to America with him he, and a large faction of the community, would reveal the truth about their past impious agreement and the consequential rape to the superiors of his church. This, he stated he would do, regardless of the potential consequences he would have to endure. And for good measure, grandma's brother made it clearly understood that should he have to carry out his stated threat, he would make sure that in addition to advising every one of the missionary's church associations about his pedophilic and sacrilegious indulgence, he would personally make sure that the news traveled to his wife's and children's ears as well. Although probably feeling that this trifling and dispensable shadow of a black man who was, and always would be, in a subordinate position, should be wiping the dust from between his toes instead of standing erect in an eye-to-eye position making audacious, recusant threats, the missionary man, swallowed his pride along with his surging nausea, and mutely nodded his head in agreement.

I don't exactly know the specifics surrounding grandma's expectations and dreams of the New World—America. But I gather, from the bits and pieces of Mama's fragmented memories about her unsuspecting declarations, that grandma believed that America was verily the land of milk and honey—the promised land that rumors described as having streets of gold, sparkling crystal towers, innumerable opportunities, opulence to be shared by all, and a democratic governmental system that espoused the policies of equality, liberty, and justice. Although nobody in the community had ever been to the cinema, or dreamt of going to one for that matter, stories and descriptions were passed from word of mouth of those who had heard information from their relatives in the capital, Santo Domingo, seen pictures, or perhaps knew someone who had once gone to the movie cinema. And grandma believed with all of her remaining might, that she had successfully fulfilled her maternal obligations by providing her child with a one-way ticket to the promise of a good life, although she would never have the opportunity to wait around and see.

Anyway, given the missionary man's probable uneasiness about grandma's brother's threat, things moved rather quickly after their little meeting. I'm not exactly sure how he negotiated all of the requisite paperwork that facilitated their quick getaway, but I surmise men of the church have their ways. Although the time period involved remained a hazy blur in Mama's memory, her best conjecture was that it took about one week for the paperwork to be processed and her departure date for the New World to arrive. And as she sadly recalls, she had that same one week to share life's precious gems of time, and bestow her last words and gestures of love and affection, on to her dying mama.

Despite the fact that the preacher man had allowed himself to be blackmailed, the truth was nobody else in the village had really known the circumstances surrounding grandma's conception, nor would they ever since my grandmother's brother would never have had the actual balls to come head to head with anybody of a superior status. So, although grandma had disclosed the identity of her father to Mama, as well as the fact that she was going to spend some time with his relatives in America, the community's inhabitants knew nothing of Mama's pending migration. All of their conversations and farewells were held in hushed whispers.

Mama did not want to go, and in no uncertain terms, did she want to leave her mama. She cried and she whined and she pleaded, but when it was all said and done and Mama knew she was defeated, she raised her little chin with a rising sense of strength and courage, and with rivulets of tears streaming from her eyes, asked with a quavering voice if she could bring Felicita along too. From what I understand of this situation, Mama, in her not-so-naive, childlike manner, understood that grandma was dying and that she was never going to have the opportunity to see her again, comprehended that she was going off to some strange, distant land with a white man who grandma avowed was her father but who had not yet once cast a glance in her direction or so much as uttered her name, and sensed that her entire life was about to be turned upside down. But, Mama somehow managed to find strength and solace in two things. One was in the tangible comfort of possessing Felicita, and the other was in an emotional resource that had not as yet been stripped from her. Mama still had the ability to place her trust and faith in the people she loved. And with these two things, along with the meager clothes on her back, Mama walked alongside the missionary man, away from her shack, from the Dominican community, from the only life she ever knew, and from dying grandma, head tall, down the dusty road, toward the awaiting vehicle that would transport them to a plane destined for New York City in the United States of America.

Though several details were added and gaps filled from her deathbed, Mama provided me with the foundation of her story about her life in the Dominican Republic, and subsequent migration to New York City, during the sunset hours of that ordinary summer night after she observed me fussing with the nameless, dark-skinned Jamaican girl, whose older sister's ass I had diligently kicked the day before. Although Mama bore a hole right through that part of my soul that was responsible for my moral conduct and convictions, she never exactly spelled out her point in telling me her story that night. But the messages were nonetheless crystal clear, and carved an edict on my personal code of ethics that would remain unchanged for the rest of my life. While I might have placed smoke screens over the messages with my own war stories and need for personal drama, the seeds were permanently planted, patiently waiting for water, a little sunlight, and a display of love, to fully come into blossom.

Message number 1:
Don't ever use someone's race, ethnicity, or even religion against them out of anger, or as ammunition in a fight. We all come from somewhere and we all have histories. Each of our histories is as precious, unique, rich, bittersweet, and sometimes as tragic as the next persons. But each of our origins and our ancestors' pasts are worthy of tantamount reverence, as they contain the gossamer, almost invisible, threads that bind us together to form the human race to which we currently belong. Like it or not, we are all but one people.

Message number 2:
Don't ever tell anybody to go back to where they came from. We, with our own personal narrow perceptions and points of references, truly have no idea from where another came, or what they needed to endure to get where they are now. We should never make light of, nor make assumptions or judgments about, another human being's journey, about which we inevitably do not know anything about, with the exception of the palpable knowledge that most journeys are difficult, painful, and irreversible, while all are virtually never ending.

CHAPTER FOUR

*If you can make it there,
you can make it anywhere,
it's up to you, New York, New York.*
—Fred Ebb and John Kander

ABOUT FOUR YEARS ago when I was struggling with a half-hearted attempt to live a drug-free lifestyle, I was arrested on three counts of assault for going buck wild on two drunk "yuppies" who must have been leaving an after-work Happy Hour party in mid-Manhattan on a wintry Friday evening. I broke the taller one's nose, and then cut the shorter one's when he blocked his face, fending off a splintering beer bottle that I had snatched from him, smashed over a parked car's hood, and attempted to use to slice his face. I am quite sure that I would have mutilated both beyond repair had it not been for two off-duty police officers, one white and one black, who jumped from their car, wrestled me down to the ground, and in doing so, saved the two yuppies from undergoing major plastic surgery. The reason why I attacked them was simple, but yet so complex, that it took six months of therapy to figure out, and yet a couple of more years of personal growth to ensure that it wouldn't happen again. In fact, I still occasionally need continued support in this area. In essence, the reason why I went off on those men was because one was urinating in public, the other had looked in my direction and said "Ooh baby" as I passed by, and both of them were drunk and white.

At the time it happened though, nobody was more shocked by my behavior than me. (Except for my knight in shining armor—Trevor. He was my dutiful, very codependent boyfriend at the time to who I often owed my speedy releases from jail on bail, and virtual slap-on-the-wrist sentences. He was also one of those people who enter your life for "but a season" for reasons that make absolutely no sense at the moment, but which are of monumental importance in terms of your growth and development, if you give yourself the luxury of viewing the larger picture of your life at a later more relaxed and personally serene point in time. I'm not so sure Trevor would share the same philosophy as me, although I genuinely pray he does. The dope fiend and the hope fiend. God, our pain did spiral. But Trevor is another story, or at least another chapter.)

At any rate, I, in all of my newly acquired personal wisdom and intermittent drug-free lifestyle, was shocked, puzzled, and even appalled by my seemingly irrational, swept-under-the-rug behavior from my past. But, when Trevor rescued me in less than forty-eight hours from the city jail, I said "fuck it" and went about my business. Until about two days later . . .

I had this nagging, overwhelming urge to go to the dentist. Now every drug addict knows that long-term use of drugs, particularly heroin, combined with the typical chaotic lifestyle, does wonders on their pearly whites. I firmly believe that every methadone maintenance program and detox clinic should have an adjacent dentist office in an attempt to preserve what few teeth might be left in the mouths of recovering addicts. Although I know perfectly well that such a detox/dental clinic dual relationship would never occur due to the simple fact that no dentist in his or her right mind would subject himself to a fate of working in the bloody mouths of junkies all day long. Not unless they were masochistic or suicidal or something.

Anyway, I, along with most of my cronies, had an assortment of rotten molars that I began the grueling and painful process of attending to once I started being released from various jailhouses and placed into halfway house drug-rehabilitation programs. Fortunately, with the exception of two, all of my teeth were salvaged and I was able to say my temporary good-byes to my friend the dentist about six months prior to my little violent incident with the "yuppy" gents. And then, out of the clear and crystal blue, as if I had lost my mind completely, I experienced this overpowering obsession with thoughts of returning to my dentist's reclining chair. I swear, I craved it more than having some hard core, wet-and-wild sex with good old Trevor. Now ain't that a bitch?

So, what did I do? The usual. Nothing. Nothing, and then eventually, relapsed. And then, started the process all over again.

The last time in my life that the cycle of having dentist dreams surfaced, what did I do? Nothing. Nothing until one day I couldn't go on anymore. I was jumpy, irritable, virtually unable to sleep, and very, very, very angry. All of my old violent and grisly thoughts and fantasies crept out of the beds in which they had been lying dormant, and haunted me through my every wakeful hour.

I hated the world, hated life, hated just about damned-near everything. What was the motherfucking point anyway? We were born and we died, and everything in-between was just some useless madness that sucked anyhow. I was born black and poor to a throwaway, illegal alien dope fiend that AIDS took away from me when I needed her the most. Nobody ever helped me. Nobody ever gave a fuck. The system fucked me up the ass every time I bent over. I learned that lesson a long time ago. Sodomy Systems 101. And, when I didn't bend over, it pushed me down and fucked me up the ass anyhow. So what was the use? I was on and off clean for almost two years and where did it get me? I was still poor, without my own apartment, without decent clothes, without a fucking thing except a bunch of therapists, drug-rehab clients, and scheduled meetings with coffee-drinking, donut-eating, cigarette-smoking NA folk who had made a substitution for their drug of choice—NA instead of dope or crack or whatever the hell had happened to turn their asses on. It's a selfish recovery program anyway. Who the hell wants to be selfish? It was all the rich white bastards' faults anyhow. They were going to make sure that we remained slaves in one form or another. The prisons and the drug rehabs were just another variation of the Old World plantations, and the ghettoes were Jim Crow reincarnated again and again and again. So what did it all matter anyhow?

I was in trouble, and I knew it. But fortunately for me, buried deep beneath my impacted anger, way below my raging thoughts, bellicose fantasies, rantings and ravings, laid a small, frail inner voice that occasionally surfaced to remind me that everything mattered and that I needed to plod ahead no matter what . . .

Then one day when I felt like my internal battles and festering hostility would suffocate me or bust me wide open and land me in a mental institution or a dope den, some unidentifiable force triggered a switch in the deepest part of my soul, and while my inner flame was flickering on-off, I started tearing and trembling in the middle of my vocational evening prep class and fled from the small makeshift classroom as if his satanic majesty was upon my heels. I ran like hell, with the velocity of a gazelle, and the keen goal-mindedness of hounds on the scent. About ten blocks later, I collapsed against the sturdy embrace of a huge tree trunk in a secluded area of Central Park, screaming and crying out for what seemed like an eternity. And then from somewhere close, came a change over the spirit of my dream, my eternal flame caught, and I saw a flickering light.

You see, I had always been one of those people who knew everything. I mean, after having lived my crazy, one-of-a-kind life, with its unrelenting lurid experiences and difficult precarious life situations, who could possibly teach me something new that I hadn't already learned in my past on the streets? I thought I knew everything about everything, and particularly everything that had to do with everyone else. And then, after finally achieving the goal of living an almost two-year, practically drug-free existence, I was certain that I had aced my recovery and truly, truly could make my claim to fame with regards to my omniscience. But somehow, while sobbing in a crouched position beneath the dense foliage of that mammoth tree, I got in touch with my prolonged blindness to the inevitability of my smallness and powerlessness in terms of my position in the universe. And somehow, as the waves of recognition washed over my callused spirit, long forgotten seeds of acceptance took root and began to sprout, slowly and tentatively. While remaining grateful for my almost one-year complete abstinence from drugs and alcohol, I now understood how a little learning could be a dangerous thing. I had chanted the first step of the twelve steps of Narcotics Anonymous several hundred times over this past year, but the words, for the first time in my recovery process, adopted a new personal and profound meaning. Whether it was my newfound appreciation for the magnificent size that nature bestows upon trees, my learning about the disease of attitudes, my incumbent need to learn about triggers and venture on to the paths of genuine self-exploration, a celestial trinket of wisdom, or I was opportunely for the first time in my life at the right place at the right time, I honestly admitted that I was powerless over my addiction, and that my life was still, very much so, unmanageable. Armed with a new strength, I collected myself, went back to my home, sought out my sponsor, and reached out for help.

As the weeks evolved into months and I plunged myself into therapeutic avenues of self-exploration, I discovered that my most recent yearning to return to the dentist was, in reality, my addict self's embellished need to relive the socially and medically acceptable drugged sensation from the gas I received while in his chair. I later learned that the inebriated yuppies from my past, my accompanying anger, and subsequent violent response, had aggravated a whole host of triggers, previously masquerading as excuses, to get high. Though I had begged Mama on her death bed to provide me with every minute detail of her ending life, I was unprepared, and way too vulnerable, to hear Mama's unabridged rendition of her "rites de passage" migration experience to New York City.

According to Mama, her entire trip was made in silence—a dead, bone-chilling silence, much like the kind that drapes itself over cemeteries after dusk. Her preacher man-father did not cast one direct look in her direction, much less utter a shred of conversation, during the all-day journey from Mama's run-down village in the backwoods countryside of the Dominican Republic to the metropolis of New York City. There was a nonverbal agreement of sorts between them. Namely, that the preacher man would walk with a stride of complete confidence and independence, as if oblivious to life's troubles and encumbrances, including that of my mama's presence, struggling with her boney, knobby-knee legs, Felicita dangling from her side, so she could live up to her end of the speechless pact and keep up with his obscure shadow. In fact, when her father in name seated her on the plane, which Mama always referred to as the metal monster flying machine, he seated her in a window seat several aisles behind him, undoubtedly very grateful that his God did not make us with eyes in the backs of our heads.

The one detail that stood out prominently in Mama's recollections of her first and last plane trip was that she peed on herself about midway through the flight. With an indifferent shrugging of her shoulders, and a simultaneous look of shame seeking immediate refuge behind the curtains of her lids, I remember Mama disclosing how with so many strangers around her, when her kidneys need to release reached painful proportions, she didn't dare do anything except fearfully position Felicita between her legs to provide additional squeezing traction. When this prop failed her, she shamefully pissed on herself and Felicita's bottom limbs. Mama's father never noticed.

The rest of the details, factual or emotional, associated with Mama's flight were either irrelevant or so painful that Mama had stuffed them deep down into the bottomless pit of her soul to a point of no return. Reflecting back now, I remember Mama used to have a crazy expression to which, at the time, I paid absolutely no attention. Mama used to say "that shit there that happened to me was so fucked-up, it ain't even none of my business." I think I know what she meant now.

Anyway, the story goes that father and daughter arrived in New York City—at Kennedy Airport from what I can tell from Mama's description—disembarked, passed through immigration by what must have been God's will or Mama's father's unctuous pastoral connections, secured a vehicle, and headed out on to a busy, car-littered highway like Mama had never seen anywhere in her entire life. Mama's memories included: it was chilly; it was dusk; she was frightened; she was awestruck; she missed her mama; and, she had to pee again. While on the highway about fifteen minutes later, the preacher man uttered his first words to Mama. He pulled over, got out of the car, walked around to the passenger side, opened the door and said, "Ven conmigo—voy al bano." (Come with me—I'm going to the bathroom.) Mama graciously followed him away from the car. When her preacher man-father walked into the dense foliage, pointed for her to go in one direction, while he walked off toward another, Mama didn't think anything was unusual. When she completed urinating on some dry leaves and fallen bark and didn't immediately hear him call for her, she also didn't entertain the possibility that anything was irregular. Even when she heard one lone car screeching off into the distance while she remained waiting in stillness, Mama still didn't put one and one together and understand the gravity of the situation nor that something was dreadfully amiss. But, when she heard the darkening sky shriek a thundering cry, saw the yellow flash of zigzagging light that followed, and felt the first of the New World's silvery teardrops on her face, she instantaneously knew that something was very, very wrong. With all of the reality-based practical thinking that an eight-year-old, frightened, newly migrated, and about-to-be-motherless child could muster up in such a grim circumstance, Mama understood that her father had coldheartedly abandoned her along a highway somewhere in New York City.

So, Mama did what any other eight-year-old girl would do in a similar situation. She wailed and wallowed in the hopelessness of her predicament until she eventually could not distinguish her tears from the wetness of the ashen rain on her face.

Although Mama had no recall of the sequence of the next few events, it must have eventually stopped raining while the darkened skies transformed into a starless gloomy nightfall, because Mama's next memory was of waking up cold, drenched, and feverish on top of a damp mound of leaves and rubbish under a hazy morning sky. Mama's memories of the next couple of days were about as opacious as was the hazy sun on the first morning after her arrival to the land of milk and honey. She remained in the seclusion of her foliaged domicile amidst the numerous weeds, less plentiful trees, and assortment of discarded beer bottles, cans, and additional decaying evidence of human civilization. Immobilized by fear from the rush of the wheels of distant cars, and numbed by a festering fever, Mama preferred to remain inert by day. However, as the noise of the rushing cars dimmed by night, she occasionally ventured out toward the highway, stumbling through the debris, in search of some scraps of nourishment. Regardless of her efforts, Mama's frail, childlike body had entered through the gates of the straits of starvation.

A day or two later—Mama could never be sure—she was awakened from a febrile, turbid sleep by the sensation of a warm pungent liquid streaming over her face, accompanied by the drunken, raucous laughter of three drunk, very out-of-control white men. At the time, Mama thought they were hairy, stinky giants. But, as an adult looking back through a more mature and realistic lens, Mama remembered them being three white men who were rather thin, in their twenties, sullied with dirt, and reeking of alcohol stench. Two of them had unusually long hair for men—at least from what her understanding was of proper hair length for men from her Dominican cultural reference point. And finally, Mama remembered the experience of being the target of their hungry, wild, glassy eyes as if it was yesterday. The passing of years never totally abates the firsthand experience of terror or pain. If the poets were right in their belief that "the eyes are the windows of the soul," then she must have been looking into the infernal chasms of the insane and the accursed.

While on her death bed, Mama's insight into the good, bad, and folly of human nature, far transcended that of her typical "ghetto mentality." Perhaps her few jewels of wisdom were charity gifts from the imminent angels of death. Or maybe, her seemingly more clearheaded, newfound insight and awareness were always present, lying dormant in her heart in physical environments in which only her street dog-eat-dog survival skills mattered, in anticipation of the day when circumstances would have it that they too could sprout wings and fly away. Maybe.

What happened to Mama during that first week in New York City is something that should never happen to any human being, particularly to a sickly, eight-year-old, innocent and frightened-to-death little girl. But it did. It happened, and continues to happen, to thousands of other defenseless, pure little boys and girls. And it's going to continue happening until we stop considering the problem to be somebody else's problem. Although she hadn't spoken about it until her last few dying weeks on earth, I know that what happened to my mama during that first week in New York City affected her until the day she died. It probably changed her life's script in a mammoth way—set it off-kilter. But, without a doubt, because Mama was one pebble on a beach of millions, her brutal rape had repercussions and ramifications that touched the lives of those with whom she came in contact throughout her remaining years on earth. Including mine.

According to Mama, when she was awakened from her twilight sleep by the wet sensation on her face, the numbed fingers of her cerebral connections eventually locked hands with their correct partners, jolting her back into a state of consciousness to face the realization that there were three dirty white men glaring down at her and one of them was pissing directly on her face. Paralyzed with fear, she remained motionless for a moment, clamping her mouth and eyelids shut in an effort to avoid having the urine run into her eyes and mouth. When the spark of self-preservation that lies in all of us ignited and propelled Mama to her feet to attempt to flee, the force of hatred that lies in some of us simultaneously triggered an offensive reaction in one of the three intoxicated predators, propelling him to grab her by the wrist while walloping her in the face with his free hand. Nose bleeding and head pounding, Mama fell limply back on to the ground with about as much strength in her as Felicita who lay on the ground beside her. In between slapping and kicking her, two of the long-haired men raped Mama. One did it from the front. One did it from the front and back.

Although Mama could not understand English at the time, she understood the universal language of savage, heartless laughter and the offbeat panting of animalistic sex. She also remembered the use of one particular phrase that the men repeated over and over while striking her with their hardened fists and feet. A phrase, that as her English improved and came to understand the translation, she later heard many a time throughout her life. "Little nigger bitch."

When Mama had lapsed into a state of semi-consciousness, the third man who had not yet penetrated her, took his position and stood directly in front of her bloody, quavering body. The other two men, probably feeling quite satisfied in their sexual release and masochistic conquest, lay prone on their backs a few feet away.

Mama guessed that they were going to kill her—just abandon her used, lifeless body right there. She believed that when the third man tried to subtly nudge her body, as if to prod her back into a state of consciousness without his two cronies observing, he was giving her permission to save her life. I always believed that the motherfucker was just so drunk he didn't know what he was doing. I mean he sure didn't come to anybody's rescue, fly in with his red cape on and save the day, when either of his two friends had their dicks up Mama's eight-year-old ruptured pussy or ass. So how was it that he was going to give a fuck about anything at the very end? In like a villain, out like a hero. I don't think so. But, Mama insisted that he saved her life, or at least part of it. I told Mama that he was just plastered and unthinking. Mama said I wouldn't know because I wasn't there. She got me on that one. I wasn't there. But my spirit has carried around the shadow of the burden since its inception.

Whether there within the third man lay a morsel of good, or whether he was just plain drunk, we'll never know. But what we do know is that Mama took that nudging on her foot to be symbolic of her last stab at life. Without having to be cued by any other method, Mama caught her breath, rolled over, snatched Felicita by one of her limbs, scrambled to her feet, and ran like hell. And those goddamned bastards with unnatural hearts picked up and ran after her. Although in significant pain, Mama streaked forward, fueled by the adrenalin that was pumping through her lifeline. Fortunately, the monster men, who on a regular day could have overtaken Mama in the blink of an eye, most probably never caught up with her because they were so dizzy and uncoordinated from the effects of alcohol. Instead, Mama got her bearings straight and headed in the direction of the highway, wild-eyed and naked. (Mama insisted that it was God who carried her at least half of the way.)

Mama said that it seemed like she had been running up that highway forever before two policemen, who appeared out of nowhere, arrived and ran after her. They overpowered Mama in a matter of seconds.

Talk about the power of perception. Mama's capture by the NYC police would have most probably been viewed by most hysterical victims as the climactic point of their trauma. But, for Mama, it was only one more, seemingly never-ending, crescent of pending disaster and ultimate doom.

For all intents and purposes, up until this point in her life, Mama could probably count how many white men she had encountered and had contact with on one hand. Namely, her preacher man-father and the three monsters. So, while her terrified, aggressive reaction to her capture by the two white policemen might have appeared insane to an unknowing onlooker, it was in truth quite sound. But, obviously, the policemen didn't understand this. They began to lose patience with Mama as she relentlessly shrieked and struck out at them with the unbridled savagery of a frightened infant-beast. I guess it was the last straw when Mama somehow managed to bite down on one of the policemen's arms because it unleashed a response from him that was somehow akin to that of her recent predators. It unleashed anger, frustration, and perhaps some hatred, because shortly after extricating his arm from Mama's mouth, the same police officer backhanded a slap across Mama's face that ricocheted her head from shoulder to shoulder and caused the flow of blood from her nose to begin again. However, that slap also knocked Mama back into a subdued enough state to make transporting her naked body to the nearby police car quite easy. I believe that since that day she remained a bit subdued, never quite regaining all of her "fight," as if the final sting of that policeman's slap reverberated throughout her spirit forever.

When, in 1986, a group of racist white males chased Cedric Sandiford to his death on the Belt Parkway in Howard Beach, Queens, I shuddered from the thought that Mama's "chase" could have very well occurred on the same stretch of land more than two decades before. I wondered if Mama's spirit had been looking down from the heavens observing the chase, whether spirits had memories, and if her pain had been rekindled. I also wondered when it was all going to stop.

CHAPTER FIVE

Give me your tired, your poor,
Your huddled masses yearning to breathe free
The wretched refuse of your teeming shore.
Send these, the homeless, tempest-tost, to me
I lift my lamp beside the golden door!
—Emma Lazarus

ONE DAY DURING my mid-adolescence, after Mama had already been infected with the virus, I came home early from school after getting into another run-in with one of the faceless Caucasian teachers and asked Mama, "Don't you hate white people?" She looked at me quizzically and asked,

"All white people?"

"Yeah, all white people."

"Now why would I hate all white people?"

"Because of what they've done to you. To all of us."

"Victoria, all the white people ain't done shit to me or anybody else. Ain't even possible for one person to know all the white people in this world, or even in this city."

"Mama, stop messing with me. You know what I mean."

"Yeah I do, but I really don't. Listen here—imagine if a woman saved up and bought her the best outfit in the whole department store to wear to church on Sunday. Now imagine that Sunday comes and she puts on that there outfit. Man, she struts all the way to church just knowing that she looks as fine as wine. And then just about when she's turning the corner about a half a block away from that church, a big, old, fat pigeon comes along and shits all over her Sunday's finest. A real big fucking shit—you know, the slimy, gooey, green kind with all that there white stuff in the middle."

I looked at Mama like she was crazy. "Mama, you crazy you know. What kind of bugged out story is that?"

"The kind that has a point. It's really very simple Victoria. You see, only one bird shitted up on that woman. Now I can see her hating that there one pigeon, but why should she hate all the other pigeons that were only living their lives and flying by?"

With that, I rolled my eyes and went out on the fire escape with my portable radio to drown myself in its far less meaningful drone of beats and stream of songs. As far as I could tell, Mama hadn't copped her regular fix for the day, and Mama had a way of exasperating you when she wasn't high. Mama also had a way of exasperating you when she was high. But the methods of exasperation, plus the results, were two very distinct and separate animals.

After the "chase" and finding "safety" in the custody of New York's finest, Mama was transported over to the closest city hospital's emergency room. She drifted in and out of consciousness throughout all of the initial medical procedures. Partially due to the administered sedatives, but mostly due to the fact that her mind was temporarily shut down from an overload of fear and pain, Mama's memory of her stay at the hospital was very spotty.

While feeling the effects of low dosages of tranquilizers, Mama recalled a faceless tribe of white people in white uniforms poking in and out of every inch of her body. Their voices fell upon her ears like a meaningless low grade cacophony—words spoken in an unfamiliar language like the endless drone of distant bees.

Two memories stood apart from the rest. Two of the blackest cells in an ocean of darkness. Two emotional nightmares that not even the sedatives alleviated.

The first hospital trauma involved Felicita. Somehow Felicita had managed to stick by Mama throughout the entire ordeal, right up to the point during which Mama was admitted into the children's ward of the hospital. When Mama awoke from a groggy sleep for the first time, she found Felicita placed in a plastic bag beside her on the night table. (Mama surmised that one of the policemen—probably the guilty one—had identified it as her personal property. Her only personal possession to her name.) With what little energy remained in her reserve, Mama reached over, pulled Felicita out from the bag, embraced her in her arms, and fell back into a troubled sleep.

She woke up to a state of alarm as she sensed one of the nurses attempting to ease Felicita from her grip. With eyes that must have been bulging in fear, Mama snatched back her prized possession. The nurse, in turn, pulled back. After a brief tug-of-war session, Felicita's worn and delicate body gave out. With the nurse's final irritated yank, off came Felicita's head. A swift decapitation.

Mama went hysterical. Placing the remains of Felicita's freakish body at a safe distance, Mama shrieked and shrieked what must have been the most bloodcurdling wail that ever traveled down the hospital corridor. A lament that lacerated the soul and made the heart bleed.

The end result was that the good hospital staff quickly came to Mama's aid and injected her with an even stronger dosage of tranquilizing medication that had an immediate effect on her central nervous system. Hence, with dissipating breathy sobs, Mama drifted back off into a drugged slumber. If nothing else, the experience provided profound instruction about how drugs could bring about a numbed relief from life's worst ills.

Felicita, or what was left of her, remained in Mama's possession. Partial evidence of a headless human travesty. The nurse must have forgotten about the grave importance of removing her from Mama's possession in all of the commotion.

Mama's second dreadful memory of her hospital stay marked her introduction into the world of Social Services and helping professionals. It initially involved the endless onslaught of nurses, doctors, and technicians who persisted on addressing her in English and then stood around waiting for a response, as if Mama had only been pretending not to understand them all along. (I guess they assumed that black folk spoke English, even if they did throw in a little slang and rhythm once in a while, and Mama, to the naked ignorant eye, sure enough looked black.) After being barraged by incessant questions, with underlying traces of festering irritation, the hospital staff finally arrived at the far-reaching ingenious conclusion to send for one of their few bilingual nurses in an attempt to determine whether Mama was dumb, selectively mute, or monolingual Spanish-speaking.

The elderly, squat Puerto Rican nurse who arrived during the next shift quickly assessed that Mama was quite fluent in her native tongue—Spanish, with a heavy "campesino" Dominican accent—even if she did look black. Although Mama felt something akin to relief after having had someone with whom to communicate, a different form of desperation and helplessness overcame her when it became painfully apparent that she could not generate satisfactory responses to the majority of posed queries that were then roughly translated by the Puerto Rican interpreter. Mama said that it went something like this:

"What is her name?"
"Anita Rosa Gonzalez."
"How old is she?"
"Eight."
"When is her birthday?"
"Don't know exactly—sometime around Christmas."
That got a mild rise out of some of them.
"Where's her mother?"
"Back home."
"Where's home?"
"The Dominican Republic."
"What part of the Dominican Republic?"

"The country part."

The next question must have been tainted with irritation.

"Which country part?"

"Somewhere not too far from town. By the river."

"Which river?"

"I don't know. I don't think it has a name."

"Does her mother know she's here?"

"Yes."

"Why did she send her?"

"Because she's sick. She's dying."

"How does she know she's dying?"

"She knows."

"How can she get in touch with her mother?"

"Don't know."

"Does anybody there have a phone? Does she have a phone number or an address?"

"No."

"Did she go to school? What was the name of the school?"

"She never went to school."

That response must have generated some knowing nods too. The staff then went another route. There's always more than one way to skin a cat.

"Whose her father?"

"The white preacher man."

"What's his name?"

"Don't know for sure."

"Don't know for sure?"

"Yes. I think they call him Preacher Juan."

"Is that his name? Is Juan the first or last part of his name?"

"Don't know."

"But, he's her father. How could she not know the name of her father?"

"She doesn't know him very well."

"Is he Dominican?"

"No. He's white."

I bet some of them had their doubts about that.

"He's white, and his name is Juan, and she believes he's a preacher?"

"That's right."

"Where is he?"

"Don't know. He carried her here and left her on the road. She doesn't like him."

"Her father brought her here from the Dominican Republic?"

"Yes."

"Why?"

"Because her mother was dying."

"And then, after bringing her here, he abandoned her on the road?"

"Yes, yes."

"Where are her immigration papers?"

"She doesn't know what those are."

"Tell her it's her papers with her birthday. Her proof of citizenship. Her permission to be in this country."

"Don't know. Maybe he got them. She doesn't really know what that is."

"Her mother. Ask her if she's Dominican."

"Yes, she thinks so. She thinks she's Haitian too."

"Haitian too? Ask her why she says that."

"Don't know. That's what she said. That's what she heard."

"Ask Anita Rosa if she has any other relatives—maybe someone here in New York."

"No, not in New York. But in her country, she has an uncle."

"She has an uncle?"

"Yes."

"What's his name?"

"Francois."

"Francois what?"

"Francois Gonzalez."

More looks of exasperation.

"So both her mother and uncle are Dominican. They have Spanish, not Haitian, surnames."

"I think so. She thought that everybody where she lived had Dominican names so they could stay living there."

I can imagine how the silence following that statement spread like milk on the floor.

"Well, uh hum, we only have a few more questions."

"OK."

"Can she read or write?"

"No."

"On what day did she arrive? Does she know the airline or maybe the flight number?"

"I'm sorry. She doesn't know. She believes that it was many days ago."

"Many days ago? But, she doesn't know a specific date?'

"No."

"Well, tell her that will be all for now. Thanks a lot. By the way, ask her how she feels."

"Better."

"That's good. Thanks again."

The Bureau of Child Welfare must have had a field day with Mama's existence and trying to tie together all of the bureaucratic tape. They knew nothing except that Mama only spoke Spanish, must have been abandoned by her parents, and was definitely the victim of a rape crime by the Brooklyn/Queens border alongside the Belt Parkway Highway. If Mama was a U.S. citizen, then the solution was relatively simple. Place her into foster care, attempt to trace down her biological parents—it's called "a diligent search," I believe—and then, after an exhaustive search and the passing of time, free her for adoption—which usually amounted to a childhood and adolescent sentence to foster care anyway, particularly if you happened to be a child of color.

Anyway, due to the fact that Mama's case was such an enigma, and therefore had thrown such a huge monkey wrench into the system's general procedures, she remained in the hospital for about another four or five months. From there, she was placed into a foster home in Harlem. A bad foster home. Then she was removed and placed into a good foster home. Then, at some point during the midst of all this, she lost her identity as a human being and became a number. Spin, spin the wheel of fortune, and where you end up nobody knows, or cares. Although she was unable to provide details about the order of her travels, Mama's number landed in many a different foster home, residential center, juvenile detention center, and eventually, drug treatment program, until she finally removed herself from the game of chance and took full-time refuge in the streets. And while, for the life of her, she could not be sure in which borough the one act that had the most impact on the course of her life occurred, Mama remembered that approximately one and a half years after her arrival in the United States of America, she followed a fourteen-year-old boy up on to a project roof top to try "sniffing something that would make her feel better." It did.

CHAPTER SIX

Star light, star bright
First star I see tonight
I wish I may, I wish I might
Have this wish I wish tonight.
—Short Verse Nursery Rhyme

THE FIRST TIME I was sexually abused was when I was five years old. Maybe five and a half to be exact. It was during the same time period that I learned that the grass is not always greener on the other side of the fence. I learned about human mirages. How we never really know what happens behind closed doors. About how things aren't always what they appear to be. How sometimes those quaint, white, picket-fenced suburban homes with the 2.5 kids, two cars in the garage, and the one shaggy dog stretched out on the lawn, also house their share of resident witches and toads and sleeping beauties. I learned that one should never wish too hard for something unless they are completely sure they want it because the mouth is powerful and they might get what they are asking for.

Some wishes come true. And then they break our hearts in two.

As I believe I've already mentioned, I was placed back into Mama's care when I was about a year and a half. Our long-awaited opportunity to continue laying down the bricks of our foundation. A slender baby, I had taken my first few steps several months before our actual reunion. A wise baby, despite my incessant gurgling and overuse of the sound "da da" to identify anybody in my visual sphere, I reserved my first articulation of the word "mama" for when I was at least one month back into Mama's care. After that, my speech development launched off at a pace of its own.

Being a toddler in Mama's care meant three things. Having a precocious induction into street life. Having the opportunity to bid acquaintance and spend time with an assortment of folks—often undesirables—when Mama frequently, unknowingly, but neglectfully, placed me into their temporary care "for just a minute" so she could take care of her business. (Later on in life, after I had traveled through the ranks of the foster care system and gained a meager understanding about the maternal patterns of addicts, I observed that some of the other children had mothers who dropped them off at their friends or relatives and never came back. Mama, despite her constant taking advantage of her friends' babysitting hospitality, always came back. I'm not appending a value to either maternal pattern. Just making an observation.) The third thing that being a toddler, or any age child for that matter, in Mama's care meant was constant moving. When I attempt to visualize "home" during my early childhood, I come up with a blur of homesteads unwinding haphazardly on my mind's first memory reel. An endless flashing of shutters and scenes from shelters, welfare hotels, dilapidated tenement apartments, and "friends'" homes, without one extended focus on the shutter that would, even briefly, highlight one main place of residence—my real home.

When I was younger, I used to say that I had lived in so many different welfare locales that the city could pay me a salary to critique and rate all of the nooks under its charitable umbrella. People used to laugh. I didn't think it was funny.

Mama's big drug then, and always really was when she could get to it, was dope. Heroin. Mainlined straight into her veins. By the time I was six, Mama had so many puncture wounds on her arms that she could have been a poster board for that game "connect the dots." She started capitalizing on her other body parts with accessible veins shortly thereafter. Hence, Mama's major maternal liability was related to her frequent and extended "nods." When at "home" and in my presence, Mama generally waited until nightfall to get high, after I had hopefully already fallen asleep. Usually, she left me with a "babysitter" and did her business elsewhere. I used to think that Mama and some of her other addict-friends had this babysitting exchange program going on. Some nonverbal agreement about who would go out, and who would get stuck at home with "the kids." Looking back in retrospect, I realize that that was a pretty silly and naive notion. I've since come to learn, mainly through my own experiences, that addicts, ninety-nine times out of a hundred, have a shortage in the planning and organization department. Except with regards to making plans and manipulations to secure their drug. There's always a hell of a lot of strategizing and plotting with regards to their chase. Drug addicts are like skilled runners in a race that nobody wins and never ends.

I should have known even then that the babysitting system was not really a system at all, but rather a random disbursement of children from whoever happened to be in the leading running positions that night. The problem was that sometimes running positions abruptly altered and babysitters quickly searched out other babysitters to oversee their posts "for just a minute." Sometimes they just up and left. Except for those fortunate souls who had the benefit of having sweet and blindly indulgent grandmothers built into the equation. Those, who seemed to be the chosen few, I later learned, were characters from similar, albeit sometimes worse, woeful tales.

While she had swept many a bright, sunlit, daylight hour under the rug in "a nod," Mama generally got her fix late at night in the streets. When things were status quo, Mama got high late at night, was pretty alert and energetic through the wee morning hours, went into "a nod" shortly thereafter until late morning, became a little antsy around late afternoon, calmed her nerves with a joint and/or beer around dinner time, and was basically "fiending" by the time the *Ten O' Clock News* was inquiring whether folk knew where their children were. But, like I said, when she did get high at home, she usually waited until after I was asleep, regardless of whether she had her stuff earlier in her possession or not. However, like the inevitable monkeys on their backs, dope fiends are always finding monkey wrenches thrown into the race. Each and every one of them could sit down and write their own books about Murphy's Law because dope fiends, particularly those who survive on the streets, are forever encountering nuisances and obstacles in the way of getting high. That's why the rituals involved in getting high are such a big deal—they've beaten the odds and the obstacles and are partially celebrating the fact that they have successfully secured their shit. The primary nuisances are the law, the police, and jail. Secondary nuisances are court-mandated out-patient drug-treatment programs, family members, and in some far and few between extraordinary circumstances, employment. The main obstacle is keeping a steady flow of cash money on hand to cop on the regular. So while the police pose periodic annoyances, especially when one gets arrested, money problems, which translates into irregular supply or losing the race, is the street dope fiend's greatest impediment. And, believe it or not, there ain't that much stealing, dealing, or hooking in the world to maintain a street addict's regular supply and keep him or her in the first place running position forever.

Mama encountered a few nuisances and many obstacles. So, she sometimes had to jockey her daily rituals and get high where she could, when she could, and with what she could. It was one of those obstacle-related occasions that landed me in the foster care system again at the age of five. The same occasion that landed Mama in the emergency room, at Lincoln Hospital in the Bronx, nearly dead.

One day, Mama, who hadn't been able to cop for over forty-eight hours, out of desperation robbed a woman of her purse on the subway platform. She then copped as much dope as the purse's contents allowed from an unfamiliar dealer. Out of desperation. She then returned to our shelter, checked on me, and made a beeline for the shelter's communal bathroom. Out of desperation . . .

It was I who, an hour later in search of my mama to tell her I was hungry, found her sprawled out in front of the dirty toilet, head bent forward, eyes rolled up in the back of her head, foaming at the mouth, saliva suspended in midair and needle protruding from her skin. Mama had overdosed on some bad shit. My five-year-old heart plummeted down the psychological shaft of terror crashing somewhere beneath my subconscious.

My screams eventually elicited help from the shelter staff, who in turn, dialed 911 that elicited further assistance from the NYC police department and emergency ambulance services. Mama had her stomach pumped and miraculously lived. I ended up in foster care, and was not so miraculously, sexually abused.

I ended up in one of those homes that I had always fantasized about from television. A big sprawling suburban home in Jamaica Estates. A clean home with a backyard complete with swings, slide, pool, and doghouse. Rooms with beautiful furniture, flowery-papered and paneled walls. Tiled floors. Extra conveniences like a big color television and a well-stocked playroom. Necessities like stacked kitchen shelves and an overstuffed refrigerator. A chance to start school in a brick, complete with gleaming monkey bar playground, rich kid fantasy-type school. I thought that I wouldn't be moved out of this foster home so quickly, and that I'd even be able to complete my first year of school without having to be transferred at some point in the middle.

I had always wished for these things. Wanted them so badly. While there was always a part of me that wanted to be with Mama, once in foster care and having learned that Mama was all right, I pretty much figured that it would take Mama some time to get herself out of her latest predicament. So I decided that I had better make the most of it. I could tell her all about my experiences when she got "better" and I was returned back to her care. Tell her all about how I lived in a fantasy house for an entire year. Tell her how my wish came true. Then she could tell me all about her experiences too.

With all of my almost kindergarten-age wisdom, I had not thought of one very minute detail. I had failed to consider that houses, even fantasy houses, contained people. Real live people, with their strengths and weaknesses, character defects, and insanities. And in doing so, I had wished myself into the fantasy house from hell.

The Bronx Family Court didn't return me back to Mama's custody for another two years. I remained in the fantasy house from hell for the first six months of that long, twenty-four-month placement period. (I never did complete a whole school year there.) Then I was shuttled about to three more foster homes until I finally wound up back with Mama. Two of the foster homes were far better than the house from hell. One was slightly better.

I never did tell Mama about the fantasy house or about how my wish came true. She didn't tell me about her experiences or where she'd been since being released from Lincoln Hospital's detox program either. Instead, we just kind of picked up from where we left off. Two silent, but more hardened soldiers.

Oh, and by the way, I also didn't make any more wishes.

When I first moved into the McNeils' home, I didn't sense that anything was amiss. I met Mr. and Mrs. McNeil and saw two typical, rich, white people. Mrs. McNeil, with her long beak-like nose, ruddy complexion, and skinny body, impressed me as a nervous, lean creature who repeatedly chirped about the fringe benefits of living as a foster child in her household. Her husband, Mr. McNeil, who was a little on the pudgy side with huge monstrous hands and an equally prominent handlebar moustache, was a smiling man, although as quiet in his demeanor as his wife was a seemingly endless chatterbox. They had two children—a boy and a girl. Both teenagers, and both as different as night and day. Their son, Mark, who was sixteen and a die-hard rock-n-roll fan, had long hair, which he kept tied back in a pony tail, a slender body like his mother, and tattoos branded on each arm—one of a skeleton's head and one of a half-coiled snake. Mark, who brightly introduced himself and kept saying weird words like "cool" and "awesome," always seemed to be strumming his fingers to the beat of an invisible guitar. His sister, Lisa, on the other hand, who was fourteen, grotesquely obese, and plagued with a pasty complexion and acne, made brief eye contact at our introductory meeting and then quickly excused herself. Probably to eat.

The most interesting of the entire lot was David. David was another foster child who the McNeils were in the process of adopting. He was eight, blonde with freckles, of average build, and the most frightened and sad little white boy I had ever set eyes upon in my entire life. Even though I was younger and smaller than my new foster brother, I immediately wanted to try to soothe away that perpetual look of fright and pain from his eyes. David, by the way, if you took away his constant look of anguish, was also the most handsome white boy I had ever met in my entire life. At five years old, I believe I had developed my first crush.

Sizing up the situation, without even taking my little crush into account, I quickly assessed by process of elimination in terms of household members' ages, that David was destined to be my close comrade—my friend. I was hence very disappointed to learn that it was probably easier to walk on water than it was to befriend David. David was about as emotionally distant as the moon was far from the earth, and I could tell that that was pretty far.

Whenever I spoke to David, he usually mumbled back inaudible replies. Although he was never blatantly rude, nor did he exactly directly reject my friendly overtures, David just kind of stood there, moving in a numbed slow motion, as if oblivious to the social skills required of him in such an impromptu interpersonal situation. I never took it personally. I knew it wasn't that David didn't like me. He had somehow gotten lost in the childhood development thing, and was having difficulty finding his way to the next level. I then began to sense that he had stopped trying.

One day when I was looking quizzically at David when he was not responding to my five-year-old friendly efforts, Mark explained that he was still sad about the loss of the little foster girl who used to live there and who I had replaced. Mark told me that the other foster girl was six years old and used to spend a lot of time with David. When I questioned Mark about what had happened to the other little girl—why she had left—he quickly turned away and said that she had gotten real sick and real bad.

I later learned that Shirley, the foster child who I had replaced, killed the neighbor's cat via strangulation. I also learned that poor, sad, little handsome David was one of those children from large biological families whose mother had singled him out, scapegoated him as the object of her unbridled anger and frustration, and subjected him to inhumane forms of abuse and torture. For seven years of his life he had lived in constant terror and despair, bereft of any display of love or affection, and instead was victim to the whimsical torments of his raging demented mother. For whatever reason, David, the third born, was selected by his mother out of five other children, to relentlessly beat, burn, poke, kick, humiliate, starve, and stuff in the closet, while she cared for the others with excessive indulgence.

David was removed from the home dazed, damaged, and half dead, when his next-in-age older sister finally broke down and cried to her teacher that she was afraid her brother was dead and rotting in the family's basement closet. David had been living with the McNeils for one year when I met the hollow shell of his remaining soul.

In the beginning I just went about my business as I had been trained well to do during my earlier years with Mama. Don't think. Don't analyze. And, don't ever ask any questions. Simply go about your business and hope that everyone else will do the same. My old familiar pattern of daily survival served me well for the first couple of weeks.

It was late fall when I had arrived, and since social workers always take so long registering new foster kids in school, I had ample time to romp around the McNeils' large yard, throw myself on to the fallen crisp autumn leaves, throw myself on to the dog, and throw myself into endless play activities with a myriad of toys and play materials that before, in my past life with Mama, I had only caught glimpses of on television.

Within a day or two of my stay at the McNeil home, I thought I had their family daily schedule down pat. Mr. McNeil was the first to rise in the morning. He was a vice president of a bank in the city, which required long work days, beginning with early morning hours. Mark, who was a senior in high school, was generally awakened by his father when he was on his way out the door. He, in turn, took responsibility for rousing David, and then later me, for school. David, who was even more comatose during the early morning hours than he was late at night, dragged his clothes on, moving to and fro as if sleepwalking through all of his morning grooming rituals. No matter how many times Mark screamed at him to throw water on his face, his countenance remained glazed with somnolence. David attended a special education school for the emotionally disturbed, which meant that he was picked up by "the cheese bus" and ate two of his three meals in school. David also attended school during the summers.

Lisa and Mrs. McNeil were two entirely different stories. Lisa, who was a freshman in high school, and probably as wide as the school's front entrance, frequently "felt sick," and thus remained balled up like a buried whale beneath her blankets most mornings when other fourteen-year-old girls were effervescent and exuberant about the prospects of a fresh new day.

Mrs. McNeil didn't typically rise from her sleeping barracks on the living room sofa until noon. And even when she did, she usually stumbled into the bathroom to relieve herself, only to return to her security blanket in front of the family's large screen television. When Lisa remained home from school, as she usually did, the mother-daughter rising duo didn't usually occur until the little hand was on the three and David's cheese bus was set to return. I, who was a pro at entertaining and caring for myself, adjusted quickly to the McNeil household's time schedules and patterns, whose chimes struck many familiar chords, and whose secrets, I was quickly able to unravel.

The first secret I unraveled involved Ms. McNeil's addictions. In addition to her "I don't do mornings" statements and behaviors, I was observant of her afternoon sluggishness while lying about in her robe, hair unkempt, eyes bloodshot, and breath sour, next to her adjacent, but substantially larger, couch-potato counterpart, until about an hour before her husband was expected to return home. In that one hour before Mr. McNeil returned from a hard day's work at the bank, Mrs. McNeil straightened out the living room, started dinner on the stove, bathed, groomed, and dressed with the end result being a 100 percent improvement in her overall appearance. She then shooed her whale of a daughter into her upstairs hiding quarters and prepared tumblers on a tray for her husband's welcome home toast from the dreaded frontiers of the outside world. It wasn't in her late night hours, late morning wake-ups, or long afternoon hours languished away on the sofa in obvious oblivion to her daughter's clinical depression that first aroused my codependent antennae, but rather the quickness with which she snapped her fingers and prepared herself every night at 6 PM—the cue that signaled that both she and her surrounding environment would be metamorphosed within the parameter of an hour. It was her magical speed and abrupt contrasting display of emotions that hastened Mrs. McNeil's skeletal bone for picking from the closet. It was all too familiar. Mrs. McNeil used a little assistance from uppers—probably cocaine or some form of speed—to sprint over the bridge back to the land of the living after being on a diurnal visit to the darker side via the transportation services of Alcohol Unlimited.

Although it took perhaps one week longer, the next secret I discovered was that mother and daughter—fat and skinny—were both in cahoots with Lisa's virtual non-attendance in school. In fact, as time passed and I fine-tuned my self-protective radar, I figured out that it was Mrs. McNeil who tempted and overindulged Lisa with high-calorie foods in abundance, and then enabled her to escape from the painful realities of the world by addressing her with bated breath maternal advice such as, "You still look a little peaked dear—perhaps you need to rest another day. Have another cookie."

I guess all types of misery needs a little company. Even the wealthy maternal type who, when palpably drowning, dismantle their children's already feeble lifeboats and dare them to swim ashore.

Mark's secret, although I didn't become aware of its looming existence until I had been a resident of the McNeil domicile for at least three weeks, was really not a secret at all. Perhaps that was why it took so long to discover. There was really nothing to discover. Mark smoked great quantities of marijuana—its pungent odor wafted up from his closed, but unlocked door until the wee hours of the morning. Mark also worshipped different elements of the occult. And although his parents might have ran interference for him and defensively stated that "it was that rock phase he was going through," evidence of a vulnerable teenage boy's blind allegiance to demonology and "black magic" was spread throughout his cluttered room.

The only secret I didn't discover—the one that was wrapped in smoke, left in a dark corner, and virtually invisible to the naked steady eye—was the one that fate would eventually unravel, and literally disrobe me and my sensibilities.

After having lived the sterile, materialistic life of a princess for about three months despite my lack of birth rights, I came to learn that there was quite a high price attached to holding my impostor crown. In much the same way that all that glitters isn't gold, sometimes the genuine glittering gold isn't shit compared to the price one has to pay to secure it with.

One night, after having drunk too much soda before bedtime, I awakened in the middle of the night to use the bathroom. Being that my room was located at the far end of the hall, I had to pass by David's room while stumbling down the dimly lit hallway in order to reach my destination. At the moment I was passing directly in front of his bedroom door, I heard it. A barely audible, but portentous sound that stirred somewhere from behind the solemn silence. Coming events usually cast their shadows before their actual occurrences. Stricken with fear, I remained glued to my spot in front of David's bedroom door, and while my auditory senses were unable to decipher the sound's source, my second nature relayed danger signals to my brain with an unfaltering quickness. The power and accuracy behind our inner voices has always amazed me. While they usually only speak to us once during the first few seconds of our thoughts' formations, their clarity and veracity are seemingly one of the few things in life that are without flaw, and yet, they are typically ignored. I once heard a religious woman say that our inner voices receive their knowledge and direction from God. Unsolicited advice that did not have to be sought through prayer. One of the fringe benefits of "grace." I wonder . . .

While I remained afraid, frozen in front of that door, dizzy from the hundreds of thoughts that were dashing fluidly through my mind, I followed suit with the majority of this world, and tossed the message of my inner voice into my mind's wastepaper basket. The message was "Flee, you're in grave danger." Instead of fleeing, I eventually found my way to the bathroom when my legs became less rubbery. Then, I went back to bed. On the way back to my room, I heard the sounds again, but this time, my auditory senses detected that their source was the combination of a child's whimpering and an adult male's moans of pleasure. I went to sleep anyway.

Following the aforementioned night of the full-bladder condition, I began to experience nightmares on an intermittent basis. Nightmares of an endless fall into a dark abyss. Nightmares of being chased by a murderous, faceless suitor. Nightmares of being stalked and assaulted in my sleep. Nightmares of pending death. Nightmares that signaled the spirit was restless and estranged from serenity.

While I typically awoke from my nightmares breathless from terror, my pajamas stained by the salty sweat of fear, and my heart beating out of control, I generally opted to remain alone in the darkness in my paralyzed position and willed myself back to sleep. Approximately two weeks later after having experienced a particularly frightening dream in which my suitor almost overcame me during the chase, I decided to go to the bathroom for a drink of water. Although I had not given much thought to the nocturnal moans over the past couple of weeks, memories of their past existence flooded every nook and cranny of the space in my head as soon as I set foot out into that dimly lit hallway again. After having only taken a handful of steps away from the deceptive security of my door, I realized that the sounds I was hearing were no longer coming from my memory's recorder, but from David's bedroom, of an even greater volume, and with more clarity than the time before. But, this difference in the sound's quality was no great wonder given that this time someone had carelessly left the door slightly ajar. Just like the white people in all of those horror movies who go right up into those haunted houses knowing that something oppressive and sinister is lurking behind the doors, I dumbly headed to David's room and peaked into the expectant darkness. I couldn't quite see, so I nudged the door open a bit more. It was at that moment that whatever was left of my childhood innocence, my belief in magical fairies and Christmas angels, and my vision of the underlying purposeful order of the universe, flew right back to never-never land, never to return again. It was also at that moment that I wholeheartedly wished that I had stayed my curious black ass in bed.

The damaging factor of sexual abuse lies not in the actual physical assault, but in the less tangible abrupt strangulation of the unknowing spirit. At some point while gasping for air, we lose our fight and experience a painful emptiness somewhere deep down in our gut. Future assaults only serve to stretch the sensitive, taut walls of the bottom of our gut further, into an even more painful position, while simultaneously sucking out more and more air.

Mr. McNeil never laid a finger on me that first night when I was sexually abused. He never removed a stitch of my clothing, nor cast one vulgar suggestive word in my direction. But due to his selfish, perverse sexual appetite and concomitant inability to contain his impulses, my spirit was asphyxiated nonetheless when I viewed him and David engaged in an unnatural sexual act. Before stepping back from that ghastly sight, Mr. McNeil lifted his head and caught my widened eyes long enough to make me understand that I was next. My inner voice said nothing.

About one week later, the induction of my late-night visits from Mr. McNeil commenced, along with my physical introduction into the adult world of sexual pathology. I was never actually penetrated, but instead guided through multiple acts of oral sex while having my naked body kneaded by Mr. McNeil's monstrous hands. With his seeming pattern of alternating nights between me and David, I often wondered when he had time for Mrs. McNeil.

When David and I were eventually removed from the McNeils' home, it was because someone from David's school noticed that he was in serious pain from, as it later was discovered, severe internal damage to his rectal area. During my physical examination in the medical team's concerted effort to determine whether I had been penetrated, I wondered if the doctors had any special equipment to detect the penetration that had occurred through my spirit's protective covering. They didn't. Oh, and before I get off the subject, in case anyone's wondering why I didn't snitch, reveal the secret, say something during or after my stay in the McNeils' fantasy house, just remind yourself that when in the midst of gasping for air and experiencing intense pain from a gaping hole deep down in the depths of your gut, you can't talk. It just isn't humanly possible. Sometimes you can't even think or remember. Along with my temporarily quelled inner voice, my ability to talk was inhibited on the night I had a bad dream and my throttled, unknowing spirit was left gasping for breath.

Years later, after Mama had died and I was placed upstate into one of those Residential Treatment Centers, I was feeling so bad that I decided to give therapy a chance to ease some of my gnawing anguish and pain. Needless to say, I had never given those dozens of other counselors, social workers, and psychologists from my past a fair chance of relating to me with my guard down. But at the point that I was placed into Residential Treatment, I was even becoming tired of my seemingly futile efforts to effectively negotiate this thing called life, and I decided to try something different. At least I thought I did.

My assigned social worker was an overweight woman who was reportedly schooled in much theory and academia. So much so that I believe she lost touch with intuition and the inherent teachings of the human heart. My advancing interest in seeking emotional solace was met by an inopportune moment of bad timing. "Que sera, sera."

My first and last individual session was over in a matter of minutes. It went something like this:

"Okay Victoria, you say you want to work on some issues."

"Yeah, that's right. I think it's time."

"Good, good. Okay, so do you want to talk about the first time you were sexually abused?"

"No, not really."

"But I thought you wanted to work on some issues. Now you have to be honest with me."

"I am being honest with you. I don't want to talk about that. Not now anyway."

"But I believe that would be a perfect place to begin in order to start making you feel better."

After much hesitation on my part. "Okay, but I'd really rather not."

"Okay, good. Now just tell me what happened the first time you were sexually abused."

"Well, I got up in the middle of the night to get a drink of water and I saw my foster father forcing my poor little foster brother to give him head. And, my foster brother, I think he was crying."

"But what actually happened to you Victoria? Did he touch you?"

"No, but I thought he would and I was scared."

"But he didn't actually touch you, didn't physically violate you in any way?"

"No, but, but . . ."

"Well, that means that you weren't really sexually abused. Were you ever really sexually abused, Victoria?"

"Look, I already told you. You asked me to tell you about the first time I was sexually abused and I told you. Now what the fuck else do you want from me?"

"I want honesty, Victoria, nothing else. Now this anger for no reason—is this what the cottage staff are talking about happens whenever you don't get your way?"

"Man, fuck this shit. I'm out of here."

"Victoria, you can't keep running from your feelings."

"Whose running, me or you? But anyway, fuck it. I'm out of here. See ya'."

With that, I got up and slammed the door behind me and on any other future emotional stirrings to seek emotional solace through talk therapy for a long, long time.

Not every woman wearing a white linen dress is a real nurse. Not every adult in front of a chalkboard with a pointer in their hand is a real teacher. Not every man with a white collar is a real preacher. Not every woman who gives birth is a real mother. And, not every person who reaches out their hand to help is a human being with a real heart. Human mirages. It is sometimes difficult to distinguish the beauty from the beast.

CHAPTER SEVEN

*What's love got to do with it, got to do with it,
What's love, but a secondhand emotion . . .*
—Terry Britten and Graham Lyle

WHEW, THAT WAS hard—going through all of my early childhood stuff and all. Feelings. You can't live with them, and you definitely can't live without them. Sometimes I hate feelings. They have a way of unhinging you and knocking you off course, leaving you open for all types of madness and bad decision making. Some of my worst enemies are feelings, particularly fear, helplessness, powerlessness, and weakness. (That little name idea of Mama's—Victoria equals "strength, victory, and power"—hasn't seemed to do me much good.) Feelings, obviously, are the recovering addict's worst nemesis. I mean hell, ain't they the main reason why we got ourselves into so much trouble in the first place? I believe that was the case for me, but that concept there you'll have to chill on since I think I'm going to make it the primary focus of a later chapter.

I finally shared all six chapters with my sponsor and she said I was doing really good. To be honest, the process of retrieving my past from oblivion got me aching so bad that I haven't been able to write another word since chapter six for about a month. My sponsor suggested that I get back into the swing of things—try to reopen my life on paper again. She said I should try to jump in at the present, and then ease my way back into the past so I won't feel the water's changing temperature so acutely. Try swimming in more shallow depths first. Less likely to experience the panic of drowning that way. She also questioned me about whether I've come any closer to God, whether I've even momentarily perceived his shadow across any of the memorable visions of my life. For the most part, I haven't. But every once in a while, I feel an alien stirring, sense an evanescent movement somewhere in a distant part of me, and then nothing but the soft echoing sensation of my heart's steady beat. And when I had erroneously believed that my truthful response would trigger a long discourse on my sponsor's part about the importance of turning my life over to that of a higher spiritual power in addition to another boring rendition of her favorite "Footprints" epigram, it only produced a knowing smile. Who can figure?

Anyway, I've spent the past month venting my feelings at NA meetings and to my sponsor on almost a daily basis. While it is true that some of my most intimidating feelings have since lowered their ugly heads and slithered away, I'm still stuck with a few of those damned uninvited guests. But I didn't pick up. No, I didn't pick up. My body has been clean of chemical substances for about thirteen months. Give me five! You go girl! Much respect! (My sponsor's husband is West Indian, so she'll know what that means.)

OK, so let's catch up on some formalities. I seem to recall promising you that I'd describe my physical attributes a few chapters ago. Might as well fulfill my promise. Avoidance is, in no uncertain terms, a motherfucker.

Well, let's see, I'm black. You sure can't spot any of my no-good, preacher-man grandfather in my skin coloring. But, I do have good hair which, as of late, I keep tied back in a pony tail or corn rolled down beneath some short, weaved in black braids. My hair color, like my skin complexion, is one, perhaps two, shades lighter than the color of milk chocolate. I'm of average height and build, although I've been pathetically thin during the days when my arms were always reaching out for the crack pipe. My eyes, much like the rest of my coloring, are a medium brown color with faint specks of coppery gold, which were undoubtedly inherited from Mama. Out of all of the many traits I acquired from Mama, why couldn't it have been her eyes? Anyway, I've got an oval-shaped face, marked by run-of-the-mill soft features, which are highlighted by thick luscious lips. The men always used to say "the better to kiss you with . . ." Yeah right, you know what they were thinking. The same thing that I was thinking and capitalizing on during many past days of groveling on my knees. I believe we've discussed my teeth before. Let's just say, we're working on it.

While my shape is clearly not a 10, keeping my modesty in check, it definitely clears at least a 7. I've got full breasts, a decidedly small waistline, and well-rounded hips and bottom that are supported by sturdy, shapely legs. My hands are small and dainty, and while marred by their share of scars and blemishes, also retain their aura of femininity. In sum, when I put some time and effort into my appearance, you wouldn't be lying if you said that I had it going on.

As for what I'm doing with myself now, in addition to playing paper-and-pen tourist guide through the mountainous dark regions of my life, I share a small apartment in East New York, Brooklyn with another recovering female addict, attend NA meetings almost daily, and work at a check out counter in a neighborhood low budget department store. I've also begun to participate in some new, previously unheard of, recreational activities with my growing, newly acquired circle of friends. I go out for lunch, to the movies, to flea markets, and sometimes to the shopping malls "just to look around." Now that last one there was truly a novel and unprecedented concept—going to a shopping mall just for the purpose of leisurely strolling about and browsing. Prior to this year, I have never stepped foot in no shopping mall without a previously planned, although often loosely constructed, boosting agenda since I was taken shopping by the hand by an amorphous procession of foster parents when I was a very young child. Even then, although I was usually too afraid to act on my impulses, I believe the notion of taking what didn't belong to me had already sprung roots in the weedy regions of my moral thinking. I probably started doing some "light" stealing from stores and my classmates by the time I was seven or eight. By the time I was a pre-teen. I was damn good. I stole food, toys, school supplies, and cosmetics. By mid-adolescence I had graduated to sneakers, coats, clothing, and electrical appliances. In fact, when I was an early adolescent I remember thinking that I preferred wintertime to summer because boosting was so much easier to negotiate when it was cold and people naturally wore layers of clothing and big coats with deep pockets. But as time passed, I learned to make compensations for those hindrances too. My pre-teen and adolescent boosting strategies were pretty uncreative and commonplace. Although I was smoking increasing amounts of marijuana, I never indulged in boosting when I was high. Moreover, I wasn't greedy, made a conscious effort to execute good judgment, and with few exceptions, always did my work by myself. I had a hard enough time fine-tuning my own judgment. There was no way I was going to depend on someone else's. I always weighed everything against the risk factors involved in getting caught. I was very clear in my thinking about not wanting to get caught, so I modulated all of my thinking, strategizing, and organizing with that one very important goal in mind. Looking back now, while I'm certain that a part of my dogmatic thinking on the subject was clearly tied into my fear of being separated from Mama again and having to leave her alone to fend for herself without the non-verbalized assistance of my stabilizing presence, I believe my adamant refusal to be arrested was mostly motivated by my need to keep my tottering personal life out of Mama's sphere of cognizance, in an effort to spare her any further feelings of disappointment. Although our far and few between conversations rarely touched on moral issues or my personal life goals, I knew she'd be disappointed nonetheless. In the end, I wonder how much of a secret my secrets really were.

With rap music and many forms of African-American consciousness-raising movements on the rise, many of my boosting peers felt a surging desire to steal from the white man and allow black-owned businesses the opportunity to flourish. In small units of two and three, kids from the inner-city neighborhoods of Brooklyn, Queens, Manhattan, and the Bronx trekked off with lots of roomy pocket space into the unfamiliar territories of the Long Island suburban shopping malls and midtown Manhattan's upscale fashion department stores. Many of their asses also ended up right there in the suburban and/or midtown Manhattan precincts. Me, I played it safe. I stole where, and from whom, it was the safest. While it would have given me great pleasure to steal from the white man in his own neighborhood, it would have given me even more displeasure to end up in his jails. So, as a young person, I always boosted from stores in inner-city neighborhoods, usually not my own, in the areas in which I was most familiar, and frequently, from other people of color. No matter how much I was tempted, I took it as plain fact that I would be a much easier target for some wary security guard in a ritzy suburban store. And I was quite certain that if I did have to run, the odds of my successful escape were a lot higher on familiar streets amidst people of similar coloring and garb.

My early boosting techniques pretty much revolved around stuffing items into my pockets and shopping bags, dislodging metal detectors and then stuffing items into my pockets, wearing one, perhaps two, layers of clothing into a store and then three, perhaps four, layers on my way out, and running like hell when the rare occasion dictated such an extreme form of getaway. Although I surely wasn't the forerunner in successful sneaker boosting, my peers always marveled at the alacrity with which I was sporting the new Adidas and Puma foot fashion. Many of them just didn't think about the going into your basic sneaker store, bagging your size sneaker off of the display rack, going into the next sneaker store, requesting a pair of sneakers of your choice in your size, and then bagging the needed sneaker for your match while replacing the missing sneaker with a same type sneaker from the display rack trick. I did, but I sure didn't spread the word. That would have increased the odds of getting caught and arrested. And, like I said, I was very clear about the significance of avoiding that outcome.

Like I said, I was damn good at what I did, and unlike my unknowing mentor (Mama), I never got caught. I maintained a rather low-profile boosting career until I was past my fifteenth birthday, right up until the point I virtually stopped attending school, said "fuck it," and started flirting with the infamous Mr. Snow, and on some scared, anxious, and despairing adolescent level, acknowledged that Mama's days were numbered, as were her depreciating T-cells.

Out with the old and in with the new. My initial levelheaded, periodic proclivity toward helping my pocket and wardrobe rather quickly transformed into a spiraling irrational, greedy, often senseless, eventually aggressive, and seemingly out-of-control-cycle of relentless, passionate crime. In addition to my growing love affair with magical, white, powdery lines, I became wed to the climactic high associated with risky criminal activity. I was a fifteen-year-old high school dropout who thought she was making her way into the first-place position in the high-stake races, but had instead mapped out the already quite familiar life pattern of going round like a blindfolded horse in the mill. At age sixteen, I was arrested for the first time on charges of armed robbery in the first, second, and third degrees.

Just for the record, while my unknowing mentor, Mama, was quite a skilled laborer herself, the patterns and objectives involved in our criminal activities often differed. First of all, with the exception of stealing a little extra food to prevent me from going hungry, Mama always stole with the goal of obtaining just enough cash to keep that clawing nasty monkey off of her back. And believe it or not, as opposed to stealing, she often preferred to acquire her dope honestly via keeping company with male addicts or dealers with charitable natures. In moments of increased desperation, she would then procure her drug of choice by making even exchanges for sexual favors. In the beginning, I stole "just because." I didn't know from stealing out of need until a couple of years later. By that point, I was also very much able to relate to the sexual favor bartering system as well.

Another difference between me and Mama was that Mama hardly ever ran when she got caught. Instead, she'd typically argue with whatever poor store man or security guard who had unfortunately, for his sake, happened to catch her in action, flailing her arms and hurling enough profanities in his direction to make any onlooker become momentarily confused about which party had actually committed a crime. Oppressed pride often surfaces at unexpected times, and despite her lifestyle, I don't believe Mama perceived herself to be a member of the criminal element. No, Mama hardly ever fled from the scene of her crimes, nor did she ever carry or use a weapon. In those few isolated incidents of sheer desperation during which Mama was driven to commit a crime against an actual person, she never inflicted any imagined or real harm. She simply picked their pockets for their wallets or snatched their purses, and then in those few isolated instances, ran like hell.

There was only one item that Mama openly and admittedly stole throughout her entire life. One item of which no sentiments of shame were associated with its theft. One particular item that I sincerely believe I never observed Mama purchase in a typical conventional manner throughout my entire childhood. Toilet paper. Word to mother, Mama stole toilet paper from public rest rooms like it was going out of style, as if it was her God-given right and it was the most natural thing in the world to do. We always had an odd assortment of toilet paper rolls in our closets. Our toileting needs were never a source of stress, although when I was about eight, I did begin to worry about all of those poor individuals who suffered from the runs and made it to the bathroom just in the nick of time after Mama had already made her daily rounds.

Finally, I don't think Mama ever knew anything about that staggering high that I used to experience after engaging in risky, potentially violent, forms of criminal behavior. While I, on many levels, enjoyed that shit, with the exception of her little toilet paper quirk, I believe Mama was actually ashamed of her periodic need to steal. She sure never bragged about any of it to me, and with one or two rare exceptions during which heroin had transported her into a completely foreign-mind zone, Mama never directly exposed me to her extracurricular stealing activities. I mainly learned from her when she thought that I wasn't looking. I wonder if she saw things when I thought that she wasn't looking as well. So, while I usually refer to Mama as my unknowing mentor, much of my past cannot be unquestioningly explained by social modeling theory. While it is true that this apple didn't fall very far from the tree of its initial seedling experiences, it similarly came up with some pretty innovative ideas about which part of the ground it chose to roll around on.

As you can see, the shopping mall and browsing thing is replete with many a live trigger. But, since the angels permitted Mama an after-hours prison visit during my last incarceration and I concomitantly made a full-fledged oath about remaining drug-free one day at a time, I have not taken one thing that didn't belong to me. Not even toilet paper. Now, before I end my long-winded discourse on my current daily lifestyle, allow me to add that I, Victoria, have begun to casually date a fine, sexy, intelligent, sensitive, and seemingly normal man. Things are going kind of slow. We haven't even consummated the relationship yet, although that's admittedly his doing because, trust me, when he gives me the word or even the slightest gesture, I swear I'll get it on with him at that very moment. But like I said, we seem to be taking things kind of slow. His name is Thomas, but instead of formally introducing you to Thomas right now, there are a few others that I'd really like you to meet—Ms. Cathy O'Connor, her disappearing and not-so-devoted husband, Mr. Leroy Stinkdog, and last but not least, her very faithful, eternally present lover, the ghost of Jose—"el salvaje."

Ms. Cathy is one person from my childhood that I'll never forget. Do you know how some people enter and then leave your life without much further ado? Their exit virtually goes unnoticed, while their shadow quietly leaves a remote trace of an imprint on your memory wheel that never quite spins into full focus again unless a more important, personal association is triggered. It's as if with or without their passing acquaintance, it would all be the same a hundred years hence. But then, there are those few others who have been absent from your life for years, play absolutely no role in your daily existence, but yet for some unexplainable reason, have their imprints poignantly and vividly transfixed in your wheel's reflection no matter in what direction it spins. Ms. Cathy is one of those people whose essence was inconspicuously absorbed into my mind's mirrors during the latency stage of my childhood. Although I never particularly liked Ms. Cathy, her immanence had left its mark as if we allusively bonded under an eclipse.

I met Ms. Cathy when I was eight years old and still, I guess, somewhat impressionable. Mama, who was always thinking up new plans with which to dupe the system, carted me off early one morning to some Victims Service Agency in the Bronx with the hopes of concocting a woeful battered wife's tale believable enough to manipulate some green social worker into pointing us in the direction of an improved housing situation. According to Mama's duplicitous reasoning, if old fat Ms. Martha and her roost of hoodlum children could be pitied by the city and placed into a nice and decent tenement building just because her drunken husband kicked the shit out of her every once in a while, blackened her eyes, and misplaced a few of her teeth, then why shouldn't the city find some pity in its heart for her as well? Like Mama said, "I've been knocked around by a few niggers myself, and I sure is missing some teeth." The fact that Mama's "beat downs" were typically caused by her own poor judgment about who she let into her rooming quarters to get high with, connive out of money, or rob blindly once they seemingly lost consciousness in a nod, was obviously not one of her top ten considerations. And since we're all in complete understanding now about the origins of her few missing and rotted teeth, we won't even go there. But, getting back to my point, Mama, along with her primly donned, selfless demeanor of entitlement, busted right through that Victims Service Agency's door and demanded that someone immediately find a refuge apartment for her broken and battered self and traumatized child. Despite her fire-and-brimstone performance, we were directed to the waiting area, and it was there that Mama and I bid acquaintance with Ms. Cathy O'Connor for the first time. Mama's little wife abuse hoax didn't pan out too well with the seasoned worker who was assigned to her case. Whoever that man was, he quickly read through her ruse and saw through her disease of attitudes, as if the long-sleeved shirt she was wearing was transparent and he could count the needle trademarks on her arms. By the time the man was done generating a list of all of the required documents that Mama would need in order to substantiate her cries for assistance, Mama was up in his face and cursing him out, telling him that it was people like him who gave men the license to keep women suffering and in a subhuman position. A black security guard escorted us to the agency's door, but not before Mama had the opportunity to form what would prove to be an enduring friendship with the only white woman client in the place. Sometimes bad comes out of good intentions. Sometimes good evolves from bad intentions. And then sometimes, there are simply divine appointments. Mama's and Ms. Cathy's chance meeting was one of those.

Ms. Cathy was a skinny, chain-smoking, blue-eyed blonde Irish girl who had finally conjured up enough courage to seek out some information about the obviously insane and recurring pattern of abuse that characterized her marriage. It was an increasingly worsening pattern in which her blue eyes were periodically blackened, her skin bruised, her mind numbed, and her heart left heavy. She wasn't seeking divorce, separation, or even a temporary escape from her marital union, nor was she seeking counseling or assistance with housing. She was simply seeking some semblance of peace and clarity of mind and an answer to the rhetorical question, "Why does he keep doing these things to me?"

Mama left the agency without any prospects for improved housing. Ms. Cathy left the agency with her question left unanswered. But, thanks to Ms. Cathy's efforts with "pulling a few strings," Mama landed an improved housing situation in the form of a one-bedroom apartment on the floor right beneath Ms. Cathy about one month after they had bid each others' acquaintance. And as for Ms. Cathy, well thanks to Mama and the ghost of Jose "el salvaje," her peace and clarity of mind were finally returned to her at some point in time right before my tenth year birthday, but with minds and hearts being what they are, who can exactly be sure when?

Other than for all of the escapades leading to the disappearance of Mr. Leroy Stinkdog, Ms. Cathy's memory always stands erect in my mind in association with the concept of weatherless and undying romantic love. In fact, it was Ms. Cathy's description of true love, along with the saga of Jose "el salvaje" and she, that ultimately swayed me to sever my noxious ties with Trevor and stop using the "love" word in vain. Until the day I die, I will never forget Ms. Cathy's misty azure eyes, nor devout soul-stirring words, when Mama sat her down one day and asked her what it was like to fall in love. Her words came as easy as the love she professed . . .

"Falling in love is like being reborn emotionally. The first time your eyes meet an invisible wand leaves your heart and casts a spell on time so that clocks never tick the same in your life again. It's as if at that very moment you meet, the angels sprinkle love dust from the heavens that keeps you intoxicated with thoughts of each other forever. You never have to spend much time familiarizing yourself with your soul mate as there is no question that your chance meeting was contemplated by fate in a past lifetime. Questions about right and wrong become scarce when you are with him as the meaning of life is found in his embrace, and curiosities about your future, in his kiss. Once you experience true love, you know with an unprecedented certainty that no matter how close or far your beloved may be, your souls are entwined by the perfect, pliant threads of the gods. Your heart sings a sweet melodic song of rhapsody, and your eyes behold the world with the unfamiliar luminescence of Cupid's fireflies, embossed with beads of color from a different, flawlessly beautiful dimension in time. The way I see it, love, like people, comes in different shapes, sizes, and colors. If I had to choose one color, I like to think of me and Jose's love as if it were the color blue. It was radiant yet serene, vast but buoyant and effortless, pure and unfledged while being as ageless and unflagging as the cerulean skies. When you're truly in love, you remain with him always because you know that if you don't, the world just won't seem right, and besides, you're sure that no matter how willful the nature of your character may be, your heart will never successfully be able to set the clock of timeless love back again . . ."

In addition to permitting a shaft of light to enter my thinking about the concept of true love, Mama's and Ms. Cathy's chance meeting allowed me, when I bothered enough to focus, to have fleeting insight into the principles of mutual friendship. Along with all of the oddities, ineffable quirks, and personal hardships that are endemic of interpersonal relationships, I caught intermittent glimpses of the affectionate sentiments and exchanges that evolve when two human beings form a genuine bond of amity. I wonder what color of the rainbow Ms. Cathy would have likened to her friendship with Mama. Probably one that was intense and deep and fluid.

Mama and Ms. Cathy were the epitome of an odd couple. They were as externally different as they were inwardly similar. Mama was street-wise, coarse, impulsive, aggressive, and in no uncertain terms, certifiably crazy. Ms. Cathy, on the other hand, was seemingly naive, sweet, responsible, passive, and to the unsuspecting eye, quite sane. However, they had one complementary tie that existed in their lonesome survival instinct, while it was nurtured by their identical characterological traits of mystery and depth.

Other than her childhood friend Felicita, I believe that Ms. Cathy was Mama's one and only true friend in life. As for Ms. Cathy, with the exception of Jose "el salvaje," I don't think she kept company with too many folk on any kind of a regular basis either. Looking back now, I suspect that Mama's style of relating to Ms. Cathy didn't differ too much from that of her past early childhood relations with Felicita, which admittedly was the main reason behind my gnawing jealousy and discomfort with their relationship. Although Ms. Cathy was about seven years older than Mama, somewhere in the ball park of thirty-three, if my memory serves me correctly, from the very onset Mama assumed a protective, caretaker, big sister role in their bond of union, which Ms. Cathy, as with everything else, passively embraced. Putting my own jealousies aside for just a moment in an effort to turn back the hands of time from a carved-out, pure place in my heart, I guess I can relate to Mama's need to take Ms. Cathy under her porous wings. Although responsible and somewhat educated and financially independent, Ms. Cathy was such a delicate, anxious, and seemingly unknowing character who could have easily fallen prey to some dominant, wily individual who could have come along and taken advantage of her resigned and gentle nature. How she ever survived in the South Bronx for all of those years, I don't know. While I guess it's possible that the God she revered so much kept his angels on point and focused in her direction, I've come to consider the possibility that the reason why Ms. Cathy's ghetto neighbors never mistook her kindness for weakness was really because they were perceptive enough to comprehend the gravity behind such a misinterpretation. Despite Mama's repertoire of insanities and periodic faltering judgment, she quickly detected some veiled, unique quality of character in her new friend that not only fulfilled her own starving emotional needs, but likewise identified her as someone worth protecting. Perhaps it was simply Ms. Cathy's uncommon capacity for love.

During the approximate fifteen-month period that Mama and I lived one floor below Ms. Cathy on Hoe Avenue in the South Bronx, I don't believe one day passed without the two spending at least one half hour in each other's company. Don't get me wrong, Mama and Ms. Cathy didn't share in typical girlfriend activities such as going shopping or having tea, but they passed the hours away together nonetheless. The majority of their fellowshipping occurred in the early evening hours after Ms. Cathy had completed her day's work at the small furniture company office in which she was employed as a secretary. Mama used to drag me upstairs every night around dinnertime so that she and Ms. Cathy could chat "for just a while" in her tiny and clean, but dilapidated old kitchen with the fraying yellow-colored wallpaper and bruised linoleum. Upon entering, Mama always helped herself to a bottle of chilled Heineken from Ms. Cathy's icebox. Regardless of whether we had dinner together or not, Mama typically finished off at least two or three beers, while Ms. Cathy only nursed one bottle throughout the entire evening. Due to the combination of my active and competitive childhood nature, I typically became bored and openly resentful of the obvious object of my mother's passionate affection within the first ten minutes of their long-winded, sometimes hushed, sometimes raucous, conversations. Hence, I usually spent the remaining portion of the visit in the living room perched in front of Mr. Leroy Stinkdog's relatively large-screened television, which aside from his small clutter of old high school and college football trophies, was his main prized possession. Our visits typically ended around 8 PM in an effort to avoid the Stinkdog's 8:15 PM return home. Sometimes, when the Stinkdog surprised us by coming home sooner than expected, Mama's and Ms. Cathy's visit ended early and abruptly.

Before I go on, allow me to explain the origin of the Stinkdog surname. Rumors had it that the Stinkdog surname originated when his ex-wife, whose body frame and face strongly resembled that of the general population of the Amazon jungle tribes, used to kick her pitiful husband's ass, while boldly declaring not only that he was a faggot, but a funky-smelling one at that. However, my latency-age Bronx buddies and I used to like to assume full credit for the nickname's inception. All I can tell you is that it only took one whiff of the Stinkdog's one-of-a-kind body odor before the apropos title was created to identify him forever more.

If you want to know a little bit about his personals, the Stinkdog was supposedly ejected from college for some not-too-completely clear incident in which he got carried away during a fraternity "spanking" hazing ritual. It was said that he belonged to the Black Omega Psi Phi male fraternity that affectionately referred to themselves as "the Que Dogs" with boasting pride and bravado. As is the case with most men with frail egos, lean spirits, and tiny dicks, the Stinkdog attempted to camouflage his own stark character defects by vicariously living through the virile, swaggering, popular existence of the morassy group identity of his college affiliations. While I admittedly cannot provide a character analysis of any other "Que Dog" fraternity member, I can guarantee you that in the case of the Stinkdog, his trumpeted Que Dog-appointed masculinity was about as bogus as the day is long. In other words, he was a comical example of someone hollering before they are out of the wood. However, due to his seemingly cemented entrenchment in advertence, he showed off his fraternity emblems and colors of purple and gold in apparent oblivion to the fact that in doing so, he himself was making a mockery of his own beloved fraternity while simultaneously inspiring the changing of his Que Dog title into the more fitting Stinkdog misnomer. In fact, the Stinkdog name became so embedded in my mind that to this day I couldn't tell you his birth-given surname if I tried. And despite the fact that I haven't been in touch with her for many years, I bet any amount of money that the same holds true for Ms. Cathy. While his name may evade the recollections of those who used to reside on Hoe Avenue in the South Bronx during the late seventies, the memory of his unique stench will, without question, always remain logged into the memoirs of our olfactory senses.

Mr. Leroy Stinkdog was a sorry individual who most folk would have probably either dismissed as a prime example of God's good sense of humor, or prayed for, depending on their own philosophies about life and resiliency of character. Looking back in retrospect, it wasn't merely the issue of his repulsive body odor, weakness of character, or need to dilute his masculine deficiencies in the larger fraternity identity that offended most of us, but instead his obvious intentional and sober-minded objective to demean, and if possible, destroy anything that was pure and good in others. Although I am positive that his malicious pattern of relating had caused many to sustain significant emotional injuries at different opportune periods throughout his life, I became personally privy to this new form of human addiction and disease of attitudes in my observation of it in the relationship between Mr. Leroy Stinkdog and Ms. Cathy. While my regrettably delayed emotional maturation has taught me that there are always exceptions to rules wherever human beings are concerned, my observation of the so-called marriage between Ms. Cathy and the Stinkdog educated me that in many cases, misery does in fact, love company.

The story goes to say that about four months following the death of Ms. Cathy's lover, Jose, Mr. Leroy Stinkdog, the neighborhood mailman, began hanging around our building a lot longer than it took for him to insert the residents' letters and bills into their respective mailboxes. While he obviously had a hidden agenda, he began performing many small services for Ms. Cathy that, due to her grievous state of devastation, she was emotionally unable to perform for herself. He began by making sure that she had enough cigarettes for the evening, bringing her sleeping pills to ease her insomnia, and offering to make small household repairs when things needed fixing. As time progressed, the Stinkdog began picking Ms. Cathy up after work, driving her to the supermarket, and keeping her company during those lonely weekend hours by joining her for dinner or a special television program. Before her numbed mind could detect the direction in which the relationship was going, the Stinkdog had found his way into her apartment and life's rituals on practically a daily basis. Then he began staying overnight. Although he initially fell asleep on the living room couch a few times due to the lateness of the hour, as the weeks passed he found his way into her bed, and finally, into her embrace. I remember Ms. Cathy once trying to explain to Mama that, for at least six months after Jose's death, she was in a state of shell shock. Although her vital organs continued functioning, Ms. Cathy said that she passed full weeks in a mindless daze, as if suspended in a vacuum, petrified to release her tenuous grip, knowing fully well that she was unprepared to deal with the pain that went along with accepting that Jose was gone from her life forever. The Stinkdog's presence slowly pried her out of the well of catalepsy, while keeping the anticipated, potentially lethal pain out of her consciousness, floating in the abeyance of denial. I remember Ms. Cathy explaining that although the Stinkdog was not her type, nor would she ever have permitted him anywhere near her bed at any other point in her life, she unfortunately experienced that irrational desperation that overcomes a person when they are drowning in the sea of their own emotional emptiness and disoriented agony. She later acknowledged that she didn't cast one awakened eye in the direction of the person, but instead was moved by relief and gratitude because of the artificial life preserver he seemed to be offering. I guess having a heavy heart isn't nearly as bad as feeling as if you've got no heart at all.

So, in an effort to feel human, Ms. Cathy welcomed the Stinkdog's presence into her life, while clinging to his flesh in her bed. Her decision to have sex with him was more based on guilt, an uneasiness about not fulfilling her obligations toward the man who she deemed responsible for taking the raw edges off of her pain and permitting her the opportunity to, at least partially, partake in a few of life's small pleasures again. As time progressed and Ms. Cathy had seemingly mastered the trick of ignoring the corner of her being in which her grief and pain for her deceased beloved continually lingered, she acquiesced to the Stinkdog's proposal of marriage for all of the wrong reasons. Primarily because she had decided on the day that Jose was lowered into the dirt that nothing really mattered anymore. Her three-year-long marriage to the Stinkdog not only taught her to never underestimate the strength behind true love and friendship, but also that no matter the depth of our loss or agony, there's always something in this mad, mad world to hang on to that continues to matter, no matter what.

I'm not exactly sure why I have this burning desire to include Ms. Cathy's story in my sponsor-dictated recovery paper walk. Perhaps it is because it is my only childhood experience that takes on even the remotest of legendary overtones. Perhaps it is because the experience, on some profound level, moved me. Perhaps it is because it marked the first time I encountered folk who respected the power of unrequited love and considered the presence of a higher spiritual being. Perhaps it is merely due to the fact that Mama paid so much attention to the ordeal. Or perhaps, I'm almost embarrassed to admit, it is because the tale exhumes an emotional concept that I had unknowingly abandoned during the earliest seasons of my childhood. Hope. While I have as yet to analyze the implications and ramifications behind the message fully, I believe that even in its darkest moments, the meaning behind the story of Ms. Cathy is a hopeful one, with promises of even more to come.

CHAPTER EIGHT

He is not a lover who does not love forever.
—Euripides

ACCORDING TO THE story, Ms. Cathy was born and raised in a middle-class, Irish-American home in a suburban town in the state of Connecticut. As far as my subjective dysfunctional understanding of normal life goes, Ms. Cathy's early childhood environment lies somewhat in the vicinity of the top 5 percent of functional, decent family living. A Disney world, if we wanted to compare it with that of my own or the majority of my life's acquaintances. Without one iota of conflicting evidence, Ms. Cathy's childhood was blessed, as if the angels were indeed watching over her from heaven without blinking their eyes. Her early experiences were devoid of the abuse, abandonment, addictions, and chaos that characterized my own. However, despite the differences in our childhoods, the experience of pain she later endured was quite real and, if not equally, then relatively, devastating to her heart and soul.

As the story goes, Ms. Cathy's life course took an unexpected and irreversible turn during a spontaneous weekend trip to New York City. Having recently become engaged to an accountant from Hartford, completed her junior year credits at night college, and received a small raise from the insurance firm in which she was employed, Ms. Cathy decided that it was high time she gave herself a break as well as an independent celebration of her achievements and good fortune. So, on a bright and sunny morning in June of her twenty-sixth year, she cheerfully informed her parents not to expect her home for dinner as she was leaving work at noon to catch the 1 PM Metro North train to New York City for the weekend to browse through some museums as well as clothing stores in order to obtain some tangible ideas about fashions for next year's upcoming wedding. And while Bob, her fiancé, expressed a few reservations on the phone about her spending two nights alone in a hotel in the notoriously dangerous Big Apple, he quickly relaxed upon hearing that she had accommodations at a renowned metropolitan hotel, bid her well, told her that he loved her, and reassured her that he'd pick her up at the train station on Sunday evening. As she boarded the train later that afternoon, Ms. Cathy felt light, adventurous, and exhilarated, with an edge of expectancy. For while she was undoubtedly proud of her accomplishments, excited about her engagement, and enthusiastic about her prospective trip, traces of a mysterious, almost magical dream from the previous night moved through her consciousness like the fragrance of lilac on a gentle summer night's breeze. Although she had dreamt shorter versions of the same dream since as far back as she could remember, the evening before she departed for New York City was the first time she traveled through the entire dream, awakening practically at arm's length from its hidden message. Throughout her life Ms. Cathy had had a recurring dream in which she was propelled down a seemingly endless winding path, beckoned by distant comforting whispers and occasionally hastened by luminescent benevolent fairies with pastel-colored wings, toward a destiny that, while as yet unknown, was uncannily familiar, and filled with promises of enchantment and eternal bliss. Although she always took pleasure in basking in the warm but yet tingling feelings that the dream produced, she had always awakened while envisioning herself at some point on the road without one hint of a view of her journey's final destination. But on the night before leaving for New York City, the dream almost ran its entire course, leaving Ms. Cathy in front of a gilded gate. But, just as she was about to push the gate open and joyfully greet the voice behind the whispered promises, she remembered her faithful servants and turned around to bid farewell to the persistent fairies. In the blink of an eye that it took to recognize that the fairies had vanished, she awakened from her dream before having the opportunity to push the gate forward.

 Ms. Cathy did not have the same dream again until several years later. Instead, she lived it for the next three. And although she definitely passed a lapse from experiencing the dream during the time period following Jose's death when she was with the Stinkdog, my premonitions tell me that she continues to live the dream today, albeit on a much different spiritual level. I guess one can't dream anymore about things once it has become one's reality. They can't wonder about the mysteries behind luminescent fairies with pastel-colored wings when they experience such magnificence in their world everyday. They can't ponder about the identity of comforting whispers when it is the voice of their lover whose soothing murmurs quicken their heartbeat every night. And they definitely cannot question final destinations that have been indubitably predetermined a very long time ago.

 The next time Ms. Cathy experienced the dream was about two weeks before the unnatural disappearance of Mr. Leroy Stinkdog. But in this later dream, she was no longer guided down the seemingly endless winding path by fairies of magical colors, but instead by her lover Jose who never failed to keep his right arm draped protectively across her shoulder.

On her first evening in New York City, Ms. Cathy strolled through sections of the Metropolitan Museum of Art, enjoyed a scrumptious dinner at an outdoor cafe in the East Village that permitted her the opportunity to view a garden variety of interesting, but admittedly, strange people and sights, browsed through an assortment of progressive East Village shops, and at the twilight hour returned to her hotel room to luxuriate in a cradling bath before retiring in a king-sized bed of royal comfort. And while she was initially disappointed that her recurring dream evaded her slumber on that Friday evening, she needn't have been because on the following morning when she readied herself to visit Central Park, she had no idea that upon opening and walking through her hotel door, she had finally passed through the gilded gates of her destiny and entered her dream forever more.

At 11:15 AM, after she had tired herself out from trekking through several different regions of the park with no particular goal in mind except to follow her impulses, Ms. Cathy sat her weary self down on a bench to take a couple of swigs of her bottled water and plan her itinerary for the afternoon.

At 11:16 AM, Jose Velez, and about twenty of his Puerto Rican friends and relatives, arrived at Central Park to have a celebratory picnic for Jose's younger brother who had just been released from Elmira Correctional Facility after having served a five-year bid due to a finding of guilt for an attempted murder that occurred during his late adolescence. Although Jose himself had recently been released from Riker's Island after being incarcerated for eight months on assault charges when he "unintentionally" caused a foe to sustain a concussion and two broken ribs during a fight, the picnic party idea was not created with thoughts of Jose in mind due to his tendency to recidivate at least once every eighteen months since he became familiar with the revolving-door policy of the NYC Department of Corrections thirteen years ago when he was sixteen. But, unlike his brother, Jose had never served "hard time" as he was typically incarcerated for crimes of a less felonious nature. Multiple year incarcerations were an unspoken requirement if you wanted to be the identified honoree of a picnic in Jose's family. Particularly after his most recent extended time-out in jail, with all of its accompanying discomforts and life's hindrances, Jose maintained his desire to pass on all family-appointed honoree positions.

At 11:30 AM, Ms. Cathy observed a group of men beginning to set up a baseball game in a nearby field.

At 11:40 AM, one of Jose's brother-in-laws hit an outfield ball that escaped his glove and bounced off into the distant sea of grass behind him.

At 11:41 AM, just as Ms. Cathy was rising to leave the park, she observed a baseball rolling in her direction, being chased by a man who kept his head down while murmuring a string of obscenities in Spanish.

Somewhere between 11:41 AM and 11:42 AM, both Ms. Cathy and Jose looked up into each other's eyes and time came to an abrupt halt. They felt the loose threads of their souls entwine, and within a fraction of a moment, understood that their hearts would never allow them to be apart again. The ball rolled by and came to a stop about three yards away.

If she could have turned back the hands of time, Ms. Cathy said that within the three years she spent with Jose there would have been only one thing she would have changed. As the ball's yardage distance from the couple seemingly marked a foreboding of their destined time together on earth, she would have gotten down on her knees, and with the lung power of a seasoned athlete, blown it to a point of infinite distance. But, despite the magical overtones of Ms. Cathy's story, like the rest of us, her humanity placed limitations on her that dictated that her will power would always remain one step behind that of her fate.

Shortly after their chance meeting, Ms. Cathy broke off her engagement with her fiance, and she and Jose secured the very same small apartment in the Bronx that she had by the time Mama and I got around to knowing her. Although Ms. Cathy's family was initially shocked, and needless to say displeased, within a matter of months they resumed their previously established supportive and loving relations with one another, albeit from a distance. I've since come to speculate that such acts of acceptance must be the cornerstone of healthy, loving family relationships. It would seem so anyway. Due to Jose's ex-wife's refusal to grant Jose an easy divorce, the two never legally married. Instead, they bonded together from a place somewhere deep down in their souls in the name of genuine friendship, love, and human spirituality. Then they proceeded to live together in a so-called common-law arrangement and became so immersed in one another, enjoying life's little and big daily gifts, they completely forgot about the legal formalities of holy matrimony.

Ms. Cathy never completed college. Instead, she accepted an office job at a small furniture company, and anxiously waited for five o'clock to be displayed on the office's dingy clock everyday to signal the precise moment in which she would be able to take leave of her paperwork trail and make an abrupt turn in the direction of home and Jose's embrace.

Although Jose initially encountered some difficulty in his fearless employment search, particularly due to the criminal record that hovered above him like a persistent shadow, he eventually landed an off-the-books but legal job on the strength of a friend of a cousin who he also referred to as cousin due to the street brotherhood thing. Jose worked the early day shift in a busy bodega that was conveniently positioned on the corner, directly diagonally across the street from the apartment in which he and his beloved Cathy resided. In fact, rumor has it that since he met Ms. Cathy and clocks seemed to come to a strange standstill, Jose's extracurricular street activities arrived at a similar abrupt halt. With the exception of one minor scuffle with the police when Jose was involved in a menacing dialogue with some guy from Queens who had disrespected his brother, his criminal record remained unblemished during the time period in which love had helped restore some balance to his life. While I have been shown time and time again that leopards do not change their spots, I once heard an elderly prison counselor of mine say that sometimes life's experiences creates imposter leopards whose spots are merely visual images of childhood wounds that can be gently erased through spiritual healing.

With the pure hearts of children and the ardor of young lovers, Ms. Cathy and Jose worked, played, socialized, made love, and attended church together, that is when their all-night hot and heavy Saturday nights permitted them to rise before early afternoon. They talked, laughed, cuddled, occasionally argued, and then talked, laughed, and cuddled some more. So much love dust had apparently entered their pores that Jose and Ms. Cathy could barely keep their eyes, hands, and minds off of one another for more than a few moments. In a hushed, secretive tone, I once heard Ms. Cathy telling Mama that she and Jose were so aware of their mutual sweet obsession for each other that they began to lovingly compete against one another to see who would drift off to sleep first after their lovemaking sessions when they lay as one in bed embracing each other's bodies, searching into the seeming eternal liquid of each other's eyes. Typically, the score was tied, although Ms. Cathy sadly remembered how Jose used to insist that he was in the first place position by a fraction of a hair.

Since their initial encounter on a mild summer morning in Central Park, the seconds melted into minutes, and then in turn, evolved into hours, and without either of the two realizing when and how, into days, months, and eventually years. Then, on one early evening in mid-October, shortly after the leaves began to assume their autumn demeanor, two desperate young male addicts held up the store in which Jose worked with loaded guns. They quickly left with the cash register's contents, but not before firing two bullets into Jose's chest.

Jose died within a matter of minutes, way before the police or ambulances arrived at the scene. But, he held out long enough to allow his beloved to run the diagonal distance across the street, pry her arms around his bloody body, and with her eyes, search into his fading consciousness. With the last of his dying strength, Jose wrenched himself loose from death's tenacious grip long enough to focus in on Ms. Cathy's horrified eyes and whispered, "I love you . . . always." Seconds later, Jose's heart stopped beating and he made an abrupt descent into death's abyss while his beloved's tears mixed with the coagulating blood that covered his body. Then, as the iron entered her soul, clocks began to tick again, and time became a painful, cumbersome component of life.

When I was young and without many reference points by which I could define "normalcy," I used to believe that Mama, our transient lifestyle, temporary institutionalizations, drugs, and a whole lot of other insanity characterized that of the typical American family. Baseball, hot dogs, apple pie, and narcotics. I didn't know anything different, or better. So, in much the same way, I didn't understand what all the fuss was about when the South Bronx neighborhood kids cheered Mama on, actually glorified her, treating her like she was the best thing since white bread, all because she instigated this "Save Ms. Cathy" crusade against the Stinkdog. I mean as far back as I could remember, Mama was always cussing and fighting with somebody, especially when she was high, which was almost always. I never thought it was funny. Instead, I used to feel embarrassed and a little scared because I knew such scenes often escalated, and could potentially result in incarceration for Mama and foster care for me. Hence, I dreaded seeing the fire that typically ignited in the center of the irises of Mama's eyes, knowing fully well that it meant that within a matter of seconds Mama would be up in somebody's face, bellowing with rage about some perceived injustice for which they were supposedly, at least partially, responsible. Most folk, particularly those with good sense, never answered Mama. They just kind of stood there as if in shock and waited for her to go away, hurling a trail of muffled obscenities under her breath as she trudged on. On those rare occasions when someone did dare to muster up a retort, Mama blazoned forth like a jackhammer, spewing out dozens of possible ways by which she could murder her adversary, never failing to repeatedly remind them that they "didn't know her." I wonder if she believed that anyone would actually have been interested in fostering a relationship with the likes of her after she had just completed generating a list of at least fifteen methods by which she would gladly facilitate their death. In her day, Mama told so many people that they didn't know her, I believe the majority of the people from the neighborhoods in which we lived made references to Mama as that crazy lady who nobody knew. In that respect, they were quite right.

Anyway, I didn't initially understand why Mama's crusade against the Stinkdog received such publicity from my peers, and later, from the adults in my community. It couldn't have just been because of the physical abuse Ms. Cathy endured. Women in the ghetto, as well as in affluent neighborhoods, were, and still are, battered everyday. It couldn't even have been because one of my older male peers once discovered the Stinkdog hunched over a homosexual pornographic magazine while taking a lunch break in his mailman uniform in the park. Homosexuality and bisexuality, whether in or out of the closet, were not foreign concepts in our parts. I eventually stopped trying to figure it out, and instead, like the rest of my latency-age peers, blamed it on his repulsive body odor and gave Mama her props for bringing some laughter into streets that were usually reserved for blood and tears.

About two months after we moved into the apartment beneath Ms. Cathy's, the Stinkdog punched her in the mouth because he found some pictures of her and Jose buried deep down under some shoeboxes in their bedroom closet. He then tore up the entire house in search of additional residual memorabilia from their torrid thirty-nine months of time spent together here on earth. He found a few more remnants, including four stashed Hallmark cards, two crumpled-up love notes, a half-used candle, about ten more photographs, and four frozen withered-away rose petals that were preserved in a cellophane bag in the fruit bin of the refrigerator. All were abruptly stuffed down the old tenement's incinerator while Ms. Cathy held her throbbing mouth, while she was dying a million deaths due to the pain inside of her broken heart. As far as I could gather when she was trying to explain the incident in between choking sobs to Mama, she had only managed to save one last tangible item that belonged to Jose. One last relic of their love that she could stroke and relive memories with when the Stinkdog was not at home. Ms. Cathy had Jose's baseball bat hidden from view under the bed skirt on the very same bed that she shared with the Stinkdog.

Bristling with anger after seeing the swollen, busted lips of her only friend, Mama didn't even wait until the Stinkdog returned home from work. As a matter of fact, she didn't even bother putting on a coat. Instead, as if she could truly sniff out his whereabouts by his musty scent, Mama put her nose to the wind and marched off into a cold April Saturday afternoon like a crazed predator, warmed by a vengeful fury and the bag of heroin that she had recently shot into her veins.

Mama located the Stinkdog about sixteen blocks away delivering mail somewhere up by the projects. Although I wasn't personally present, about ten of my peers who had similar magnets for strife and trouble, later excitedly described how Mama came charging up on the Stinkdog out of nowhere, propelling herself against his body with such force that it caused him to crash up against the side of his mail cart, which in turn toppled over, leaving the Stinkdog with no choice but to lie inert across its strewn contents. But, of course, Mama didn't stop there. No, not my mama. She then proceeded to yell at the top of her lungs that if he ever lay one more motherfucking, foul-smelling finger on so much of a hair on her friend's head she was going to shove the entire mailbag up his faggot ass so hard that he'd be shitting out SSI checks for the rest of his life. And while it was decidedly true that the Stinkdog was a man of numerous character defects, he did demonstrate some good sense in this isolated impromptu circumstance and remained there on the floor on top of his mail cart with his legs sprawled apart, a dumbfounded look on his face, and about a third of the mail that belonged to the people in the housing project drifting aimlessly away across the cement pavement with the wind beneath its sails. Minutes passed until Mama finally exhausted herself from screeching out an abundance of miscellaneous obscenities, and then triumphantly stalked off into the direction from which she had come.

According to Mama's latency-age fan club, hundreds of curious faces came to peer out their windows to identify the source of the ruckus, laughing their heads off to a point beyond tears when they discovered that a big and historically boasting black man had allowed some female dope fiend to kick his pitiful ass. This, of course, gave my already vibrating peer posse license to keep their finger wagging at the Stinkdog, while making loud jeers about his body odor and sexual preferences.

As is the case with most exciting moments in time, the initial flurry eventually died down and people went back inside and went on with their business, while the Stinkdog scraped around on his hands and knees looking for runaway mail. However, the children never forgot. Since that cold April afternoon on the day that Mama publicly kicked the Stinkdog's funky ass, he never could finish a complete mail tour without some juvenile thug pointing their finger at him and howling something about how the Stinkdog was a faggot with SSI checks coming out of his ass. Looking back now, I guess it was kind of funny. But at the time I didn't think so when it was my mama, the adult child, who was the first one to point the finger.

Whether it was because of Mama's magnanimous threats, his public embarrassment, or the natural ebb and flow involved in moods, temperaments, and abusive relationships, I can never be sure, but to the best of my knowledge there were no displays of violence from behind the closed doors of Ms. Cathy's apartment for about the next three months. Then Mama hit a number for about $100, bought me three fairly decent outfits for the coming school year from Fordham Road, and it was time for me to precociously learn about yet another area of adult dysfunction via the instructional techniques of observation and immersion.

As soon as I discovered that Mama had won all of that money, I knew it would only be a matter of time, probably hours, before I ended up under the minimal surveillance of some misfit babysitter. Despite the fact that Mama had never previously left me with Ms. Cathy for more than just a few hours due to her hatred for, and my fear of, her unsavory husband, she entreated Ms. Cathy to allow me to stay at her house for one night while she "went out for a while." Ms. Cathy agreed. I cried and whined about the putrid smell that was upstairs. And Mama dashed off to the races at the closest shooting gallery she could possibly find.

Before I go on with my detailed account of my three night stay with my hospitable babysitters, allow me the opportunity to share my hard-learned knowledge about Mama's favorite vacation spots. Although I never entered a shooting gallery for my own personal use until months after I had cleared my seventeenth birthday, I, like Mama, eventually made them my home away from home. Although I was virtually homeless at the age of seventeen, I guess they, in a peculiar sort of way, were my home, along with the streets, rooftops, alleyways, crack houses, and abandoned buildings. Shooting galleries are man-made likenesses of hell here on earth. Although typically located in uninhabited, and uninhabitable, abandoned buildings, apartments, or basements, many inhabited apartments were transformed into shooting galleries by their afflicted tenants, by their tenants' afflicted children, or by dominating afflicted others who seized control over a weaker tenant's dwelling. Elderly parents and grandparents' apartments often easily fell prey to the unscrupulous habits of their addicted offspring. In fact, I remember how when old Mrs. Henry, who had raised her five grandchildren in the projects down by Ms. Cathy's building, went into Lincoln Hospital due to a mild stroke, she came home to find that her nice little apartment had been transformed into a dope den by her grandsons and their dope fiend friends. Poor Mrs. Henry must have lived out the next six months of her old life in terror and shame until she was eventually found dead in her bed by one of the addicts who was looking to steal something from her room. It was said that the only reason why the addict even realized that she was dead was because of the foul smell festering in her room from her stiff corpse that had already started to rot away three days before. Even so, Mama and I heard that it took at least another twelve hours for the most devoted of her grandsons to get himself together enough to clear out all of the fiends and the drugs in order to phone the necessary authorities.

When I was a child and heroin lorded complete power over Mama's life, shooting galleries were the street addict's home away from home. When I grew up and crack, the popular drug of choice, lorded complete power over my life, crack houses became the interchangeable label for the street addict's home away from home. Regardless of their so-called identifying label, shooting galleries and crack houses have always been inhabited by faceless lost souls. Souls, whose vital organs may be functioning, but whose opaque eyes reveal the coffin-like emptiness of spirits who have died a thousand deaths when, by the grace of God, they have been given one thousand and one lives.

While I have as yet to travel through death's ultimate haggard door, and hence cannot speak on the topic of physical death from a place of actual personal experience, I have miraculously survived the demise of a thousand spiritual deaths, and by the grace of God, in my thousand and first life, feel qualified to state that purgatory holds nothing over shooting galleries and crack houses here on earth. I have seen every last remnant of religious doctrine and human decency be abandoned on crack houses' doorstep. I have also witnessed and enacted every last impious principle of the "ten commandments of crack" behind the crack house's frequently knocked-upon door. I have seen people mercilessly menaced, robbed, and beaten. I've seen pregnant women stomped and pummeled for trying to scam someone out of their drug. I've seen women place minute quantities of white powdery substances into their infant's mouths to quell their whimpering. I've seen mothers struggling to steady their shaking pipes and look the other way while wasted men slithered off into the direction of their children's sleeping quarters. I've seen heroin addicts get into a nice nod and have their pockets slit open and their contents removed before their first drool of saliva even hit the ground. I've seen other heroin addicts overdose, have their pockets searched, and the syringes plucked from their limbs, before being tossed out into the hallway or down a stairwell so as to not have their pending deaths interfere with somebody else's next high. In fact, once while leaving a crack house in the early morning hours of the struggling sun, I saw a man pluck a syringe from the arm of a stiff and mumble, "This must be some good shit," and begin to unravel the cloth that would bind his own arm in preparation for the obviously lethal substance. I've seen people arouse from various states of consciousness to trample over one another in their blind and feeble attempt to escape the police. I've seen people, perhaps past pretty people, laid out on filthy floors and foam bleeding couches, having the monstrous rays of meaningless television programs highlight their varied stages of poor grooming and once-upon-a-time and forgotten hygiene practices. I've seen knives placed against people's throats, and guns placed to people's heads, to compel what appeared to be members of the living dead to turn over their fix. And I've seen the living dead cast quick glances at these weapons of pending death, but yet take one last hit before reluctantly passing the remainders of their fix over. I've seen people, tormented by the initial pangs of pain of physical and psychological withdrawal, stab some small-time, street-corner dealer in cold blood for selling them an empty bag. I've also seen other afflicted relatives of the same small-time, street-corner dealers "share" their homemade, tampered drugs, tainted with toxic substances such as rat poison or powdered ammonia, with the addicts who stabbed their relatives in cold blood to avenge their deaths and injuries and perpetuate the cycle. I've seen relatives turn against relatives, and friends turn against friends. I've seen men forget that they were husbands, fathers, sons, and brothers; women forget that they were wives, mothers, daughters, and sisters. I've seen many a person forget that they were human beings. I've seen many people forget that they once had morals, religious teachings, hope, and love. I've seen many people lie to themselves and say that they were not really addicts, and definitely not nearly as bad as the brother they just got high with back in the crack house, when they really were. I've seen many, many people busy at planting the seeds of guilt and shame that would ultimately propel them to take many more trips to purgatory on earth, and perhaps eventually kill themselves during the trip. To coin the famous expression, by the time I was twenty-seven and had decided to completely abstain from the use of all drugs and alcohol "one day at a time," I had seen it all. The fact that I can remember what I saw through my own deadened eyes can only attest to the fact that faceless lost souls continue to have vision even after their spirit has died a thousand lives, as long as by the grace of God, they have been granted a thousand and one. I've come to believe that the spiritually dead addict's continued gift of sight is one of the greatest paradoxes of drug addiction. While it certainly has the potential of planting many seeds of guilt and shame, it likewise bears promise of steadying one's feet on the recovery walk, particularly if one is living in the days of their thousand and first life.

Back on to the path of my more straight and narrow memories, it was somewhere during the first few months of my ninth year of life that Mama hit a number and the Stinkdog disappeared. It was somewhere behind a smoke screen of similar magnitude, but different texture, of those who were to disappear from my life years later. While I am certain that at the core of Mama's intention lay a genuine but poorly constructed plan to retrieve me from Ms. Cathy within a couple of hours, as drug-related circumstances would have it, Mama's couple of hours evolved into a couple of days.

I remember it just the same as if it was yesterday. The first day was a Saturday, and it passed as smoothly as a tear cascading down a freshly greased face. The next day, Sunday, was as uneventful as Saturday. The only difference was that the Stinkdog was off on Sundays and spent his entire day of leisure perched on the couch in front of the television looking like some fat turd on a cushioned log. This meant two things. One, that I couldn't watch television. And two, that I would have to stay outside on the streets for most of the day to avoid his presence and toxic smell. With the exception of having to coexist with the Stinkdog and missing Mama, my little two-night vacation stay at Ms. Cathy's really hadn't gone so badly. Ms. Cathy was always nice to me, I ate well, and I saw my friends everyday. Ms. Cathy always believed that I was worrying about Mama. She'd look at me with her blue eyes all full of concern and say, "Don't worry Victoria, your Mama will be back." She didn't have to reassure me. I already knew that. Mama always came back.

I remember how, when I was preparing for bed on Sunday night trying to escape from Ms. Cathy's gaze of concern, I had a premonition that Mama would be home the next day. I imagined that she'd probably be waiting there for me when I returned home from summer school. I don't know how much of a premonition it really was, or rather my precocious calculations about how far $70 could get you in the heroin races. But, by the time I had laid my head down to go to sleep on that Sunday night, I was resolute in my decision that Mama would be home waiting for me in the afternoon. As is typically the case with most human calculations, my prediction concerning Mama's return was partially correct. She did come home on Monday, but not before I had returned home from summer school.

For reasons that I did not understand, the Stinkdog did not get ready to go to work on that next Monday morning. Now that was highly unusual. The Stinkdog's attendance record with the U. S. Postal Service was about as regular as his bowels. And from what I could gather, that was very regular. But if Old Faithful had chosen that day to blemish his record, I wasn't going to allow it to phase me. I went about my business, said a quick good-bye to Ms. Cathy, who appeared to be preparing for work rather slowly that morning, and left out from the apartment chuckling silently to myself over the passing thought about how "every dog has its day."

I spent about one hour that morning on individualized reading, and the next three, on recreation and lunch. Afterward, I returned to the apartment to discover that my premonition about Mama being there was wrong. Instead, upon traversing across Ms. Cathy's apartment doorstep, I learned for the first time in life that we can sometimes smell trouble way before we can see or hear it. It's as if when one's star is on the wane, the scent of the mist from gathering clouds trails through the expectant atmosphere towards the olfactory glands of the attentive observer. The scent of trouble is caustic and overpowering, but as transient as the life of a bubble.

I smelled trouble as I momentarily lingered in Ms. Cathy's apartment doorway. Then I tasted it, same as if I was chewing the tinny flavor of crushed metal in my mouth. It wasn't until I went into the kitchen for a drink of water to rid my mouth of the bilious aftertaste that I actually saw anything that would confirm my higher order senses' prelude to fear. Ms. Cathy quietly entered the kitchen and I learned three things. Firstly, I learned from her presence that Ms. Cathy had not gone to work that day. Secondly, her untidy hair, swollen lip, and bloody nose apprised me of the fact that I had just entered into a scene of ugly domestic violence. Thirdly, the catatonic look of fright in Ms. Cathy's eyes taught me about a side of human terror of which I was unfamiliar. Frozen terror. Fear, that instead of stimulating the rush of adrenalin that generates quick thinking and strength of action, chills the blood, numbs the senses, and stifles the spirit, leaving one as lost and helpless as a sparrow with broken wings.

I quickly processed all of my recently acquired knowledge and searched Ms. Cathy's face for some sign or signal about what to do. The longest minute ever must have passed before Ms. Cathy smoothed down her hair as if it was any other day, motioned for me to sit down at the table, and said, "I'll be right back—you know I've been meaning to buy milk for your cookies all day," in the most lifeless voice I had ever heard a human being speak in all my days on this planet called earth. Then, from the bedroom, I heard the Stinkdog bellowing out Ms. Cathy's name all mad and crazy-sounding, as if it was him with the battered face having a right to be all angry and indignant about something. As I stood there trying to cipher through all this madness, Ms. Cathy retreated back from the direction in which she had come in such a surreal manner that I began to question whether she had really been standing before me, bruised and rendered insensible, telling me that she was about to go out for some milk just seconds before. All I could think to myself was, "Oh shit, I hope she ain't gonna go downstairs looking like that. Talking about airing your dirty laundry in public." Then I started thinking, "Oh God, now what the hell is Mama gonna do when she sees Ms. Cathy's face like that again? Oh God." I actually stood there wasting time wishing that Mama would stay away for at least another couple of days so that Ms. Cathy's face would have time to heal before she saw her. I then wondered if it was just me, or do all kids stand around thinking about dumb shit in the middle of crises? It was during this same time period in which I had started allowing my child's imagination to begin to extricate itself from the tethers of nonsensical thinking and question what I should do if more violence occurred that I first heard the somewhat distant thumping sound of flesh being punched and pummeled. Paralyzed with a fear that must have been next to kin of Ms. Cathy's, I moved up beneath the kitchen doorway's jamb and powerlessly watched the Stinkdog drag Ms. Cathy on her back into the living room by her ankles. Her head, which was bleeding profusely from a gash on her temple, left a trail of blood that occasionally spurted up along the lower portion of the wall, creating an eerie inkblot sort of design of human folly. I believe that I was so stricken with fear that my brain completely shut down until they reached the center of the living room, when the Stinkdog, dripping with sweat and savagery, heaved Ms. Cathy up by her hair and wrist to her feet, only to throw her back down on the floor before he went to go settle himself down on the couch in front of the television. My brain flickered back to life as the Stinkdog's eyes turned to meet mine. I distinctly recall thinking that if that motherfucker took one step near me, I would leap backwards toward the fire escape, but not before grabbing a kitchen knife to slice off his puny ass balls. As I tried to shake my thoughts free of all that Superhero shit, I realized that the Stinkdog wasn't looking at me at all, but was instead looking through me as if I wasn't there.

I didn't know what to do. My mind was racing back and forth from thoughts of guilt about how my presence in Ms. Cathy's home had probably caused the fight in the first place, to harried thoughts of weak plans of bravery and wit of which I could possibly enact to save Ms. Cathy's life. I didn't know who was worse off—me with my stupid, useless thoughts, or poor, battered Ms. Cathy. We both were about as helpless as two bits of waste paper. Just as I was fumbling to piece together a semi-sensible plan about how I could trek through the living room in front of the television to reach the phone in the bedroom to dial 911, I made my decision. Ms. Cathy was definitely worse off. She was staggering to her feet, blood matted down to her hair, more blood drooling from her mouth, face swollen, lip busted open, talking about how she "got to go to the store to buy some milk for the cookies." It was as if she was completely oblivious of the Stinkdog who kept one eye on his idol—the television—and a more watchful, curious eye on his beaten wife, who aimlessly wobbled around the living room repeating the same gibberish about going to the store for some milk.

The Stinkdog and Ms. Cathy were both breathing hard from the combined effect of the past struggle and exertion, and I, immersed in this new nightmarish dimension of the adult world, was hardly breathing at all. Although I never dared to turn my head to glance at the clock above the stove, to the best of my altered judgment I believe that this deranged circus continued for the better part of an hour. At some point during the hour's time span, and I swear I can't pinpoint an even approximate when, Ms. Cathy retrieved a towel from somewhere and began to clumsily dab at the gash on her head to subdue the bleeding. The most unhinging element of the entire scene was Ms. Cathy's endless mumbling about going to the store for some milk. I was convinced that one of the blows to her head had caused brain damage, or even worse, had caused her to lose her mind. I even had these flash visions of Ms. Cathy looking like a crazy bag lady wandering through the streets talking to herself like I had seen all those other crazy, homeless folk doing when I was out with Mama.

When I grew older and was unfortunately subject to many other scenes of domestic violence between man and woman, I came to learn that Ms. Cathy had indeed lost her mind, but not for any long period of time like the psychos on the streets. I believe the customary legal term for Ms. Cathy's condition was "temporary insanity." My theory about her type of "temporary insanity" is that the shock and revolting horror of the onslaught of the assault by her supposed partner somehow managed to freeze her last normal thought in her mind. Suspended reflections. It's as if the human psyche must keep its last normal cognition, feeling, and purpose in its forefront, reliving it over and over, to retain its edge on sanity. The vital organs function, while the mind comes to a halt on screeching wheels, running interference with the noise that could potentially disturb its equilibrium. And the heart, well, it just hangs heavy, with each inoculating experience adding on more weight.

Just when I began to breathe, half of me believing that the worst of the storm was over, and the other half trying to convince myself that it was so, the Stinkdog rose up from the couch without provocation, and in one fell swoop, backhanded Ms. Cathy upside her head, causing her to fall back down on the floor. With her back against the wall, her shoulders limp, legs apart, and blood dripping everywhere, he started kicking her. First in her thighs, and then in her privates, screaming between raspy staccato breaths about how "nobody wants her filthy hoe ass pussy anyway." It was horrible. He just wouldn't stop. He kept kicking and kicking and screaming and screaming. And I, who had been involuntarily inert for the better part of an hour, found myself springing forward into motion, flailing arms with a tear and mucous stained face, launching toward them screaming, "Stop, stop, stop." But he continued. Kicking and kicking, screaming and screaming. It was one loud, bloody, hateful mess.

Somewhere around my twentieth plea for him to stop, that bastard Stinkdog jerked Ms. Cathy up by her left arm and backhanded her again. This time as she fell her right foot caught hold of the back of one of the living room chairs, causing it to fall sideward on to the side table on which the Stinkdog's familiar television stood. With my vocal chords throbbing and my lungs gasping for air,

I drew in a quick breath as the table and television teeter-tottered forward. Although Ms. Cathy appeared mindless, the Stinkdog watched the wobbling table with as keen an interest and as stifled a breath as I. The television crashed down on to the floor with a loud explosion. A look of finite murderous rage etched itself across the Stinkdog's face. And that's when I knew he was going to kill her—end Ms. Cathy's life right there in front of me in the next few moments.

I had never actually witnessed a murder before, and somehow knew that I would never have survived it. Realized that my nine-year-old mind would crack into as many pieces as there were glass shards strewn on the floor. So even though I didn't believe in him, for one split second I squeezed my eyes tight and prayed to God with all of my juvenile might, that he would do something, anything, to stop the Stinkdog from killing Ms. Cathy right in front of me. Ms. Cathy later told me that she too, in her half conscious state, upon hearing the television crash on to the floor, prayed for one of God's angels to come forth and make its presence known.

I opened my eyes and saw no hand of God, nor any angels. Instead, I saw the Stinkdog moving toward Ms. Cathy with the purposeful strides of a bloodthirsty lunatic. I closed my eyes again, knowing that when I opened them, it was all going to be over.

That's when the miracle occurred. A miracle as sudden as my prayer, and as camouflaged as a tree toad in the woods. The miracle came in the form of Mama—my mama.

That door busted open with such force you'd have thought we were being raided by the narcotics squad. Her body, much like a torpedo with fire bursting forth from green watery slits at its crown, shot across that living room faster than anything I'd ever seen in life. Then she had him. Had his slimy neck in a tight grip, as they struggled chest to chest, with the Stinkdog stumbling backwards, out from the living room and down the short hallway toward the bedroom in which Ms. Cathy and he shared a bed. The same bed on which Ms. Cathy and Jose "el salvaje" once lay, and shared their love and dreams. From somewhere I thought I heard someone whisper "Now I'm going to kill you" through gasping, disconnected breaths, but I couldn't distinguish from where the voice came. Its sound, trailing on the last vibration of an echo, whisked past the base of my conscious with one lone, fine tendril. To this very day, the voices of my conflicting thoughts bicker with one another as to whether the source of the shadowy hush of a voice came from Mama, the Stinkdog, the moaning Ms. Cathy, myself, or from the distant clamor of an angry, restless spirit called forth to settle some business once and for all.

I lost sight of the tussle as both the Stinkdog and Mama moved beyond the bedroom door. I reached down to Ms. Cathy who was struggling in a lopsided wild manner to her feet, looking like she had just showered beneath a faucet that spewed blood. As we fumbled together frantically toward the bedroom, the door slammed with a loud thump in our faces. One second later, we heard a body crash up against the closed door with a loud thud, and then Mama's sunken wail.

The battle raged on. Punches and kicks, made known by sharp stings against flesh, grunts, and loud cries. Mama cursed and threatened, while the Stinkdog stood his ground with dissipating breaths. The two had obviously moved forward into another section of the bedroom, but the door had somehow managed to become locked. The noise of glass shattering and furniture falling reached our ears, while Ms. Cathy and I beat upon the door with weakened fists. My mind raced on wheels of fear for the ultimate safety of my mama, and myself.

There was then a period of silence, more deafening than any of the ruckus by which it was proceeded. It was as if all things living and breathing had simply ceased to exist. There were no more slaps, no more breaking of glass or furniture, no more threats, no more cries, whimpers, or even the rush of held in breaths. Just a mysterious dead silence, accompanied by an enigmatic energy in its mist.

Tingling with trepidation, my ears' antennae groped out for any sound of recognition that would help me to understand what had just happened from beyond the door that was locked in front of me. Seconds passed by, obviously undisturbed by my unresolved fate. I looked at Ms. Cathy as she turned to look at me. As my panic traveled down from my throat into the pit of my stomach and a weak yelp for my mama stirred from somewhere down in my gut, the door opened. And there she was, looking more confused than she was frightened or injured. Shirt torn and hair tousled, her eyes darted everywhere around the room. It was then that I realized who she was looking for. I don't believe I had ever seen Mama looking more perplexed in all my life—not even under the numbing grip of a good nod.

After my eyes quickly scanned the room's contents and I realized that the Stinkdog wasn't there, I asked Mama what had happened. Continuing to look around her everywhere, she shook her head from side to side murmuring, "I don't know."

Old Mr. and Mrs. Rivera from across the hall crept into the apartment, saw that the violence had ended and began to take charge of wrapping Ms. Cathy's head, while their pregnant daughter, who came in quietly behind them, informed us that she had just called 911 for an ambulance. Mama went over to the bedroom window, which was lifted up halfway, peered out and called down to folk who were on the street below as to whether they had just seen the Stinkdog jump from the window. Upon hearing their response, she turned back to face us, her head slowly shaking from side to side.

Such is the legend of Ms. Cathy, her lover Jose "el salvaje," and the disappearing Stinkdog. Later, when Mama retrieved her speech more fully, she swore up and down and over and over again that the last thing she remembered was breaking a lamp over the Stinkdog's head and running over to the other side of the bed to search under the skirt for Jose's old bat. Muttering a string of profanities upon realizing that it wasn't there, she then quickly stood back up, prepared to finish the fight with her own two hands and with whatever additional furniture she could use as opportune weapons, until she realized that the Stinkdog was no longer there. She said that because she initially thought that he was hiding, ready to lunge out at her at any given moment, she stood in silence, visually soaking up her surroundings to improve upon her position for the projected assault. It was when the enigmatic energy of the dead silence encapsulated Mama that she started to question whether he had truly disappeared.

The folk from down on the street swore that they never saw the Stinkdog jump down the two-story distance from the window. Mama swore that when she had looked out, she had not seen him running up the street. Ms. Cathy swore the bat was under the bed the last time she had made it that very morning. I swore that the entire ordeal had been very frightening and strange and was sure glad that it was over. As for the Stinkdog, he never came back. He had truly disappeared to whatever eternal place it is that Stinkdogs go.

The people from the neighborhood quickly spread the word that Mama had kicked the Stinkdog's ass so bad that he had disappeared forever. After all, it was possible, wasn't it? The window was partially open.

Ms. Cathy believed that God had sent forth the spirit of her beloved Jose to save her life. In fact, she changed from that day forward. She stopped drinking her little beers, started reading the Bible, and attended mass on a regular basis. She no longer sought solace from carnal relationships on the rebound, but instead from the joy of a peaceful spirit, as well as from memories of sharing love and dreams with Jose "el salvaje" when he was there with her physically in their special heaven on earth. After all, the bat was there under the bed skirt that very morning. Wasn't it?

Mama surely drank in all of the praise and pats on her back from our neighborhood residents for her outstanding act of courage and good will. And her veins definitely sucked in the few bags of dope she received from the generous drug dealers in the neighborhood who gave her her props in the form of her chosen reward. But when we were alone, and I'd look at her with questioning eyes, my lips about to part with the proverbial inquiry, she'd just shake her head from side to side mumbling, "I don't know, Victoria. I just don't know."

As for me, I just placed the entire episode into that chamber of my mind that holds space for the category of things best not thought about too deeply. The category that seemingly expands when we get older, contracts when we get wiser, and surfaces when we die. The labels that get affixed to this category in recovery are avoidance and denial.

CHAPTER NINE

The rights of a child have no boundaries...
The right to free education and full opportunity for play and recreation.
The right to learn to be useful members of society and to develop individual abilities.
The right to enjoy these rights regardless of race, color, sex, religion, national or social origin.

—Unknown

TALK ABOUT REMINISCING and taking a nice and quiet stroll down memory lane—this autobiographic experience is surely not allowing me to forget that my childhood was rather lacking in the department of niceties and quietude. But, I have to admit it has exhumed feelings and memories, some bad, some not so bad, that I thought were buried forever in one of the many mausoleums of my mind. My sponsor says that, as was probably the case with Mama, they were only temporarily resting on God's acre.

Speaking of my sponsor, who persistently goads me through this process with her weapons of enthusiasm, genuine concern, and cheerfulness, she was quite impressed with my rendition of the legacy of Ms. Cathy, her lover Jose "el salvaje," and the disappearing Stinkdog. She said that after reading the past couple of chapters she knows that like Ms. Cathy and her early adult dreams, I'm coming upon my gilded door with the answer key to my life's questions and purpose. While she admits not being entirely sure in which part or concept of the two chapters my key exactly lies, she attests, with an unprecedented clarity, that should I continue to retrace my steps through this particular childhood experience, the key will become so vividly visible that I'll be left wondering why I didn't detect it there all along. When I asked her the stupid question about why, if she was so certain about my key's approximate location and the pending nearness of its discovery, she didn't use her own experiential wisdom and study the last couple of chapters for me to save us both, particularly me, a hell of a lot of time and aggravation, she appeared to momentarily revisit a nostalgic place of her own before sighing deeply and flatly stating, "Because keys only make themselves visible to their rightful owners. I could traipse up and down the verbal or written path of your life's rough road a million times and miss a million times what was meant to be seen by your eyes only. Whether your key is hiding amidst the brush like a chameleon or is as in plain view as a Christmas tree amongst a patch of pansies, I could never understand the significance that its presence has in your world because I know nothing of God's purpose for putting it there. Beware of those superficially self-actualized know-it-all people who claim to have competence over helping you better understand and live your life. Their claims are false and speak of the incompetency by which they probably understand and live their own. No, Victoria, I subscribe to the slogan 'Live and Let Live.' I'll support you on your recovery journey as best as any human being possibly can, and when limited by the constraints endemic of the human condition, I will let go and let God."

That was about two months ago. As usual, I initially resisted taking her advice, but then as time passed, and I sorted through my apparel of fears and trust issues, discarded the ones that didn't fit right anymore, held on to some, and replaced those that were discarded with some new and improved protective coverings, I began to reread all of the painful words of the past two chapters that were splashed down on paper like verbal tears. Upon reliving my childhood experience surrounding the legend about seven times, I felt disappointed that the only recurring thoughts that struck me were the newfound meaning that I now attached to the color blue, a wistful stirring to go see Ms. Cathy in the Bronx, and a growing understanding that this paper-and-pen trail actually did have a destination of merit that I needed to continue pursuing. I shared my disappointments with my sponsor. She smiled in appreciation and softly said, "What did I tell you? God is good." Although my determination to splash some more verbal tears down on paper didn't diminish in the slightest, I once again began to question whether I, in my time of most extreme vulnerability, was under the direct tutelage of a crazy woman.

Although I started out amongst all the other eager Oedipal-age children with high hopes and expectations about beginning school, by the time I was in the latter part of my elementary school career, I had gradually fallen in among the ranks of the "bored of miseducation." As I got older I figured out that having high hopes and expectations really meant having premeditated disappointments. Sad as the realization may have been, it at least saved me from feeling disappointed so often. It similarly gave me an excuse to give up on myself and life. Just like with everything else, I guess the truth of the situation lies somewhere in between. Temperance and moderation. As far as my earlier dreams and fantasies about school though, they died somewhere during the latency stage of my childhood, disappearing into thin air like a mirage once you come close up on it. While I don't know whether or not any of my peers had been fortunate enough to switch gears after this dismal crossroad, I recognize that for me it was a point of no return.

As I believe I already mentioned when summarizing my painful experience with making wishes, I began school a couple of months later than most children while living in the glamorous foster home from hell in Jamaica Estates. Between missing the first two months and contending with all of the noisome nocturnal activities that were going on in the McNeil home, I'm not sure how I managed to learn my ABCs. But I did. Despite the fact that I was probably the only kindergarten kid in a class of upper middle-class, designer-wearing Caucasian tykes who actually looked forward to nap time due to my inability to secure any undisturbed sleep at home, I was writing my name and saying my ABCs by the time I was removed from the "dream" house and placed into a series of different foster homes. However, it all caught up to me by the time I was in the second grade and started living with Mama again in some shelter in Brownsville. It was at this point that my astute second grade teacher discovered that I was academically lagging behind my fellow ghetto classmates. The teacher sent a letter home stating that I was at risk of being left back and recommended that Mama provide me with additional tutorial supports. The caseworker from the shelter read the letter to Mama. Later, when we were alone, she asked me, "What the hell did that lady mean by additional tutorial supports?" I told her that it meant that I needed help with reading. She guessed aloud that it must be in our blood since she "always found reading hard too." Then, in one of her far and few between serious moments, Mama forewarned, "Don't follow in my footsteps, Victoria. Learn how to read. Listen to your teachers. Choose your friends carefully. And, for God's sake, don't mess around with no drugs." Her imploring eyes dug a hole somewhere deep inside of me that would later serve as a well for shame.

My second grade teacher never did leave me back. I also never got provided with any additional tutorial supports. Not until it was too late and I was locked up in some Residential Delinquent Facility and had already lost all interest in improving upon my ABCs. But I did learn how to read. Despite all of my school absences, school transfers, childhood traumas, and lack of additional tutorial supports, I learned how to read. Although she never said so, I know that made Mama proud.

While being an elementary school student in the NYC foster care system surely puts a damper on one's achievement motivation, being a student while living in the NYC shelter system certainly doesn't add anything positive to one's already doused levels of inspiration. Talk about the folly of systems. Waiting around for a school placement after moving into a new shelter can take so long that you might as well just sit back and wait until it's time to go shopping around for a GED program. This is especially true for kids like me who had the compounded complexity of having a mother who kept getting transferred from shelter to shelter due to "inappropriate social behavior," and then when she was in one housing situation for any reasonable period of time, "couldn't quite put a finger" on the location of your requisite paperwork. Given that my approximate seventeen-year-long mission with drugs did not have a fundamental, deleterious effect on my long-term memory functions, I estimate with a credulous degree of accuracy that by the time I entered kindergarten in Jamaica Estates and graduated from the sixth grade at some dingy school in the Bronx, I had attended at least twelve different elementary schools. What was even more pathetic, and definitely a primary contributing factor to my delayed academic levels and depressed achievement motivation, was the fact that during that same time period, I had missed about twenty-four months of school waiting for some system to find an appropriate school placement.

Before I go on with the details of my hopscotch school experience, allow me to provide some additional descriptive verbiage about the realities of school days of children in foster care. Firstly, when you're a kid living in a foster home everybody knows it, or at least you believe everybody knows it. This is especially the case when your white foster mother arrives at your school to confer with your teacher and you happen to be black. It is similarly the case when you've been placed into a middle-class neighborhood school and you're still wearing clothes from John's Bargain Basement because your foster parent lacks a heart and the incentive to appropriate your clothing budget correctly. And just for the record, don't let me omit that this is also the case when some heathen, jealous biological child in your foster home goes around the entire school informing all of your peers about your foster-child status while not leaving out the part about your real mother being a drug addict. Such experiences definitely function as pitfalls when, after missing so much school already, you're trying to learn your ABCs.

As previously suggested, residing in the shelter system rarely becomes a boon to your educational achievement. This is particularly true when, because of your mother's extracurricular activities, your family forever remains on the tier 1 level. Although I've lived in some shelters in which there was an observable attempt made to bring some semblance of order and dignity to the overall living environment, put succinctly, most tier 1 shelters during my childhood days were human zoos. Despite all of the strict rules and regulations that they fed you when you first moved in, people generally did what they wanted, when they wanted to do it. And when you have a bunch of poor, oppressed folk, replete with histories of social and emotional problems, doing what they want to do when they want to do it, in one rather small, uninviting, overcrowded area, there is always chaos and madness and then more chaos and madness. People stole from one another, fought each other, drank, used and sold drugs, had sex day and night, and often made so much noise that whether you believed in God or not, you'd sit there and pray for the din to be done. Forget about if your adjacent neighbors shared different musical tastes. Even if you didn't like a particular music, you'd prefer that all of your neighbors did. Then perhaps they'd all listen to the same radio station and you'd hear the same unpalatable tunes in stereo. But when neighbors shared diverse tastes in music behind those thin shelter walls, you were among the chosen and few, if you maintained your sanity. Once, when I was about eleven years old and living with Mama for a brief, three-month stay in a shelter in lower Manhattan, we had one neighbor who played soul music on our right, another neighbor who played that Puerto Rican salsa music all loud and stuff on our left, while the lady across the hall blasted gospel music, all at the same time night and day. Nothing would have brought more belief at the moment than a power outage. An abrupt electrical failure that would not be corrected until the day we moved out. Or at least a psychotic man with overly sensitive ears and a huge hammer. It was amidst this chaos and cacophony that I was expected to complete my homework, study, and rest so that I could rise bright and early for the forthcoming school day.

The fourth grade was a memorable academic year for me. Lots of change. Lots of chaos. Even more than I was typically accustomed to. My fourth grade teacher, Mrs. Gross, referred me to special education and reported Mama to BCW on allegations of maternal neglect. I was placed into a temporary foster home, again. Mama moved and was mandated by court to attend a methadone maintenance program, again. And I, for the first and last time throughout the entire span of our sixteen-year-long relationship, queried Mama about her disease of addictions.

I'll retrace my steps just a bit to clarify which era in my life I am exactly speaking. Mama and I met Ms. Cathy when I was eight. The Stinkdog disappeared approximately one month after I had turned nine. I entered the fourth grade while still living with Mama in the same apartment building as Ms. Cathy about two months later.

The minute I laid eyes upon Mrs. Gross I knew that she was going to be trouble. Big trouble. Long before I had reached this point in my educational experience, I had come to the conclusion that teachers who were employed by the Board of Education generally fell into one of three neat categories. The smallest of the groups contained teaching professionals who genuinely cared about all of their students and simultaneously sought to educate them. We'll call this commendable group the "Great Masters." The second category of teachers, which were comprised of considerably more employees than the first, included those teaching staff that hated their jobs and students, and didn't give a damn about teaching. We'll refer to this second assortment as the "Maintenance Masters." Despite their overt nastiness, believe it or not, the Maintenance Masters never really inflicted any lasting injuries on their students. Probably because their nastiness was so overt. The fact that they didn't like you, their jobs, or themselves was so obvious that you just allowed yourself to be maintained by them for the one, two, or three-year time period that you were a number on their class roster, and then went about your educational business, or didn't, depending upon whether you had already joined the ranks of the bored of miseducation or not. If you grew up in the ghetto and attended an inner city school, then you've probably already figured out that the largest, and most dangerous, of all the teaching domains were composed of those restless, insecure types who had convinced themselves that they were among the chosen few who not only cared about what happened to you, but also had the omniscience and omnipotence to effect meaningful change over your life. This third group, even more than the Maintenance Masters, perceived the city's population in terms of "us versus them." They were the monkeys who reached down into the roaring rivers in the midst of violent storms to yank the thrashing fish to the safety zones of their hairy, coarse embrace, and then quickened to anger when the fish, freshly plucked from their natural habitats, died in their arms. We'll label this disproportionately overly populated group the "Slave Masters," and then make the mental note that it is the students of these teachers who probably continue to be the most largely represented amongst the bored of miseducation.

I smelled Mrs. Gross's Slave Master beguiling scent when she first bellowed out "Good morning class" on that very first Tuesday after Labor Day that was going to mark my entrance into her dominion of bogus benevolence. Tasted it, just the same as if my mouth was bound by metal tethers. I've come to believe that children are bestowed with the natural gift of social perception at a very early age. While the seeds must be present in all, their sprouting is hastened by environments that nurture and foster their development. Ironically, or perhaps not, the seeds of social awareness thrive amongst the children of ghetto environments. We slum children didn't need too many "don't talk to strangers" lessons. We learned to read faces years before we learned how to read our first printed word. It was due to the presence of this skill that I immediately sensed that Mrs. Gross was a fake and a potential danger to my already precarious life's equilibrium. As the days evolved into weeks, I realized that my gut reaction was more than correct.

My initial wariness of Mrs. Gross, with her birdlike, bespectacled smiling face, coiffured hair, French-manicured nails, and designer dresses, was confirmed when she, cloaked in philanthropy of a chiffon texture, went after this little Puerto Rican boy named Eduardo who came to school every day wearing clean, but the same clothing. It was three weeks into the semester, and although Eduardo had come prepared with a new pencil and black-and-white notebook since day one, he had not as yet brought to class the ruler and spiral notebook that Mrs. Gross additionally required. It became a daily ritual. Directly after she checked the attendance and quieted us down, probably so that we could all clearly hear, Mrs. Gross would stand under the American flag smiling, and with a saccharine sweetness ask Eduardo whether his mother had realized the importance of purchasing her son all of his school supplies as yet. Eduardo, who was just a tiny, frail creature with wide, mahogany brown eyes, would simply shake his head from side to side before squeaking out a barely audible "no." Then, with the involvement of someone who didn't enjoy a life of her own and had spent the entire evening before dwelling on somebody else's less fortunate business, Mrs. Gross would preach a sermon about the importance of being responsible in this world, about how we children should start learning how to be responsible at a young age, and about how parents should model responsible behavior by responsibly meeting their own needs as well as the needs of their children. I can only imagine how her supposed well-intentioned words, razor sharp with points like stalactites, bore wounds the size of grapefruits through Eduardo's fragile ego. Wounds that would erupt and fester throughout his life each and every time he allowed himself to focus on the concept of responsibility. I began to wonder whether Mrs. Gross, with all of her intellectual knowledge about the importance of being responsible, had ever considered the importance of taking responsibility for her mighty tongue.

    I believe the reason why this incident stands out in my mind so vividly is because it exemplified meaningless cruelty. To be certain, I, the entire class, little Eduardo, and even Mrs. Gross knew that her daily ritualistic sermons were being preached in vain in terms of stirring poor Eduardo into any form of action. There was absolutely nothing she could say, sweetly, icily, or any mixture therein, that could have prodded Eduardo to put some pressure on his mother to buy him the requisite additional school supplies. I'm sure that even Mrs. Gross' blindfolded heart recognized that her seemingly purposeful words were, in reality, insidious in their intent. Everybody knew that Eduardo's mother, who was a nice lady, but a little slow in the head, had fifteen children from just about as many fathers, and limited resources, skills, and energy by which she could possibly care for them all. I remember hearing Ms. Cathy telling Mama one evening how it was so strange that Eduardo's mother had seemingly out of nowhere selected two of her brood to voluntarily give up for adoption. Ms. Cathy was going on and on about how she could understand it if Eduardo's mother had chosen the youngest two, but how it was completely illogical that she had selected a boy and girl who were somewhere in the middle of her children's nineteen year age range. It hadn't made any sense to Ms. Cathy, or me, with my eavesdropping ears, that is until Mama eventually chimed in and flatly stated, "Maybe she knew. She was their mother so maybe she knew as only a mother can that they were the weakest. Maybe she knew that the others had something that them two didn't and she wanted them to survive." Ms. Cathy remained quiet, as I silently conjectured that perhaps it was for reasons such as these that Mama and Ms. Cathy were friends.

Anyway, everybody also knew that that BCW was "actively" involved with Eduardo's family to help monitor the situation in which there was never any evidence of palpable abuse. His mother was merely a slow woman who lived in such a small-sized shoe with so many children that she truly didn't know what to do. But as far as Eduardo was concerned, or any of the other remaining twelve for that matter, he wasn't about to rock that small shoe by badgering his mother about any additional school supplies when she had just given two of his siblings the boot for no apparent reason.

Everybody in school knew about Eduardo's family's situation. BCW had frequently made trips to the school to investigate different allegations of abuse of which none were ever founded. I bet such news was the primary topic of conversation in the teacher's cafeteria. Without families like Eduardo's and mine to gossip about and entertain themselves with, most teachers would probably have died of boredom during their lunch breaks. This would have particularly been the case with the Slave Masters.

Mrs. Gross never tired of getting her early morning wreck off by verbally needling Eduardo about his lack of material possessions and his family's obvious lack of responsibility. In fact, somewhere after the time that we celebrated the man's birthday that discovered America and began to look forward to the coming Halloween holiday, she worsened. First she brought in our mindless principal, who could have been the King of the Maintenance Masters, pointed out Eduardo, and smugly asked for his expert guidance and assistance with the matter. The principal, whose name I can't even recall, which by the way often occurs when looking back on our relationships with Maintenance Masters, probably gave one less shit about school supplies, Eduardo, and even Mrs. Gross. He absentmindedly said that he'd look into the matter the next time a city social worker came to the school to investigate Eduardo's family, and then abruptly turned on his heels to leave the room without casting one more glance in Eduardo's direction. You'd have thought that between the two of them, one of them would have come up with the brilliant idea of reaching down into their own pockets to contribute the dollar each that it would have cost to end the entire ordeal, and more importantly, Eduardo's obvious agony. I guess such concepts as sensitivity and generosity aren't included in any of the syllabuses for courses in early childhood education.

Well, the shit finally hit the fan the week before Halloween. Mrs. Gross, who was interchangeably stating that her hands were tied with regard to helping Eduardo since his family "didn't even have a phone," while likewise bragging that she was going all out this year in terms of buying us treats for our Halloween party, finally dealt her lowest blow and informed Eduardo that since he had not as yet assumed any responsibility for bringing in his school supplies, he was not going to reap the reward of being able to participate in the party, and would instead be expected to sit in the back of the classroom. We all have different thresholds of frustration. Different straws that will break our backs. Being banned from the Halloween party must have been Eduardo's. Tears poured from his eyes as he lay his head down on his desk, trembling and crying for at least a half hour as Mrs. Gross continued on with some lesson about the kindness that the European pilgrims bestowed upon the Indians. Swallowing Eduardo's pain like his thin polyester shirt must have absorbed the effusion of his tears, I wondered when it would be my turn to deal with the Slave Master monster in the Halston dress. I also wondered whether when my turn came, I would lay down my head and cry like Eduardo.

Eduardo had one fringe benefit in life that I didn't. In fact, I often wondered how my life would have been different if fate would have given me that same benefit. Eduardo had fourteen brothers and sisters, twelve with whom he had daily contact, one of whom rose to the occasion with fraternal brilliance and temporarily saved the day. Although none of Eduardo's brothers or sisters were in our class, there were surely plenty of them in the school. And whether it was a true-blood connection or not, Eduardo also had "a cousin" Marilyn in our class, who upon seeing Eduardo weep, flew to one of his younger, but more tough-skinned and daring brothers with developing thuggish survival skills, and informed him of the fact that Mrs. Gross had made Eduardo cry for a whole half hour over the threat of his exclusion from the promised Halloween party. That afternoon, Eduardo's younger brother, who I believe was named Ricardo, put on his red cape, flew in, and saved the day. He joined some six graders and stole more than just school supplies from a neighborhood drug store. Eduardo came into school the next day with two rulers, two spiral notebooks, and a quavering smile. On the day of our Halloween party, of which Eduardo was now a permitted participant, he donated to our meager bounties by passing out large quantities of candy that Ricardo had stolen the day before now that he had successfully passed the initiation test in the school of petty larceny. The brothers' lesson about responsible behavior was well taught, and was finally over.

Interestingly enough, I ran across Marilyn years later when I was serving time upstate in prison. I recognized her immediately. She was doing hard time "for killing some bitch during a fight who thought that she was a punk." Her boyfriend, who she was really fighting over, never bothered to visit her in prison once. Glad to see me after all those years, Marilyn quickly filled me in on all she knew about our old acquaintances. Ricardo had been shot dead in the chest at the age of seventeen by the police during a jewelry store holdup. Eduardo was still alive, or so she thought. The last she heard was that he had left his wife and seven children and was living on the streets, begging for some change from strangers with outstretched crusty hands to keep him from experiencing the delirium tremors from alcohol withdrawal. Five others of the remaining clan in Eduardo's mother's household had also ended up dead, either from drug overdoses or street-related murders. A pair of fraternal twin girls who had been in the sixth grade when I was in the fourth were reportedly doing real good. Marilyn heard that both of them had somehow managed to make it through college and were both making pretty decent livings in the legal work force. The rest were basically doing their best to survive. The last she heard was that Eduardo's mother still lived in her small shoebox apartment, surrounded by more grandchildren than she had had previously with her own children. When I questioned whether she had ever heard anything about the brother and sister who had been given up for adoption so very long ago, a look of confusion crossed Marilyn's face before she cast a weak smile of recognition, eyes clouded over by distant memories, and said, "Only God knows that Victoria. But they say he takes care of the weakest of his children, so I guess they're all right."

Mrs. Gross removed her focus of attention off of little Eduardo following the incident prior to the Halloween party. In fact, since Eduardo had become the student who would typically bring in any newly required school supplies ahead of the entire class, she shortly thereafter identified him as the class role model for responsible behavior. Ironically, I believe that Mrs. Gross proudly assumed credit for catalyzing the development of Eduardo's moral character. An accomplishment about which she could brag about in the teacher's cafeteria. But, Mrs. Gross, in spite of her superficial demeanor, like most Slave Masters, wasn't stupid. On some level she understood that Eduardo, whose mother remained poor, overwhelmed, and a little slow in the head, had not made any great personal strides with regard to the growth of his moral character, wherein financial resourcefulness had been one tangible fringe benefit. I believe she understood that concept very well. I also believe she didn't care.

As the school year progressed, so did her range of target and artillery. She indirectly picked on the mulatto girl Julia, spewing forth her sociopolitical viewpoints concerning the dangers and hidden evils inherent in interracial relationships. Words obviously unchecked by any gatekeepers of sensitivity. Eyes, fixated on Julia, like sentinels of stigmatization.

She intentionally challenged and provoked "the behavior problem kids" in the class. Upped the ante in situations that could have easily been leveled off. Prodded fragile egos with nonverbal pitchforks, wedging loose raw impulses from their minimally secure confines, and then appeared a combination of surprised, repulsed, and smug when little nine and ten-year-old children began to act out their unhinged pain in front of her. Mrs. Gross seemed especially self-satisfied when one of the "crazies" was permanently removed from her class to either be placed into another class, another school, or sentenced to special education, depending upon the size of their transgression, or in reality, the sharpness of her pitchfork.

Mrs. Gross segregated our class of children of color into two very obvious and distinct groups. There were those children who came from relatively stable, usually intact homes, who were groomed better and dressed more fashionably, and who generally had more in the way of educational resources available to them at home than their student counterparts. These were the children who sat toward the front of the room, were called on more frequently, were chosen to be her special monitors, and were provided with more positive feedback about their performance and overall importance as human beings. The feedback they received, unlike ours, wasn't tainted with the marked impurities of sarcasm, condescension, and open malice. While some of the pressure we experienced might have been lifted off of these chosen few during class time, the lines that Mrs. Gross drew between us children within her own imaginary warped sandbox ended up causing her star children more harm than good. These were the same children who were isolated, teased, and physically assaulted by their peers during recess and lunch since their presence cast dim lights of recognition on our already potentially gloomy futures. They were also the same children who had rifts drawn in stone within their own impressionable psyches. Rifts that multiplied and eventually crisscrossed, causing confusion with the formation of their identities, loyalties, and egos. Rifts that would create lost adults who would still be inferior to the majority of the "them versus us" thinkers of their day. Rifts that would push both them and us one step further away from the realization that we are all but one people.

There was one boy amongst the chosen few named Jeffrey. One boy with probably just a tad bit more insight and foresight than the others who, after having experienced psychological isolation for about two weeks, and having weighed the pros and cons, stood up in the middle of science class one day and announced that he was changing his seat because he couldn't see the blackboard as well from up close. When Mrs. Gross, looking befuddled and disjointed, called out the suggestion that perhaps he could wear glasses to correct his farsightedness, Jeffrey laughed aloud without turning back as he walked toward an empty desk in the center of the room. Probably thinking that he could see distances just fine, he eventually replied, "That's all right. I can see perfectly fine from back here with everybody else." His smile was as firm as Mrs. Gross' responsive look of dismay. Jeffrey continued to earn adequate grades from his less advantaged position despite the fact that he began to experience a bit of pressure from Mrs. Gross within the classroom. He remained a free spirit during recess and lunch. Although he was no longer subjected to verbal teasing and physical assaults by his peers, he similarly chose not to join his peers in the isolation and victimization of the remaining chosen few. Having spent time on both sides of the fence, I guess he decided not to waste his energy reinforcing rifts that were ignorantly drawn in the sand.

Mrs. Gross' crusade against me began somewhere in November, directly after Mama made the mortal mistake of sending Ms. Cathy to Parent-Teacher Association interviews instead of adhering to her usual pattern of having nobody there to represent me at all.

Life was as close as to what I suspect is considered "normal" than it had ever been. Whether Ms. Cathy's newfound serenity was rubbing off on Mama or not, I really can't say for sure, but for one of the few times in her life, Mama was maintaining her habit at a seemingly lower level than I had observed during the past nine years of life. What was even more amazing was that she was managing me and the apartment off of her meager welfare pittance as well. Although she was home now more than ever, when Mama did make a customary dash in the races, she left me under the safe supervision of Ms. Cathy. Since the disappearance of the Stinkdog, Ms. Cathy was indeed the most stable, protective, babysitting resource that Mama ever had. Along with Mama's improved stability went the benefit of me having the time to form actual friendships with kids with whom I had the opportunity to share daily life experiences for more than just a couple of months. Mama and Ms. Cathy were even about to enroll me in a Saturday arts and crafts program at a local community center. Things were definitely looking up. And then fate looked down and sneered in my direction.

It wasn't that Mama didn't care about my academic progression. I believe that in spite of her bold, impudent character, she was embarrassed to have her own virtual illiteracy uncovered during the course of a conversation with some well-educated teacher. I believe she felt this embarrassment for both me and her. I also believe that she thought that school buildings had eyes with X-ray vision that could penetrate barriers of flesh and observe the sagging spirit. I knew that I was at least partially right in my supposition because Mama had made it explicitly clear from as far back as I can remember that her past school experience was a taboo topic. So I knew that deep in her heart when she decided to send Ms. Cathy to the Parent-Teacher night in my behalf, she had regrettably determined that Ms. Cathy had the least of the sagging spirits and would therefore make the most dignified impression. But, unlike Mama who functioned as if the best defense was a good offense, Ms. Cathy generally related to others with a pure and almost naive sincerity, at least until shown that it would do her best to do otherwise. She didn't discern the hostile, feline look that Mrs. Gross cast in her direction as she sat down, while simultaneously turning around to check that I was seated comfortably in the back of the classroom. She was similarly unaware that she had to rake through the subtle guile of their weedy informal chat to forestall yet another major setback in mine and Mama's lives. Later on, when she was explaining to Mama that Mrs. Gross had said that while it was obvious that I had come a long way, but yet was still experiencing some difficulty with my academics, only as an afterthought did she mention that "Mrs. Gross was unusually intent, but pleasant enough." Through the mild glaze of eyes that were responding to Mama's usual nighttime fix, there was a momentary flicker of concern.

Ms. Cathy had not thought it necessary to share the little white lie that fell from her lips when Mrs. Gross questioned Mama's absence. Quickly determining that Mama's absence could easily be explained away by saying that she often worked nights and left me in her care, Ms. Cathy must have not detected the raised brow of the coiffured woman sitting across from her. The same brow that was attached to prejudiced eyes, which had already categorized me as the daughter of a welfare recipient. I, in turn, thought little of it when Mrs. Gross nonchalantly queried me bright and early the following morning about where Mama was employed. But, I did notice her skulking smile when I uneasily stated that Mama was presently unemployed, and that's when I began to worry.

Whether or not Mrs. Gross reported her suspicions over the reported discrepant information, I can never be certain. However, shortly thereafter she began to direct the most prickly of her pitchforks toward me on an everyday basis. I, unlike the impulsive behavior problem kids, always met her pitchforks with an indifferent, standoffish demeanor. I guess I had experienced so much in my short little life span that it took quite a lot to rattle me. And on those far and few between occasions when someone's noxious needles did prick a raw nerve, I never let on that I was unhinged in the slightest. Quite unlike Mama who made a public sideshow upon the most shallow stimulation of her emotions, I typically remained calm, consistently spoke in a low volume, and maintained an affect that was as cool as the first of September's breezes. Up until very recently when I learned about the dangers associated with denying the nuances of my emotions, I flatly informed people what I thought of them or what I was about to do to them same as most people ask the time of day. Sometimes, instead of informing people what I was going to do to them, I simply did it. Although smoking huge amounts of crack admittedly put a dent in my otherwise neutral modus operandi, even while under the influence of the pipe, I tenaciously held on to my greatest defense of apathy with a doubled ferocious might. So while I didn't react to Mrs. Gross' piercing jabs in the impulsive, aggressive manner of my behaviorally disturbed peers, I similarly did not repeat little Eduardo's reaction by putting my head down on the desk to cry. But the pain of having tears stuck behind solid salt mines hurt just the same.

We experienced a bitter cold winter that year. A winter that brought with it at least two major snow storms and one unforeseen hail storm in which pellets of ice ricocheted down from the darkened heavens like bullets spraying from a giant machine gun. Despite my flimsy winter clothing, in the end I survived the war with the weather better than I did the cold war that existed in my classroom with Mrs. Gross on a daily basis. The hard frozen pellets that characterized New York City's hail storm were nothing in comparison to the icy words and glares that Mrs. Gross hurled in my direction without reprieve. My armor of indifference ended up being as flimsy as the winter coat that Mama had caught on sale the year before on Fordham Road. At some point during the later part of February, when the outside temperatures actually raised a few notches, I entered the eye of the storm.

It became evident that the more visibly unaffected I was by Mrs. Gross's subtle insults and overt sarcasm regarding my attire, academic performance, and even innate intelligence, the more unnerved and driven she became. Perhaps Eduardo's reaction would have been beneficial to mimic in the long run. Maybe then Mrs. Gross would have donned a smug grin like a Cheshire cat for a few weeks out of pride for winning the war and we all could have continued on with our business. Mine, the business of a lost nine and a half year old girl trying to survive the ghetto life with a heroin-addicted mother in a situation that, despite its palpable detriments, was beginning to look up. And Mrs. Gross, the business of a Slave Master who, under the pretense of a concerned, learned professional, stuck her righteous nose in a multitude of innocent students' lives to wreak additional havoc and pain on top of the mound that fate had already allotted them. I surmise we'll never truly know if my mimicking Eduardo's reaction would have benefited me or not since I stood firm in my Victoria character. And besides, I've come to learn that Slave Masters, and other pawns of the devil, are never predicable.

Whether she had had a bad Valentine's Day, or my lack of emotion had finally begun to wear on her last nerve, I can never be sure. The only fact of which I am completely certain is that shortly after the national holiday of love, Mrs. Gross abruptly altered her tactics of assaulting my exterior, and instead, aimed her artillery toward the most tender region of my interior. While I had taken pride in fending her off for such a long time, I decomposed quite instantaneously when her words perforated a small hole through the seemingly impenetrable safety-deposit box that preserved the treasure of emotions that I possessed toward Mama. Bull's eye.

One day, which was not so very much out of the blue, Mrs. Gross vehemently insisted that she wanted to meet Mama, talking some bullshit about wanting to discuss with her additional outside educational resources for me. I told her that I would pass the message on. I never did. Mama never came. Then, out of her obvious growing desperation to remain undefeated, she started harassing me about the fact that Ms. Cathy had provided conflicting information concerning Mama's employment status. She needled me and needled me, repeating that it was apparent that one of us was lying and she would eventually get to the bottom of it. Her next scheme included sending a letter home with me everyday demanding Mama's presence in school. When this ploy proved to be as unsuccessful in making my staid facial expression flinch, Mrs. Gross moved away from her customary insults and started to hover about more threatening territories, mindlessly looming at precarious distances from my tenuous personal space. Then, whether it was by luck or skillful aim, she pierced my emotional safety-deposit box, causing an effusive leakage of the box's contents, and I exploded.

In front of the entire class, Mrs. Gross went off on a harangue about what kind of mother would consistently ignore her daughter's teacher's invitations to come to school for an important conference. She broached the topic that lying and irresponsibility were obviously part of my family's dynamics, adding that these patterns were typically observed in very sick families in which weak people tried to escape from their responsibilities of the real world by using drugs and alcohol. Somewhere in the middle of her sentence about how "these kinds of mothers usually produce problem children since they were usually unwanted and uncared for," Mrs. Gross was suddenly silenced. Her words were replaced by quickened gasps for breath. Within the confines of what seemed to be a second, I had thrown my desk over, jumped forward and grabbed on to her neck, hissing into her face, "Bitch, if you ever put my mama's name into your mouth again, I'll fucking kill you." And let the truth be told, I would have.

I had never disrespected or threatened a teacher before in my entire life. But that didn't seem to matter. I was suspended for the indefinite time period that it would take to have me placed into special education. Ms. Cathy tried to come up first to meet with Mrs. Gross and the social worker, but was told that Mama needed to come since she was not my legal guardian. Mama, who was visibly upset by the whole ordeal, intuitively believing that she was ultimately at fault, eventually came up to the school. But during the time period that she must have been struggling with her own guilt and fear of the inevitable confrontation, she nose dived back into her habit at a progression that defied any past hints of self-preservation. After not having shown up at our apartment for two days, one day without notice Mama shuttled into the school in both a physical and psychological disarray. She was unkempt, smelling of her own stale sweat, and had a glaze in her eyes and slur to her gravelly speech that unequivocally highlighted a state of significant intoxication. It was her obvious state of intoxification that gave Mrs. Gross license to call BCW about her long-term suspicions of child abuse. It was in the same state of intoxification that Mrs. Gross seized the opportunity to have Mama sign the requisite papers that would sentence me to an indefinite stay in special education. In the end, Mrs. Gross won the battle and earned the right to wear a simpering smile in the teachers' cafeteria for the next several weeks. And I, even though I didn't recognize it at the time, was left in a weakened position to continue fighting an unnamed war.

Whether it was by coincidence or not, a memorable conversation occurred on the very same afternoon that Mama arrived at my school "with a nod" and Mrs. Gross and the school social worker unanimously agreed to inform BCW of Mama's visible, maternally neglectful demeanor. At the time, I had no idea that our brief exchange of words would secretly burrow through all of the trivia of my short-term memory and nestle in a distant frontier of my unconscious, awaiting the momentous opportunity in which it would be graciously disinterred. I didn't give the conversation a second thought. But, for whatever reason the Puppet Master of Fate does what he does, during the same time period in which I was dismissing Mama's and my words as just an isolated example of a frustrating verbal interaction between mother and daughter, the Master of Fate was focusing on two very unknowing, pathetically helpless human puppets and immortalizing their words for a preordained future reference purpose.

Since Mama arrived at my school at such a late hour on the afternoon on which she had hoped to survive the school conference with Mrs. Gross and the school social worker, the school's dismissal bell rang at some point during Mrs. Gross' long awaited showdown. She must have been so overwhelmed by her sense of righteous satisfaction for finally having snagged her prey that the small detail of detaining me in school that day despite my suspension status to wait for the BCW investigating social worker must have inadvertently escaped her. Hence, I went home.

By the time it was three thirty in the afternoon and Mama had returned, I was well aware of the impromptu school conference that had just transpired, informed by at least half a dozen of my school peers who had witnessed Mama gliding past the school's entrance and through the corridors to the beat of a very strange and different drum. So when she walked into our apartment, nodding in place while attempting to slurp down some old beer, and slumped down into a kitchen chair without even removing her ragged overcoat, I was well prepared for the next few words that fell from her lips, slurred due to her clouded mental functions and the saliva that dripped out along with them. "I think there might be some trouble again because of that Mrs. Gross teacher over in your school, you know."

I watched her for several minutes as she slipped in and out of drowsiness, eyes drooping closed only to be semi-opened seconds later. Stared at her glazed suspended eyes, set in what once upon a time and long ago could have been a strikingly pretty face. Stared at her dirty wrinkled coat with broken bulging pockets filled with junky contents of which she could not even identify or name their purpose. Stared at her lowered body that was weak, festering with germs, and awaiting the one infectious disease that would finally take her life. Stared at the sad, sagging spirit that was seated before me and thought that I had finally seen Mama for what she really was. A surge of unforeseen wisdom moved inside of me impelling me to go over to my mama and gently touch her arm.

"Mama, why do you keep doing this to yourself?"

She struggled to look up, dilated pupils trying to focus on my face. Her thoughts obviously weaving in and out through the cloudy cognitive passages of her mind. She looked at me for what seemed to be a short lifetime, and eventually sighed and said, "Because I'm trapped, Victoria. Trapped behind a curtain of dread." I digested her words, and then the surge of unforeseen wisdom surfaced again.

"But Mama, curtains can be moved or pushed aside." Struggling to not give into the nod, her pupils regained their focus for one last moment.

"Not when your curtain of dread is made of iron."

I gasped upon hearing her words, took a step back, turned, and moved in the direction of our kitchen's doorway. When beneath the door's jamb, I was overcome by one final surge of what I understood to be unfamiliar hope. It seized control of my tongue and forced me to fiercely whisper, "But there's always electric drills," as I made my way out of the room. I never turned back. Never bothered to see if Mama had heard me. Never knew. The fading sensation of hope disappeared from my repertoire of emotions for at least the next sixteen years of my life.

Mama was abruptly forced to come out of her nod when the BCW folk arrived hours later. By then, our conversation was seemingly forgotten, along with the rest of the forgotten words of ghosts and sagging spirits.

The specific details that followed the aforementioned episode bear a striking resemblance to the repetitive incidents of which my childhood days were comprised. Mama was court-ordered to attend a drug rehabilitation program, again. Mama chose a daily methadone maintenance program in the northern section of the Bronx to fit the appropriate drug rehabilitation program criteria, again. Due to her virtual abandonment of our apartment in Ms. Cathy's building and "other issues," she was asked to move out. She, once again, ended up in a not-so-decent shelter in the vicinity of the Grand Concourse. I, during the same time period, was placed into one, maybe two, temporary foster homes until the judge agreed to let me return to live with Mama in the shelter approximately two months later. After having been out of school for almost three months, the shelter social worker began the process of trying to enroll me into school somewhere around mid-May. On June 13, the day of my tenth birthday, with only two more weeks of classes remaining, I officially left the mainstream and began my educational career as a special education student amongst the vast majority of New York City's bored of miseducation.

The anonymous war raged on . . .

CHAPTER TEN

The more you judge, the less you love.
—Honore de Baltzac

AT SOME POINT during my mid or late teens, I really can't say for sure, I sat in on some therapy group with other "ill-adapted" types like myself. The group leader was a frail, petite and middle-aged Indian psychiatrist-type lady whose accent and low volume communication style made it completely impossible to hear her unless one strained their ears. One did. In fact, we all did, even the craziest amongst us. Based on her physical appearance alone, she initially impressed as though she had nothing to say or worth hearing. But there was something about the steady softness of her voice that immediately pricked all of our attention, struck chords within that needed to be stirred. It seemed that the softer she spoke, the more we strained. I don't recall in what institutional setting I chanced upon this Indian lady, I don't remember her name, how old I had been, or exactly how many times I had sat in on her therapy groups. But, with the identical purpose of the greenness of grass, I remember word for word her description of the human cup theory. And for this reason alone, I'm glad that I had strained my ears.

While perhaps the most unscientific of all of the nature-versus-nurture theories that I ever heard, the human cup theory relates a message both of which I can relate to and humbly appreciate. According to the tiny Indian lady with the accent and the soft voice, "We are all born into this world with different cups. The size, elasticity, and robustness of our cups are predetermined by genetics over which nobody ever has any control. Our unpleasant early life experiences are the forces that are responsible for poking holes into the bottom of our cups—our childhood environments, over which we likewise have no control. Strong, pliant cups combined with happy life experiences make for future cups that are filled to the brim with healthiness; fragile, brittle cups combined with early traumas make for future weak cups with bottoms filled with holes that are unable to hold on to the good stuff that passes through, and so on. Those with whom we bond, love, and love us back, help preserve the matter around the holes that hold the bottom of our cups together. Those of us who attempt to cover our holes with superficial Band-Aids usually end up with the same wide, gaping holes in the final analysis. True healing comes from within. It occurs when we diligently work at mending our holes by remembering our pain and focusing on the matter that has held our cups together all along. It is only then that we find our cups able to hold on to the good that is placed inside of them, as opposed to helplessly standing by as the good stuff leaks out from porous bottoms. It is also then that we can master the spiritual art of viewing our cups as half full instead of half empty."

With all of the suffering and pathetic unfortunate circumstances that gave rise to the bulging chasms on my cup's bottom, I am yet aware that there simultaneously existed some solid matter that held my cup's bottom together. Despite her frequent physical and emotional absences from my life, I always had Mama. And although perhaps dictated by the chapter of accidents, at a later point in my life, I had Ms. Cathy. Even Mama, who most would perceive as having not had one lucky card dealt to her in all her life, had those with whom she shared love. Mama had her own Mama for the first seven years of life, followed by me, and then later, Ms. Cathy. I have only met one human being who I honestly believe lacked any matter by which the bottom of her flimsy cup could be held together. I can state this without being guilty of stretching the truth one iota. Born into this world with probably the finest of porcelain cups, she departed as if the porcelain was made of gingerbread. May my wild waif of a friend Bruny rest in peace. Her sad and lonely life dispatched a reality in which crumbs, from what was once a sweet and rare substance, eventually chipped away from sides that engulfed a bottomless pit. It is with great hesitation that I introduce you to my beautiful little friend. While she lived, I don't believe anybody ever took the time to get to know her. Peep into her small, pure heart. Most thought of her as unworthy of their time. Neglected by all of heaven's star angels, it was as if her life served no other purpose than to have others chew on the crumbs of her shell and then spit them on to the ground when they were sated, and her crumbs' sweet flavor exhausted.

I hesitate to drudge up memories of my wild waif of a friend because of the depth of the sadness that is consequently elicited from within. I am similarly reluctant because of the compunctious, bothersome tunes that reverberate through my conscience every time I recognize that I too selfishly nibbled on her gingerbread cup until the sweetness of the flavor was gone. I, however, was never sated.

It all started out on the first day that I started doing time in special education. Sometimes the good and bad times of our lives interface to such an extent that it is difficult to append accurate rating labels to them. I was guided into a small classroom that was located down a long corridor on the dark side of a rather dingy school building in the Bronx. I was alone. After the episode that occurred in my last school, Mama's non-verbalized decision to never step foot into a school building was now cemented in granite. On the night before, Mama's unexpressed fears were illuminated in her insistence that I memorize a fabricated story that would provide a logical legitimate explanation concerning her absence. Her worries and my attempts to commit the fabricated story to memory ended up being wasted expenditures of energy. The counselor who accompanied me down the long dark corridor and later reviewed the business-type looking school papers that I held in my possession didn't seem to give Mama's absence a second thought. It was as if she was quite accustomed to conducting business with children with absentee parents. Later on I learned that absentee parents were on the list of criterion that was associated with affiliation to special education. It was especially high on the list for those of us who were classified as "emotionally/behaviorally disturbed."

While I admittedly experienced some anxiety with regard to beginning a new program in a new school, the tone of suspended animation that was set by the obviously unconcerned counselor that accompanied me to the classroom only served to channel my peaked anxiety into feelings of curiosity, tainted with a slight irritation. After no more than two words were exchanged between the counselor and my new teacher, I was left standing alone in front of the classroom. The counselor walked off with the zeal of a cow grazing in a pasture on a day where lazy, fluffy white clouds prevailed, obviously feeling that she had completed enough work for the morning on her present civil service job. Upon opening the door, the teacher had to hurry away to physically remove a rugged-looking Spanish kid from the window sill who was evidently having a hoot and a holler yelling a string of four-letter obscenities to some female passerby down on the street below. During the time period that half of the class' eyes turned to follow the teacher and half remained focused on me, I quickly appraised that with the exception of a petite, cute Puerto Rican girl who sat right next to the teacher's desk, all of my classmates were boys. There were about eight of them present, of all shades of the minority rainbow. Despite the fact that the teacher who opened the door was the only one attempting to pry the screeching Spanish kid off of the window sill, I observed that there was a second teacher seated in the back of the classroom. I later learned that this was the paraprofessional. The person who was paid a salary by the Board of Education to help manage such groups of "unmanageables." Despite what I've heard about not indulging in our first impressions of people, this was just one more case to prove the liberal and supposedly open-minded folk wrong. My initial observation of the paraprofessional who remained oblivious to the din around her with eyes glued to her own written works of interest did not alter in the two-year period that I did time in Mrs. Holloway's class for the emotionally and behaviorally disturbed. With few exceptions, she was about as useless and ineffective in adding anything to our educational or emotional development as the weathered poster that read "School is for Learning" that was tacked on to the wall in the back of the room. So I guess it was in the fifth grade that I changed my subscription to the advice that was always so readily offered about dismissing one's first impressions. At this age I had arrived at the sagacious conclusion that if upon first sight it impressed as a piece of broccoli, it probably was. Vegetables don't change—that's why we have to be so careful about with whom and where we plant them.

Since it took Mrs. Holloway so long to hush up the unruly Spanish kid, I took it upon myself to seat myself at an empty desk in the back of the room, which was at a safe enough distance from the otherwise preoccupied paraprofessional. When the boy was finally stilled and Mrs. Holloway turned in the direction of the door, I allowed a few moments to pass so that the class and I could entertain ourselves with her harried look of confusion and I could administer a brief personality test to my new teacher. When the joke began to stretch to unacceptable limits, I called out, "Here I am." The warmest smile that any teacher had ever cast in my direction washed over her initial fleeting look of shock. I smiled back. My visual memory of Mrs. Holloway has gently eroded over the years. It's kind of what happens to shards of glass when they bathe in the ocean's sea water for months. The only physical attribute that remains vividly lodged in my visual memory was her coppery, red-colored, shoulder-length hair. When she wore it down, I remember thinking that it looked like she was wearing a silky crown of autumn leaves upon her head. My emotional memory of Mrs. Holloway holds similar keepsakes of regal warmth and animation. She was, in no uncertain terms, the best teacher I ever had in my short educational career. I learned more in that two-year period under her tutelage than I did in the next five that I flitted in and out of school. I had finally won a round in life's lottery and stumbled upon one of the far and few between Great Masters. Blessed by the Spirit of Truth and first impressions.

It was about one hour after I was first seated in Mrs. Holloway's class that I formally met Bruny. Within the hour I had already learned, through vicarious instruction, that she was not seated right up under the teacher to prevent the boys from bothering what had been the only girl in the classroom. It was quite the contrary. Mrs. Holloway had obviously sat Bruny there to prevent her from bothering the boys. I had never seen anything like her—cute little girl with slicked-down brown, wavy short hair. But the things that came out of her mouth. Vulgarities and obscenities fell from her lips aimed at whatever boy who by chance was looking in her direction with the ease of rain water cascading off of flower petals on a rainy day. Her cuteness and style fit together about as well as oil and vinegar. I think the only time that Bruny's mouth was free of obscenities or some menacing banter was when she was sucking on one of her multi-flavored lollipops. I later learned that many a past teacher who had tried to do their bidding with regard to enacting the "no eating in school rule" with Bruny had been met by such fury and resistance that the rule was long ago forfeited when it came to Bruny and her lollipops. Prior to her entrance into Mrs. Holloway's classroom, Mrs. Holloway must have gotten word of the lollipop clause in the school's decree because she completely accepted the fact that at any given moment Bruny could have at least ten lollipops on her person, with one blatantly dangling from her mouth. Nobody ever challenged the lollipop clause—not any of the teachers, the students, or even the principal. There are certain psychological boats that the wiser of us recognize should never be rocked.

It was directly after Mrs. Holloway had explained the class rules and given out a short list of the required school supplies that Bruny approached me. Prior to her getting out of her seat without permission and sauntering the distance to the back of the classroom where I was seated, I was under the impression that she hadn't noticed my arrival. With 95 percent of her attention focused on the boys in her perimeter, and the remaining percentage on Mrs. Holloway, how could I have thought that she had any knowledge of my existence? But she had. Bruny approached me with sad and tentative eyes and a red lollipop filling the wide facsimile of a smile that was on her face. She held three additional lollipops in her right hand. A green, red, and yellow one. Seemingly oblivious to Mrs. Holloway's assuaging remonstrations to return back to her seat, Bruny looked me squarely in the eyes as if she was searching for something. I must have worn a dumb questioning look on my countenance, having had no idea what was really going on. It was much later in our friendship that I realized that she had been quickly assessing the depth of my potential to form a real friendship. The overture of offering me a lollipop was a mere distraction.

"Hey, your name's Victoria."

I nodded slowly, questioning thoughts held in abeyance.

"I'm Bruny . . . You wanna lollipop?"

"Nah, that's all right."

"Yeah, whatever. Maybe later you'll change ya' mind."

Her eyes remained fixated on me. Invisible fingers held my eyes open, making it impossible for me to blink. A faint sigh escaped from the corners of her soul.

"Well, what can I say?"

"Nothing that I don't already know."

I blinked just as a genuine smile crept up on her lips and she moved away slowly, still assessing me with her searching eyes, while knowing that the chord of friendship had just been struck. Then, as if we had never been engaged in conversation, Bruny abruptly turned and snatched a pencil out of a fat boy's hand, hit another boy in the head, and ran back to the front of the room. Disregarding the fat boy's boisterous complaints about his pilfered pencil, Bruny sat back in her seat and asked Mrs. Holloway when it was going to be time for lunch. Mrs. Holloway whispered something into Bruny's ear, gently retrieved the stolen pencil from her hand, and affectionately patted her on her tiny, frail shoulder. The class was ready to begin.

Bruny never cast another look in my direction throughout the entire morning. It was as if my presence was second in importance when compared to all of the impulsive, hyperactive boys in her circumference. I'm not exactly sure who initiated the first move, but we somehow managed to sit together at lunchtime, and I somehow managed to have sucked one of her green lollipops down to the stick by the time Mrs. Holloway came to retrieve her class from the cafeteria to begin the afternoon's lessons.

I've come to learn that some of life's most challenging questions don't have definitive answers. Relationship ones rarely do. Bruny was far different from the girls with whom I typically associated. Given the zeal with which I typically shunned her type, one would have thought that we would have become classroom enemies. Aggressive mortal foes. Bruny was girlie kind of cute with a big mouth who was always intruding upon somebody else's personal space with her provocations. She was a major class nuisance who never shut up. Yet, she was the most giving, sweet girl I had ever met. I once saw Bruny give away her entire snack to the only white boy in the class who was crying because somebody had stolen his snack money on the school bus. Then she knocked him upside his head about five minutes later for no rational reason on earth. Perhaps it was because she had given the snack money situation some additional thought. The white boy brought snack money to school everyday. Bruny, on the other hand, was lucky if she had snack money twice a year. To rationalize the reasons for Bruny's erratic behavior was an exercise in futility. As time went on, I figured out that Bruny did what Bruny did because she was Bruny and left it like that. I kept it simple.

Mrs. Holloway loved Bruny, although unfortunately, in somewhat of a pitying, overly indulgent fashion. In fact, I remember thinking that she loved her too much. Although with the best of intentions, Mrs. Holloway honed in on Bruny's neediness and tried too hard to placate the emptiness within. Not understanding that this treatment sucked the life out of Bruny's weak defenses, our poor teacher often fell victim to the brunt of Bruny's callow and callous remarks. As the school months passed, a pattern emerged in which Bruny was at her sweetest and most affectionate moments with Mrs. Holloway at the very beginning of each day, her numerous open wounds having had the opportunity to heal across the hours of the nighttime's darkness. It was when Mrs. Holloway attempted to reciprocate her affection in an overly effusive manner that Bruny turned on her and became the wild waif of a girl who I came to know and love.

Bruny never cursed at Mrs. Holloway. I guess that was the one line she had decided not to cross, regardless of how much tenderness Mrs. Holloway lavished upon her easily bruised psyche. She reserved that for her peers, particularly the male ones with whom she would pick fights on an hourly basis. I believe it would be a fair estimate to say that Bruny had more fights during our first month of shared school experience than I had in my entire life. That includes my stay in residential treatment centers, drug rehabilitation programs, and multiple incarcerations with some of the most violent and provocative females in New York State. Bruny loved to fight, and fight is exactly what she constantly did. When she wasn't fighting, she was talking about fighting. She was a crazy girl. Despite her small, almost coquettish presentation style, she was one of the craziest fighters I had ever seen. There was an unfailing abundance of strength in that little body of hers. And where her physical strength left off, a whole lot of mental craziness picked up. Everything was a potential weapon—from pencils to desks to the heels of her little shoes, if she could remove them quickly enough. But since speed was never one of her weaknesses, she usually did. By the middle of the fifth grade, Bruny had been suspended for fighting so much that I almost expected to miss her presence in our classroom on at least a biweekly basis. I think the only thing that kept her from being transferred to one of the more special, special education programs was the combination of Mrs. Holloway's overly sympathetic and pitying attitude and my learning how to divert her attention away from precarious, aggressive situations on to other areas of interest, like our friendship. Our friendship, I came to learn, was the one thing that she valued and needed more than fighting, aside from her lollipops. Strange as it may seem, with all of her fiery venom and unsettled impulses, Bruny never cast one nasty look or heated word in my direction. I, instead, received all of her sweetness and all of her loyalty. Bruny adored me, and at times, seemed almost obsessed with the hope that I would adore her back. I did, you know. I really did. How could one have helped from adoring a little wild waif of a girl who would have given anything to make me smile, make me feel happy and needed? It would have been impossible not to. Yet, I'm not so sure Bruny felt any adoration on my part. In fact, I'm not so sure at all. I'd almost bet that my cute little Puerto Rican friend with the never-ending assortment of lollipops propped into the comfort zone of her mouth felt like she was anything but the recipient of some significant other's adoration. Who am I kidding? The truth is the truth.

It's most likely that Bruny was the one who initiated our friendship. I honestly cannot remember, but she must have been the one who sat next to me in that smelly cafeteria and offered me one of her prized lollipops for a second time. Many years later when we were sitting on some project park bench hitting the crack pipe together, I remember feeling confused and asked Bruny how we became friends. Since it was her lips that were sucking the shit out of false happiness at the time, I answered my own question, "Must have been when you gave me a lollipop during lunch at school." She inhaled deeply, looked down briefly with glazed eyes and corrected me, "No, it was when I came across the room and looked into your eyes and knew that you were one of the good ones."

Mine and Bruny's friendship developed with the ease of the setting of the sun. Although in the beginning our "odd couple" status almost matched the seemingly odd nature of Mama's and Ms. Cathy's everlasting friendship, we both evolved into slightly different people during our relationship's course. Perhaps it was the effect of two prepubescent girls' natural maturational processes that was responsible for the transformations. Instead, I like to think of it as a personality trade-off between two little needy girls. A compromising of the egos that tied us together in a harmonious fashion. Each compromised character trait serving to add on to the largest of the invisible cords that connect the most vital of all little girls' organs together. For it was our hearts that ultimately bound us to one another and made us feel more complete.

As our defenses lifted and we became closer, Bruny became somewhat more wary and pensive. Her past pattern of constantly becoming involved in physical altercations for the hell of it waned. To a degree, she traded in her impulsivity for self-constraint, tainted with the ability to be more artful and strategic in her warfare tactics. I, on the other hand, who had previously only entered into fighting situations as a mere means of taking care of personal business, survival if you will, developed an itch for increased social excitement in my life. The fighting words that started to fall from my lips were censured less by my past hold on pacificism. They were instead increasingly fueled by a recalcitrant energy that, for the most part, had previously lain dormant. Although Mama may have functioned as an early role model for some of this behavior, in actuality Mama usually ended up being more mouth than she was anything else. I had mouth accompanied by an aggressive adrenaline rush that seemed to race with faltering brakes throughout my body. Besides, it didn't take a genius to discern that Mama's mouth was a rudimentary defense that functioned to buttress her sagging spirit. Most of her menacing tirades were generally about nothing and served no viable purpose in the minds of the general public. Or so I thought. Mine, contrarily, were typically about something, fueled by a non-intoxicated tongue, and served many self-serving purposes in my homeland of the ghetto streets over which I proudly sauntered and preyed. The fact that my tongue often bit off more than it could psychologically chew was of little consequence to me. It was my ungovernable tongue that made me slash two girls before I was even out of elementary school. Two girls, who on two distinct occasions, challenged my threats and seemingly left me with no choice but to make me force them to swallow their words, while at the same time did not allow me to relish the emotional digestive process of my own actions. It was at the point that my aggressive displays were galloping away on hooves of a new and different animal that Bruny clung to me the most. I first thought that she only wanted to come along for the ride. It was only when she was gone from my life that I more accurately concluded that she had clung to me in her loving, but feeble attempt to anchor me and slow me down. No matter how many of our traits subconsciously merged, Bruny never surrendered her sweetness. She was definitely one of the good ones.

After we spent lunchtime together for approximately one week, Bruny and I were running the streets together after school and on the weekends on almost a daily basis. We jumped rope, did each other's hair, listened to music and danced, talked and giggled about boys, and began the practice of marking our territory in the hood by making gut, heartfelt decisions about which other girls were acceptable associates. Our ethnic differences didn't seem to bother either of us in the slightest. Although I, who had typically only befriended African-American girls in the past, encountered difficulty at times convincing the other black girls that this little "goya bean" fit the criteria of "cool" and could be trusted. Before she met me, Bruny seemed to be somewhat lacking in the female friend department, particularly amongst the female gender of Puerto Ricans. Despite her tiny size and cuteness, she lacked that passive air that ordinarily characterized the Latina femininity that so many of the other girls seemed to possess. While they were individually intimidated by her, as a group, the other neighborhood Spanish girls typically shunned her, making it quite clear by their body language that she was not one of them and therefore not welcome into their small cliques. The couple of older and rougher Puerto Rican girls with whom Bruny used to associate in her aunt's project accepted me just fine. In fact, they were quite awestruck by my proclivity for the art of stealing. Despite her menacing mouth and seeming concomitant aggressive nature, Bruny's two or three older friends never got too far in their attempts at convincing her to steal for them. I guess they had figured that with her small size and overall adorable appearance, she'd be thought of as quite an unlikely thief. But Bruny claimed to be scared. When they really put pressure on that part of her that needed to please and be accepted, she'd eventually concede to serve as a decoy, although she'd outwardly deny her role as an accomplice to her dying day. Regardless of the untruthful quality of her conscious admittances, Bruny spent many a day intentionally looking all cute and innocent in one corner of some neighborhood store, while her artful older cronies were making out like bandits in another. A bag of lollipops was the only compensation that she ever asked for, or received, in return for her theatric efforts. It was no wonder that these older girls frequently sought to employ

Bruny's cheap labor services. No matter how often I tried to convince her to be more assertive and demand an equal ration of the "goodie bounty," Bruny refused. As far as Bruny was concerned, she wasn't stealing and she didn't want any conscious part in taking something that didn't belong to her. Could she help it if she happened to make some junior high school girls so happy by merely looking cute while they browsed through stores that they felt it necessary to compensate her with lollipops? No. I guess transparent suits of armor come in all shapes and sizes. As for me, I tacitly understood that throwing a larger, not-so-cute black girl into the mix wouldn't have made for such good stealing business. So, I usually kept my distance whenever Bruny's older friends took her "shopping." At first, I used to wait across the street. When I came to realize that they typically detained her for about five or ten minutes, I began to do a little brief "shopping" on my own from whatever store happened to be in the closest proximity on the avenue. Later on when we were alone and Bruny would happily be sucking on one of her sweet rewards, I'd pull out some of my loot. She'd always look at me all wide-eyed and exclaim, "You didn't."

"Nah."

"Ya' sure?"

"Yeah, here I got you another lollipop."

Relief would always wash away her facial expression of doubt.

"Red, oooh, that's my favorite."

It worked just about every time. My little friend's need to hang on to lucid lies that were as easy to pop as soap bubbles sometimes scared me. It was as if the bubbles' filmy outer coverings provided the flattering unction to her soul. Veteran of pain that she was, Bruny chose to believe that it was silver sparkles, instead of rain, that fell from the sky a little too much for me.

At the time we met, I was living with Mama in a shelter. Towards the end of the fifth grade, we moved into a run-down apartment in the Bronx, further south from where we had been living. For whatever reason, I was allowed to remain in the same school. This meant that I had to then walk about fifteen blocks in order to get there. Mama slowly stopped attending the methadone maintenance clinic. And when she did attend, she only sold the little bottles of methadone that they gave her on the streets for drug money anyway. In my ten-year-old mind's appraisal of the situation, her habit appeared to be getting worse. By my eleventh birthday, Mama had adopted the very embarrassing behavior pattern of picking things out of the garbage when she was high, which was just about always. It is possible that Mama had always engaged in such behavior and I had never noticed. There are certain things that even the most vicious amongst us refrain from telling little children. But, by the time puberty had set in, few people felt the need to hush their whispers concerning the fact that they had seen Mama bent over somebody's garbage even if I was in their presence. Most, however, were tactful enough not to say it to my face. The one boy from the projects who unfortunately suffered from a tactless moment, and called himself teasing me about Mama's shopping sprees in his project's garbage, found himself crying all the way home to his Mama with a bloody face after I had smashed him over the head with a garbage can's metal lid. Most of my peers practiced the art of tact after word of that incident filtered throughout the neighborhood.

I do believe some clarification is in order. When I say that Mama had turned into a garbage picker, I'm not suggesting that her behavior was akin to the mentally ill derelicts that you would find out on the streets of New York City eating food out of the garbage as a means of survival. Some heroin addicts, and as I later learned, some crackheads, in the latter course of their disease's progression, engage in garbage shopping behavior to serve two very real purposes. Firstly, with few exceptions, garbage shopping behavior is a solitary act. It also requires a rather focused type of concentration. And lastly, the act of searching from garbage can to garbage can and mulling around through different contents is repetitive in quality. There is something that happens in the chronic addict's brain, some chemical reaction that serves as a numbing agent on the senses, that creates an internal desire to engage in seemingly mindless, but focused repetitive behaviors in isolation. Distractions, particularly of a social quality, are frowned upon because they bring down our high. While some engage in other behaviors, such as repetitive cleaning, of which dusting is an all-time favorite, with garbage shopping comes the possible fringe benefit that one will find something of actual value with which to purchase more drugs. That brings us around to the second major purpose of garbage shopping for the addict. Mama, and many others like her, had big hopes of finding a buried treasure from amidst the debris of our neighborhood trash cans. And when in usual actuality there were no real treasures to be found, Mama's numbed, intoxicated mind had her convinced that some pieces of junk were little treasures in disguise. Maybe the disease truly progresses to a state in which one's perceptions are grossly distorted. Or perhaps by the time one's addiction has reached a chronic stage, and the addict is feeling so low about themselves, so guilty about all that they have not given to their loved ones, the need to give supersedes their reality testing, thereby causing them to see many valuable and wondrous qualities in virtual pieces of junk. And God help you if you challenge the addict about the value of their find. Not a wise move. Not after they've been out all night sifting through multiple areas of garbage and just so happened to find you the very thing that you've always wanted. Even if it is slightly used.

By the time I was eleven, we often had more garbage in our apartment at night when Mama returned from her shopping extravaganzas than was left in the pails outside. Mama brought home furniture. Worn, tattered, and broken furniture that never matched anything in our apartment. She once brought home a large mirror with a crack dead up across the top, talking about if you turned it sideward nobody would notice. Mama brought home books. Tons of irrelevant, useless, and often ridiculous books. She said she wanted to start a library. I guess the fact that she didn't know how to read hadn't crossed her mind. Mama brought home nursing textbooks, mechanical books, and books about how to grow a garden. When I once made the stupid mistake of asking her how we were supposed to start a garden when we were living in a tenement building with no front or backyard, she said that was beside the point and got mad about my lack of appreciation. Mama even brought home a book about how to care for your pet hamster when we hadn't had a pet in our house since I was born. The closest we ever got to having hamsters were the look alike numerous rodent families that intermittently squatted in the open spaces of our apartments. Mama brought home rusty, disgusting costume jewelry that "just had to be cleaned." While I had the good sense never to put any of the offensive metal on my person, Mama started sporting the stuff like it was made by Gucci. Looking back now, I believe her most embarrassing prized possession was this broken Mickey Mouse watch with a frayed pink band. The damned thing didn't even work. Beneath the scratched glass surface, a motley array of Mickey's body parts used to slide back and forth against the glass covering and get caught up on the minute and hour hands. This made a very dull tinkling noise every time she moved her arm. Other than the watch's appearance, the most controversial moments were when we were out on the street together and someone would inquire whether Mama had the time. She'd flatly say no, and they'd be steady looking at her arm with suspicion and bewilderment, collecting their thoughts as Mama would go off about her business as nonchalantly and undisturbed as before the question had been asked. While I was generally mortified in the very beginning, an edge of nonchalance, and even humor, replaced my mortification as time progressed along with her disease.

I think the most bizarre thing that Mama ever brought home was a pair of broken snow skis. I wouldn't know if they were usable or not because to this day I don't know what skis are supposed to look like. This occurred when I was older, about fourteen, and we were living in Manhattan. God knows where she had found them. The only thing I could think of was that she had probably taken to traveling uptown to where all the rich people lived. I couldn't imagine that any resident on the lower east side of Manhattan had just rid their domicile of a pair of skis. Although at this stage of the game I knew better, I just couldn't help myself from asking Mama what she expected me to do with a pair of skis when we were living in NYC. As was expected, she was offended by my question and in her usual slurred speech said, "Never mind, I'll use them myself." The vision of narcotized Mama attempting to mount skis to glide through the busy streets of midtown Manhattan on a snowy day was sufficient to permanently cement me in my decision to never question one of her overtures of intoxicated love again. I learned about halfway through my eleventh year that the best method of handling Mama's garbage shopping sprees was to pretend that she was as brilliantly lucky as any valiant pirate at sea for finding so many riches, wait until she went into a deep nod, and then throw just about everything back out into a neighborhood trash can. Typically, if I left her one of the more innocuous components of her past night's find, she'd never know the difference. There were, however, one or two rare occasions in which Mama actually found something that was worthwhile. Those were the things I kept.

Whether it was due to my inevitable entrance into prepubescence, or the steady progression of her addiction and the accompanying, almost daily shopping sprees in our community's trash, Mama began to detach from me in noticeable increments during the same year I met Bruny when I was in the fifth grade. Since her emotional availability had never been one of her hallmarks to motherhood, this detachment basically translated into her increasing physical absence from my life. With the exception of our once-a-week ritual of trekking across the Bronx to spend the day with Ms. Cathy, who conveniently always had many beers on reserve, I was lucky if Mama was in my presence for one hour each day. This, in turn, translated into my spending the majority of my days and nights in the bowels of the streets, often being affected by surrogate parental influences whose seedy characters were a far cry worse than Mama's.

Bruny, whose dysfunctional family background remained a mystery to me in terms of the particulars, had an even greater amount of personal freedom. On occasion, Bruny stayed out all night without her absence ever being detected by either of her parents. While it was true that she did have a paternal aunt in the projects with whom she often visited, neither of her parents ever bothered to verify the exact nature of her whereabouts. She was the most uncared for little wild waif that I ever knew.

Bruny never invited me to her home. It was as if there were things inside that she didn't want me to see. If we didn't hook up in school, she'd either come by my apartment or shelter, depending upon what month we were speaking, or she'd just miraculously appear wherever I happened to be on the streets. It was as if she could sniff me out. I'd turn around from whatever I was doing with whoever I happened to be doing it with, and there she'd be. Always smiling that same knowing sad smile with a lollipop dangling from the corner of her mouth. She had no problem bringing me to her aunt's house when she wanted something more substantial than a lollipop to eat. Her aunt seemed nice enough, in a distant sort of way. At least she didn't appear to mind when Bruny served me a portion of whatever food was sitting out on her greasy stove. She was just cool and unresponsive. The bubbling pots on her stove displayed more enthusiasm about their content's boiling process than she did about anything in her environment, including her small niece. Since the door to her project apartment was often left unlocked, Bruny usually walked right in unannounced and uninvited, with me tagging along like a simpering shadow slightly behind in the rear. Once inside, Bruny would head straight to the kitchen that always possessed the aroma of stale grease and spices. A warm and potent cultural smell that in another lifetime might have warmed the cockles of my heart, but instead in Bruny's aunt's kitchen corridor, made me slightly nauseous when we stayed there too long. Her aunt would occasionally appear out of nowhere, display an instantaneous sign of visual recognition, and mumble one or two words in Spanish, stiffly wait for Bruny's one or two word response, and then retreat, probably back to wherever it was that she had just come. Throughout their entire thirty-second interaction, her aunt would never cast one glimpse in my direction. It was as if my physical body, and the spirit it housed within, were invisible. Sometimes there were other strange people in the apartment. An older man with bored eyes, a fat woman, and several kids with stony faces in the adolescent spectrum. While I'd observe Bruny nodding or mumbling something to one or more of these anonymous relatives, she'd usually repeat her pattern of heading straight to the kitchen same as if there was nobody in the room. And I, feeling awkward and confused amongst invisible strangers, would stumble along behind her. I used to feel relieved when we'd enter Bruny's aunt's apartment, eat, and leave without ever having encountered one family member. I used to wonder how Bruny felt, what ran through her mind. I eventually concluded that her sensation of relief was probably experienced when she had her ritualistic thirty-second exchanges with her aunt. Because, as far as I knew, that was probably the only personal interchange she'd have with another human being who shared her same blood line all week.

    As far as Bruny's own living situation was concerned, I had no idea, and we didn't talk about it. Even at ten years old I was wise enough to know that there were certain questions that were better left not asked, and certain things better left not said. I never saw Bruny's father. In fact, she never spoke of him until we found ourselves incarcerated several years later. I knew she had a couple of older brothers and a dead murdered sister. I never saw her oldest brother Fernando, who by the time Bruny and I had met, was serving an eight-to-fifteen year sentence up North at Elmira State prison. Her brother, Luis, who had a heroin addiction that placed him close to Mama in the races, was rarely around. Bruny told me that he used to stay in Bushwick, Brooklyn with a girlfriend whenever he wasn't in jail. It was once and only once that I believe I laid eyes upon Bruny's mother. Bruny hadn't showed up for school that day, and since Mama and my after school visit to Ms. Cathy had ended, by evening I wanted to know where and how she was. I knew what building she lived in. It was hard to miss, being one out of the only two on the block that wasn't burnt out. I asked an old lady who was struggling to drag her shopping cart full of groceries up the steps which apartment Bruny lived in. She simply stared at me, but when I held the building's door open for her, she told me. I must have knocked on that door for about three minutes before a woman's voice asked me what I wanted. I thought the old lady had been a hag prankster who had intentionally told me the wrong apartment. When I identified myself and inquired whether Bruny was home, a gruff feminine voice flatly informed me that she wasn't. As I was retreating back down the dark unpleasant hallway, the apartment door opened and a short, once-upon-a-time-and-long-ago pretty Puerto Rican woman stood leaning against the door jamb watching me from the corner of her hauntingly hollow eyes. Although she didn't appear to be high, they possessed a blank, eviscerated look that I had come to associate with die-hard addicts. Eyes that had long since belonged to a living soul and caused a chill to trickle down my spine like dripping ice water. It took all the energy I had to regroup and extricate myself from her constraining gaze. When I reached the staircase and turned back around, she was gone. An invisible cloud of mystery and depression left in her stead.

When Bruny located me a few hours later in the park demurely fending off some thirteen-year-old boy's rap, I never mentioned anything about going to look for her at her house. As the days passed without her uttering a word about it, I just figured her mother never told her—if, in fact, the mysterious woman with the sad and empty eyes was her mother. It was obvious that she had her own personal reason to keep our relationship separate from whatever she experienced at home on a daily basis. After meeting the woman whose pained eyes temporarily imprisoned me in their mesmerizing gaze, I consciously decided to respect her wishes.

Throughout our childhood friendship, there was only one occasion during which Bruny volunteered any glimpses of insight into her past. On a blustery, cold January day that marked an approximate eighteen-month anniversary of our friendship, Bruny arrived late to school wearing the same clothes that she had worn the day before beneath a ridiculously large man's jacket. Although she seemed more quiet than usual throughout the morning's academic rituals, she came bounding over to me at lunchtime with the usual red lollipop's stick protruding from her chapped lips.

"Wanna see something?" she asked me with half a smile.

"Yeah."

"Ya' sure?"

"I said yeah," wondering what this was all leading to.

"Look."

From a pocket within the oversized, worn jacket that she had opted to leave on all morning, Bruny withdrew a weathered photograph. It was a picture of her when she couldn't have been any more than three years old, obviously taken in a park on a bright sunny day. In the picture, Bruny was wearing an adorable yellow dress with white socks and shoes. She had the same short haircut and the usual lollipop stick visibly hanging from her jaw. Just as I was about ready to tease her about the lollipop, I noticed that Bruny's eyes were slightly turned in the direction of a large adult male silhouette whose muscular arm was the only body part clearly captured by the camera's lens. As I further scrutinized the old photograph, I realized that whoever it was that Bruny was cautiously inspecting in her peripheral vision had filled her eyes with substantial awe and trepidation. Her look elicited the black shadow of a sickening familiar sentiment to momentarily waft up from the basement of my heart and hover gingerly above my consciousness. A psychological eclipse that piqued my spirit, but dissolved into a gray smoky vapor before I could identify the matter at the bottom of the chimney from which it had come.

"Well, whatcha think?" came her impatient voice.

"Nothing, uh damn, you were real cute. Uh Bruny, whose that over here?" I pointed to the muscular arm. An unforeseen cloud swept across her face.

"That's papi, uh, my father."

"Oh." I didn't know what to say. So I said nothing, silently.

"Okay, give me." I guess she had had enough of clouds and silence. She snatched the photo from my hand and buried it inside a worn pocket. "You wanna go by Fat Joe? He got a radio. Let's go get it. Come on."

We started to cross the school cafeteria. A gnawing, awkward, uncomfortable feeling lingered on my spirit. I knew that the weathered photo in the ridiculously large man's jacket meant something. Something that Bruny was trying to tell me. Knowing that I should say something, I finally blurted out, "Bruny, you sure did look cute in that picture. Really cute. And now I know that you've always had a thing for lollipops. Were you born with a lollipop in your mouth or what, huh?" I forced out a weak laugh.

As if Bruny didn't hear my remark, she changed the subject and went on about her lunchtime social business. I figured that old photos of baby doll girls with scared eyes and lollipops in their mouths were a forgotten business. That was until about two hours later when Bruny sprung out of her seat in the middle of art class and ran over to me in the back of the room. She looked at me dead serious-like, with the same vacant pained expression that characterized the eyes of the woman who I believed to have been her mother and said, "I didn't always have a thing for lollipops, Victoria. Not always." She stared at me deeply for about the inside of a second before turning around and racing back to her seat, intentionally knocking Fat Joe's radio off of his desk as she dashed by. The familiar, familial wounded look was erased from her face when, in a few more minutes' time, she turned around and called out to me about the finer details of her art project. It was never, however, erased from my memories. Same as a picture of a tiny cute toddler named Bruny with frightened eyes.

Looking back now, my two years spent in Mrs. Holloway's special education class was kind of special. I met Bruny—a genuine friend with whom I would share some of my most significant and intimate life experiences when my head was still young and impressionable. I was also identified by Mrs. Holloway as having the most responsive and absorbent brain in the classroom. Our teacher, Mrs. Holloway, was one of those rare birds who, once tucked away into the private nest of her classroom, left her own book-learned teachings at the door, and spent her time concentrating on giving us that which she believed we needed most in our lives. A wise hen who understood the importance of feeding each of her chicks a different kind of worm. It was this quality of hers that made her classroom an inviting and nurturing academic haven. It was similarly the quality that won her the title of Great Master.

Bruny, as I previously hinted, received an abundance of affection, praise, and attention in our special education nest. And although she hurled it right back at Mrs. Holloway almost as fast as she could bestow it upon her, by the end of the two-year time period that we spent with her, Bruny began to digest compliments and truths with much greater ease. She had even learned to accept, and seemingly appreciate, physical embraces for what they were. Her learning to accept hugs from Mrs. Holloway generalized into the occasional spontaneous gesture of embracing me during our future shared emotional climactic experiences. A behavior to which I had previously been unaccustomed, but secretly cherished. I'm not suggesting that Mrs. Holloway performed any miracles in her little special education classroom that was tucked away at the end of the school's long dark corridor. Certainly no miracles were performed that turned Bruny's life around on to a different course. She merely shone a light upon a different way. Planted the first seed and raised the curtain on Bruny's potential to experience happiness in a healthy manner. Had the astral influences parceled out a few more Great Masters along her early path, who could say the exact direction that her life would have taken? Seeds that go without water and sunshine for too long eventually die.

The worms that Mrs. Holloway fed me were of a completely different nature. They nourished my intellect, while covertly stimulating my appetite for more. In addition to raising my reading level to three years above grade expectancy, Mrs. Holloway instilled within me the courageous belief that I, Victoria, the fatherless daughter of Rosa the dope fiend, was also a human being of substantial intelligence. A star angel had briefly descended into my life.

Before I lay the subject of visiting angels to rest, a brief description of Bruny and my vacation stay in heaven is in order. Knowing that our parents were just about as useful in accessing resources from the community for us as the welfare institution was in combating poverty, Mrs. Holloway took it upon herself to arrange a two-week stay for us at a Fresh Air Fund sleep away camp as a kind of graduation present for us when we were promoted out of the sixth grade. After she organized all of the paperwork, Ms. Cathy took over with all of the remaining details. I don't know who did the same for Bruny. Her spirit of independence must have negotiated it herself, because on the day that we departed on the big bus, she was about as efficiently prepared as I was. Who even knew if her parents ever realized that she was gone.

We spent two entire weeks being children. Real children. We climbed. We explored. We participated in sports events. We ate toasted marshmallows around a big, orange campfire. We rolled around and did somersaults on grass that looked like emerald green tinsel and danced in the summer breeze. We told ghost stories at night. We sweated, and we laughed, and we cried normal tears of pain when we scratched our knees. Of course, we had to break out a little of our ghetto mentality up there in the camp wilderness. Bruny had about three fights. I had one. We cursed and taunted the boys, but then later sneaked into their quarters late at night when we weren't supposed to. I stole a few carbohydrates from other juvenile campers when they weren't looking. And we definitely availed ourselves of the opportunity to smoke weed along with the rest of the inner-city contingency whenever we believed that the breeze was blowing in a direction that wouldn't give us away. But when it was all said and done, we enjoyed what I believe is often referred to as good, clean, and wholesome fun. On the very last day before we had to return to the city, I surprisingly learned something new about my little friend with the battered ego.

There was a nun up there who wasn't exactly a staff member, but volunteered her services for arranging the summer's yearly talent show. Sister Anna was a red-faced, fat and jolly nun who exuded love and an internal tranquility from her every pore. Bruny adored her, and she was constantly in her presence trying to absorb all of her saintly drippings. We were all supposed to identify one skill that we wanted to further develop, and then perform that skill on the evening of the talent show. Of course, since stealing and fighting weren't viable options, Bruny and I were at a loss about what skill to decide upon. When we were right down to the wire of the time frame reserved for making such decisions, Bruny, who appeared more unsettled about my indecisiveness than she did about her own, made a statement to me whose essence was quite a foreign concept.

"Ya' know, Victoria, I don't know why you're stressing this. You could do and be anything that you want to. You're special."

I was stunned. "You too Bruny. So could you. You're special too," I stammered.

Her eyes saddened and clouded over with faraway burdens.

"You don't have to try to make me feel better. It's all right. I'm different, but you . . ." Her eyes brightened again, "You could be something, Victoria. Don't you ever forget that."

I didn't know what to say. What could I say to my adorable sweet friend who was already so damaged that she was resolute in her vision of what little her life held in store for her? I stared at her for what seemed like a life time before I reached out and gently stroked her fingertips with my own.

"Why don't we go get a lollipop, Bruny? It's been a long time since you ate a lollipop."

This is what I said to her, but before I lifted my fingertips from on top of hers I had decided to recite one of the poems that I wrote in Mrs. Holloway's class about hope at the talent show.

Bruny never did perform along with the rest of us on the night of the Fresh Air Fund Camp's youth talent show. Instead, she sat in the audience, smiled, and provided us all with good cheer and support. I know that Sister Anna was especially disappointed about Bruny's absence from the makeshift stage floor. Perhaps her disappointment even surpassed that of my own. Sister Anna seemed so attuned to Bruny's inner world. It was as if her spirit's fingers gently explored each internal crevice of pain and self-hatred that my little friend's body tried so hard to cover up with cuteness and ardor. In spite of her disappointment, Sister Anna let her be. A healing tactic that we could all benefit from using sometimes.

Later that evening though, when the stage had been cleaned and we were all herded out by the campfire for our last night of song and toasted marshmallows, Bruny disappeared. When more than ten minutes had passed and I realized that she must be up to something of far greater significance than using the bathroom facilities, I left the others and began my search. After looking inside all of the individual cottages, I headed toward the main reception area. From the distance I saw Bruny slowly approaching Sister Anna who was standing in front of a little church vehicle in the small parking area reserved for staff. I hid in the night's shadows, believing that my friend merely desired to say farewell to her for one final time in private. After a brief verbal exchange, of which I could not decipher one word, I heard it. The most beautiful pure and melodic voice that I had ever heard. A voice whose strength and splendor pierced my heart and brought me down on to my knees as if in prayer. Her song, while delivered in Spanish, clearly reflected an exulting tale of bittersweet love as only understood by the hearts of few women. The rhapsody of the music was so breathtaking that it silenced all of the competitive chirpings of crickets for miles in the distance. I was certain that all of the forest's animals were similarly robbed of their breath and bowed at the knees. When the song of rhapsody was complete and the chorus of nature's children slowly resumed its previous tempo, Sister Anna lovingly wiped tears away from Bruny's eyes, made the sign of the cross over her, and held her tight for their final embrace. It was only when Sister Anna's car drove off into the darkness and Bruny turned to head back toward the mainstream of the camp's nocturnal activities that I was able to slowly rise from my knees and step out of the shadows.

"My God, Bruny, your voice. You never told me that you could sing. Your voice is beautiful."

She stared at me with a look of confusion on her face for a matter of seconds. Then the look of confusion was washed over by a look of irritation.

"Let's get back to the campfire."

"But, Bruny, your voice," I stammered with incredulity rising within. "You could be somebody someday too. You could be singer."

She turned on me, a look of desperation and deep-rooted tumult in her eyes. "No, I can't. I only did it this one time. I did it for Sister Anna."

"But, Bruny, that's stupid, you could . . ."

She cut me off. "I said no. I only did it this one time for Sister Anna and I'm dead serious, Victoria." That's when she popped a lollipop into her mouth and began to fumble with the plastic foil of another.

"Okay. Okay." I've always been the type to avoid getting into fights that I knew for certain I was going to lose. I could tell that Bruny's cup was especially brittle right then. It was also vulnerable and likely to break and spill out all of her emotional contents. We walked in silence and returned to the campsite with the others. As usual, Bruny sucked on the sweetness of her lollipop while the rest of us carried a discordant tune around the perimeter of the fire.

Later that night when we were lying down in our bunk beds with me on top and Bruny on the bottom, I tried to reach out to my little friend one final time by whispering out into the darkness, "Bruny, can I just ask you one more thing? One more thing and then I swear I'll never ask you one more thing about singing again."

The sound of air being sucked opposed the silence. "Yeah, okay."

I carefully thought about how I should word my question, since I was only permitted one. "Bruny, why was it okay for you to sing for Sister Anna and it's not okay for you to sing to the rest of us?"

Her response came quicker than I expected, "Because she listens with the ears of God."

Even though my allocation had been exhausted, I didn't have anymore questions.

Such were the threads that wove the fabric of our friendship together. Our similar penchant for mind-altering substances and self-destructive behavior were incidentals that slipped in and out between the threads like flammable tinsel. Try as I might, I cannot pinpoint my first experience with the seductive stepping-stone drug—the one whose natural herblike qualities are propounded by many who embrace personal self-serving perceptions and generalizations. Marijuana. A drug is a drug is a drug. Mirages are always illusions and lies are never truths. He who runs from reality for even but a second has spent one second of his life living an illusion. One can only find beauty in truth. When we live our lives on roller coasters of lies and illusions, we strip ourselves of beauty every time we go for a ride. And then there are additional truths. There are truths for those of us who are unable to mount roller-coaster rides at whim. Those of us who because of our genetic foibles never exactly fit snugly into our own skins. There are more truths. Truths for those of us who, despite our snug fit, need to come out from within our skins for just a while to forget the hurt with which living in our skins is associated. Whether our cups are debile and emaciated from birth, or whether our life's experiences have punctured multiple gaping holes into our cups' bottoms, is of little significance. The message that should be posted in front of every marijuana drug-dealer should be a glaring, "Ride at Your Own Risk."

If they were at all present, Bruny and I neglected to heed any of these invisible signs. While we mounted separate rides in different parks, the insidious progression of the roller coasters' ups and downs wreaked tantamount destruction in our lives.

CHAPTER ELEVEN

*We admitted that we were powerless over our addiction,
that our lives had become unmanageable.*
—First Step from Narcotics Anonymous

IT'S BEEN ABOUT five months now since I started to write this journal. Since my sponsor continues to praise my efforts, remarking that I'm proceeding along my journey quite nicely every time she reads a new chapter, I gradually stopped barraging her with questions about my conscious, persistent deficits in the spiritual arena. For at least in the last three months, I've continued writing from energy reserves built upon blind faith. Or at least, this has been my experience from the naked eye.

Although I've never bothered to mention it to my sponsor, I've observed that over the past four or five weeks my Narcotics Anonymous fellowshipping has increased from about two-three to about four-five meetings a week. My increased attendance at meetings did not result from any conscious decision of my own. It just simply happened. The one lesson I learned shortly after the infancy stage of my recovery walk was that drastic shifts in behavior patterns don't just simply happen. On the contrary, there are usually quite distinct internal explanations for the seemingly surprising shifts. So, by about the third week, it dawned on me that my increased attendance at meetings was not the product of some amorphous coincidence. I approached my sponsor with my concern and question. I received support for my concern and validation for my question. I still, however, did not get an answer. When I queried my sponsor about the very small matter of a response, she smiled, hugged me, and then with me standing as limply and confused in her embrace as Mama's beheaded rag doll Felicita, she declared with bushels of certainty into my ear, "Answers are always one step away from the questions Victoria. As a matter of fact, they're typically one step in front of the questions. It's just that most of us ask the questions first as part of the process of gearing up our courage to face the answers."

When my rhetorical question was abruptly transformed into another soul-searching exercise by my sponsor with her seeming endless supply of unrequited wit, I addressed her with one more loaded question that was increasingly plaguing me with concern.

"Okay, well, can you tell me something else then? The more I write of my past life experiences in my personal journal, the more my lifelong tendency to blame everybody outside of myself for my misery seems to be a valid attribution. My childhood did suck. My mother was a pathetic creature. I was abused, poor, deprived, and surrounded by sick people. Even my best friend . . ." My words were choked down by tears and welling memories. I tried to hide this. My sponsor observed it anyway. "Go on, go on, Victoria. Your best friend Bruny, what was she to you and what did she do?"

Shit. If she had all the damn answers, why didn't she just give them to me? Answers are free, aren't they? My soul squeezed out one lonely drop of salty liquid from the corner of my right eye. My better eye—the stronger one.

"I don't know. I don't know. She didn't do anything. She just died. But that wasn't her fault."

My sponsor looked at me intently for a long while. What I initially detected to be a look of exasperation on her face, slowly evolved into a sigh, followed by an expression of inner peace and resigned acceptance.

"You're right. That wasn't her fault."

I met her gaze halfway and gingerly held hands with her guiding spirit for one intimate moment. "Look, Victoria, as I've told you, you're so very close to the answers for all of your questions that you're beginning to shiver from feeling their breath on your neck. Relax, continue with your journey, and be willing to receive the answers. Your shivers are bringing memories of my own early painstaking recovery steps to the surface and I genuinely feel for you and with you. I'll tell you something that my first sponsor once told me when I was struggling with conflicted accusatory feelings from my past. When life doles you lemons, you can always make lemonade. Don't stress yourself out too much Victoria; you've been sipping on the sweet, sour syrupy substance for several months now. You just haven't figured it out yet."

Somehow I knew her answers to both of my questions were intertwined, in a convoluted sort of way. It felt like all of my truths were floating by, perhaps just an arm's length away, quietly protected in a web of mystery. But who was the spider responsible for the intangible threads, and how could I gain access into this amazing tapestry?

I ran home from my sponsor's apartment that night. I waited until she shut her door before I ran. For some unknown reason, my need to run embarrassed me. As soon as I returned, I laid out her verbal responses on paper and attempted to fill in the blanks of my psychological crossword puzzle.

Why do I attend meetings? To experience a sense of universal love, tranquility, and personal validation.

What was lacking from my life during my latency-age and pre-teen years? A sense of inner peace, personal direction, acceptance, and self-love.

What was the significance of having Bruny in my life? I loved her and she loved me. And from somewhere deep within the heart of our friendship, parts of myself began to be reflected back on to me.

What did Bruny do? She died, even though that wasn't her fault.

My sponsor was right. I was very close now. The breath of the Spirit of Truth was raising all of the hackles on my neck.

What did I do? I lived, and even though I haven't figured it out yet, I'm sipping on the sour syrupy taste of squeezed lemons one day at a time.

Damn it, so why the hell then am I attending so many fucking meetings?

The communications cable to the spiritual world temporarily went out of order, but in the residual buzz, I heard "to experience a sense of universal love, tranquility, and personal validation." The line never quite went dead.

On the following evening, I relaxed, picked up my pen to continue wading through my past, and privately and humbly asked the spider to help me to become more willing to receive the answers that were close in my reach and intricately woven into the mysterious web. It was with this improved clarity of thought and vision that I found the courage to tackle the beginning threads of my life of addictions. I began with the first thread, which was tied to the roots of the cannabis plant.

About two weeks after my first and only deserved graduation ceremony out of elementary school, Mama must have cracked another deal with the housing authority with regard to their inner-city housing accommodations. Whether Mama had more in the planning ability department than I gave her credit for, or whether I did in fact have a star angel employed on a very part-time basis to watch over me, remains among the top ten haunting but comforting mysteries of my life. Regardless of which nurturing agent was responsible for the provision of my shelter during my latency-age years, they were on the ball when they designated the fifth and sixth grades as being the two years in which my housing situation would remain relatively stable. I needed some stability. I definitely needed the completion of my experience of having Mrs. Holloway in my life. And, as I'm beginning to realize, I needed to meet Bruny, although I haven't figured out exactly why as of yet.

If Mama had, in fact, held it together for my benefit, she sure made up for it as soon as that two-year time period had expired. While she had managed to keep her simmering impulses beneath a covered pot on top of a low flame for quite some time, the fire was eventually turned on high, causing the lid to fly off and all of her unbridled instincts and habits to recklessly pour down the sides and splatter around her surroundings. The progression of Mama's addiction had reached an all-time high. Her deterioration was visible now, even to the most casual of onlookers. It was not only discernible from her increasing outlandish behaviors. It was conspicuous in her physical appearance, as pronounced in her unkempt, poorly groomed daily existence as it was in the foul-smelling pockets of pus that oozed from rotten skin and collapsed veins that she was no longer able to hide beneath her meager clothing. Perhaps the truth was that Mama's disease had progressed to a point in which she no longer cared about hiding the wounds of her flesh. She certainly no longer cared about hiding the wounds of her spirit. In fact, it appeared as if she no longer cared about much of anything anymore. Not even me.

One night, right before we were forced to leave the run-down, dirty, small apartment that I had come to affectionately associate as home, I went to this kid Flip's house with the premeditated agenda of smoking a little reefer and chilling with my homies. Flip's moms was out on the town, partying to the beat of her own private drum. Flip lived on the third floor of an old building whose bathroom window looked out over what had come to be known as Dead Man's Alley. This small passageway that ran like a thin capillary between two blocks of endless cement structures acquired such a daunting name more because of its combined effect of its dark, dank, and dirty appearance with its occasional gray corpuscles of temporary human squatters than because of any unusually high incidents of discovered corpses amongst its narrow trail of debris. As was the case with most alleyways that were located within New York City's ghettos, human corpses were occasionally found in various stages of decomposition within the subduct of Dead Man's Alley in the Bronx too. The supposition that there was more than the usual number of dead bodies found there, murdered by the hand of another or by the hand of the deceased's own addiction, was quite suspect and a notion that was only really entertained by children with overly active imaginations. The honest-to-goodness truth was that most creatures who slithered in and out of Dead Man's Alley, whether they were members of the rodent, feline, canine, or human genre, had hearts that actively pumped blood throughout their veins. In addition to their shared common ground with regard to being on this side of the grave, all of the passersby who, for even but a minute, borrowed space in Dead Man's Alley, shared the similar traits of being amongst the nutritionally impoverished, physically languished, and spiritually dead. While an occasional thief might have opted to seek a brief refuge in the shadowy corners of Dead Man's Alley to escape detection from the brightly illuminated rays of a police car's light, its human visitors were typically comprised of die-hard junkies, alcoholics, and mentally deranged bums who actually preferred to experience their more black and insane moments in privacy. Even the most sick amongst us have been spared one clipping of pride. It seems to be attached to that part of our heart's muscle that squeezes out the final beat. On the late summer night that I chose to spend in Flip's unsupervised domicile to hide from all of my young life's troubles behind a cloud of marijuana smoke, I learned that Mama had gravitated to Dead Man's Alley along with her last clipping of pride.

It was about one in the morning before I tired from watching Flip's television screen in between wrestling with some dark-skinned, fifteen-year-old boy in the flickering darkness. It was about the same time that my hang-out partner for the night, Nora, must have tired from taking care of her business with Flip's brother in his bedroom. Emerging from the bedroom with her blouse on backwards, Nora possessed the single-minded goal of embarking upon a serious munchies mission in Flip's mother's cluttered kitchen. Flip, who had smoked more than any of us that night, was passed out on the couch. The television's lights periodically passed oblong shadows across the relaxed muscles of his face. I rose slowly, steadying myself on my feet, before I carried me and my buzzing thoughts into the bathroom. After I released myself and was splashing water on my quiescent face, I heard the familiar voice. The voice of one of whom I was created. Mama's voice. Its muffled sound reached upwards and spread itself thin across the bathroom window's small ledge. Without giving it a second's thought, I climbed up upon the cushioned toilet seat and stuck my head through the window's tiny square space, peering down into the unsuspecting darkness and insanity. While the quarter moon's candescence precluded any fulfillment from my visual senses, my strategic position along with the intensity with which I listened, maximized my ability to see all that was happening down below. The picture was so clear that I was certain that a sixth sense had surfaced to compensate for my hindered ability to see anything through my eyes. Children like me who have mamas like mine must often rely on stimuli outside of the jurisdiction of the standard five senses, lest they would perish shortly after departing from the womb.

There were two voices down below. Two female voices. While I was able to tell that the second voice was nearly as gruff and devoid of life as Mama's, I was unable to recognize the exact identity of its source. Just another faceless junkie. A discomforting thought liberated itself through the trap door of my quickly dissipating buzz. Had anybody else from any of the neighboring apartments had the initiative to perch themselves up upon their toilet seats to peer outside and listen to the two gruff voices down below, they more than likely would have been unable to distinguish the exact identities of both of the voice's sources. That is, of course, unless they were the child of the woman inside of the other gruff voice. The conflict that arose within as I struggled with the recognition that, with the exception of me, Mama was inclined to be viewed as just another faceless junkie by almost every other person in the world, caused me to lose the buzz in my head as well as my tenacious footing on the toilet seat's edge. I, in turn, shifted my weight and thoughts, before refocusing my strained senses down on the happenings below. Mama's voice parted the silence first.

"Come on, come on. What you moving so slow for? I ain't got all night."

"Shut the fuck up, Rosa. Whadya mean you ain't got all night? You got a date or something? What the hell else you gotta do?"

"You got jokes huh, shut the fuck up and come on."

"I'm coming. Damn. I'm coming. Can't see shit. I ain't got no cat eyes like you."

"You ain't got shit. Not even no legs to walk with seem like, you so slow. Here over here, come on."

"Where the hell are you, you crazy bitch. I can't see a thing. Shit."

The sounds of a bottle rolling and a quick gasp rose up through the darkness.

"What the hell you doing now?"

"I don't know. Knocked into a bottle or something. Damn. You sure there ain't no rats here Rosa?"

"Fuck the rats. Would you come on."

"What? Fuck the rats! Is you crazy? Rosa, I . . ."

"God damn, you don't ever shut up, do you? Is you gonna come on or what?"

"Okay, okay. Damn."

The sound of hushed, hoarse whispers was followed by the dull scratch of a match being struck. More hushed whispers. I assumed they were preparing their works for their nighttime injections. After about three minutes of more maddening silence, I heard Mama's voice again.

"This Cocoa Delight is some good shit. Real good shit."

The sound of matches being struck again. This time to light cigarettes for two who were obviously about to relax into a deep nod. I was about ready to step down from the toilet. Being in the presence of other people's nods was boring business, particularly when the other person was your mama.

"Yeah, you right, this sure is some good shit. Hey, what's that over there?" cried out the obviously startled and frightened voice of Mama's faceless twin.

"Damn, what the fuck you talking about now? What? Where?"

"Shit, over there, Rosa. Don't you see him?"

"See who? Damn, see who? What shit you talking about now? I swear you a stupid bitch, even when you high."

"Fuck you Rosa, I'm serious. There's a body over there. You know what, I'm out of here."

The sound of clanging metal made me understand that Mama's scared friend must have rose to her feet very quickly. But not nearly as quickly as the fear that rose in my chest.

Mama's voice was becoming increasingly irritated. No wonder. Her partner was running interference with her high. "You is both a stupid and a noisy bitch. What the hell you doing? I don't see no damn body, but just hold still a minute and I'll go check it out."

The slow movement down the alley of a small orange light quickened my fear as I realized that courageous Mama had gone to check out the accuracy of her friend's perceptions with cigarette in hand. The addict's ever-ready flashlight. I was too petrified to cry out in alarm, although every nerve in my body had shifted to the fright and flight mode.

The flatness that characterized Mama's voice with her next remark did little to allay my rattling fears.

"See, it ain't nothing to get all stressed out about. The man's dead. It's just the body of a fucking dead man."

"What the fuck you talking about? It's just the body of a dead man? There's a dead man's body over there? Shit. What you saying?"

"Come over here and look for yourself."

"Rosa, you really is crazy telling me to come on over there. You sure he's dead?"

"Hell yeah, I'm sure he's dead. I'm going in his pockets."

"What? Did I hear you right? You gonna do what?"

"I'm going through his pockets. And, if you don't come on over here and help me, I'm gonna keep everything this dead motherfucker's got."

I heard a muted "Shit" as I saw another glowing light slowly move through the alley to come in closer proximity to the first.

"How much he got?"

"I don't know. It looks like only about six fucking dollars. Shit, look over here."

"Damn, what now?"

"The brother must've had something real good."

"What you mean? What shit you talking about now?"

"He got the needle still sticking out of his fucking arm."

"Yeah, and so the fuck what?"

"And, I'm gonna take it and get me some of his good shit, that's the fuck what. You down?"

"That's it. You really is fucking crazy. How you gonna take a needle out of a fucking stiff? What if the shit killed him? Is you crazy?"

"I'd be crazier if I passed me by some good shit. He can't use it now. Fuck it, it ain't gonna kill me. Ain't no shit ever killed me yet."

I heard more gasps from the shadows of the darkness down below. They echoed in the silence after my own. Two of the longest minutes in my life passed before I heard Mama say, "It wasn't all that. Shit. Come on, let's get out of here before someone come looking for him. Got me six dollars here for some more Cocoa Delight. Now that's some good shit."

"Huh?"

"Come on, ya' chicken white girl. Ya' feelin' that Cocoa shit now huh? Come on."

"Yeah, yeah. I'm coming."

The sound of shuffling footsteps, accompanied by one orange light, made its way out of Dead Man's Alley into the distant black shadows. Without having been able to see their faces, I knew that Mama was in the lead, guided by her small glowing torch and clipping of pride.

I remained seated on the toilet's edge, transfixed in an unsettling trance until the dark-skinned kid came banging down the door.

"What the hell you doing in there?"

I bolted up quickly on to my feet and opened the door only to find my evening's get-high partner with glassy eyes and a dumb look plastered across his blunted features. The sight sickened me, although at the time I couldn't figure out why.

"Nothing," I walked past him.

"Now where you going?"

"None of your fucking business."

I slammed Flip's mother's apartment door behind me.

Mama didn't come home until about eight o'clock that morning. By then, I had already been startled awake twice by horrific nightmares that contained vivid images of languishing, faceless corpses slowly moving through Dead Man's Alley with little orange flashlights. When the sound of the closing apartment door caused me to awaken for the third time, and I saw Mama's haggard, numbed face drift in through the doorway, the painful reality of the larger-than-life vision before my eyes affected me more deeply than any of the creepy nocturnal images that I had recently dreamed. Nonetheless, I fell back asleep. This time though, I only dreamt images of vapid thoughts.

Following our cordial eviction from the apartment building in the Bronx, Mama and I played hopscotch with the shelter system again. We hopped from Brooklyn to Manhattan to Far Rockaway before hopping right back to Manhattan again. The only thing was that the master card shuffler upstairs must have hollered "game over" around the time that we hopped back to Manhattan for seconds because this was when Mama's tired-looking Panamanian friend threw the dice in the direction of the basement apartment in Spanish Harlem and we moved in on a "permanent" basis. As far as I was ever concerned, when one remained in one housing situation for a year or more, one was living there on a permanent basis. Since we didn't move again for almost three years, I considered our basement apartment in Spanish Harlem "very permanent."

If I had to choose one-time period in my family's never-ending roller-coaster ride that marked the point of our maximum deterioration, I'd choose, without hesitation, the almost three-year time period that we called Spanish Harlem "home." While it is regrettably true that our ride together rarely rode on tracks that were on an upward slope, our life together in Harlem sapped the foundation of our already pathetically dysfunctional family unit and left each one of us standing alone at a low ebb. In the beginning, I just thought that our roller coaster was on a downward slope that was steeper than usual. Now I realize that our move to Spanish Harlem marked the end of the ride. Without my knowledge, both Mama and I were ejected from our seats and pitched downward into an abyss, more affectionately known as hell. At the time, I guess the reason why we didn't realize that we were being ejected was most probably because we were high.

Being the seasoned itinerant that I was by my twelfth birthday, I believe my appraisal of Harlem, USA. in the early through mid-eighties was an accurate one. As far as my early adolescent acumen could discern, Harlem was the ultimate in drug capitals of the tri-state area. It was probably the ultimate in drug capitals of the entire United States of America, but since Mama and I had never traveled beyond the state of New Jersey, I didn't feel comfortable making any firm conjectures of such an expansive quality. While it was always true that drugs could easily be found close right outside of Mama's and my previous doorsteps, its presence in Harlem gave new and improved meaning to the word "abundance." For the likes of a street addict such as Mama, such an omnipresence of narcotics proved to be overwhelming, and eventually fatal.

It just seemed like everybody shot heroin. Everybody. While there were some who limited themselves to "girl" (cocaine), they were definitely amongst the minority. Baseheads were making their presence known in increasing numbers, but dope fiends still ruled in Harlem in the early eighties. I believe the sovereignty of the poppy plant became most visible when the product became scarce. While I'm told that nothing in the eighties ever came close to the dope panic of 1976, there were brief one and two day periods of heroin famines that uprooted the most cryptic of heroin dependents up through the cracks of New York City's five boroughs. When this periodically occurred because of some major federal cartel drug bust, it seemed like all of the city's dope fiends gravitated to Harlem like a patch of dried-up weeds in the middle of a drought, withered and mindlessly searching. Addicts combed the streets from the 111th to 118th in droves, hoping to chance upon someone who could hit them off with a "one on one" or some discrete news about a dealer who just happened to have a small stash remaining. It used to look like an addict's convention, with the streets and parks being the meeting halls. Mama was always amongst them, sick and tired, but never tired of being sick and tired, "fiending" for that one bag of dope that would make her feel normal again, even for just a little while.

Fortunately for Mama and all the others who played similar but different roles in the greatest of life's tragedies, heroin shortages were a rare occurrence in Harlem in the eighties. On the contrary, there was typically quite an abundance available for those who cared to, or needed to, indulge. As a result, Mama became an increasingly distant and scarce object in my life. Regardless of how limited her past parenting skills had previously been, I experienced her increasing absence as quite a loss. Whether it was the result of the rapid progression of her disease or her reaction to my increasing maturity, I can't say for sure, but by the time I was about twelve and a half, the reality of my situation was that I was pretty much left to survive on my own. A roof remained over our heads simply because welfare took to directly paying for its presence. Food made its way into our cabinets because I took to following Mama around like an annoying fly on the days of the month when her food stamps were expected. It was I who led our grocery shopping missions, and I that prepared us anything that resembled a hot meal. It was also I who often ate over at friends' apartments or boosted additional comestibles out of the supermarkets to fill in the seemingly forever present empty spaces in our pantry. Sometimes Mama would dupe me and not come around for one or two days before she was due her food stamps. This was when I further developed my acclimatization skills and set about to master the art of resourcefulness. Since my early childhood had provided me with an excellent foundation course in the art of survival, it took me no time at all to figure out how to dupe a duper. Within a few months of my stay in Harlem with Mama, I became a "superduper." I was intent on surviving, and while Mama's lifestyle might have presented me with a few stumbling blocks, the reality was that her heart was not intent on thwarting my efforts. Mama was always able to be found. Most times I was able to locate Mama in one of the many shooting galleries in the Clinton Arms Building up on 117th Street and Eighth Avenue. Although there were shooting galleries all along 112th to 120th on Eighth Avenue, Clinton Arms was one of the only buildings in which there was a shooting gallery in virtually every apartment. It also seemed to be Mama's favorite. Sometimes I'd have to go knocking on doors and stepping around folk nodding in chairs or over their works and cleaning buckets to find Mama. On occasion, an alert addict would point me in the direction to the right apartment. If I could locate a reliable touter, he would usually make my search that much more the faster and easier. Touters were like low-paid street advertising agents who stood out on the corners putting addicts on to what was good out there on the streets for the day. For example, let's say that on a given day there were five different brands of heroin circulating on the street—Victory, The Hulk, Good Pussy, DOA, and Poison. If the dealer of Victory had a great deal of his product and was intent on selling it, he'd hire himself a few touters—low-grade street hustlers who usually had habits themselves—to go around verbally spreading the word to all the addicts with whom he came into contact that Victory was the best buy of the day, and then point the drooling addict off in the right direction. All the touters knew Mama by the time we had lived there for a couple of weeks. By the time I was thirteen, they also all knew me. So whenever Mama pulled one of her disappearing acts, I'd just meander up to the most visible touter and inquire about her probable whereabouts. Touters, despite their occasional annoying sexual remarks made for my benefit, seldom pointed me in the wrong direction.

In the beginning, I used to feel a fleeting sensation of embarrassment when I had to pluck Mama out of some shooting gallery. But after a few months time, it became almost routine and neatly fit into my normal existence. Besides, the more shooting galleries I entered, the more times I saw mothers toting their small toddlers along with them. I then felt relieved, that at least during my earlier childhood, Mama had managed to keep this segment of her business more private. On the few occasions that the man who owned the shooting gallery had yelled, "Hey, get that kid out of here" when he saw me, I waited for Mama out in the hallway. She always came out of the apartment within a half hour's time when she knew it was me who was waiting for her outside.

Despite all of the sexuality that I had been exposed to before then, I think I learned the most about the adult anatomy during my occasional searches for Mama in shooting galleries. Addicts will inject themselves in any vein from which they can experience a quick get-high. For the most part, the general consensus is "the quicker, the better." I learned that lesson from counting the increasing number of dots on Mama's body throughout my childhood years. When one vein becomes infected or collapses, they turn to another, and then another, and then another. Injecting certain veins also gives different sensations of rushes. The neck and underarm, for instance, produce quick and intense rushes, while the leg and finger bring one's rush on with a more gentle ease. Some dope fiends went after a rush from out of their private parts and seemingly had no shame about getting their rush on from their dicks or pussies right out in the open, even if twelve-year-old me happened to be walking by.

I think my most memorable early shooting gallery experience occurred about one month before my thirteenth birthday. It was check-and-food-stamp day, so I knew I had to go find Mama. It was also May and pouring down rain in buckets that didn't make my search any easier. Even the touters seemed to be tucked away into their own dry hideaways. Finally, after searching through about five different galleries in Clinton Arms, I came across Mama in what was supposed to be a kitchen in a second-floor apartment. She was cleaning her works. Just as we were getting ready to leave, the Newark Boys entered. The Newark Boys were a group of addict-thugs from Newark, New Jersey who periodically held up galleries to make more money for their own get-high. Usually they wore masks, but they always had guns. They made everybody, except the owner of the gallery, of course, hand over their money, drugs, and whatever was left of their boosting products for the day at gunpoint. Then they made everybody strip so nobody could come running out after them when they made their exit. That's when I started to laugh. There was this one big, fat, black lady who sat half undressed on a dilapidated bed and started to cry. The more they screamed at her to shut up, the more she shrieked and cried. Then, because I was laughing so hard, they turned to me and told me to strip too. Mama, who was used to such stickups and standing there numbly in her birthday suit, told them that I was a kid, which meant that I didn't have to strip too. They argued back and forth for awhile until one of them finally told Mama that if she didn't shut the fuck up, they'd shoot her just on principle. Mama, who loved a good fight anyway, told them that they could go on and shoot her if they wanted to, but that still didn't mean that I was going to get undressed. Finally, the Newark Boys got tired of arguing with Mama and left. I never did get undressed, but at some unknown point during their verbal clash, the fat lady stopped crying and I was no longer laughing. While to the most preoccupied of observers it might have appeared that the emotions of the fat lady and I were on opposite poles of the map, even at the age of twelve I realized that our raw sentiments were probably more similar than anybody else's in the room. One thing was certain—we both still possessed the capacity to feel.

Two weeks later, when I needed to go search for Mama again from the same gallery in Clinton Arms, I recognized the guy who was shooting up beside Mama as being one of the same armed Newark Boys from my memorable stickup incident from the time before.

In much the same way our move to Harlem marked the point of our family's decline, junior high school identified the point of my academic decline. It was a disastrous decline on all accounts. By the time I was enrolled into my appropriately designated seventh-grade special education class, it was almost Christmas time. Why bother starting school three days before a ten-day holiday was my precocious logic. Since I couldn't arrive at a rational response to my own rhetorical question, I didn't attend. I also didn't attend many days after the Christmas vacation ended either. In fact, if I attended thirty days in the entire semester, I was doing good and probably would have been proud of my accomplishment. Despite my record of chronic truancy and virtual absenteeism from all crucial citywide examinations, I was promoted to the eighth grade, and then with only one iota more of a concerted effort on my part during the eighth grade, I was promoted once again to the ninth.

Much like the rest of my childhood, my memories of my junior high school years are wrapped up tightly into a dense and blurry misshapen keepsake, with residual traces of marijuana smoke shaped like an umbrella hovering above to provide the illusion of protection. I was smoking "trees" on practically an everyday basis. When I wasn't smoking, I was hanging out with other young, wounded souls whose socialization skills were limited to copping weed to smoke, and then copping some more to smoke again. Our adolescent burgeoning sexual hormones merely served as adhesive to keep the weed bags tighter together. A friend was someone with whom you smoked. A good friend was someone who always managed to have a large supply. A boyfriend was a male somebody who you wanted to smoke with, and have sex with, after you smoked. Smoking and hanging out with other potheads was a time-consuming business. When I wasn't doing either, I was honing up on my boosting skills. By this point in my life I had made some alterations in my boosting goals. My adapted goals included boosting for survival purposes, like to put additional food products into our apartment and mouths. It also included boosting for vanity purposes, recreational purposes, and moneymaking purposes. Sometimes I boosted just to polish up on my technique. Other times, I boosted just for the fuck of it. Although I might have been telling myself a lie at the time, today I realize that I was also boosting to support my daily marijuana use. I have since exposed the lie. When I wasn't smoking, hanging out, or boosting, I was running around looking for Mama. With my hectic schedule, how could I possibly have had any time left for school?

Just like I was seeing less and less of Mama, once I moved away from the Bronx I saw Ms. Cathy and Bruny on a less frequent basis as well. For whatever the reason, Mama always traveled back and forth to the Bronx to spend a few hours with Ms. Cathy on check days. Although we never discussed the particulars of any of her strategies or maneuvers, I assumed that she used to cop herself a healthy stash, get herself feeling nice, and head on off for the train to see her one and only true friend in life. Why exactly I didn't do the same, I couldn't tell you. While that inner voice that resounds from the deepest part of our soul continuously reminded me that Bruny was my one and only true friend as well, I put up all kinds of excuses to lie down comfortably in my out-of-sight, out-of-mind bed of self-deceptions. I was fortified with a well-developed, multi-layered defense system by then. So I was usually able to rest peacefully with few disturbances. There were one or two isolated occasions, however, that no matter how carefully chosen my pillow, and no matter how attentively I had picked out the warmest and fluffiest of comforters, the truth beneath my decisions kept me tossing and turning all night long. The princess and her pea didn't have nothing over the ghetto girl and her lie. It wasn't as if Mama never asked me to accompany her on her biweekly excursions back to the Bronx. Her invitations had become as religiously carved into her habitual behaviors as her daily copping and mainlining of heroin. It was I who usually opted to decline. As if in collusion with her consistent invitations, within the fraction of the second that it took for me to verbalize my decline, the echo of a lone inner voice struggled to be heard from deep within. Indeed, without fail, the spirit of truth had knocked on the door of my conscience at every critical turn of my life. It was I who ignored the knocks and didn't let it in.

In my prepubescent confusion, my reasoning for letting go of my friendship with Bruny was tied to her behavior, and my reactive feelings of personal shame and embarrassment about her behavior. In essence, spending a great deal of time with Bruny would have meant my having to take a step down off of the stage on which I had begun to stand amidst my peers. I was cool, belonged, and was very popular. Bruny was not. It wasn't that Bruny didn't try with all her might to remain closely knitted in friendship with me. On those rare occasions that I did assent to Mama's invitations to accompany her to the Bronx, Bruny urged me to return more often and begged me to invite her to my apartment in Harlem. My feelings of shame and embarrassment caused me to lie to her about our housing situation. I told her that we were still jumping about from one precarious shelter housing situation to another. Since it was tacitly understood that such a housing crisis preempted the importance of social visits in one's life, I was freed from having to face the guilt that directly denying her visitation would have caused me to experience. If it wasn't for the occasional surfacing of that one lone voice, I would have been spared from experiencing any pangs of guilt at all.

In addition to the fact that Bruny lacked any manipulative and charming social finesse, she had developed quite a reputation for sucking dick throughout the entire South Bronx. It wasn't that I was mad at her for being, as they said, so skilled at it, it was just embarrassing to be so closely associated with a dick-sucking hoe. What was so bad about it was that none of the many dicks that Bruny sucked were attached to the bodies of boys who at least honored her by identifying themselves as her boyfriend for even one day. In fact, throughout all the years I knew her, Bruny never had a boyfriend. By the time I got around to asking her whether she wanted a boyfriend, she must have serviced all the young thugs in training across at least three different zip codes, and my question held little significance. By this point, she had either played lollipop with every available young heterosexual in the hood, or he had repeatedly heard rumors about her competence in the life skill area of fellatio from his boys. Nobody with even a half ounce of pride would risk losing face by going out with her. Even new jack thugs who had recently moved into the neighborhood heard about Bruny and her generous gifts. By the age of fifteen, all of New York City must have known that Bruny gave the best head in the Bronx. Everybody knew that if you wanted the best dope, you went to Harlem, and if you wanted the best head, you went to the Bronx and asked for my little friend Bruny. I never approached Bruny about her behavior, nor did I speak on my feelings or question her about her own. Instead, like a soldier, I marched on with all of the communication skills I had learned at home. By then I was armed with ample artillery to survive the war of the living dead. Don't analyze. Mind your own business. And never, ever, under any circumstances, honor your feelings with an honest tongue. And so, the internal and external wars between habit and heart raged on.

In the beginning, I believe Bruny serviced guys for free. However, as time progressed and she started enjoying her own billowing escapes in clouds of marijuana smoke, the lollipop game took on different dimensions with additional rules. COD. Namely, cold cash or cannabis on delivery of competent cocksucking. In much the same way that I had dedicated ample time to perfecting my boosting skills, Bruny dedicated equivalent time to perfecting her performance at sucking dick. She became so proficient at it that by the time she did start hitting the pipe, she had quite a lucrative business with which she could support her habit. In fact, it wasn't until Bruny got wise, or more entrenched in her addiction, and started charging niggers on the regular, that I began to hang out with her on a more frequent basis. Hell, the truth is the truth. Bruny's truth was that she was the most competent dick sucker in town. That translated into her having more money, weed, and cocaine in her possession than any other fifteen-year-old girl in our neighborhood. I was definitely down with that program. I wasn't so worried about reputations and popularity contests by that point. Fuck any of them stuck-up bitches and their rumors if they didn't understand that. It is funny how when our needs change, we're so apt to alter values that had previously appeared to be cemented in stone. Years later, each and every time I decided to trek on up to the Bronx to share some of her earnings, the Spirit of Truth knocked on the door of my conscience with its usual hollow thud from bygone days in which I had ignored Bruny's existence. I still didn't let it in.

We remained in our hole of a basement apartment in Harlem where windows were considered luxuries until, with my persistent pattern of truancy, I managed to sneak through the cracks of the Bored of Education's system one final time and was unjustifiably promoted to the ninth grade. Due to the fact that my birthday fell in June, I became eligible to participate in New York City's Summer Youth Program prior to entering my first legal year of high school. I was assigned to work in a day care center for disadvantaged toddlers. I was basically responsible for assisting the licensed teachers throughout the day during all of the recreational programs designed to meet the physical and developmental needs of young children from the ghetto. This typically translated into my having to chase after wild-ass little hyperactive boys who escaped down the hall, clean up mess after mess of examples of three-year-old artistic and destructive tendencies, diffuse seemingly incessant verbal disputes that had the potential of erupting into explosions of pre-oedipal violence, and attempt to maintain my own sanity by dissociating from the ever-present shrilling shrieks and clamor. Once I realized that smoking a joint or two in the morning facilitated my being able to endure all of the aforementioned job-related duties, stressors, and hazards, I did so with the same applied regularity as the rest of my morning grooming rituals. I was fired somewhere in the middle of my third week of employment. Whether it was due to the continuous presence of my bloodshot glassy eyes and accompanying space cadet attitude, or to the fact that I had already accumulated three unexplained absences, none of which I had bothered to phone in about, remained an unsolved puzzle in my life. At the time, I personally didn't give a fuck. Since I was already quite adroit at the art of accumulating small quantities of wealth by several other viable means, I viewed my termination as a blessing in disguise—one of the far and few between favorable acts of the gods in my life. It not only got me away from those bellowing babies; it also provided me with even more time to do what I enjoyed doing most, which, as I sadly dare to admit today, was virtually nothing.

Until my recently acquired employment in the mini-department store in East New York, my almost three-week stay at the Day Care site at the age of fourteen was my only legal job experience in life. I guess the notion of acquiring a Social Security fund was of minimally perceived significance at the time. Surprisingly enough, however, I clutched on to one goal throughout the haze of marijuana smoke and repressed concern for Mama's security on this planet. I strongly desired to buy Mama a memorable gift from my first paycheck. Although I could have stolen, or legally bought with my trade-off monies, Mama a present of much greater monetary value at any given point during my early adolescence, for some unexplainable reason latched on to a dangling invisible value, I needed to purchase this gift with money that was earned by socially acceptable means. So I did.

I had already snorted a few lines of cocaine by the age of fourteen. It goes without saying that I earnestly believed that this was one of life's ultimate highs. However, once I started out on my mission to Chinatown to purchase the perfect gold piece without having indulged in the use of any mind-altering chemicals for at least the past sixteen hours, I even had to admit that I felt a different, but almost equivalent high. A high that had minimal reminiscence to that which I was accustomed to experiencing from my purchases at the street corner pharmacies in the past. After approximately two hours of searching and haggling over prices with men with slanted eyes, I stood in front of an honest vendor with the perfect piece. On its triangular-shaped polished gold face, which I figured must have represented the Holy Trinity, protruded a delicately carved figure of Jesus on his cross, complete with all of the requisite artistic finishing touches to make his facial expression appear real and beseeching. Beneath the crucifix in raised bold print read the words "God Loves You." Even though I had sufficient money on my person to buy the piece along with a twenty-four-inch-long, thin but solid, rope chain, I haggled the price down about $10 more, cut the deal, and then requested that the honest vendor inscribe "And So Do I, Victoria" on the back. After smiling sweetly in my direction, he did, and then I left. When I completed the long train ride back uptown, I bought two bags of weed with the money I saved from negotiating the price of my purchase. I do not believe that my life afforded me any additional opportunities to experience the natural kind of high that I felt on the beginning of my journey to buy Mama a memorable gift since then.

My choice of purchasing Mama gold—a possession which she could easily sell, pawn, or trade in for smack, and by which she would definitely be tempted, must have been overlaid by several issues of deep psychological significance, of which genuine naivete was not one. I can't imagine that my choice of purchase exemplified the sanguine expectation of dope fiends attracting hope fiends into their tragic circumferences. Life can never be explained by too simplistic a theory, or can it? Deep in my heart I knew that Mama would not be able to hold on to my gift for more than a day or two, unless, of course, she simultaneously hit the lottery or robbed a bank. In the case of either of these latter scenarios, the odds of Mama keeping my golden gift for more than a couple of days greatly improved. Even in these cases, however, the odds were inevitably subject to decrease over the passing of time.

I wrapped the little crucifix and chain in gossamery paper and expectations, and gave it to Mama at the end of July. She had just showered and was slumped in front of our only window trying to forestall the already steady accumulation of body sweat. Upon unwrapping the dainty box and beholding its contents, Mama's chin slowly rose so that her eyes met mine. She then stared at me for what appeared to be the better part of a lifetime. I had never felt so uncomfortable in my own skin. While locked inside her gaze, I observed the full range of human emotions waltz by. Each one—pain, love, sadness, and wonder—separately danced forward, bowed, and then retreated to allow its fellow emotion to step on stage before Mama blinked and the final curtain fell. The last emotion to curtsey before the intimate revue came to a close was hope. It was also the emotion that took center stage and held hands with the rest right before Mama blinked, shuffled to her feet, and hoarsely whispered, "Even though we both sometimes forget. God ain't never forgot the reason I named you Victoria."

Mama wore the gold rope chain with the delicate crucifix and personal inscription for two days. On the third day, she disappeared and didn't return for another two. When she returned, her neck was bare. Neither of us ever uttered a word about the gesture of my gift again. I guess we separately understood that we both did what we had to do.

CHAPTER TWELVE

"Oh, I've been a victim all my life," he said.
"No, Joe," she said. "Your whole life is ahead of you."
—Joe and the Volcano

HOW DOES ONE say good-bye to their mother? How do they look into her coffin after looking into the coffin of her eyes for a lifetime? How does one look into their mother's face for the last time, knowing that this time when they say good-bye it will be the last? Saying good-bye in death's company is not just like any other good-bye. It isn't "see you later," "ciao," or "so long"—it means good-bye forever. It means that last glimpse of your mother—the one who has held you along life's path, even if she did drop you a few times—will be shelved as your ultimate memory. It means you won't hear her speak, watch her shuffling down the street, or nodding out at bedtime before your only apartment window. It means that you won't ever have your mother to laugh with, cry about, or share in the merry-go-round of life's ebbs and flows again. It means this when you love your mama in spite of all of her character defects. It means this no matter what the size of your family is, but when you are the only child of a street addict, the only surviving next of kin, it also means that you are now completely alone in the world. It means this whether you ever figured out how to say good-bye or not. I never did.

Mama learned that she was HIV positive a few months short of my fifteenth birthday. I was in the ninth grade at the time for the first time. She, like most addicts of her kind, learned about her HIV status by sheer accident. And, like most of the others, upon acquiring the information concerning her status, did not alter her lifestyle one bit. In fact, her inextricable grasp on to the drama of the streets appeared to move one notch up from the sublime to the ridiculous.

Before I get into my last humbling days spent with Mama, descriptions of the effects of AIDS-related diseases on the human body, her lying dead in the coffin, and all of the other gory details surrounding Mama's death, I feel a need to paint a more poignant picture of Mama when she was still among the living. Or, to put it more accurately, when she was still on this side of the grave. My point is that I want everybody to understand that I grew up with a mother whose spirit kicked the bucket before I was born. Die-hard addicts like Mama and I pretty much follow the proclamation cited in all of the Narcotics Anonymous literature: We end up in prisons, other institutional settings, or dead. That is, of course, if we are not among the chosen few fortunate enough to be reborn. Since we've never physically died, we are reborn when some ministering spirit breathes life back into our own spirit. Ministering spirits speak to us through human voices at times. Other times they don't. Those of us who have gone through the experience say it's like receiving mouth-to-mouth resuscitation from a morning star. While I may still choke or require assistance from an inhaler auxiliary device at times, my revived spirit has, through little understanding of my own, rejoined my body to strut and fret my hour upon a stage again. Mama was less fortunate than I. Her spirit died a thousand deaths, while in between, her life was spent attending the funerals of each. Out of all of the many psychological theories I was exposed to during my multitude of "treatment" experiences, the one that held the most practical meaning for me and my life was Kubla Khan Ross' five stages of grief. I think Mama's entire life was an expanded version of these stages. I believe that once Mama experienced the loss of her spirit, her living physical and emotional selves spent the remainder of her time immersed in the various stages of grief. Shock, denial, anger, sadness, and acceptance. I knew them all quite well. They were like my childhood chums. By the time Mama learned about her fatal diagnosis, she had long since moved into the acceptance stage concerning the loss of her own spirit. Discovering the news about her perishing immune system did not perceptibly move her in the slightest. Not until the very end anyway, and by then, I believe her decaying immune system had already taken a toll on her sanity.

 A few chapters back I outlined the primary and secondary nuisances that dope fiends must fend off in order to achieve their main goal in life—getting high. I suggested that such obstacles as the police, jail, family, and employment frequently mar an addict's direct and easy access to the cop spot. While all of these nuisances may, particularly in the beginning, be perceived as annoying and tiresome, most diehards will soon enough adjust, appearing to swim through the irritating mire as if in smooth and untroubled waters. The willpower that identifies most addicts is ironclad and quite amazing. It's a shame that it is usually accompanied by the flimsiest of headgear to mastermind its purpose. Don't pay any attention to those naive, addled counselors who prattle on and on about the lack of willpower of addicts. They're ignorant, quite wrong, and need to seek assistance from a vocational counselor concerning a change in careers immediately. Trust my word on this one: Addicts want what they want when they want it. When the thing they want is a drug, they will do what it takes to get that drug, no matter what. Mama couldn't find the money to buy herself a new winter coat since I was about nine years old, but she typically had enough money to buy at least two bags of dope a day, and that was when times were hard. Bruny once had to cop out to "unlawful solicitation" charges after she'd been picked up for prostitution at least four times by the same cop. Since she had promised herself that she was going to go on a long run on the pipe for her birthday, she managed to sneak crack into her court-mandated in-patient detoxification program. True to her word, Bruny puffed on the pipe intermittently on her birthday all day long every time she went back to her hospital room to pee because of her "weak bladder condition." I, who almost got fired when I was first hired at the department store because of repeated absences on stormy weather days, used to boost come rain or shine in my heyday. I went out in the rain, snow, or hail. I went out during heat waves and inclement windstorms, even when my low body weight from the crack pipe placed me at great risk of soaring past somebody's fourth-floor project window along with the rest of the street debris that weighed less than ninety pounds. My deceased friend Tomcat—strapping giant who was like six foot four inches, two hundred and forty pounds in his sweat socks before he took the plunge—constructed makeshift syringes out of hollowed-out, sharpened car antennae and the soft parts of the plastic from eye drop bottles when he couldn't get his big hands on any more conventional form of works. Imagine the breadth of the imagination of someone who would devise the option of inserting a fucking TV antennae into his arm. Then imagine the potency of the willpower that resides behind that imagination. Then join forces with me and the penniless Bowery winos who always manage to remain at least partially charged and snicker at the ignoramuses who claim that addicts have a dearth in the will power department. Ha, ha, ha.

I just got lost in the verbal sauce again. Sorry. Back to Mama and her dead spirit inside of the functioning flesh. During my early teens, I started to observe that Mama began experiencing a hindrance that plagues all intravenous heroin addicts whose armor-plated willpowers are impervious to the whispers from heaven's hosts. At least it was then that I began to make my observations about Mama's struggles with tertiary level obstacles. The obstacles could have been present before, but it was then that I began to take notice.

The human body will take but so much abuse. It is also equip with but so many blood vessels that can withstand being constantly punctured. Most heroin addicts begin their injection careers with the more visible and easily accessible veins in their arms. As time and their addictions concurrently progress, what were once pumping leathery vessels of life's source, evolve into mashed and stanched conduits of flowing human refuse. It is then that other limbs and body parts are sought. This is followed by the progression of time and the deterioration of more blood vessels. Subsequently, dope fiends capitalize on body parts that, at an earlier stage of their disease's development, they never would have considered as viable entrances for narcotics into the human body. In my lifetime, I've seen armpits, necks, penises, toes, gums, and a variety of different sections of the female vagina used to get off from. And these are only but to name a few. The problem is that once an addict starts to stray away from the more popular use of limbs, the other less resilient passageways of the human anatomy begin to atrophy quickly. Inevitably, addicts will continue to inject their poisons into veins at various levels of degeneration until their flesh begins to crawl away in repugnance on its own. One can tell this is happening when the flesh is oozing pus and veins are no longer functional. This will occur after the addict's emotional self has moved into the acceptance stage of grief over the loss of their spirit. This is also at the crux of why whole-spirited individuals cannot relate to the behavioral extremes of addicts. Animated spirits cannot echo the mindless thoughts of those whose souls are empty. Never ask an addict why they do what they do. It's not that they won't understand your question. You won't understand their answer. I once asked one of Mama's running partners who, of course, was a decidedly less threatening subject, why she continued injecting herself in veins that were obviously collapsing and infected. Her reply was "Well, how the hell else am I gonna get the shit into me?" As I walked away and reflected on all of my experiences with Mama over the past thirteen years, I was more stunned by my own stupidity for asking the question than I was by Mama's friend's response. Like I said, never try to comprehend the self-destructive machinations of an addict. You'd receive more satisfaction from expecting your linen to dry after you've hung it outside on a rainy day.

While Mama and the majority of her running partners all exhibited a multiplicity of extreme behaviors that might have fringed on bizarre to certifiably insane, the idiosyncratic details describing the infamous Claw of Harlem during the early eighties would have caused even the most demented of Bedlam to be awestruck with bewilderment. I met the Claw shortly after we moved to Spanish Harlem. I heard about him shortly after moving in. Marietta—a fourteen-year-old girl who met the status of neighbor/acquaintance in my life at the time—painted a crystal clear picture of the Claw as an appendum to her critique of one of the latest Freddie Kruger movies. Marietta, a biracial early-eighties version of today's "hoochie," who was of mixed African-American and Puerto Rican extractions, lived part-time next door to me in Spanish Harlem with her alcoholic mother. She also lived part-time with her forty-year-old boyfriend farther uptown. The disparity in ages in their relationship was not what identified Marietta as a "hoochie," but rather the fact that every time she came back home "to help" take care of her intellectually challenged younger sibling, she played what she called the "Give and Take" game with several aspiring young drug dealers in the neighborhood. As per her own verbal description, "I give them good pussy and take their good money." Marietta and I never got tight because you couldn't trust her. She also seemed to be quite intellectually challenged herself. She was, however, someone semi-decent with whom I could pass the time when I was trying to suppress my internal concerns over Mama's whereabouts and wanted to lay low and in close proximity to our basement apartment. Despite her flagging intellectual deficiencies, Marietta usually provided updated and accurate information about contemporary cinema. Everyone has their own portfolio of strengths and weaknesses. One day, while describing "all that fucking blood" caused by Kruger's metal nails, she paused as if in deep contemplation, abruptly switched gears, and embarked on a verbal mission to nowhere about the Claw missing his big break in Hollywood, "except they probably wouldn't want no black dope fiend 'round all that expensive equipment stuff." I, who hadn't heard of the Claw before, didn't know what the hell she was talking about. Before I could open my mouth to say this, she must have picked my confusion off of my face because she stopped dead in her tracks again and said, "Don't tell me you ain't seen the Claw yet." My dumbfounded facial expression confirmed that I had not. "Shit. Girl, wait till you see the Claw. He make Freddie look fine." Marietta then went on to explain that the Claw was Harlem's infamous male dope fiend who was probably "in his thirties or something." His disease, as described by Marietta, had progressed to a point that was both unbelievable and reached by few, if by anybody else at all. With the exception of his face, which was purported to be surprisingly handsome, the Claw was a self-made freak—a vascular anomaly caused by the regular and repeated poking, pulling, and palpating of his various blood vessels in order to inject heroin into his body. The Claw was often observed manipulating his veins with tweezers in an effort to inject needles through their rubbery flaccid walls. He reportedly used to probe through one of the several abscesses on his skin, already moist and oozing with pus, to come into closer contact with one of his veins. Pens, keys, and an assortment of other common household items were similarly used in his own personal handling of his blood vessels. The Claw was gaunt and identified by the oddest shuffling gait in Harlem. Due to the fact that all, or nearly all, of his blood vessels had collapsed in his forelimbs, what were once fingers had transformed into deformed claw-like members that were quite limited in their fine-motor coordination. Everybody in Harlem knew the Claw, from children to adults. He was harmless, although incredibly loathsome if you stared too long at any part of his body, aside from his face. I immediately recognized him from Marietta's description when I first saw him. He was usually in the streets, and his grotesqueness made him quite visible. Unlike other addicts of whom many were afraid or shunned, the Claw was viewed as pitiful in a unique sort of way. Hence, he was mainly self-supported via charitable donations from decent Harlem folk and generous drug dealers. And, of course, like Mama and all of the others, the Claw always had the opportunity to find treasures during his garbage-shopping sprees while on a seemingly perpetual nod. I don't know whatever became of the Claw. I surmise he died. Probably by some form of vascular failure or gross infection. Or perhaps, he too, succumbed to the grip of the deadly virus. I can't say for sure. All I know is that I associate him with my early teens and Mama's death.

Although as far as I knew Mama never pulled any veins out of her arms with any tweezer-like instruments, her skin also became a mosaic of abscesses in different stages of infection by the time I was fourteen. When I saw that she could no longer control her limbs' abscesses' putrid smell by regularly anointing them with alcohol and/or Bacitracin, I begged her to go see a doctor. She eventually went to Harlem Hospital in response to my verbal insistence and her own probable physical discomfort with the foul-smelling wounds. It was there that Mama was tested for the HIV virus, and a few days later, was apprised of her positive status. I learned about her positive status approximately one month later by sheer accident. Mama was out on an overnight run and I had decided to do some superficial cleaning by tidying up around the apartment. I came upon hospital papers with Mama's blood work results buried beneath a heap of dirty clothes. I think I was angrier about her not telling me than upset by the results. I don't remember thinking about it much afterwards. I never cried, nor spoke on the subject with anybody, including Mama. Looking back now, I also don't believe that I ever queried Mama about any health-related issues once I learned that Mama was going to die from some AIDS-related disease. My use of marijuana, alcohol, and cocaine increased just about as much as my school absences did. On Christmas Day, when I was fifteen years old, I blurted out our little family secret while en route to Ms. Cathy's house for Christmas dinner. Out of the blue, with my mind flirting with unrelated thoughts about innovative stealing strategies, against the din of the train's metallic roar, I involuntarily threw off my protective muzzle and let "Don't you think you had better tell Ms. Cathy about your being sick?" fall from my lips and heart. Mama absentmindedly looked at me as if she had discussed the topic with me in an open, therapeutic manner for at least the past six months and replied, "That's what I planned to do." The emptiness that I felt at that very moment could have filled infinite vacuums. I had never felt so alone.

Although not using much more discretion than I, Mama did disclose her positive status to Ms. Cathy that day. She did it over dessert, somewhere in between the serving of coffee and apple strudel. Mama flatly informed Ms. Cathy of her "death sentence," and then before allowing her to slide back down into her seat, dessert tray still locked within her grip, asked her if she could assume legal guardianship of me when she died. The silence that followed could have been sliced as easily as the thick fruit-filled pastries that lay before us on the table.

My initial thought was that Ms. Cathy must have already known all along. I based this premise on the fact that she didn't show much of an emotional reaction, nor even get up to light another cigarette. My second thought was that Ms. Cathy hadn't exactly known, but had her suspicions that such a fate lie waiting to unfold within the next few chapters of our lives. This also could have explained the fact that no look of shock ever registered upon her face. Then, of course, there was also the possibility that Ms. Cathy hadn't correctly heard her. After considering the range of possibilities that involved other people's emotional relationships and reactions, I started thinking about my own. I first considered that Mama had never told me either because she forgot or couldn't. As I continued thinking, reason and logic increasingly highlighted the fact that the odds of the latter supposition being true were probably substantially higher. This paved the way for my understanding that she most likely informed Ms. Cathy the way she did because she didn't know any other way. Besides, Mama had experienced a shortage in the tact department throughout her entire life. And then, since enough had been said and thought, Mama didn't say anymore and I stopped thinking. Ms. Cathy simply nodded her head in agreement.

Interestingly, the one memory that stands out in my mind to illuminate the time period of Mama's discovery of her HIV status, like a bright florescent lamp that is bothersome to the eyes, is associated with my ultimate, albeit unsuccessful, stab at becoming a normal student. As is already known, I was virtually a non-attending student by the time I went to high school. I never amassed any credits during my initial enrollment at Julia Richmond High School in Manhattan. Then we moved. Mama and I were forced to move out of our Harlem basement apartment due to a fire that ruined most of the lower level floors of the building and the fire marshall's subsequent decision to condemn our living quarters. Neither of us was home when the fire started. I guess I should have felt grateful for having accidentally missed what could have been yet another traumatic experience in my life. The fire occurred on a school night at about one o' clock in the morning. Both Mama and I were hanging out, separately. We were lucky that the few articles of clothing and belongings that we had were salvaged. The two items that were ruined beyond repair—the mattress and old raggedy sofa Mama and I slept on, respectively—were so battered and rotted that we never would have bothered to lug them with us to another apartment anyway. The fact that the raging fire had busted out our one window, seared the cruddy linoleum, blackened the walls, melted the cabinets, and burnt a large gaping hole in the living room's ceiling, didn't phase Mama in the slightest. After the initial shock and all the accompanying "Oh my Gods," "Oohs," and "Ahs" were over, Mama would have told the super to fix her ceiling, thrown a couple of pictures from somebody's garbage on our walls, and gone about her business. If it wasn't for the fact that the fire marshall condemned the building, she would have spent the rest of her life living in that burnt-out basement apartment in Harlem. However, the fire marshall did condemn the building. So, we moved out into the city's emergency shelter system again, playing our familiar game of shelter hopscotch every four or five months. We knew all the moves. This time, though, the level of the game differed slightly in that most of our shelter residences were coincidentally located in the Bronx. After leaving Harlem, Ms. Cathy enrolled me into another high school in the Bronx. I remained in a MIS-II special education category while on the roster of that Bronx school system until I was court-mandated to a non-secure residential facility upstate. This was true regardless of whether we were temporarily shuttled to a shelter in another borough or whether I hadn't seen the inside of a school building for six months. One day in early February, when I should have been in the second semester of the tenth grade, Bruny and I made a pact to return to school. When I hunted down the assistant principal of special education for my class schedule and to inquire about the process of being decertified from special education, I was derisively informed that I was one of those "LTAs." Long-term absences. Yeah, well. I surely knew that already. I thought that was one and the same reason that I hunted her down in the first place. Looking back now, what I think neither she, the majority of her staff, or even I realized, was that more than being one of those "LTAs," I was one of those "LATs." Lost angels in transit. The schools are filled with us. It's a shame that the public school system hasn't recognized our presence and created an official category for us as of yet.

When I returned to school, I attended classes for about one week straight. Then I started to cut. It wasn't that I wanted to cut. It was just that I couldn't stand being in those special education classes and lacked the ability to see the forest instead of merely the trees. In addition to the fact that I already knew everything that was being taught and was bored out of my mind with the teachers' slow and repetitive teaching styles, Bruny and I were still the only two girls in the classes, surrounded by a bunch of nasty, excitable, acting-out young boys who spent more time attending to Bruny and I than they did to what lesson was being taught. With few exceptions, nobody learned anything. It was a vicious cycle that bored me close to tears on a daily basis. Bruny quit regularly attending classes first. Probably after the first two or three days. In addition to being bored, I believe the work was a little hard for her. Bruny was somewhat challenged in the areas of reading and writing. I also believe that she had only agreed to come back to school because she believed I wanted to and felt it would be good for me. The fact that she might have chanced upon some fresh young stud with whom she could swing an episode in a dark stairwell was probably perceived as one of the fringe benefits for putting my needs first.

    I hung in there longer than Bruny. Although I started arriving late to school, leaving early, and on occasion, missing one or two of my classes that were scheduled in the middle of the day, I could have earned four or five credits by the end if I had stayed. Since I liked English and Social Studies, and consequently rarely missed any of those class periods, believe it or not, I pulled eighties on my first report card. My test scores and class participation warranted grades in the nineties, but I rarely completed any homework. Needless to say, I also never studied. My temporary drive to plod along was initially fueled by the verbal pact I had made with Bruny, as well as by whatever unconscious motivations decided to float to the surface and take a breath of fresh air at this particular time in my development. A day or two after enrolling back into high school, it was stroked and reinforced by a relationship that I had formed with a new guidance counselor who had come to the school. Her name was Miss Rivera. In many ways, Miss Rivera fit the role of the fantasy mother that I never had. Miss Rivera was young, pretty, and smart. What made her more appealing was that she seemed to know and understand my life's language. She also understood the streets. Within two or three conversations I was convinced, luxuriating in my newfound sentiment, that I had finally found someone who understood me. The only problem was that she was not my counselor. She was Bruny's. I met her in my efforts to drag Bruny into her office to meet her on the first day of school. Laughing down the hallway, I lightly told Bruny that perhaps her counselor could figure out her obsession with lollipops. Bruny did not find my statement very funny and struggled even harder to unleash herself from my grip. Miss Rivera's later efforts at engaging Bruny were futile since no matter how nice and dedicated a counselor seemed to be, "you just can't trust nobody." I wonder if Bruny's appraisal of the untrustworthiness of the world's inhabitants applied to me as well. Anyway, I had no problem comprehending that Bruny and I were two separate people with individual minds. Control had never been one of my issues. I allowed Bruny and her convictions to rest in peace after that first day and instead focused on my own need to wade the waters of a relationship with Miss Rivera, gently and discreetly, one member of my body at a time. With all of the prudence and nonchalance that I believed I had mustered over the years, I was quite disconcerted upon realizing that it was my heart that jumped into the water first.

    My own counselor was a pudgy, middle-aged black man who seemed to possess only two concerns during the school day. These included whether he could read through the entire newspaper and when he would be able to clock out. My problems and I did not fit into the parameters of his range of concerns.

I picked up on his lead immediately, took the hint, and stayed the hell away from him. Instead, I had voluntary "informal" counseling with Miss Rivera everyday during her lunch period. Tales of my past and plans for my future were discussed in an office that was the size of a big closet and always redolent of mayonnaise and tuna fish sandwiches. How Miss Rivera could stand the smell or the same menu day in and day out, I never knew or bothered to ask. I guess we all have our little quirks and idiosyncrasies. It didn't really matter much anyhow since I tacitly understood that all of our time together began and ended with the spotlight on me. We spoke about Mama, foster care, the shelter system, friends, and my own solidifying patterns of existence. I don't remember how detailed any of my descriptions of my life were. It didn't seem to matter. Miss Rivera always understood what I was saying even when I wasn't exactly saying it, and she never pushed me into the section of the pool that I feared was over my head. While we tap-danced across the foundations of many subjects, the one topic that we always came back to was my future and what I needed to do for my future today. Since I was raised to be a present-oriented type of person, I had some difficulty with this concept. I eventually accepted that I might have to consider doing something different if I didn't want a future that was hopelessly bleak. After swirling for a while in foreign waters of contemplation, I dug my heels into the notion that the beginning of any personal changes in my life should start with my decertification from special education. Nobody, not even Ms. Rivera, could budge me from my irreversible line of reasoning. Two weeks after returning to school, I was running down my wearied Mama on the streets who was in search of "a little extra shit for later." I wanted to get her to sign her name on a request that I had written asking the Board of Education to remove me from special education classes. I don't know if Mama understood why she signed the piece of paper that I held before her over the hood of a car on a cold and wintry early March evening that seems like it existed epochs ago. She just signed it, muttered something about going to get something to eat, and left. It was a good thing I had gotten Mama to sign the request when I did. She didn't return to our shelter that night. On the next day when she did return, her mind was so zoned out that she probably wouldn't have known who she was to sign anything anyway.

 According to some difficult-to-decipher fine print in the Parents' Guide Book to Special Education, the Board of Education must respond to a parent's request to remove their child from special education within thirty days. Their response must come in the form of a psycho-educational re-evaluation of their child's "overall functioning and current educational needs." From what Ms. Rivera explained to me, this boiled down to two separate employees administering weird tests with me on an individual basis, my teachers providing a summary of my current school performance, and a social worker conducting "a brief social" history update with Mama. I should have known I was doomed before the process had even commenced. While I was successfully fanning the embers beneath my own personal short-lived achievement motivation, and therefore felt relatively secure about my ability to perform well during the administration of the two weird tests, I immediately recognized the bad breath of defeat when news of the importance of my teachers' commentaries was placed before my face. I had a bad reputation in my school. I had an even worse track record, and with the exception of Ms. Rivera, no supportive allegiances or allies who could even momentarily divert the majority of the educators' attention away from my predicted rueful future. A future, that in the prejudiced minds of the greater number of professional civil servants, was already carved in stone. The fact that Mama had to endure a "brief" social history update interview in her condition with one of these civil servants, who would more than likely perceive her as an anomaly to humanity, was merely the icing on the cake. Forget about focusing on the final objective of being decertified from special education. I had to worry about the consequences of Mama being hassled and lassoed into a conversation with one of the "Bored of Miseducation's" unqualified social workers. When I expressed this fear to Ms. Rivera, she told me that I needn't worry, at least about Mama being interviewed by an unqualified social worker. Ms. Rivera explained that it would most probably not be a social worker who conducted the social update with Mama at all. She told me that the NYC school system used "educational evaluators" instead of licensed social workers to conduct social history updates in an ingenious effort to save money. Educational evaluators were teachers who had voluntarily received additional training in individualized academic test administration in exchange for the blessing of being removed from the classroom. Glorified teachers who knew as much about social work as Mama did about not using drugs. It was a person with credentials of such a nature that would most likely be scheduled to probe and extract sensitive and vital personal information from Mama—an inveterate heroin addict. Information that would then contribute to possible future decisions and courses in the life of the inveterate heroin addict's daughter. Me.

 Upon learning about this requisite part of the decertification re-evaluation process, many fantasies surfaced about the possible contents of the looming social history update. Mama informing some burnt-out teacher about the latest word on the best shit out there on the streets. Mama appraising some Long Island resident about the perils involved in shelter living. Mama verbally menacing some naive Republicans who, in their subtle condescending mannerisms, were not so subtle. For reasons of which I continue to be unsure, my darkest and most unhinging fantasy was locked into my fear that Mama would somehow disclose what was supposed to be kept confidential. I feared that some prying quasi-professional would elicit information from Mama concerning her HIV status. I was afraid that the educational professionals would then follow suit with their typical behavior of not keeping confidential information truly confidential. While I was aware that BCW could not remove me from Mama during the last of her days as long as she was ambulatory and semi-coherent, I cradled these fears nonetheless. I presume that an undeveloped personal shame lay beneath the cradle's blankets. A shame that was as vaporous and real as a shadow's shadow.

Consistent with the usual results of excessive worrying, no harm resulted from the brief social history update that was conducted with Mama. Since it was less work for the educational evaluator to conduct the interview via the telephone, it was quickly determined that this would be how matters would be conducted. Since it is very difficult to successfully reach somebody who lives in a shelter by telephone, and next to impossible to find a street addict like Mama at home in a coherent state, I quickly offered the suggestion of having Mama call the educational evaluator "at her convenience" since we "were not in possession of our own phone." All involved readily agreed. Without hesitation, I convinced Ms. Cathy to call the obviously unseasoned worker and impersonate Mama. Ms. Cathy acquiesced as soon as she double checked that Mama "couldn't give a shit one way or the other who spoke to the bitch on the phone." After successfully managing the icing on the cake, I approached the testing business with increased optimism and determination. I should have known that in the end my dreams of decertification would fly away on wings of human ignorance and intolerance, instead of being harvested by benevolence and goodwill.

Given that I've been a pessimist for as long as I can remember, I don't know whether I hoisted myself over the line of reason to accomplish my stated goal or to prove to myself that the goal I had dreamt up within Ms. Rivera's office could, in fact, not be accomplished. One would think that once one mastered the lesson concerning premeditated disappointments during their childhood, they wouldn't have to voluntarily enroll into a refresher course during their adolescence. My actions went against the grain of normal human expectations. It is for this reason that I am more inclined to believe that my short-lived, socially questioned zest for self-improvement was a parody of the worse kind. Ugly in its well-contrived base of self-deception and lack of regard for the depth of disappointment capable of being experienced by the young human heart. Whatever the reason for my plunge may have been, I put my mind, heart, and soul into the one month evaluation process. It was a gambler's gamble. My chips were placed on the table with players who often do not play fairly and tend to lack integrity. My five senses trying to gain true insight into a game whose rules were as colorful and varied as the autumn leaves sprayed on the school's park bench in late October. When I lost the bet I, as would any other hurt child, picked up my marbles and ran. I ran as fast and as far as I could from any accepted edifices of society, from any hint of a fragrance redolent of hope. I ran directly back to the life with which I was most familiar, played future games with players with whom I shared the same rules. I foraged the streets for any experiences that would further entrench me into a lifestyle from which there was no easy return. I ran then because it was easier to run. I was no longer conflicted.

My microcosmic experience with the special education re-evaluation process was a mockery of due process, and as far as I was concerned, equitable with the general nature of the entire school system. Years later, when I was to become quite familiarized with the New York State criminal justice system, I expanded my previous identifications of viable mockeries to include that of the many municipal courts I visited. The politics of prisons, on the other hand, make the reproachable courts look like an enactment of excellence and perfection. Hidden away from the public's eye, what is in the dark is that much more likely to stay there. I grasped on to the belief that mankind, in its feeble attempt to mold a noble legal system into smaller functional institutions with equally noble and functional employees, had unequivocally failed. Additional years later, when I was fighting "assault and robbery" charges for a crime of which I had been falsely accused, my young, fresh-out-of-law-school, yet-to-be-tainted, male Caucasian legal aid attorney apprised me that my contemporary theory was all wrong. In fact, he laughed at me. According to my lawyer, our judicial system, and its facsimile branches thereof, upon which our country was founded, suffered from a deficit in the nobility department from the very onset. The law, he stated, was in truth a mockery unto itself. Perhaps it was for this reason that the members of my school's special education support team failed to decertify me. Perhaps there were deeper and more insidious reasons at large that I was too distracted by the mockery of it all to see. Perhaps it was just one of those things.

The process that followed my mother's supposed request for decertification began with a clinically untrained imposter social worker conducting a social history update with Ms. Cathy by telephone. Ms. Cathy graciously assumed the role of Mama for the three minutes that the telephone interview lasted. During this brief phone conversation between the two imposters, the employed wolf in sheep's clothing came to believe that Mama continued to be gainfully employed as a bank teller, was temporarily housed in a shelter apartment due to an unforeseen tragic fire that destroyed our family's home, supported my educational advancement, primarily through the provision of consistent tutorial services and culturally enriching family outings, and occasionally suffered from migraines for which she was seeking treatment in the form of alternative medicine. On the day of my conference when the stand-in educational evaluator read the results of the social history update aloud, I could have cast bets on whose jaw dropped open first. Mama's or mine. While I was left wondering whether Ms. Cathy was referring to my past and painful periodic visits to the Clinton Arms shooting galleries as the sources of cultural enrichment in my life, I was certain that Mama was merely trying to decipher the meaning of all of the three or more syllable words contained in the educational evaluator's brief verbal presentation. As for all the professionals in the room, I'm sure they didn't believe a word of it. The confession that we were currently residents of a shelter was probably the one exception. I'm also sure that no matter what the contents of my social history, it wouldn't have mattered in the final analysis. Nobody really cared. While Ms. Rivera was probably the one exception in this regard, her passivity and political insignificance cancelled out any potential of her making a stirring impact on my life. The world goes round and round.

My individualized testing ran its course with minimal difficulty up until the very end. For whatever reason, somebody in the ranks of administration made an error and scheduled me for a bilingual evaluation. Something about my last name sounding Latin. So, in the beginning, when a pudgy, rather dark-skinned man with thick glasses that made his eyes look like two-dimensional, soft brown coins initially summoned me to a dank and windowless room and jauntily spewed forth in Spanish as if both he and I had just stepped off of a banana boat, I figured that this was either a test designed to measure patience or I was doomed to a future education with the mentally retarded. Fortunately for me, the Latin man with the fish tank eyewear must have read somewhere that it is advisable to question your client's language dominance after having been stared at dumbly for more than five minutes. Once it was determined that I was not retarded and devoid of any verbal communication skills, but instead monolingual English-speaking and a mere victim of an inadvertent error made by some civil servant when they were scheduling the evaluation, the remaining portions of what I later learned was a psychological assessment proceeded rather swimmingly without further ado. Shortly after the two-hour long testing was completed, which was about two periods after my lunch hour, I was advised that I would be receiving the second and final component of the overall assessment process within a matter of moments. During the two-minute intercession between tests, I somehow managed to pee in the girl's bathroom, throw some cold water on my face, and convince Bruny to stop lingering outside the door in anticipation of anything that resembled a timely departure. Disgruntled and unappreciative of my situation, Bruny exited the school without me. Subconsciously disgruntled and unappreciative of my situation myself, I returned to the dank and windowless room and was begrudgingly welcomed by the second judge of my educational worth. This meticulously groomed middle-aged Caucasian woman with sinewy arms, dyed auburn hair that was pulled back into a bun the size of a pearl onion, and a smile that gave new meaning to the word "shallow," used English from the very onset. I momentarily relaxed into a passing feeling of gratitude for the obvious communication that must have taken place between the examiners concerning my language dominance while I was in the bathroom. When the shadow of a false smile crept back on to its rightful post on my examiner's face, my brief encounter with relaxation and gratitude was quickly replaced by wariness and the bitter taste of trepidation on my tongue. The assessment of my levels of academic functioning was conducted formally to the point of sterility. That is, until we were at least three quarters of the way through. At this point, Miss Posterboard for-the-elite-of-the-Artic received a phone call that erased any curiosities that I might have had about her social life, particularly with regard to her athletic-type arms. Plans were discussed, fine-tuned, and then finalized about a tennis date set for later in the evening. Then the appropriate shade of shoes for an upcoming wedding, the ins and outs of dining in Manhattan while diligently adhering to a Weight Watcher's Diet plan, and the never ending trials and tribulations involved in finding a reliable housekeeper were all discussed while I quietly sat stewing in the juices of my own simmering patience. However, it wasn't until the dismissal bell rang and the woman who was made of glass hung up the phone, sighed, and irritably mumbled something about my needing to hurry up so she could maintain her four o'clock manicure appointment, that I reflexively recoiled and rolled my eyes. While her blindness was evidently selective in that she had previously failed to notice my occasional discomfort and shifting motion in my seat while she was on her personal phone call, the rolling of my eyes did not go by unnoticed. The taut air that lay between us spelled out that a worse sin had never been committed. In fact, with the exception of my "overly rigid stance and limited ability to establish rapport," it was the only interpersonal nuance cited in her report. Another noteworthy feature of this session centered on her impromptu decision to ask me only two additional questions following the rolling of my eyes and the coincidental accompaniment of the signaling of the school day's end. As I silently left the dismal room with thoughts settling like dark clouds in my head, when she no longer thought that I was looking, I saw my examiner quickly giving me scores of zero for successive questions that were left unasked, and therefore, unanswered. The darkness of my loitering mental clouds prevented me from making any commentaries about her blatantly unethical behavior at the time. It similarly subverted my ability to make any unveiling remarks on the day of my conference when neither examiner was physically present anyway.

 Approximately one month after I handed in the request that contained Mama's crooked signature, a formal meeting was held to make the final determination concerning my educational fate. Those present included my guidance counselor, the extremely nervous, and obviously somewhat disturbed, tittering orthodox Jewish psychologist who was assigned to my school that year, a Southern European and ancient-looking woman who I had never laid eyes on before and received a salary for functioning in the role of my school's educational evaluator, my first-period gym teacher whose class I had never attended, Miss Rivera, who invited herself since she was not my legal counselor, and myself who, upon entering the buzzing special education office, wondered whether I had mistakenly stepped into the shoes of Alice when she was in Wonderland destined to arrive at the Mad Hatter's Tea Party. I quickly shook this possibility from my leaping mind when I realized that there was no tea being served. Mama was the final party to arrive at our little conference. She arrived approximately five minutes before it was over. During her brief stay, Mama managed to force herself to remain in at least a "semi-conscious" state just long enough to drop her jaw when she heard the information that Ms. Cathy had shared during her telephone impersonation act, offend four out of the six of us that were in the room by going into a deep nod shortly after being seated, and sign the conference attendance sheet after being prodded to do so by me and Ms. Rivera. Looking back now, I have to admit that Mama's disheveled appearance replete with her raggedy coat, matted hair, and residual rancidity from infected oozing epidermal pores, along with the salivation and eyes rolled back into her head full effect of her nod, must have been some sight. It surely caused the unfamiliar old educational evaluator to push back her chair and open her eyes as big as saucers quicker than she had probably moved in the past twenty years. About three minutes after Mama's entrance, the gym teacher simply put a tissue over his mouth and left.

I couldn't even be angry with Mama for her seeming complicity in this comedy of errors. I don't believe I took out any of my frustrations afterward in her direction, not even one. The truth was that Mama had never even been formally invited to the meeting. As she was not accessible by phone, "the team" was required to invite her by written correspondence. The team did. I received and opened her letter of invitation two days after the conference had occurred. Its postmark was one and the same with the stamped announcement of the conference that was written inside. Nobody had any intentions of being blessed by Mama's presence. The written invitation was merely an extension of a bureaucratic formality. Whether "the team" had learned about the true nature of Mama's essence, or they typically conducted business in this fashion, I cannot say for sure. Of what I am decidedly certain is that no team member was quite prepared for the likes of what they saw and felt when Mama surprisingly arrived. I am also sure that they must have engaged in discussions for days about how to prevent such faux pas from happening again. Mama had inspired a new kind of preventative service.

As a result of my final experience with the "Bored of Miseducation," I've had the impassionate words from Elizabeth Browning's poem "How Do I Love Thee" drifting through my memory's marrow ever since. Thoughts that breathe and words that burn. Whether on the hustler's prowl, cast alone in prison, or in my dreams, I have periodically felt the familiar hush of Browning's expressions of love, cautious to not arouse any accompanying emotions as if a timid child on tiptoe. About one week before my conference, Miss Rivera was informally told that I had performed poorly on the section of the educational evaluation that purports to measure literacy and verbal memory skills. Although I wondered if this was due to the fact that these skills were measured by the section of the test that was virtually omitted as a result of my examiner's whimsical behavior, I agreed that I would choose a short verse from one of our class' contemporary books to discuss with the team members in an effort to demonstrate my genuine motivation and effort. Instead, I got carried away and memorized E. Browning's "How Do I Love Thee" in its entirety. When Miss Rivera ran into me in the hallway and inquired as to whether I made any attempt to commit a popular literary title and author to memory, the kernel of my deep-rooted sense of shame stirred, and I scoffed her off by saying that I had memorized two new rap songs instead. She ignored my unprecedented jeering tongue and laughed along with me. Since the mockery of the overall situation was seemingly aimed at Miss Rivera almost as much as it was toward me, she could not laugh at me, only with me.

On the day of my conference, Dorothy's scarecrow could have predicted the eventual verdict without going through all of that trouble to acquire a brain. He could have simply held up a mirror to the eyes of the conference members for an accurate reflection of a future that was about to unfold. The eyes of the team members were dull, distant, and without concern, drooping moons of varying colorless shades. When I entered the room, everybody stared at me as if I had grown another head next to the original. When I looked down at my watch to double check that I was on time and realized that four sets of eyes were still boring through me, I decided that my two-head theory might hold more than a kernel of truth. Miss Rivera finally cut through the silence with a genuine salutation of welcome. The religious psychologist attempted to repair the sear by reminding Miss Rivera of the lack of need for her presence since all of the paperwork pronounced that the black man who was reading the paper to her right was my official counselor. Miss Rivera looked at her askance, although the fact that her words had obviously sprinkled the salt of fear on her tongue did not elude me. Although I knew nothing about politics except for the politics of the streets, I sensed that my decertification from special education was not the only item on the day's agenda. It was merely the only one that was written down.

After all of the members of the Mad Hatter's Party introduced themselves, the educational evaluator, who also conveniently wore the hat of social worker, questioned Mama's absence. As pleasantly and straight-faced as I could, I explained that the bank could not release her from her duties, not even for just a few hours. My counselor looked up from his paper just long enough to murmur something about slave labor and returned to an article that was obviously captivating the preponderance of his interest. Had I known at the time, I would have not held back from communicating that Mama could not very well be present when her invitation letter was still sitting idly in someone's drawer or the school mailroom. Ironically enough, both Mama and her letter shared similar states of being. They were either in transit or in the dark. Some papers were rustled and the lady beneath the chadal and the impervious invisible parasol of religious doctrines began to spew off my psychological test results. I understood her jargon just the same as if she was talking Yiddish. I heard something about my verbal abilities being better developed than my nonverbal abilities, and then wondered what nonverbal abilities were. I also heard that while I had many weaknesses, I was superior in some areas. She smiled without looking in my direction when she said that. My counselor was looking at the paper, my gym teacher was looking at his watch, and the educational evaluator was looking out the window. So everybody missed her wasted smile. At the end of her diatribe of psychological gibberish, I heard something about my hidden ability to do better. Aside from understanding that my brain often plays hide-and-go seek, I had as many blind spots in my understanding of my cognitive potential as Mama had holes in her arm. With the exception of Miss Rivera, when I looked around the room I realized that I still had a greater understanding of it than those who currently shared the same air with me in the room. I cared.

Following the psychologist's presentation, the educational evaluator read some numbers off of her report, adding a word or two about my limited ability to establish rapport with the consulting examiner, and then looked back out the window. It took my counselor about three minutes to realize that about three sets of eyes were staring at his balding temple before he lifted his eyes off of his newspaper to say that he doesn't really know me very well since I resist attending counseling sessions with him. Something about a possible underlying difficulty with male authority figures, as he returned his eyes to the paper that was spread open beneath him, he added an additional comment about my seeming tendency to take advantage of Miss Rivera's naïveté, time and kindness. My gym teacher then rounded the conference up by stating that I am one of the many ghosts in his class. He then stepped on very precariously laid stones and supported my counselor's aversion-to-men theory, thinking aloud about how often this occurs to young girls who come from broken and troubled homes or have histories of sexual abuse. Thanks for sharing. If I had a gun, I would have shot him, right in the gut where it felt like he had injured me. Instead, I shot him the dirtiest look I could conjure up in my state of humiliation and disbelief. I was consoled somewhat by the fact that Miss Rivera did the same. As I was collecting all of my runaway thoughts and quelling my impulses, Miss Rivera pertly provided a summary of my recent significant improvement in class attendance and academic performance, empathizing that I had earned two grades in the eighties in major classes. She attempted to make eye contact with each and every team member as she stressed the positive effect that such a decertification would have on my self-esteem. She was successful with all but one of us. My counselor's eyes remained fixed on his newspaper. Once Miss Rivera's obviously prepared speech wound down to the tossing out of a few remaining dangling unformulated thoughts, the educational evaluator interrupted her by making a comment about their need to complete all evaluations in a timely manner. With my counselor deep into his article, the gym teacher focused on the time, and the orthodox psychologist looking up into space as if she was praying in silence, the educational evaluator looked squarely into Miss Rivera's face and told her that after having reviewed all of the necessary documentation, the team believed that I would continue to benefit from the provision of special education services. As if one of Alice's familiars gave me back my stolen tongue, I blurted out, "But why?" She danced around my question, cavorting across my fate, stating that I had just started to improve my attendance, not forgetting that I continued to cut some classes with regularity. When I made a statement to the effect that I thought special education was for students with disabilities and not mere truants, her face stood at attention before generating an upside-down smile. At this point, the psychologist took an express rocket ship back to earth from out of space and reminded me of my history of school-related behavior problems. When I truthfully stated that with the exception of cutting classes and nonattendance, I did not knowingly have one incident that tarnished my conduct record since elementary school, the gym teacher reminded the educational evaluator of the approaching lunch hour and the psychologist silently blasted back off into outer space. It was in the middle of the educational evaluator's final feeble rationale for prolonging my stay "on the far side" that Mama banged on the door, as if in active pursuit of a thief who had stolen her stash of dope. Before anybody could respond to the loud thumping noise, she opened the door on her own and shuffled into the room. I later learned that Mama's presence at this meeting was the direct result of Ms. Cathy mentioning the importance of it to Mama the last time they spent time together. To the best of her ability, Mama always tried to show up for that which she truly deemed as important. Unfortunately, she was not in possession of a functional sane mind in order to make these distinctions or to see her good intentions through.

Mama's uninvited presence was the only thing that lifted my counselor's attention from his paper and kept it roused. My gym teacher simply left. Distracted and perturbed about the unwanted interruption, the educational evaluator greeted Mama in the most artificial and begrudging of fashions, reviewed the results of the social history update as if repeating a task that she had already performed, and went on to explain that the overall test results revealed "just a few weaknesses" in academic spheres that could best be addressed in special education classes. Feeling protectively jittery and wary, as well as pinched emotionally, by Mama's nodding figure before me, I lost the necessary energy to further argue the point that I was not originally placed into special education because of any intellectual deficits in much the same way that I wasn't enrolled into any classes for the learning disabled at the time. Words leaked out in the form of stammers and stutters in my state of emotional disorientation. It was then that Mama must have located my energy and sucked it up into her own pores. Her head lifted out of her nod and her eyes adjusted back into their rightful place, staring at the motley crew that was seated before her on this planet called Earth. Mama then stared at me with a look of keen intent with the depth of which only a mother is capable, as if her essence was commanding my pain to vault forward through my skin, even if she needed to quaff it up when it reached her side of the room. She then turned and rested her eyes on Miss Rivera for a minute, and relaxed her body posture for just a moment when she felt her kinder spirit. Mama's eyes darted across the next three inhabitants of the room with cursory indifference.

"Why don't you people let my daughter speak her mind with your ears open? She got something to say, ya' know."

"Missus, uh Miss, uh Missus . . ." the educational evaluator said with a not previously heard choppy speaking style.

"Rosa, my name is Rosa."

"Ms. Rosa then. Victoria already had an opportunity to speak. You are aware that you are fifteen minutes late?"

"You are aware that you better back the fuck up or . . ."

"Mama," I cried, "it's all right. I already spoke."

The psychologist looked as if she was now silently praying for her life.

Miss Rivera jumped in and summarized the previously held meeting in simple terms. Mama calmly asked her a few questions about my scores and possible future choices. Miss Rivera responded pleasantly as if she was the only professional in the room who realized that she was talking to another human being. My mama. The educational evaluator looked over at Miss Rivera as if to say thank you a thousand times, an unspoken gesture that communicated that she owed her one. When all was still and five sets of eyes fell upon me, making it quite clear that the ball was in my court, I read off Mama's countenance that while she did not completely understand the ramifications of all the verbalized fine print, she nonetheless understood the groups' dynamics and was ready to wage a war on my behalf. Miss Rivera's visage disclosed that she would be at Mama's beck and call as her first commanding officer as soon as I fired the pistol. Our three adversaries were shaking in their intellectual boots. I weighed my options deeply before arriving at the conclusion that while we would definitely kick some ass up in here and win this battle, we'd eventually lose the war. Not even Mama could fight a system that traversed across the moral foundations of nobility and justice on stilts. Besides, Mama's days were numbered and I didn't want to add any more shameful experiences to her life's list. I curtly stated that I felt my appeal had been addressed fairly and assured everybody that I would follow through with all of the previously offered helpful recommendations concerning study habits and attendance practices. Mama rose and walked proudly to the door as if to make a quick exit. Just as the most aged of the three was beginning to breathe a sigh of relief, she turned and knowingly stared at me, stared through me, as if she was telling me that she understood all of the thinking that had gone into my final decision and was pleased by the person who had developed from her egg. She made one more comment before she left us for good.

"I see you've got the strength Victoria. Ask God for the power and the victory will be yours."

The psychologist's face dropped one notch beneath awe, two from wonder.

As I watched Mama's receding figure go through the door's glass panel, her shoulders increasingly relaxed into their usual slouch. So much so that she was eventually shuffling down the school's corridor—moving with her familiar gait through the one municipal building that she feared and dreaded entering for most of her life due to God knows what trauma she experienced during her own youth.

On the day of the conference, I appreciated that she had entered it for me. Yet, I also understood that her brief display of pride was the direct result of her love for me, separate from any positive sentiments possibly felt for herself over her accomplishment. After the door was shut and Mama was at a safe enough distance, I turned to what was left of the team and glared so hard that I almost expected to see the visible results of skin scorched by fire.

I shook my head slowly from side to side and said, "You know what, fuck ya'll." I reached down to pick up my school bag and Miss Rivera grabbed my hand. I looked at, through, and past her after I gave her a look of acknowledgement.

"Do you understand what you're doing and about ready to do?," she asked.

"Uh, huh, I understand all of it." I lied. I only understood some of it.

As I gently moved past Miss Rivera, I said, "Oh yeah, I almost forgot. I did something for all of you."

"What's that?" the educational evaluator croaked with a nugget of fear obviously still lodged in her throat.

I snapped my head from Miss Rivera to her direction and with as defiant a stare as I could muster began to quote E. Browning's poem in its entirety. My voice boomed as loud as a voice can possibly go without being legally screaming.

"How do I love thee?" With a head as high and tall as Mama's, I exited through the door jamb. "Let me count the ways." I turned the corridor's bend on my third "I love thee for," but the remainder of the poem could still be heard by all, resounding in the distance. At some point in the very beginning of my distinct performance, I thought I heard Miss Rivera say to nobody in particular something about the fact that "too many mistakes were made here today. One too many that hopefully can be undone." Who knows? It could have been portentous thoughts from the recesses of my own imagination.

I never returned to school after my conference when it was written that my individualized educational plan would remain the same. Instead, I informally dropped out. No truant officer ever came searching me out to question Mama or me about my long-term absence. Nor did Mama query me about my obvious decision to drop out and sleep through most of the day. I believe she tacitly understood the reasons and feelings behind my behavior. She had probably lived it once herself in another lifetime. Different characters, same story. I sent Bruny to Miss Rivera with a note about one month after my conference. The note read, "Thanks for all of your help. I'll always remember you."

I did. That time I wasn't lying.

Mama died approximately one year later in March, just a few months before my seventeenth birthday, about thirty-four years after she was born. As I said, Mama never took any of the vitamins or medications that purported to have increasing success with slowing down the deterioration of the immune systems of HIV positive individuals. It wasn't even that Mama concurred with any of those eighties folk who assessed that the medications' negative side effects outweighed their benefits. The truth was that Mama just didn't have the time for anything of that nature. She was too busy killing herself slowly.

Mama was hospitalized twice before she died. The first time at Harlem Hospital, and the latter, at Lincoln Hospital in the Bronx. The primary medical diagnosis behind both of her hospitalizations was AIDS-related pneumonia. In August, she remained at Harlem Hospital because one of her regular get high partners dragged her there. I believe that the only reason why she didn't resist was because she was so sick that she wasn't able to carry out the majority of her get-high rituals anyway. At Harlem Hospital, she was assured to receive sufficient amounts of methadone and rest to make the thought of hospitalization a more appealing option. During Mama's initial hospitalization, I stayed with Ms. Cathy and visited Mama every couple of days. It was the only reasonable thing to do.

Once Mama was hospitalized, the irrefutable fact that Mama was going to die became increasingly lucid, as if time had finally made the correct adjustments on my binoculars' lens to facilitate my being able to see into the future without any of the prior confounding blurs or distorted fragments of denial. After gingerly allowing myself to be sentient while processing this improved vision, I found myself concentrating more and more on the narrow file in my mind that highlighted all of the redeeming qualities of the smudged lenses, wherein one's limited ability to experience the pain of what one is incapable of seeing was the one that stood out most in bold print. I responded by intentionally further sullying my perceptions, by staying high on marijuana, cocaine, and alcohol as often as I could. The fact that I was simultaneously moving up in the ranks of notorious boosters also took the edge off any unbearable percept or accompanying feeling that might have escaped through any part of my lens that had remained unfogged. When one is successfully boosting hundreds of dollars worth of clothing on a daily basis, patterns of risk-taking, egocentricity and emotional constriction preside.

My life seemed to take off on a course all of its own directly after I dropped out of school and Mama's imminent death became as acutely apparent as her gaping pores. Along with all of the changes and furthering of bad habits, went my gradual withdrawal from Bruny again. Bruny dropped out of school shortly after I did. Her reputation for being a slut only escalated at this point from a level that was already pretty close to the roof. At the time I became involved with a drug dealer who was called Smooth. Smooth occupied most of my free time with activities that were either of a sexual or drug-related nature. The other thing that threw a small-sized monkey wrench into my friendship with Bruny was the fact that he, as well as most of his boys, had his dick sucked by her in the past, and when high, spewed forth comments about the "lollipop hoe" without apparent regard for my presence. I admittedly lacked the backbone to find a happy medium between those two opposing forces in my life, and as such, went with the boyfriend.

Mama's lifestyle perpetuated directly after her release from Harlem Hospital. In fact, she lied about her release date so that neither Ms. Cathy nor I could meet her there, and thereby hinder her burning desire to run to the cop spot as fast as her weak legs could carry her. By the time Mama surprised both of us by announcing her premature release date and the fact that I could return to the shelter apartment with her, her pupils were already dilated, and her ability to feel, numbed. Shortly afterwards, Mama went on a very long run. She continued wearing her hospital identification band as a bracelet throughout her frenzied trot on the streets.

Mama was hospitalized again for the same debilitating medical diagnosis about six months later. The only difference was that Mama now experienced multiple physical infections, a marked low body weight, and the constant presence of painful sores and blisters. This time Mama wasn't released from the hospital until about four weeks had passed. Ms. Cathy and I were both wise enough to inquire about Mama's discharge date from the hospital's nursing staff. Despite her infirmed condition, Mama's sense of personal volition never altered. Mama managed to leave the hospital in the absence of our company again by sneaking out in the middle of the night before her discharge date, against sound medical advice. The only surprising factor was that when Mama arrived at the crack of dawn on the following morning, her eyes were shining with a brightness of which I had never known heroin to produce. They looked like bright lights inside of green bottles. She was also smiling. Smiling a relaxed, contented smile that did not hide any of the gaping spaces in her mouth from her missing teeth. She was adequately groomed, continued to be in possession of her personal tote bag, and in the most unfamiliar of ways, was exuding a glow that was contained and wholesome in quality. I wondered whether I had missed out on hearing about a new drug that had hit the streets. I was also curious about whether Mama had taken it in dangerously large qualities.

Mama died exactly six weeks after her second hospitalization. She had grown incredibly weak, was virtually incontinent, and could not stop coughing from the seeming ever presence of phlegm inside of her lungs. Her ability to breathe deteriorated to the extent that it appeared as if her body's only purpose in burning calories was to help her not die sooner from asphyxiation. Rotting skin sloughed off of her body away from her infected pores so quickly that no amount of bandages could effectively hold her together any longer. This time it was obvious even to her that she was in dire need of some form of life support. Heroin no longer served as a panacea. It was time to go, from the familiar comfort of her mattress, from our shelter, from this world.

Mama remained inside of our room without leaving to cop heroin or having any of her get high partners visit to bring her any as a token of their discomfort over having to bid farewell to such a loyal, old friend. Perhaps they stayed away because they didn't foresee the imminence of her death. Perhaps they didn't like looking into mirrors. Eerily enough, Mama, who had never acknowledged or practiced religion in her life, remained in our room praying with a newfound ability to absorb serenity from the air. Her only requests of me were for an occasional glass of water and to make sure that her Bible, which had mysteriously appeared in our room about six weeks ago, was placed close to her bedside. I figured that she must have stolen the Bible from Lincoln Hospital during her prolonged stay. On the third day after this pronounced strange behavior, after having hacked away in obvious discomfort all night long, Mama rose, asked for my help with getting dressed, and told me to go downstairs and call for an ambulance to take her back to Lincoln Hospital. She was too worn and weak to consider taking a cab. Once in the presence of the paramedics and about to make her final exit from our room, Mama beckoned me to come over to her side. Smiling, in the absence of any fear or doubt, Mama told me to prepare to go over to Ms. Cathy's for a while. She also told me that she wanted both of us to visit her in the morning. Mama must have been too tired and worn to wait. Her lungs took their last breath in the middle of the night. Mama died.

Ms. Cathy used some of her own personal savings to finance the burial for her only friend. Since we figured that aside from the two of us, nobody would bother attending a wake, which probably would have tipped the scale of Ms. Cathy's budget anyway, Mama's funeral rites were restricted to a quick and simple internment with a clerical assistant who was expected to say a few words. I used some profits that I had recently earned from boosting and brought flowers. Ms. Cathy bought a small half moon-shaped tombstone the color of a pale rose in memory of her name. I chose the words "May the Victory be Yours in Heaven" to be inscribed in script on her tombstone, directly below her name and the announcement of the almost thirty-five years that her slowly dying spirit dwelled on this earth.

Mama's funeral was held on a cold and bleak Wednesday morning in March. Our coats whipped around our bodies with the harsh quickness of leather belts. The biting wind stung our eyes, making it difficult to decipher whether the moistness in our eyes was a reflection of our sorrow or a physical reflex to the biting cold. In accordance with her lifelong restless, and anything but predictable character, Mama's funeral generated two surprises, both equally unexpected, but soothing to my heavy heart. The first occurred shortly after the half frozen clergyman cleared his throat to begin an abbreviated sermon in Mama's behalf. From the far side of the cemetery grounds emerged a group of about fifteen people, all unfamiliar, appropriately dressed, clear-eyed, and able to consistently stand at an angle that was perpendicular to the ground. It was obvious that none of these serene and decent-looking people of color were any of Mama's get-high partners or associates from any of her many street activities. Yet, they gathered in a respectful small half-circle behind Ms. Cathy and I, heads bent, hands clasped together in prayer, obviously intent on hearing the dirge that had been prepared for Mama. The only conclusions that seemed reasonable to me at the time were that they were either "mourners for hire" or I was bearing witness to a flock of very lost sheep.

The second surprise came directly after the service, before any of us had the opportunity to draw a complete breath. Lifting up from behind us, the sweet voice of a songbird circled our ears and reached into our souls with its richness and purity. The rustling leaves provided a soft natural background rhythm to the melody's silvery sound. Ms. Cathy's head snapped around, apparently stricken with the simultaneous sentiments of awe and curiosity. Unlike Ms. Cathy, I did not have to turn my head to identify the person behind the sonorous voice. I knew it was Bruny. I also knew that once I turned, she'd be gone. Another of love's fleeting presences.

I kept my focus on the plain coffin in front of me. The coffin that was soon going to be lowered into the ground. The ordinary structure of wood that embraced Mama. After being the not-so-gracious recipient of a multitude of affectionate looks and words from the pack of strangers, I sighed, turning as one with Ms. Cathy, and walked away from the only human being with whom I was truly familiar and comfortable. My only known relative. Mama, who I loved, and for whom my story has in part been written. She was no longer with me in this world.

CHAPTER THIRTEEN

God, Grant Me the Serenity to Accept the Things I Cannot Change,
Courage to Change the Things I Can,
And the Wisdom to Know the Difference.
—Reinhold Niebur

IT WAS ALL downhill after Mama died, or uphill, depending on how or why one looked at it. Life's perspectives always seem to be dependent upon something else. Or at least this is how it seems to me.

After Mama died, I moved in with Ms. Cathy. While our apartment share wasn't exactly a marriage made in heaven, the two of us did all right. I considered our genial coexistence to be a mark of good fortune, considering the fact that once the common denominator of our love for Mama was removed from the equation, Ms. Cathy and I were as about as different as chalk from cheese.

By the time I moved in with Ms. Cathy, I was pretty immersed in the street life. I wouldn't say that I was a thug as of yet, although such an identification was undeniably imminent. I had abandoned any whimsical thoughts about the possibility of returning to school. I was an adroit booster of anything that wasn't nailed down to the floor or larger than a twenty-seven-inch television. I indulged in the "recreational" use of marijuana, alcohol, and cocaine, regularly and interchangeably. Smooth and I were still going strong. Since he was moving up in the ranks of notorious drug dealers, at least three levels above that of the common street pharmacist on the corner, I was vicariously gaining the respect and status that was my due. On the streets, it was the equivalent of being "the doctor's wife." While I couldn't accurately be described as a thug when Mama died, this no longer held true shortly thereafter.

Ms. Cathy had no real control over me once the courts placed me into her care. It's not like Mama did either, but I resisted indulging in particular impulses, and certain behavioral extremes, when I was with her to avoid having contact with any governmental "support systems" and additional disruptions in our lives. Perhaps I always suspected that Mama's and my time together was limited and I didn't want to squander it. And while the rules and messages were often unclear, I certainly didn't want to disappoint her. Life with Ms. Cathy was different. I liked her and all, but had no great need to avoid upsetting any delicate apple carts. Ever since the disappearance of the Stinkdog, Ms. Cathy transformed into a meditative and self-possessed type of individual. I knew that there was nothing that I could possibly ever do to take that away from her. It was obvious that Ms. Cathy was never going to allow anyone to steal her joy up from under her ever again.

Ms. Cathy provided me with clothes, food, and an impeccably clean apartment. While willing to provide me with conversation, guidance, and nurturance, she was reserved and passive in her approach. I tacitly understood that Ms. Cathy would always be there if I needed her. I similarly knew that I wasn't emotionally ready to receive that which she was most inclined to offer: honesty and unconditional love. I still had many a lesson that I needed to learn.

In September of my seventeenth year, I was arrested on charges of "armed robbery" when I went down to the Cyprus Projects in Brooklyn to avenge a robbery. A robbery in which I had initially been the victim. My objective was to stick up a girl with a blade whose boyfriend had recently held Smooth up for his money, gold, and drugs when he was checking on one of his spots in the East New York section of Brooklyn. Me and my sorry-assed luck, of course, had to be with him. As most big and growing bigger drug dealers will do, Smooth had acquired several enemies along his slow rise to quasi fame. His foes blossomed out of the envious and greedy facets of human nature, particularly flowering in abundance in those parts of the city in which such concepts as "The best defense is a good offense" and "Life sucks and then we die" reigned. Many drug dealers, I've come to learn, often possess quite a dearth in the benevolence department. While their egos operate the steering wheels of their lives on almost a full-time basis, they are simultaneously prodded by the character defects of envy and greed. These are the character traits that occupy the passenger seats. It is a rarity to have easy access to their positive qualities. Instead, most drug dealers I've come to know, have discarded their more humane qualities in the trunk, or out of the tinted windows of their seemingly recklessly racing vehicles. Such was the case with Smooth, his increasing number of enemies, and the small-time drug dealer who eventually caught up with him and robbed him when I was in his company.

I met Smooth in a club downtown. When our eyes met, it was definitely a serious case of hormones crying out to hormones. Our chemical attraction endured for months. And as backwards as it might have been considered by any preaching moralist, a true liking of one for the other actually evolved somewhere in between our hormones' cries and moans. Smooth was originally from the Pink House Projects in Brooklyn. He lived there for as long as it took BCW to realize that his alcoholic mother was as physically abusive toward him and his younger sister as any hired Chinese torture specialist. This determination on BCW's part occurred somewhere before his ninth birthday, around the same time that his teacher could no longer deny that the fresh sears on his dominant hand were not an accident and Smooth had already developed a hatred for himself and toward the world in which he had been born into. After it was determined that his mother was a raging alcoholic whose maternal behavior revolved around the use of excessive corporal punishment, Smooth and his sister were sent to live with an aunt in Queens. When this same aunt was incarcerated for helping her boyfriend deal marijuana and crack out of her apartment, Smooth and his sister were shuttled back to Brooklyn to live with their paternal grandmother in the Marcy Projects. Then he stayed with some cousin in Queens, and then with another man in the Bronx. I believe after this, he was sent back to Brooklyn. By the time I got around to meeting Smooth, he had internalized the migratory patterns of living that had been imposed on him so many years before. Within a month of knowing him, I gave up on writing down my man's phone number. The "S" section of my phone book had more black marks than a leopard, and more erasures than a first grader's notebook. As it was, I left it up to Smooth to contact me. He always did, from a variety of different homesteads and numbers. By the way, if you're surmising that it was Smooth who filled me in on all of the juicy details concerning his painful past, you are as astray as a ship in the desert. It was his sister who possessed the barefaced tongue. Smooth, on the other hand, just remembered "having to move around a lot."

Smooth participated in the operation of several different busy drug spots in Brooklyn. For the most part, he stayed away from heroin. Instead, he profited from facilitating the distribution of marijuana and the new drug crack-cocaine throughout the various Brooklyn ghetto communities. Crack hit the streets in 1984. While some old-timers were still standing over stove ranges with baking soda and bottle caps, most folk who sought that speedy, powerful, and wonderful new high were beginning to hit the crack spots. This meant that Smooth was making lots of money. He was even considered to be a high roller by some. To me, however, he was just Smooth—my man with the money who kept the clothes, gold, and drugs rolling right on in. One day, after driving around my hood for a while, Smooth decided that he ought to go check out one of his spots around Sutter and Blake avenues in East New York. Since the police were combing the streets on this particular night, he decided to park his car about one and a half blocks away from the spot. At least that's what I thought the reason was. Smooth and I were never big conversationalists and he certainly never shared his decision-making processes aloud.

I went with Smooth to check on his spot, indulged in a couple of white lines, and was seriously feeling his body next to mine on the walk back to his car. I was feeling it so much that I wasn't quite sure who exactly pulled who to the side of the car to tongue the other down. Whoever was the responsible party had made a grave mistake. We both opened our eyes to the sound of a gun cocking up besides Smooth's head. I later learned that the body of the hands that were connected to the gun belonged to a drug dealer from the neighborhood that had beef with Smooth over some territory business. Whatever the case might have been, I knew at the time that this wannabe dealer was definitely not a wannabe stickup kid. He was quite real when it came down to the potential of using the gun that was in his hands. More real than the color of yellow on the sun. Despite all of Smooth's typical black male gangster posturing, the commanding nature of the situation registered as quickly in his brain as it did in mine. He didn't resist handing over his money, gold, or drugs to the body that was connected to the hands that held the gun. I, on the other hand, who was feeling the full impact of the adrenaline rush from the cocaine right about then, and who typically demonstrated a scarce amount of sense in situations in which I was being directly challenged, was quite resistant to the notion of handing over my new big gold chain to the ugly motherfucker who was standing over me with a gun. In response, I shirked back further toward the car, giving him one of my coldest Victoria stares ever. In light of my awareness of the absurdity of my response, I should have almost expected to be pistol whipped by the accomplice who popped out from the shadows behind the car to swiftly remove my cold stare from my face. This was one expectation that would never have evolved into a premeditated disappointment. With a knot upside my head the size of a large lemon, gushing blood, and an ache in my temple as mammoth as Mount Everest, I had to listen to Smooth rant and rave about what he was going to do to those two motherfucking punks all the way to Brookdale Hospital. After I was sutured, given an ample dose of painkiller, and it was established that I had not sustained any permanent neurological damage, I started counting my blessings. I felt especially blessed that I had not opened that mouth of mine that I had clearly inherited from Mama and still possessed a mouthful of teeth. I also started devising a plan to get back my gold chain and piece. Smooth had just bought it for me and it had cost a pretty penny. Quite a lot of pretty pennies—about $800 worth of them. I knew I didn't have to worry about avenging the fact that I had been pistol whipped. Smooth would take care of that triple fold. Of that I was as sure as oceans are blue.

Upon putting my "feelers" out on the streets, I quickly learned that the wannabe drug dealer was as stupid as most other wannabe drug dealers. He had given my specially made chain and piece to his wannabe drug dealer's girlfriend. And, of course, she was so stupid that she not only brazenly wore my prized possession on her scrawny neck, she also had the nerve to run her big mouth about the story behind its origin all around her hood. Give or take, it took me about thirty-six hours to learn who the stupid bitch was and where she lived. When I found out, I took the train to Brooklyn and walked the distance to the Cyprus Projects, packing a small .22 in my pocket, and covering the injured side of my head as best as I could with a red-colored bandana. The fact that I had a visible bruise on my face and was openly asking different youth on the street where I could find this chick named Latonya, girlfriend of wannabe drug dealer Tee, did not seem to phase anybody. After all, I was in the PJ's of Brooklyn, USA. After about ten minutes of my diligent search, a young light-skinned girl pointed her out to me. She was standing in front of the corner building on Fountain Avenue. Fortunately, she decided to go upstairs within a matter of minutes, giving me the quick and easy opportunity to get her alone in the elevator. The bitch was petrified. She handed over my piece before I could even get my entire menacing vulgar threat from out of my mouth. I also believe that she pissed on herself. (However, that part might have been my dramatic adolescent fantasy addition to the actual situation.) Everything went just about as smooth as Smooth adhered to his name. I didn't run out of luck until I was about three blocks away from the projects, way on my way to the subway station with my chain in the pocket of its rightful owner. When I heard the police sirens, I ditched the twenty-two through an opening in a sewer. Since no weapon could be recovered and the scrawny scaredy-cat girlfriend of the wannabe drug dealer could not identify any real details about me, the robbery, or about anything much else, the original "armed robbery" charges were lowered. I eventually copped out to "robbery in the second degree" and was sentenced to one year at an upstate minimum security residential facility that housed youth offenders, basically for stealing back my own gold chain. Smooth personally shot the wannabe drug dealer in front of a Kentucky Fried Chicken restaurant and left him for dead. He didn't die, but he never snitched on Smooth either. I guess he wasn't that much of a chicken. One of Smooth's boys stuck up the guy who had pistol whipped me. Rumor had it that he left him with one functional eye. Smooth and I didn't have much of a relationship afterwards. While my being incarcerated for a short spell might have put a damper on the relationship, I believe the real reason we grew apart was that our hormones finally let up some with their moans. In fact, when I absconded from the Mickey Mouse facility the criminal system had placed me into about three months later, I considered myself quite single. That was, of course, until I hooked up with one of the big boys who ran the majority of the cocaine sales way uptown in what I've always referred to as "Dominican Land" (Washington Heights). I forgot all about Smooth and that $800 bullshit chain after I met Johnny and all of the others whose lives revolved around highly destructive mounds of white powdery substances.

In terms of my life's other areas of importance, my relationship with Ms. Cathy dwindled away to that of a fond, but distant acquaintance. Although we both convincingly played the roles of concerned family members during my court proceedings, I believe we had long ago come to the realization that I was going to stray from the nest in just a matter of time. Although we can never truly read the minds of others, I also believe that we both similarly understood that I'd never be back. Ms. Cathy was Mama's anchor, not mine. At this point in my life, I was still searching for my own.

Anyway, we both went through the rituals. Ms. Cathy hired a private attorney for me to fight my case. Don't ask me why she put out the $3,800 when she did not need any crystal balls to foresee the direction in which I'd be flying when I left the nest, but she did. In fact, one day after my blue pinstriped lawyer had maneuvered to place me back on the streets for a meager $250 bail, my curiosity got the better of me and I asked her in as direct a manner as I was emotionally qualified to do at the time,

"Ms. Cathy, I'm thankful and all, but to tell you the truth, I never thought I'd be bailed out or have a private attorney."

"Oh no, why not?"

The rhetorical question of the century.

"I don't know. I just didn't." One more ditched effort. "Ya know?"

"Uhmm. Oh well, you're welcome anyway." So much for last-ditch efforts.

Feeling quite uncomfortable in my skin right about then, feeling the combination of the pressure from my need to get high as well as from the presence of so many unsaid words in the room, I'd figured I'd make a good closing remark. A closing remark that was about as direct and honest as the rest of my conversation.

"I'm going out. Maybe I'll go try to track down Bruny." Despite the fact that Bruny had sucked on every male organ in at least a two-mile radius, she was still among the top three of my friends in Ms. Cathy's book.

"Anyway, thanks again. Maybe the reason I never thought that it would happen was because nobody I knew ever had a private lawyer is all." I felt Ms. Cathy's eyes kindling a burning sensation on my back's surface as I turned in an attempt to slip quickly out the door.

"Victoria, you've been provided with a private lawyer to remind you that you still have another chance."

I turned around. Stared numbly at her first, dumbly next, before looking away and half mumbling, "I'm afraid I don't know what you mean." But I did. We both knew that I did as I moved hastily out the door, away from Ms. Cathy and all of the unsaid words that hung in abeyance, along with the rest of my life.

Despite our perfected (or should I say almost perfected) roles, my low bail, private attorney, and the presence of alternate choices, I was nonetheless sent away for a twelve-month period. Ironically, it was Ms. Cathy who was ultimately responsible for this decision. Or at least, this is how I read the situation at the time.

After my lawyer diligently worked at having my gun charges dropped and was swiftly heading in the direction of an eighteen-month probation sentence along with some court-mandated community service hours, we all approached the bench and a withered, older-than-God judge directly asked Ms. Cathy a question that would be the final deciding factor in my case. From translucent bluish lips, he asked, "As her legal guardian, Ms. O' Connor, do you believe that you can effectively supervise and manage her behavior at home? Can you with confidence ensure the courts that Victoria will abide by her court-mandated curfew, attend school on a regular basis, and refrain from associating with undesirables?"

The length of Ms. Cathy's silent response frightened me. Finally, old blue lips spoke again, "Ms. O' Connor, the courts presented you with a question. Are you able to respond or would you like the question to be repeated?"

Ms. Cathy sighed. My heart sank.

"No, that will not be necessary. I heard the question the first time. I was just trying to figure out how I could answer it and still remain honest with all of the parties involved."

Ms. Cathy looked at me sadly. I knew for sure then that I would not be sleeping in my own bed for too much longer.

"Your Honor, I cannot ensure the courts about any aspect of anybody's future behavior except my own. I've come to learn that over the years. What I can ensure the courts is that I will support Victoria in her attempt to comply with all of the court's mandates. Whether she will make use of my support is a question that can only be answered by her."

While I shortly thereafter swore on all of the bibles in the world that I'd make use of my guardian's support and abide by all of the court's dictates, the "court" interpreted Ms. Cathy's acknowledgement concerning her powerlessness over other people, places, and things to mean that she didn't want to be held responsible for my predictably negative future behavior. Nonetheless, even at the time, I didn't hold her response against her. While I might not have known anything about the Twelve Steps, I somehow sensed that Ms. Cathy had always done the right thing by me and was only trying to do the right thing by herself the best way that she could at the time. No matter how hard I tried, and believe me I tried very hard, in the end not even I could find fault in her way of trying to be fair and honest and responsible. Had the "court" been to a few Twelve-Step meetings and understood the true meaning behind Ms. Cathy's words, I probably would have been placed back into her home on an eighteen-month sentence of probation. Had I had any more insight into her words, I most likely would have never seen the inside of a courtroom again. As it was, the "court" was ignorant about the Twelve Steps and I was sent upstate. As it also was, my limited insight prevented me from learning many a lesson it would have behooved me to learn at the time in an expeditious fashion. Hence, I traversed across the floors of many a courtroom in the days and years that followed my escape from my first felony incarceration.

    I was sent upstate shortly after the rest of the world had just celebrated the New Year. Barring my memories of the extremely cold temperatures and the seemingly endless fields of snow that looked as if a satin wedding dress with glistening sequins had been draped over the earth's surface, I remember little of my short stay in my first correctional facility. It had as minimal an impact on me as my previous five-day stay in the Women's House of Detention at Riker's Island. I guess since I had been born there, it was a "going back to the womb" kind of experience. Aside from having spent about twenty hours in the Women's Receiving Room at Riker's Island, I only spent about three days in Building Three before Ms. Cathy bailed me out. Nothing much aside from a few medical tests and a few social contacts had occurred before I had found myself back on the streets. I believe I spent even less time "on the rock" once I was remanded and scheduled to spend the next one year of my life in some quiet rural county in the northern end of New York State. Due to my age, I lucked out with my first bid and ended up in some Mickey Mouse Minimum Security residential setting for adolescent females with felony convictions that were on the lower end of the severity scale. I never quite got into the routine of things in my new home. I guess that somewhere buried in the archives of some therapist's progress notes exists a notation negating that I had made a positive adjustment to my new "highly supportive and structured" residential setting. I assume that little wise voice inside of my head informed me from quite early on that I wouldn't be remaining in my new home very long. This more than likely became the most clear to me when I realized that my correctional institution was an "open setting" whose New Age philosophy on the subject of reform and rehabilitation for wayward young women teetered on the end of the liberal scale. I'm actually ashamed that it took me until practically the end of March to head back home to the Bronx and the insanity that I thrived on. Since there were no bars or barbed wire fences constraining me, I believe it must have been the humongous piles of snow that delayed my departure. I had enough sense to know that if the going got tough, the "New York City tough" could not get going through avalanches of snow. A resourceful hustler I was, the Abominable Snow Woman I was not. By the end of March though, my distaste for the wintry stuff and increasing longing for other varieties of white powdery mounds prodded me to make a break for it. I escaped on a morning when everybody was in school—just walked right out the fucking door. So much for all of those "great escape" scenes that I had observed in the past on TV. It was so easy that I was almost embarrassed. I remember sliding down the great hill that separated the facility from the rest of the terrain of nothingness, one eye and one ear always kept open, thinking that if I ever had an occasion to compare "great escape" notes with my peers, I'd probably have to borrow a bit from my active imagination. Upon making it to the road that plows had already cleaned and salted some days back quite nicely, it occurred to me that while my escape might have been just as easy as pie, I just might have some difficulty trying to explain to some truck driver why a black girl with state issued boots was hitchhiking in the boondocks surrounded by cracker counties. As I was relying heavily on the most competent of my executive functions, a truck driver of color came driving by and offered me a ride in the direction of New York City without asking any personal questions. At least he didn't ask any personal questions for the first hour of the ride. At some point, however, when we were approaching the outskirts of Albany, he asked me to suck his dick. I told him that that would be a small price to pay for all of his kindnesses and suggested that he stop at the nearest truck stop so I could accommodate his needs as soon as I accommodated my own in terms of using the facilities. As you can probably figure out, the horny old bastard readily agreed. When we stopped and he stepped down from his seat to come around to my side, within the parameters of five seconds I busily emptied all of the loose change that he kept in the ashtray and stuffed it down into the deep pockets of my jeans. Had he presented me with one second more, I probably would have stolen his truck from right before his eyes. As it was, my bounty added up to about $7.50—a sufficient enough amount to purchase a one-way bus ticket in Albany and a token once I reached the Port Authority Bus Terminal in New York. Given the situation, I couldn't have asked for anything more. After completing my business in the facilities, I remained there peacefully and unnoticed for the better part of an hour. Upon exiting and seeing that the old horny bastard driving the sixteen-wheeler truck had probably long ago realized that he had been played and was gone, I pled a sob story to some sappy, vulnerable-looking middle-aged white man about how my rotten, good-for-nothing boyfriend had abandoned me at the truck stop when I had informed him about my pregnancy. He felt so badly for me that he not only drove me way into the city limits, but also gave me an extra $10 so I could "make my way to my paternal aunt's home in the Bronx with little trouble." I graciously thanked him aloud. Silently, I graciously thanked his past life's circumstances that made him so extremely dumb. Upon hitting the streets in the Bronx, I decided to stay at my "friend" Sabrina's crib that lived north of Ms. Cathy around the Grand Concourse in the 180s. As I was well aware that a warrant for my arrest had been issued shortly after my escape, I stayed away from Ms. Cathy. I stayed away from her for additional reasons as well, more complex psychological ones. The same kind that I continue to grapple with to this day in my daily struggle to live life on life's terms. I stayed with Sabrina and her ancient great grandmother for almost one month before I moved in with an older acquaintance, Cheryl, who lived in the Marcy projects in Brooklyn and who largely contributed to the perfecting of my boosting skills and techniques. While with Cheryl, I sometimes went back to the Bronx and stayed with Sabrina. Sometimes, I stayed with Verna, who also lived in the Bronx and was on welfare, had three babies, and was hitting the pipe on the regular. I was becoming a street nomad of sorts. Sabrina, Cheryl, and Verna. They were all acquaintances as far as I was concerned. I knew that with little provocation, they were all capable of stabbing me in the back. Some were capable of gutting me. I stayed far away from Smooth who I heard was fucking some prissy, designer clothes-wearing Puerto Rican chick from Brownsville. I figured she and I were bound to have beef and she would just be the type to rat me out on my warrant to the police. Despite the fact that I inwardly acknowledged that I couldn't turn my back too long on any of my acquaintance hostesses, I had no problem finding a place to lay my head at night. Accomplished, resourceful boosters were always welcome in the homes of those apartment doors on which I found myself knocking more and more frequently. While never having to ever approach the generous mark, I was a welcomed house guest all the same.

One day, when I was returning from Bloomingdales, having earned at least $400 for a half a day's work, I ran into Bruny. She had lost some weight and looked kind of tired, but she was still the same old Bruny. Within a matter of minutes after having informed her of my recent activities at Bloomingdales, she slapped me five, exclaiming that we could now become boosting business partners. I had never trusted anyone before, especially when it came down to boosting. "Solo is better" had always been my motto. Without her having to say so, I also quickly deduced that Bruny had succumbed to the pipe since we last ran together on the streets. Notwithstanding all of the above, I also knew that I could trust her. Bruny would always be my ace and I knew it. She had shown up for me more than any friend or acquaintance ever had. No matter what her personal issues might have been, I knew that she would continue to do so. It was for this reason that I agreed to Bruny's proposal about becoming business partners after only a few moments of deliberation. It was for this same reason that I agreed to spend the night with her at her cousin's house. While I never regretted the former decision, I came to regret the latter.

Due to reasons that she never discussed, Bruny had been forced to move out from her mother's apartment into some one-bedroom hell hole with a cracked-out older Puerto Rican woman who had all five of her kids removed by BCW because she used to force her two oldest to do sexual favors for money or crack. By the looks of the situation she was about ready to have her sixth child removed as soon as she gave birth. My experienced naked eye appraisal of pregnant addicts told me that although she only looked about four or five months pregnant, she was probably somewhere in the third trimester. I similarly would have put money down on the fact that she would probably give birth prior to her expected due date, probably somewhere around her eighth month. That is, if the addicted, underweight fetus could even wait that long. Bruny referred to the wizened woman whose face looked like a hand-me-down prune as "prima" (cousin). I had my doubts.

While in the small, smelly apartment that reeked of mildew and stale urine, and made any of Mama's old apartments look like Beverly Hills mansions, Bruny refrained from hitting the pipe in my presence. However, she graciously shared the lines of coke that I put out across the rickety table for her intranasal use. Bruny's "prima," on the other hand, who obviously now had to support her habit via the prostitution of her own wasted body, had no qualms about lighting her pipe up in our faces and then smoking it until she could barely push on the stem. The fact that the "prima" had barely earned a $5 bag for all of her night's dick-sucking efforts seemed to be a matter of course. I began to alter my initial judgment about their not being blood kin. Perhaps dick sucking was a family past time and she and Bruny were close cousins indeed.

Despite my great trust in Bruny and her hospitable gestures, after sharing a few lines of my good cocaine with her, I lied and told her that I had forgotten that I had made some plans to meet a guy that night. The reason was that as far as I could see in the dim light, the squalid and small surroundings was crawling with cockroaches, rats, and vermin of a variety of different genre. Don't get me wrong. I wasn't exactly lodging at the Hilton myself, nor had I not been in similar, perhaps worse, environmental conditions when Mama was still alive. I guess I just saw myself as being in a different class at the time. In a different upgraded class. Talking about delusions of grandeur. I was drowning in them, steadily and unwearily, mistaken in my belief that I was managing my own life that much better. Misguided in my thinking that it was I who was managing my life at all. My erroneous notions held about as much weight as soap bubbles suspended in air. Their life expectancy, an analogous amount of time.

Whether Bruny understood the real reason for my abrupt departure, I have no clue. She was, however, probably somewhat grateful that she'd have the opportunity to take a little push on the stem herself away from what appeared to be my judgmental eyes. We met bright and early the following day. Nine in the morning sharp to be exact. Business partners seated together on the number 4 train, clanging our way downtown to moneymaking Manhattan for a day's work. To most passersby, two seemingly very normal young females of color. We never spoke of many things. But we were a moneymaking duo, and until I changed playgrounds and toys, we thoroughly enjoyed each other's company.

Forgetting that Bruny had originally been my second boosting instructor, Mama having been the first, I was initially surprised to see just how competent and well-paired a team we were. My biggest fear had been that Bruny could not pull herself together enough to blend into Manhattan's finest department stores without standing out like a squash in a grape vineyard. She fooled me. Along the mountainous path of her boosting career, Bruny had acquired two professional suits that she used "to go shopping" interchangeably. And she wore them both well. Once she put one on, covered her typically poorly groomed hair with a matching hat, and removed the forever present lollipop from between her lips,

Bruny was able to pass for decidedly more than halfway decent. Her worn facial pallor was easily camouflaged by makeup, and her extremely gaunt physique, by the tightly knit polyester, but classy winter white raincoat that she wore prouder-looking than most pictures of any peacocks I ever saw. Her rotted teeth were entirely another issue. But, if she kept her mouth closed, Bruny was in business.

Bloomingdales and Lord & Taylor were our primary stomping grounds, although we occasionally ventured downtown to Macys when one of us felt any pressure or heat spreading through the air further uptown. Sachs Fifth Avenue was always tight. Whenever I went through their heavy glass doors, I felt the fingers of fear gently caressing my spine. My take on the situation was that they paid their security staff more than their competitors. My sixth sense told me that I was playing with fire having my ass inside, and that soon enough one of the better paid employees was going to earn their salary by being responsible for carrying my ass back to jail. Although I later learned that it was my better thinking that usually caused my greatest troubles, my decision-making processes worked to my advantage in this situation by propelling me away from the store in which the security staff probably had fewer monetary complaints.

Fortunately, it was winter. This afforded us the luxury of being able to store large quantities of the fruits of our labor down into oversized coats. If practice indeed makes perfect, Bruny and I had came to perfect the crawler booster technique after about a month of working together. This involved cutting out the bottoms of our long coat pockets, and quickly shoving out hands through to drop the pricey merchandise of our choice down into the coats' deep pocket linings. I'm proud to say that it was I who was the forerunner in learning how to disconnect the little, metal-and-plastic store alarms that annoyingly pierced every damned thing. Then I taught Bruny. She never quite got the hang of it, probably because it took a fair amount of strength and dexterity, something that she was coming to lack more and more. Despite my greater proficiency with "alarm removal," Bruny did quite well. It didn't matter all that much anyway since she disengaged alarms with her boosting tools quicker than most people inhale on a good cigarette. Between the two of us, Bruny and I netted about a grand a day. There were days when we were less lucratively fortunate. There were similarly days when I netted about a grand all by myself. Those days, however, were far and few between. While we lost some in the end by the time we fenced off our shit, Bruny and I were quite satisfied with our renewed and improved careers. The fact that our friendship had been revived through our business partnership was decidedly the most significant of all the fringe benefits.

I was making money with Bruny by day and building a social life amongst the indecorous and unctuous by night. I immersed myself in the club scene so deeply that it became increasingly difficult to awaken in time in the mornings to run and catch the train to go and meet Bruny. Typically, I barely had time to meet Bruny by ten, after leaving some shadowy after-hours spot by eight or nine. Had it not been for the large amount of cocaine that I was putting up my nose, I wouldn't ever have been able to meet up with her in the mornings at all. I was on a perpetual run, finding fewer and fewer hours in a day to meet my basic needs for sleep and rest. When I did eventually allow myself to "crash," I'd remain in a comatose kind of sleep for days. All of a sudden, things like my nails, hair, clothing, and jewelry took on an unfamiliar importance in my life. I worried about these aspects of myself constantly, and likewise assumed that others did the same. I grew tight with this Dominican chick that lived up in Washington Heights. I met her in the ladies room at an after hours spot in the Bronx. After eying me down for the entire duration that it took me to snort two hits of coke and then apply two fresh coats of lipstick, she finally started laughing and shared that she just remembered where she had seen me before—in the holding pen at Central Booking when I was arrested on armed robbery charges. Maricella had passed one unhappy evening behind bars on multiple drug-related charges. That is, until her relatives from Jersey came and bailed her out. Maricella lived with her two brothers, Miguel and Johnny, in Washington Heights. All three of them, especially Johnny, were responsible for moving a sizeable portion of cocaine and heroin throughout the streets of New York City. Although their connections in upper Manhattan and the Bronx were the largest, Maricella and her brothers made their mark in the other boroughs as well. Nobody ever discussed additional familial influences, but I was pretty sure that drug trafficking in its many forms was a family business. What I did come to learn after my friendship with Maricella was more firmly established was that at the same time that she was bailed out of jail, both of her brothers were easily bailed out as well. Between the three, the bail bondsman received $100,000. This made me believe that Maricella's relatives from Jersey were rolling in dough. Dough that would be considered blood money in other circles.

 Hardly any time had to pass before Maricella and I realized that we had lots in common. I was eighteen by then. She was twenty. We were both obsessed with our appearances and fast money. We were both the quiet types who, nonetheless, gravitated toward excitement and insanity and possessed an impulsive, crazy edge. We had both given up on school, been arrested, and had dead mothers who were permanently resting in cemetery plots. Maricella. She was my home girl. My ace. The fact that Mama was born on Dominican soil made us like sisters, almost . . .

 In addition to hanging out together in clubs, Maricella and I did girlie things together. We shopped, and got our hair and nails done. Things like that. Things that I'd never been able to do with Bruny, and generally had always done by myself. Maricella never asked me how I made my money. Even when she asked me to get together during those afternoon periods that I had already reserved for boosting, Maricella always nonchalantly accepted my declines to her offers, without blinking one curious eyelash. It became apparent that Maricella felt that how I made my money was none of her concern. The fact that I had a sufficient supply of it was the only thing that mattered. As I grew to learn more about her, I came to understand that in much the same way she kept her nose out of other people's business, she expected others to do the same with her little family-operated drug distributing company. It wasn't until she introduced me to her two brothers one night after we had already been friends for months that I received an invitation to their apartment. My invitation came from Johnny. Johnny, the older of Maricella's two brothers, was the finest specimen of a man that God had ever placed in my path before. He was the type that Hollywood paid big bucks to be in their movies, and rich women paid comparable amounts to in terms of their money, blood, sweat, and tears, to keep in their beds. Johnny's eyes and ass alone were worth at least two years of the average civil servant's wages, and that, was only for one night's rental.

Being young and all, Maricella forsook her culture's nightlife on Friday and Saturday nights, and instead, would typically go club hopping with me to the city's best hip-hop spots. Maricella conveniently also had a thing for black men. Not only had I heard her repeatedly say "Once you go black, you never go back," I believe that she was also in strong agreement with the adage, "The darker the berry, the sweeter the juice." I was always able to find Maricella in the most dimly lit of spots. Given my understanding of her choice of men, I would simply just look around for a curvaceous shadow standing beside a figure with glow-in-the-dark teeth and eyes. Then I'd know that I had found her. Anyway, on this particular Saturday night, Maricella told me that her brothers wanted her to accompany them to a big Dominican Merengue party at the La Vega Night Club that was located just as far uptown as one could go. She looked at me hard then, as if trying to figure something out, relaxed, and pleasantly asked if I wanted to come along. Even though I realized that I'd probably be the only one there who didn't understand the music or anything that anybody was saying, I figured then was just about as good a time as any to expand upon my cultural horizons. Besides, I had heard that Dominican men who lived in New York were not cheap with their money. That was a cultural trait that I was definitely feeling, then and now as a matter of fact. I accepted Maricella's invitation within moments after it had passed through her lips.

Johnny and Miguel picked up Maricella and I from an upscale R & B joint in Harlem at about 1 AM. It was about 1:01 AM that I decided that Johnny was about the finest man I had ever laid eyes on in at least half my life. At 1:02 AM, I knew that I wanted to get with him and have his baby, or at least go through the motions. By 1:05 AM, I knew that Johnny felt the same.

The three-to four-year period during which I had relations with Johnny is about as difficult for me to retrieve from memory as the shadowy captions of my childhood. From what I do remember, I believe I spent almost four years at a long and very crazy party. A party that I invited myself to. A party of superficial joy. A party that had such a tight grip on me that before I knew the seasons were evolving, my hold on it was just as tight. A party that was devoid of Jesus' blessings.

Within a few weeks, I moved into the apartment with Maricella and her brothers. Since I was fucking Johnny, I slept in Johnny's room. I don't believe that Maricella was too thrilled about my new living arrangements and bed partner. In fact, I know she didn't like it one little bit. Whether her reasoning was of the "too close for comfort" persuasion, or whether she felt that I wasn't good enough for her brother, I'll never know. However, on the first morning that Maricella and I woke up under the same roof and passed each other in the hallway on the way to the bathroom, her malcontented attitude was easily identified. As her dark eyes bore into mine with a matching clamped mouth that contradictorily squeezed out a "Good Morning," I realized that our short-lived friendship was not only strained, but probably over. Defunct, if you will. Whatever her issues were, she kept them to herself and I never prodded. Better not to open Pandora's box and let sleeping dogs lie. I was my mother's daughter. Besides, I really didn't give a damn at the time anyway. I had what I wanted, what I thought I needed. Johnny. Fuck Maricella and her opinions. As long as she kept up with her saccharine smiles and hollow laughter, I wasn't about to look under any rocks.

I continued waking up bright and early to go boosting with Bruny at least four days during the work week. But, as time passed, Johnny's street pharmacy business began to boom. And then it boomed some more. One night Johnny pulled me close to him and whispered softly into my ear that he hoped I would be winding down any of my past business involvements since there would be no more need for me to work. In fact, he made some subtle remark about me being family now and family should work for family. I was slowly breaking away from Bruny again anyway. There was no hiding from the fact that she was a bona fide crackhead. She walked the walk and talked the talk. If that didn't convince one, her appearance told it all. Her work skills were also becoming more and more sloppy and loose. The bottom line, though, was that I was just traveling in too much of a different circle. At least I thought that this was true.

The way things worked out, I didn't end our business partnership. Bruny did. She went to jail. I wasn't glad about the way it happened, but her arrest got me off the hook of having to do something that at the time I just seemed not to be able to do. Not easily anyway. This is the way I used to think. The never-ending party already had its grip on me, shaking my shoulders ever so gently that only an angel's eyes could perceive the last vestiges of virtue that fell loose from my spirit.

It happened on a Monday morning. Early. The weather had already begun to chill. Perhaps it was for this reason that I doubly resented slipping loose from

Johnny's warm embrace from under the covers to traipse all the way down to midtown Manhattan to meet Bruny at East Fifty-ninth. I'm sure the fact that I was snorting lines of coke followed by much ass waxing until about four in the morning didn't do much for my mood as well. Once again, as I closed my eyes to ease the dull ache from beneath my lids, which seemed to be throbbing to the beat of the train's whirling wheels, *rattatat, ratta tat, ratta tat*, I swore to every God that ever rented space in people's souls that this would be the day I would inform Bruny that I was resigning from our little business partnership.

We met, and because we had already played Bloomingdales out, we decided to travel further downtown and try our luck at Macy's. Somehow we ended up in Sach's Fifth Avenue. Don't ask me why or how. I truly have no recollection. We probably went to Macy's and found that it was too hot. I really don't remember. The bottom line is that we ended up in Sach's Fifth Avenue, giving my ominous premonitions one more opportunity to be transformed into realities. This time the bad luck fairies seized the moment.

Since I had found a new Puerto Rican fence that moved designer silk dresses very quickly, and it was an extremely easy item to steal when the alarm gadgets weren't clasped on too tight, we usually began our day exploring dress departments of various expensive clothing designers. Once that alarm was removed, we could slip at least eight to ten dresses a piece down the linings of our jackets via the crawler technique.

On the day that Bruny was arrested, after having about four dresses from two particular designers, we decided to move to another section of the store where the clothing was even pricier. Just as we were about to leave, Bruny looked at me with a strange, intense facial expression as if her life depended on how well she studied the contours of my face. She asked me to go and wait for her downstairs in the area where they sold pocketbooks. Just as I was about to ask her about what happened to the idea of moving over into another section of designer dresses, Bruny gave me a silly smile and told me that she wanted to practice a new coat boosting technique that involved switching coats. Still smiling, she told me that she had peeped a classy fur that looked like it had a loose alarm on it and wanted to try out her new skills with it. She said that the coat was selling for two grand, on sale. Thinking that that was some pretty good fast money, an interest in learning new techniques for fur boosting surfaced inside of me. The combination of this thought along with the faint throb inside my temple rented all of the space in my head. So when Bruny asked me to give her my coat for a while until she met me in five minutes downstairs, not a single irregular thought crossed my mind. There simply wasn't any more space. I handed her my coat, told her that I'd see her in five, and ambled away. I was glad for the break, and although I didn't recognize it at the time, would have trusted any directive that Bruny would have given me anyway.

When Bruny didn't show up in five, I didn't think anything of it. However, by the time fifteen minutes had passed, beads of sweat began to collect above my brow and under my arm pits. Once twenty minutes had passed, I knew something had gone dreadfully wrong. Setting my brain on a self-protective channel, I figured it was best to wait outside. This way, I could always run. I wanted to know what happened, from a safe distance. In five more minutes, the police pulled up alongside the store, and about fifteen minutes later, I peeped Bruny being led out in handcuffs to the squad car by two uniforms. From my safe distance, I could see that she was trembling. And then, as if she knew exactly where I'd be watching her, her face grimaced as her eyes cut diagonally across the street in my direction. Her lips mouthed something as one of the uniforms pushed her down into the back seat of the police car. The car drove away and then she disappeared for the next year or so from my life.

Three days after Bruny was arrested, I was driving to the Bronx with Johnny to make a pick-up. While waiting for the red light to turn green on a deserted corner off of Jerome Avenue, I casually looked through the tinted glass windows of his BMW and saw a crusty, black, crippled crackhead perched on the edge of his seat in a wheel chair. As his eyes sought mine and he started to inch forward, he thrust his arms up high in the air and began to bellow, "I wish I was a drug dealer too, so I could be rich and famous because God ain't done shit for me." I looked over at Johnny as we pulled off to see if the crackhead's words had registered in his mind. They hadn't. I guess they hadn't left any marks in mine as well.

I later learned that Bruny had observed an undercover store security guard peeping us in the dress area at Sachs that day. It was when he turned around for a minute to radio in for assistance that Bruny told me her little white lie about the new fur boosting technique. She intentionally took the rap. Bruny told me what happened when we happened to come upon one another months after her release. When I asked her why she did it, she flatly stated that since I already had a warrant out for my arrest because of my past escape she had figured that it would be better for me if she got caught alone. I intellectually understood, but could not relate. I especially couldn't relate since I hadn't bothered to check up on her once, nor had sent her even one commissary dollar throughout her entire bid. I didn't make one move to help Bruny during her incarceration even though I had always known deep down in my heart that the reason why it was Bruny and not me who had gotten arrested had nothing to do with accidents or bad luck fairies at all.

CHAPTER FOURTEEN

If we do not change our direction, we are likely to end up where we are headed.
—Ancient Chinese proverb

I BELIEVE THAT I must have started working with, or should I say for, Johnny on a full-time basis before Bruny's case had even been heard by the grand jury. Let's just say that I surely didn't waste any time. If she took three months to cop out to a plea of a lesser charge, I was, by that point, pretty much solely responsible for bagging all of the dope and coke that was set aside to be sold out on the streets in smaller quantities. Namely, trays and bags. At first I believed that Maricella would just add my taking over of her job to the list of cardinal infractions that she already held against me. Strangely enough, she didn't. Of course, she didn't exactly stop participating in the family business either. In fact, her new assignment was probably a hell of a lot more prestigious and important than being "a bagger" anyway. Looking back now, I was never exactly apprised of the details involving Maricella's new job description. All I knew was that she was doing it outside of the apartment. It was around this same time period that I ingeniously arrived at the conclusion that I wasn't family. I was merely somebody who was fucking a family member. Important family business matters were only discussed amongst family, typically not in my presence, and always in Spanish as a final safeguard.

As crazy as it sounds, none of the above bothered me. Not even in the slightest. I was, you see, doing my own thing. Feeling my oats as they say. Squeezing myself into the narrow identity that had been carved out for me over the years. Or at least this is what I figured I was doing. I later learned that while my past experiences may have helped shape a crude mold with little promise, I never for a second lost grasp of the invisible chisel that was placed into my hand at a time when the ideas that formed my negative identity were mere fumes of fancy. Shuttered grace.

Johnny and his family fulfilled my needs at the time quite well. Johnny satisfied my sexual needs. His feared, almost ominous presence in the neighborhood likewise vicariously fulfilled my need for, what at the time I thought was, respect. Because I was his "wifey," I had mad props. Props that I had basically been denied throughout the course of my childhood as the daughter of a drug addict. Johnny's family, regardless of the fact that they were consistent in their subtle communication concerning my alienated status, still provided me with a group of live human beings with which I could maintain an illusion of belonging and intimacy. And last but not the least, when all else failed and one of the truths of my existence dared to defiantly poke its poignant head through the clouds of my fantasies, Johnny and his family provided me with a seeming endless supply of drugs. Mind-altering substances that kept both my head and emotions buried in the sand, allowing me to cruise through many situations as if they were all creations of a poetic frenzy. Guns, frantic cries for help, and other people's blood and tears, floated by my conscience for many years, like castles in the air. It wasn't until I was arrested, having probably been set up, and was sitting in somebody's overcrowded, cold, and smelly jail cell without the benefit of any numbing white powdery substances to summon forth any illusions, that I began to see Johnny and his family for what they were, and my situation for what it was. My insight, however, was a day late and a dollar short. At the time, it was only at the budding stage. Its weak seeds lost root as soon as I was released nine months later from Riker's Island on a Wednesday and Johnny asked whether I'd rather start bagging up again on Thursday or Friday. The fact that he had never once visited me or responded to any of my attempts to contact him became irrelevant. In comparison, it was even one notch less relevant than the fact that upon my return to his apartment, there were enough foreign traces of femininity left behind in his bedroom to apprise me of the fact that my side of the bed had not been empty. Since clues of his infidelity never actually materialized into a live bitch stepping up into my face, I looked away from this truth as well. Such concepts as fidelity and pride lose their relevance when one has joined the race that nobody ever wins.

My second arrest occurred during the early part of the second decade of having my physical presence felt on this planet. I was doing one of Johnny's cousins the favor of running a few ounces of cocaine across town, finding myself in handcuffs as soon as I entered the building in which I was supposed to make my drop off of bags of goodies. Although I could never prove it, or even get my finger anywhere near the truth, it felt like a set up to me. It felt like a set up to me even then when at best, I processed truths like beveled whispers. It felt as if the police were expecting me, as if I was a guest who had been cordially invited into their snare. However, since it happened so quickly and I was being charged with possession and sale of a controlled substance in Manhattan Criminal Court before I could organize any semblance of logical thought in my head, my conscious shook itself loose of such considerations. Instead, I maintained my focus on my case. My greatest fear was the price I would have to pay for absconding from the Residential Facility during my adolescence. Fortunately, the political climate for drug-related crimes of addict offenders was favorable in the eighties. This was particularly true if one happened to be female. Even though the odds were better for addict offenders who also happened to be white, two out of three kernels of luck could not be scoffed at by someone in my predicament. When it was all said and done, I copped out to possession of a controlled substance in the third degree, appealing to the judge's capacity for empathy by stating that my illegal proclivities were all associated with my out-of-control addiction to drugs and alcohol. Fortunately for me, the government had recently invested large sums of money into drug rehabilitation programs in hope of reducing crime and recidivism rates. Also of good fortune for me was the fact that the pudgy Caucasian scholar clothed in flowing black robes who was seated before me on the bench that day had a bleeding, open, and very forgiving heart. He believed me. The only unfortunate part of the situation was that I didn't believe me. I didn't believe in anything that I said about struggling with an out-of-control addiction. I simply believed that I had successfully managed to manipulate yet another system in my life. Hence, the court's decision to place me into an in-patient drug rehabilitation program in lieu of my going to jail did nothing to help me. It only served to reinforce my confidence in my ability to manipulate and deceive the world in which I lived. I was not ready to accept life on life's terms just yet. In fact, I still had a very long way to go. Six months of drug rehabilitation only served to convince me of how much I couldn't wait to do that very first line of coke.

I started hitting the pipe shortly after I was released from an in-patient substance abuse program. I chased that first "crack" high ever since. Needless to mention, up until my very last push on the stem, I had not caught up with it. That is, even though I wasted the next approximate six years, thousands and thousands of dollars, and almost my life trying to do so. It was quite a high price that most of us paid to be bums. About four or five years later when I was attending one of many court-mandated drug rehabilitation facilities, one of my more astute individual counselors dared ask why I had ever gone after that first hit on the pipe when I had already seen the consequences firsthand with Bruny and so many of the others. At the time, I believed the question could have been placed quite high on the "Most Stupidest Questions Asked by Drug Counselors" list, became angry, and reacted to my anger in my typical fashion. I made some form of an insulting sarcastic remark to the counselor, abruptly ended the session, hit the streets with the best of intentions of copping a couple of bags, and in my head, blamed my immediate "need" to use on the counselor's stupidity and lack of competence. On those occasions, when my attempts at copping were thwarted by some unforeseen trick of the devil and I had to wait longer than expected to feel the familiar glass texture of the crack pipe between my subtly twitching lips, my reasoning about why I continued to remain in this crazy race became more expansive. Not only did my externalization of blame include my singular incompetent counselor, as my levels of frustration mounted, the driving forces behind my addiction took on several different faces of varying degrees of familiarity. It assumed the faces of many past counselors. Society in general. The blurry countenances of all the Caucasian peoples in the world, including those who were addicts in a worse position than myself. At the very pinnacle of my frustration, it assumed the visage of my mother, if only but for a fleeting moment. I had not yet learned about the powerful experience of looking at oneself in the mirror. Today I still forget and need to be reminded at times.

In the end, it wasn't Bruny who was responsible for influencing me to get hooked on the crack pipe. Ironically, I was once again avoiding her and all other forms of "low lives" at the time to successfully maintain my status amongst Johnny's clan. I needn't have bothered. Whether it was directly related to my newest form of addiction or not, Johnny kicked me to the curb about a month after I had decided to give it a try when I was hanging out with one of my old running partners from the Bronx. Big-boned, crazy Theresa who ended up with a life sentence a year later when she threw her boyfriend and his brother out of the sixth floor project window for raping her six-year-old retarded daughter. Even though we all thought the judge would let Theresa walk under the circumstances, he threw the book at her for leaving her daughter alone in the hands of two crackheads in the first place. The fact that Theresa herself was a crackhead made the situation all that much more understandable, and all that much worse for Theresa. The end result was that both mother and daughter probably spent the rest of their lives in separate institutions, with vivid memories of one for the other locked up as if they were inmates in the cells of their brains.

With reference to the incompetent counselor's question, I had no reservations about taking my first hit off the crack pipe even after observing the progression of Bruny's disease. Had such thoughts rented space in my head, I would have been in a much healthier space and not as prone toward making such frivolous choices. At least that is the way I see things. The most ironic detail of the whole tragedy was that throughout the course of my approximate six-year downward spiral as a crackhead, I never once considered myself to be on the same "low life" level on which I had placed Bruny. It wasn't until I embarked on an honest, soul-searching journey in my recovery that I realized that the lines I had always drawn to separate people into different categories were invisible and only held meaning in my own head.

Johnny kicked me to the curb by intentionally having me walk in on a romantic episode between him and a sexy, but younger than young Cuban chick. She was so young, maybe fifteen at best, that I even felt stupid when I considered kicking her immature ass. Before that part of the brain that is responsible for the defense mechanism of denial had an opportunity to register, I realized that I had been set up again. Leading me by the arm into his sister's bedroom, Johnny explained that he thought it would be best if we separated for a while, while continuing to see each other from time to time. He added that since I wouldn't be living there anymore, it would make sense if I gave up my "bagging up" job, although I could still "participate" in different types of business opportunities for the family from time to time. It was then that I no longer held any doubts that both Maricella and he had learned of my fondness for my newest drug of choice. Johnny threw out the chick and I packed up my things. I didn't express any resistance. I guess I had resolved myself to the fact that things, both on the outside and within, were changing. I had lost insight over which of those things I had control quite some time ago. Today I still forget and need to be reminded.

Once I moved out of Johnny's house, I stayed in different living arrangements for as long as I was permitted. I got along as best as I could. True to his parting statement, Johnny sought me out from time to time. I was able to keep myself together enough to still be considered a wild, but presentable enough Saturday night partner in any of the Dominican bars or clubs that he frequented. With me, for whatever reason things happen like they do, my physical self was the last part of me to deteriorate. My spiritual and emotional were among the first to go. So, Johnny kept me around for a rather long time, both as his weekend partying and sexual fling, as well as his part-time employee of small "running" jobs in the neighborhood. I was good for doing major exchanges with the girlfriends of others like him in the bathrooms of clubs and bars, and even better at doing little runs to Brooklyn and the Bronx. Although I was always sufficiently rewarded in bed, Johnny never neglected to give me the more tangible reward of cocaine in crack form for my jobs well done. As time passed, this evolved into the only singular reason why I continued hanging around. When I wasn't running for Johnny, I was boosting. Somewhere in my early twenties when my sense of morality recessed into the shadows of my conscience, I became active in pulling off robberies. I usually went along with this crazy brother named Deion, who we all referred to as Dee, to do such jobs. I met Dee one night when I went to this crack house in the Bronx with my latest running partner Ann. On our way in, we met Ann's cousin Dee, who was on his way out. We spoke for a few minutes and then he went back inside with us. Fifty dollars later when I was feeling as good as it got, Dee asked me if I was interested in doing a job with him later that night. I agreed. About three hours later, we robbed a small-time street-corner drug dealer further north on the Yonkers' border. Dee simply put the gun to his head, and as the fear registered in the dealer's widening hazel eyes, I growled that he had better hand over all of his fucking money, drugs, and gold between clenched teeth. I had never exactly robbed someone before, and the fact that I was able to do it so easily, so detached from any censoring considerations, slightly unhinged me. I dealt with my nagging internal discomfort by robbing two more drug dealers on the Lower East Side with Dee the next day. In much the same way as practice makes perfect, it also makes just about any behavior more familiar, and therefore, less repulsive and easier to rationalize. As it was, creating a rationalization for robbing drug dealers proved to be quite an effortless task. Firstly, Dee and I never had to worry about whether one of them would press charges against us. Secondly, I figured they were behaving in as equally a perverse, if not more, manner against society than I was. I perceived Dee and my little robbery activities to be nothing more than a present-day practical example of Darwin's survival-of-the-fittest theory of evolution. An egotistical, self-profiting version of Robinhood in the Hood, if you will. It gets better. As time passed and Dee convinced me to participate in our form of "gay bashing," I began to lean on additional little sick forms of rationalization as well. Namely, I wasn't at fault because I wasn't exactly sure that Dee was going to go through with his presented plan. Although it wasn't as yet obvious to the naked eye that was only focused on the superficial self, my disease was progressing at an alarming rate.

"Gay bashing" as per Dee and myself, was basically defined as having Dee, who was fortunately a good-looker in a pretty boy effeminate kind of way, allow himself to be picked up in any of the downtown Manhattan parks or gay bars with me waiting expectantly in the paling gloam. Our "gay bashing" behavior was planned, ruthless, hard of heart, but unfortunately accurately depicted a good example of one of our more tender mercies. For whatever the reason, rich gay white boys were continually attracted to Dee. They were on him and his cute tight plump ass self like white on rice. As for Dee, he played the part well. He swished and swooshed, batted his eyes, flashed wide and juicy flirtatious smiles in their direction, and accepted their love taps on his pronounced shoulders and generous behind. Even though he was richly rewarded with top shelf alcoholic beverages, I often wondered how Dee was able to shelf his pride in his masculine identity so easily. While his performance as a homosexual could have won him an Oscar, it was a very sad show. The show typically went on for about forty-five minutes from beginning to end. Once Dee got himself picked up by a good prospect, he'd allow himself to be courted. If his suitor didn't make any aggressive moves in a half hour, Dee would become more assertive and prod the conversation along a sexual course that would inevitably get him invited over to the fag's apartment with a quickness. During our running days on the streets together, Dee and I must have gone after at least fifteen or twenty fags. There was only one who Dee was unable to manipulate back to his apartment. I'll never forget him. A blonde, all-American jock type with a goofy smile that looked as if it had been painted on his face in error. Dave, the telephone operator, who also did some choreography and dancing on the side, who was likewise interested in boating and drama, but was looking for more for himself than just a one-night stand. Although Dee never admitted it, I think his confused ego was slightly wounded by the fact that he couldn't convince Dave the telephone operator that he wasn't just a smooth-talking, one-night stand sort of guy. Even though we headed back uptown empty-handed that night, the memory of the look of dismay and mortification on Dee's face as he approached the shadows in which I lay crouched in silence was enough to make a petrified statue guffaw. As for me, it kept me laughing for at least the next three months and made the entire failed adventure worth while. Although Dee was never able to fully appreciate the humorous aspects of the situation, my laughter eventually became contagious and he grew accustomed to laughing at an image of his rejected self walking away from a prim fag.

Along with Dave the telephone operator who gave us cause to laugh, Dee and I came across fifteen or better open fags who gave us easy access to their money and gold. Once Dee was able to convince his bushy-tailed victim for the evening that it was love at first sight and he could turn him out as soon as he got him under the sheets, they'd usually sneak away, arm in arm, in the direction of the fag's apartment, with me staying behind at a safe distance, my thinning body blending in with the evening's shadows. Fortunately, the majority of the fags lived in walking distance of the pick-up spots. On one occasion, a fag led Dee away to the train station and I lost sight of them as they spontaneously embarked a train at Grand Central Station hand in hand. Dee, who was led to a very exclusive building complex in Scarborough, ended up "deading" the fag off for everything of value that he had in his apartment single handedly. On another occasion in which Dee was led off to some fag's car, he showed a look of surprise that rapidly developed into glee as he started to quickly calculate the bounty for that evening in his mind. He gave me "a thumbs up" when the fag wasn't looking as he demurely slid into the passenger seat of the car with an exaggerated, overly dramatic air of femininity. His self-possessed look of satisfaction was equally as exaggerated when he picked me up in the same car a few hours later. I actually believe the fool was disappointed that he'd have to sell the car immediately given the heat that could possibly follow behind the situation.

Typically, once Dee and the fag arrived at the fag's apartment, I'd remain in the shadows until Dee gave me the signal that the fag had unlocked the door. At this point, I'd come bounding forward as Dee would fling the naive man into his own home with his buried strength as easily as if tossing coins into a lake. By the time I'd lock the door behind us and Dee would be removing his concealed .22

from his sock, the fag would usually be cowered down on the floor, crying and begging for mercy. As a rule, we never touched them except to dig their pockets. Dee would hold the gun on them for good measure while I ransacked the place in search of gold, drugs, or more cash. On a few occasions, one of us would make an empty verbal threat in order to prod some compulsively neat and organized fag to disclose where he kept the goodies. On one occasion, toward the end of our gay-bashing adventures, we all plunged into a fag's apartment to find another fag, an extremely ostentatious one at that, standing in front of us with his arms and eyes crossed and foot tapping on the floor. As if he hadn't noticed me at first, the foot tapper proceeded to rant and rave about the pain that his partner's infidelity was causing him, claiming that he had been hiding in the darkness watching with disgust as his partner made his smooth moves on Dee. He then proceeded to cry, fling his arms about in despair, and continued to rant and rave. I had never seen anything like it in my fucking life. To make matters worst, the other fag, Dee's fag, started to cry. To this day I'm unclear as to whether Dee's fag was crying over his partner's evident pain or about the fact that there was a gun pointed at his head. Dee and I had no choice but to stare at one another in astonishment for the better part of two minutes. Finally, through poorly controlled snotty snobs, Dee's fag choked out, "Sssh, Snuggles, we have company right now . . . we'll talk later." It was my laughter that broke into the crying, whining raucous first. Then Dee's loud exclamation of "oh shit." It wasn't until then that Dee's fag's partner finally realized that I too was in the apartment, wielding a gun at his lover's head and laughing hysterically. This fag could have won an Emmy for drama queen that night with his reaction to my presence in his otherwise seemingly comfortable abode. Apparently still not understanding the exact nature of the situation, he began to cry out that not only did he have the most disloyal lover that ever existed in this world, but one that was so amoral and freaky that he picked up married bisexuals as well. Moaning at the top of his lungs, he droned on and on about the fact that his lover's lack of consideration had finally caught up with him, screaming that he was now about to taste the revenge of a spurned woman. Throughout all the screaming and weeping and my own giddiness, none of us could hear Dee's attempt to clarify that, while unbeknownst to at least half of us, we were actually in the middle of a robbery situation that we needed to attend to immediately. I was laughing so hard that I couldn't catch my breath. At this point, I opened the door behind me and beckoned Dee to follow, trying to blink away the tears of laughter that were spilling down my face. Stomping his feet and shooting a cutting look of disappointment in my direction, Dee reluctantly followed. Above my own laughter, I continued to hear the incessant tortured cries of the jilted lover as I made my way down the hallway and into the street. Those were definitely the days.

My last gay-bashing robbery occurred about three victims later. This one, who was even more weak and effeminate-looking than most, shocked the shit out of us when he desired to play fag he-man and fight back. It was the first time that we had to show that our bite was equally as big as our bark. Although it couldn't be helped, I didn't enjoy doing so. I had to pistol-whip the guy, and later, Dee had to tie him up. I couldn't suck enough times on the crack pipe that night to erase the image of that fag being knocked down on his own floor. It was an image that I imagine will remain forever in my memory. My memory of past behaviors of which I am ashamed. Dee went on earning money through the gay-bashing business with another partner once I told him that I quit. We remained together on and off as partners for drug-dealer holdups and future prosperous street activities for a couple of years. That is, until the day that Dee was shot in the head by a drug dealer in Brownsville during one of our more desperate robberies. The only reason why I wasn't killed was because the gun proved to be without sufficient bullets when he turned it on me. By then my disease had taken me to the point where I was beyond benefiting from any earthly lessons. I laid low for about two days, shrugged my shoulders, and found myself a new holdup partner within the next day or two.

Violence was never an essential ingredient in my life. While growing up, I met several individuals who fed off the stuff. It was an all-around turn-on for them. Without it, life just didn't feel exciting, complete, or familiar. It was a companion addiction of most addictions. In much the same way that having one's Saturday night's drink without the accompanying cigarette just wouldn't feel right or be "the same," violence served as a spice of life for many of the people with whom I spent my younger years. For whatever the reason, this had never been the case for me. In fact, never having been much of a fan or follower of violence unless I was truly pushed to the limit, I generally avoided violence as one would another contagious malady. Should one be able to avoid making contact with the infirmed without causing greater harm to another life area, one would surely graciously do so. But should such avoidance potentially afflict an even greater harm in one's life, most would weigh the probable consequences in both directions and proceed, albeit with perhaps greater than usual caution. Such was my lifelong strategy for dealing with violence. I graciously avoided it until the price of avoiding it outweighed the benefits. When applicable, I looked for discounted ways of buying into it. That is, until I became more deeply entrenched in my addiction. At this point, I stopped worrying about cutting corners when it came to making my points known through physical force. I similarly no longer worked hard at avoiding violence. As a result, violent situations identified my existence for many years, particularly those in which my use of crack was most active.

I believe the most unnecessary violent incident that I ever got myself involved with occurred when I was about twenty-two years old and hooked on the pipe with a fierceness. I'll never forget it. I was virtually homeless at the time, and about one hundred and fifteen pounds. Mind you, I still thought I looked cute. Although this addition really has nothing to do with the story, I was only about two months short of doing one of my first relatively long bids in prison. Bruny, this nameless, wild, plus-size girl from the Pink House projects in Brooklyn, another nameless cousin of Bruny's, and myself, all went down to the Lower East Side to cop one very, very cold night around Christmas time. I remember it was Christmas because all of the holiday gifts and extras were on display when Bruny and I had attempted to successfully "go shopping" that day. Since our appearances left a great deal to be desired at that point, our successful boosting days in high-fashion clothing stores were a thing of the quickly fading past. Not only did all of the security guards recognize our disguises for the day with the identical quickness of a mother for its young, but even those who did not know us sniffed out that we were in foreign and unfitting waters within moments of resting their eyes on our tired and used appearances. This translated into the undeniable fact that it became more difficult for Bruny and I to make any money through at least partially "honest" means anymore. As a result, Bruny increasingly relied on her $5 blow job specials while I predominantly depended on my freelance robbery jobs. However, on one unforgettable day when both Bruny and I were unable to earn anything from either of our hustling techniques and went downtown with money sufficient enough to cop less than one dime bag a piece, we ran into two nameless, but vaguely familiar chicks who were in as about as desperate a situation as we were. For simplicity's sake, we'll refer to these two chicks as "plus size and cousin." We all copped from the same guy on a corner off of Avenue B. We all put in about $10 if I recall, and we all got beat. Needless to mention is the fact that there wasn't one amongst us who wasn't heated about having been sold bad drugs. In fact, approximately three days later on Christmas Eve, there wasn't one amongst us who wasn't still stressed out and wasn't laughing and bragging about what they would do to the motherfucker should he be stupid enough to allow himself to be seen. And then, lo and behold, as if summoned by the collaborative effect of our imaginations, the guy who had beaten us started crossing the street in our direction. I don't think anybody thought twice. We all surrounded him, razors, knives, and garbage can covers pulled out uniformly. After we demanded, and then received, our money back, we were still not ready to go. We were unwilling to call it quits, unable to walk away. Words had already been hurled and blood boiled. Fragile, virtually non-existent prides had sauntered to the plate, unaware whether this would be their ultimate display of bravado while still resting in the hearts of the living. When it was all said and done, the young man, who had sold us the bad drugs, was emergency-room material, unconscious and bleeding from infinite lacerations on his face and above his waist. The only thing I recall thinking about as we all scattered away was that since none of the blows seemed to be fatal, he probably wouldn't die. I also wondered exactly how long it would take before I had the opportunity to wash his blood from my hands. I ran into Bruny about two days later. She told me that she heard that the young drug dealer had been in intensive care, but had since been removed. The word out on the streets was that he was going to survive the assault. Although I was high at the time, and therefore rather impervious to entry from any uncomfortable feelings, I remember being overtaken by a foreign sense of astonishment and shock.

"What you trying to say? You mean we almost killed him?"

"You got to be kidding, right? Damn, Vic, you don't remember leaving that boy's face looking like chopped meat?"

I thought deliberately and deeply for the better part of a minute.

"No, Bruny, no lie, I don't."

"Damn, that's why I stepped back you know."

"Huh?"

"I stepped back when all you fucking crazy soldiers pulled out your blades and shit. I know what can happen in the heat of the moment with a blade in your hand, so I stepped back. I got enough fucking problems in my life as is. I don't need nobody's damn blood drying up on my hands to cause me any more grief. You know what I mean?"

I pondered real hard and slow on her question again.

"I think so Bruny. I think I do now."

A couple of days before I was arrested on drug possession charges again, I learned that the young dealer was definitely going to live, although his face and upper torso would be seriously maimed for life. I also learned that he was the son of an addict who had abused him throughout his childhood when he lived in Boston, and that as a result, had come to New York to live with his aunt who would hopefully help provide him with the promise of a better life. It was then that I learned that he was only twenty-two years old at the time we assaulted him and scarred his face and body for life. Remembering Bruny's words, I questioned whether it wasn't better to step back sometimes. I also regrettably understood that even though our victims don't usually die, their dried blood is always difficult to wash from our hands.

Another memorable incident that occurred shortly before my first jail bid stands out in my mind apart from the rest, not because of its uniqueness, but because of the succinct fashion in which it crystallizes the insane existence in which I lived. For over one year, Bruny and I had worked well with a Puerto Rican fence from West 109th Street in Harlem who used to buy our freshly boosted high fashion ladies wear on a regular basis. Despite our slight conflicts of interest surrounding the topic of profit that always exists between business partners, the relationship was characterized by mutual respect and demonstrations of amicability. That is, until the day my addiction took over and took our relationship to another level. Not having been able to locate Bruny on that particular morning, I went out boosting by myself and had no luck. Tired, but not tired enough, I crawled back into the hood on my stomach without any money with an overwhelming need to hit the pipe. It was in this condition that I dragged myself into the crack spot begging for a high. Knowing that I was a good credit risk, a familiar basehead took pity on me and temporarily satisfied my gnawing urge. Once my head cleared and I was able to think of something other than my next pull on the pipe, I overheard two brothers with whom I was slightly familiar talking about how they wished they could get into the fence's apartment on 109th Street. As far as most fences' philosophy concerning self-protection went, if they didn't know you, they didn't let you in. As far as my dog-eat-dog philosophy was at the time, forget everything and everybody and go for yours. I acknowledged my familiarity with the fence to the brothers with whom I had previously never conversed—our only commonality being our desire to make quick money due to our shared obsession with our drug of choice. I later learned that their names were Mike and Will. Had their mamas called them George and Troy, there would have been no difference.

That same day, I went with them to the fence on 109th Street. It was because of the sound of my voice that the fence so freely opened the door. It was then that Mike and Will pushed their way into the apartment with guns in their hands and a look of base desperation in their eyes. A poor strategy for someone who wanted to make it appear as if I had no involvement in the robbery. Nothing could have been more plainly obvious. I had my girl, Lakeisha, waiting outside. It was she who had to hail a cab afterwards. After Mike and Will made sure that the fence and another female member of his family had turned over all of their money, we left. Upon dashing down the hallway and out the building's door, we all panicked and cried out in dismay upon realizing that Lakeisha had been unable to locate a cab. Shit. Mike and Will had taken the money from the fence's mother. It was always the Puerto Rican mothers who held on to the money of their protective sons. And it was she who was still bellowing her head off from inside of the apartment as we quickly made our way down the block. The shrill sound of her voice pressed down hard on my panic buttons, like frosted icicles tapping in unison on my every pressure point. I could only imagine what would become of us should even one of her protective sons with the sensation of vengeance vibrating through his bones decide to come out after us. Lakeisha jumped up and down, flailing her arms in the direction of every car that even slightly resembled a Lincoln gypsy cab. She beseeched Jesus to please make one of the motherfuckers stop. Finally, one did. We jumped in, drove uptown to 117th Street, copped, and laughed our heads off at the thrill of it all. Both Lakeisha and I got $350 each for our efforts. From there on, however, I could no longer accompany Bruny to the fence. They rightfully believed that she had not been involved. Since 112th Street seemed to always be the dividing point for Black Harlem, I didn't have too much to worry about if I didn't let my crazy ass cross down any further than 111th. Such was the way we functioned thereafter. I waited on 111th while Bruny continued doing business with the fence and watched my back for several weeks. It was in this manner that I destroyed my business relations with the Puerto Rican fence with whom I had enjoyed at least a one-year-long friendly relationship. Such was the essence of my life when I lived my life on the streets as a crackhead during my early twenties.

Ironically enough, it was during those same years that I scoffed at Bruny's overly promiscuous behavior, and neglected to see my own relationship with Johnny changing into one of sex for drugs. If I wasn't running Johnny's drugs somewhere for profit, then I was fucking him after a night of Hennessey and good coke. But I still didn't see any similarities between Bruny and myself. Although I can never say for sure since I was never actually present, I was repeatedly told that Bruny never had sexual intercourse for money, but instead found a way to have her penchant for sucking on lollipops pay off in dollar bills and nickel bags of crack. Thinking about what she had told me about my potential so very long ago in summer camp, I sadly realized that it was sucking dick that had become Bruny's greatest skill. Since practice makes perfect, and Bruny had lots of practice, her skills reached a level of competence unmatched by most by the time the news got out that she was wanted by a government health agency. At the time, she was staying with an alcoholic aunt in the Farragut House projects in Brooklyn. Within two weeks of having moved in, word of Bruny's competency in this skill area spread like wildfire. Niggers who smoked weed or just hung out in the doorways of the project buildings uniformly sought Bruny out every time they felt a rising heat sensation in their groin area. Until the very end, I don't believe Bruny ever needed to solicit clients herself. In addition to having her regulars, her client base was always on the rise due to word of mouth. No pun intended.

When I first learned of the fact that Bruny was being sought out by a government agency, I figured that it was either a parole officer, a BCW social worker concerning terminating her parental rights on a child that she may have bore without my being aware, or an unknown special service unit of the police. Shortly thereafter, I learned that it was the Department of Health who was in such earnest pursuit of my childhood friend. As the story goes, Bruny was infected with the HIV virus and syphilis, and was being accused of spreading her diseases rampantly across the many men who exchanged $5 for some of the best head on their side of town. The Department of Health never caught up with Bruny, but one of the men who she reportedly infected did and beat her down to a pulp. After spending a week's stay in Brooklyn Hospital, Bruny packed her meager bag and took herself back on up to the Bronx where she intermittently lived between the streets and different friends' homes for the remainder of her years. Learning about her HIV status didn't markedly impact upon any of Bruny's behavior. She continued to hit the pipe with the same force and frequency, boost whenever she could, and suck on any guy's dick that was horny, blind, and stupid enough to ask her to. That is, of course if he was willing to pay her $5 for a nickel bag of crack.

Such was the manner that I bid farewell to my teen years and entered my twenties. I stole, occasionally took advantage of opportunities in which I could trade sex for money, and was arrested on at least six occasions on different misdemeanor and felony charges. Sometimes the charges against me were dropped. Sometimes I spent a few nights in the city jail. After living the lifestyle for more than two years, I was caught boosting out of Lord & Taylor. I was high as a kite, and in my enthusiasm to reach the department store before closing, had neglected to remove my pipe and two emergency $10 bags of heroin that I had for sale purposes from my inner pocket. As the men in uniform pushed my face down on the concrete pavement outside of Lord & Taylor, I figured I might as well kiss the streets goodbye since I probably wouldn't be seeing them for a good long while. As it turned out, I admitted I used drugs in court and copped out to lesser charges. I ended up spending two months at the Women's House at Riker's Island and the next four at an in-patient drug rehabilitation program. The program referred me to an out-patient day treatment program once I completed my court-mandated six months. Instead, I became involved in more of the same that had led me through many court room's doors in the first place. At that point, I believed that things could be different the second time around. I believed that they would be different if only I'd be a little smarter and control my use of crack just a little bit better.

CHAPTER FIFTEEN

You cannot create a statue by smashing the marble with a hammer, and you cannot by force of arms release the spirit or the soul of man.
—Confucius

SOMETIMES I SIT back and wonder how I survived it all. Then I think a little bit deeper, a little bit harder, and question why Mama and Bruny didn't. At this point, I prod myself a tad bit more and reconsider. Perhaps they did in their own ways. Just differently, I guess. On the days that I permit myself to poke at such disconcerting areas of thought, I do so sparingly and with caution, as if stirring the charred embers of a fiery furnace at arms length.

These are the thoughts that surface each and every time my sponsor and I unravel more thread from my memory wheels from my days of "using." Sometimes things got so crazy and downright ugly that I don't know what veiled force motivated me to survive, urging the oxygen to continue filtering into my lungs, the blood to plough through my veins, and the ephemeral will to fight in my heart. Don't misunderstand me. I had my share of good times too—the wonderful feeling of being high, a multitude of blissful hours donning the carefree attitude of rustling daisies in a sunny meadow. There was also the insane and illogical camaraderie between myself and my addict-peers, the excitement of taking the streets by the balls and squeezing, holding on day to day, moment to moment. No, it wasn't all bad. Drugs made everything better until they made everything worse. And when things got bad, they got worse pretty quick. Progressively and insidiously. It almost felt deceptive, as if a major lover's promise had been broken. Broken, twisted, and stomped out until even the slightest shadow of it memory was obliterated. By that time, there were no more good times. Only pain, shame, anger, disappointment, and revulsion. Revulsion toward a self that was stupid enough to believe that the good times would outweigh the bad and stay around forever.

Revulsion toward a self that was cocky enough to believe that they alone had the golden grip from which the balls of the streets could not lurch free. Promises, promises, promises . . .

    I'm trying hard not to jump around too much with my storytelling. Not an easy task when my own memories are broken and fragmented, and my tolerance for crossing over all memory terrains with evenly distributed patience and care, virtually nonexistent. As I believe I recently disclosed, after learning about Bruny's exposure to the virus, I drowned out that, and every other painful fiber of my life, by losing myself in the streets, and in the various "highs" I chased from the chemicals I abused. I went on a sabbatical from my self-destructive walk during the six-month period that I was incarcerated and mandated to attend drug rehabilitation programs. As the years evolved, jail became more and more like an alternative to vacation, a respite, especially when I was only incarcerated for a few days or weeks at a time. Mandated drug programs were also like vacations, albeit of a different flavor. They were the epitome of vacations from hell. For the next few weeks, I'm going to dig deeper into the recesses of my memory to try to convey the highlights of the four years that precede my last incarceration and accompanying genuine burning desire to stay clean. Johnny, Bruny, Trevor, me—we're all in there. Characters as tragic and sad as we are real. While I'm certain that this is true, I still become confused with the "whens" and "wheres" of our times together. In my passing through of several chaotic stages during my first year of recovery, I've come to learn that the actual "whys" and "whats" become less and less relevant. For lack of a better place to begin, we'll start by going on a tour of my alternative to vacation spot—jail, namely the Women's House at Riker's Island and Albion Women's Medium Correctional Facility. These were my homes away from my home in the streets. Places where I could sleep, be fed, and share chow with friends and acquaintances. These were the places where, much like on the streets, I often needed to sell my soul.

    Never in my life had I wished that I had been born the opposite sex. Not even when I experienced the despairing and internal anguish associated with sexual abuse. While other aspects of my entity may have been considerably unbalanced on occasion, my sexual and gender identities developed quite "normally" and seemingly without event. It was only after my first extended stay at the Women's House of Detention that fanciful thoughts of being male blossomed in my head. These thoughts were solely born out of the reality that nothing, and I indubitably mean absolutely nothing, could be worse than being confined with a bunch of crazy, nasty bitches. Nothing that I had ever experienced in life, that is. First of all, remember that with few exceptions, judges and jurors are often more sympathetic and lenient toward women, particularly women with children. This is true regardless of the fact of whether they are actually of the maternal persuasion or not. This means that if you are a woman, especially a woman with one or two kids to your credit, you have to do something pretty grimy to get your ass locked up in the first place. Or, at least they have to say that you did. But, as a rule, the population of incarcerated women versus men differs from the onset. Depending on whether you are incarcerated within the inner city versus the suburbs or within a lower versus higher income community sets the stage for measuring just exactly how large this difference between the sexes can be. Second of all, without wanting to put down my own sex, the truth is that whether they are at a garden party or locked up in some penal institution, women are just some petty, not being able to mind their own business, bitches. Plain and simple. This, in addition to the fact that their urges for closeness and intimacy keeps them dipping and dabbing into lesbian relationships, makes it virtually impossible for them to ban together on the strength of one sisterhood. From what I've heard, male inmates run their own penal institutions, whereas the female inmates inadvertently have the guards do it for them.

Sisters can be nasty, dirty individuals. Especially a bunch of poor and oppressed, drugged-out, diseased sisters from the streets who are in various stages of both physical and psychological withdrawal. The person who stated that there is no place in the world that smells worse than a boy's junior high school locker room must have been a male, a sheltered male who never had the opportunity to visit the women's holding tank at Central Booking. I know I'm right because as sure as I'm sitting here sixteen months in recovery, I know that had that same person visited a women's jail house, he would have immediately recanted his statement about the unbeatable stench of a prepubescent boy's locker room.

Once I had to instigate a minor uprising when I was locked up at Central Booking in Brooklyn. This occurred during the time period that I swung in and out of one long sick episode with Trevor and still retained an artificial sense of dignity. Within the overcrowded, small dank cell, lay what was obviously a very sick crackhead whose filthy, stained stretch pants must have contained the rotten fecal combination of at least three different forms of human discharge. I was willing to bet that the woman's drawers were a breeding plant for every species of body lice and bacteria that existed. Being that I was coming down off of crack and whatever else I had put into my system, I was in no way, shape, or form feeling pathetic. Without question, I wanted that bitch out of my space. The only way one was ever prematurely removed from the holding pen was for reasons of a serious physical condition or a life threatening display of aggression. The foul-smelling woman was seemingly comatose and not presenting any aggressive threats. Since she was similarly not drawing any attention to herself with any cries of physical pain, and I was not about to get any closer to her to draw any of her diseased blood, I egotistically concluded that routine procedures would just have to be altered with regard to acceptable reasons for the immediate removal of inmates from the bull pen. Trevor and I jockeyed different ideas and strategies back and forth across the many collect phone calls that I made to his apartment. Finally, after about four phone calls and two and a half hours of having to put up with the most putrid smell imaginable, Trevor made a suggestion that I figured might actually work. Definitely one of the fringe benefits of going out with a codependent guy who was studying labor law. The other, of course, was easy access to money. Anyway, once Trevor conceived the idea, I refined it, molding it into a practical working plan to fit the circumstances. Without going into many details, I basically convinced the majority of my temporary roommates to carry on like a bunch of banshees in unison until they achieved their vocalized goal of having the beastly human figure removed. My plan was sort of a group effort version of Mama's general approach to problem solving. Anyway, it worked. Approximately fifteen minutes after the correction officers' initial empty threats about what would happen to us if we didn't shut the fuck up, two obviously extremely disgruntled officers entered the bull pen, awakened, and then at arm's length, pushed "the rotting one" out to a cell in which she could take refuge in solitary confinement. It occurs to me now that throughout the entire ordeal, I never once thought of the woman's feelings, what it must have felt like to have been her. The next day when I was sitting in one of the holding pens of the Brooklyn court house waiting to be seen by the grand jury, I overheard one court officer tell another that "the rotting one" was up on multiple charges of prostitution and solicitation. Just like me, I guess there were many others who simply did not think.

Typically, I was not as diplomatic in getting my point across in jail as I was in the case involving the worst smelling woman in the world. I fought. Not as frequently as some of my peers, but I fought. Between my fairly long-known allegiance to Johnny, my constant moving days across the ghetto neighborhoods in at least four out of the five boroughs, and my hanging out days as a very young adult in bars and clubs ingesting drugs and alcohol that made me feel as if I was drinking stars, I was pretty popular among the female contingency of street people. This meant that I was typically left alone, encountering virtually no hostility from my fellow jailhouse residents whenever I paid my regular visits. From what I've read, a member of an established sorority shares a sense of sisterhood with other members of the same sorority that she may come upon in other parts. I like to think of my experiences across the different jails of New York City from the same perspective. For the most part, I was a welcome sorority member regardless of the borough in which I found myself incarcerated.

Jail is a funny place. A woman's jail is even funnier. The Women's House of Detention at Riker's Island is the funniest. Just like in every other social community in the world, each jail has its own ambience, its own set of rules, a larger set of rules that it shares with other jails, and then despite popular belief, an even larger set that it shares with society as a whole. The jail concept, with its own interface of institutional demands and expectations, combined with the unique distribution of personalities across the inmates, correctional officers, and outside dwelling populations, all contribute to the exact flavor of each correctional institutional setting. The Women's House of Detention at Riker's Island is a prime example. Its particular flavor is derived from the combination of one of the largest inner-city political correctional administrations that ever existed. An administration comprised of an infrastructure of adjunct social service agencies, a diverse ethnic and socioeconomic mixture of female inmates of which women of color from lower income backgrounds are the most largely represented, an interesting distribution of correctional staff with a powerful union that attempts to modulate the underlying political pressures, and one of the most heterogeneous, backdrop city populations in history. The Big Apple. It's no wonder that life on the female side of the rock is such an experience.

The primary rule that I quickly adopted into my own personal guidelines shortly after I was sent to the Women's House for the first time was to always maintain your sense of self while doing your time. This was first and foremost. It basically referred to not allowing anybody or any one situation to stress you out, particularly to the point of no return. Those who required "protective custody" or ended up in the "MO" ward learned this lesson the hard way. Subtle in this primary rule lies the auxiliary message: "Use and/or manipulate whatever person or system you must in order to maintain yourself." The rules I learned in jail similarly reinforced everything that I learned during my childhood upbringing concerning shutting down my capacity to feel as needed. There are many other jail specific rules as well. Rules about snitching, preferring to stick with your own kind, getting too close to the police, and minding one's own business. As far as the sex scene in jail went, I typically didn't have to pay attention to any of the rules concerning jailhouse sexual relationships. I simply didn't have any. Perhaps this was because I continued to get high in jail, and was therefore, emotionally unavailable. Perhaps this was because I could not see myself crossing over any heterosexual lines. For whatever the reason, busting a nut and falling in love were the two last things on my mind whenever I was locked up.

I believe the most difficult part for me about the jail experience was twofold. Firstly, I could not get high when and how I wanted. Secondly, I observed so many reviled human behaviors that not even I could stand it, particularly without being high. Women can really be cruel toward other women. Human beings, in fact, can really be cruel toward other human beings. In jail, I saw so much cruelty, so much inhumanity, so much blasphemy that even I, with all my horrendous childhood experiences and immunizations, often needed to close my eyes. The only reason why I didn't leave them closed was because I feared that somebody would stab me in the back if I did. In jail, I saw some of the most vicious forms of aggression imaginable. I saw one sister impale another sister's cheek with a homemade knife because she thought she had gone into her cell. In jail, I saw one dyke bitch forcibly fist fuck a little petite Trinidadian sister with whom she had previously had beef with on the streets. In jail, I saw four correction officers, three white, one black, literally club a woman down to a pulp. I never found out why they did it. I'm not even sure that they knew. In jail, I saw women rip up other women's children's photographs out of misdirected feelings of anger and vengeance. I saw the riot squad come in and put the fear of God in the toughest, most impervious eyes on the block. In jail, I saw three sisters pull all the hair out from a white woman's head simply because she was white. I similarly saw correction officers mercilessly beat inmates simply because they were black. Sometimes they beat them simply because they were inmates and available to be beaten. In jail, I saw the purest looks of hatred in the eyes of women. Looks of hatred that were intense, unadulterated by chemical substances and distracting external forces. Looks of hate that bred reactive looks of hates. Looks of hate that had once been looks of pain, once upon a time and so very long ago.

Like anybody else who has ever spent any time to speak of being locked up, I have plenty of jail stories to share. Some are horrid. Some are actually warm and funny. Some are empty and light and meaningless, like little children's jokes. Some are substantial and deep, like anecdotes from the gods. It's no wonder that the one jail story that stands out in my mind—the one with the most significance—involves Bruny. It almost seems as if it was the will of heaven to place Bruny into my life when and where I would need her, and the lessons that accompanied her presence, the most.

I don't remember the exact year. But Bruny was still alive, I wasn't attached to Trevor yet, and I somehow remember myself being on the younger side. Lumping all of these memory factors together, plus the fact that I recall the time period as being sweltering hot, I believe we're talking about the summer of 1992, or possibly 1993. Perhaps it was 1994, but I'm inclined to think not. Some intangible part of my spirit is crying out that it was the summer of 1992, so I'm persuaded to believe that this must be the case. Intangible parts of the spirit rarely lie. When they do, they're still not lying. They're making wishes.

Whether it was in the summer of 1992 or 1993, I ended up in jail on "unlawful solicitation" and "criminal possession of controlled substances" charges. While the former were dismissed for insufficiency of evidence, the latter charges stuck, sticking me in jail for the duration of most of that long hot summer. I ended up being placed on probation with mandated out-patient substance abuse counseling at the broiling summer's end. It took about two months to fight the case from the inside. From what I can recall about the incident, I had been found just about ready to go down on this drug dealer from the Lower East Side in his car. I already had drugs on my person, although where exactly they were from and how I had gotten them into my possession eludes me at the moment. I was probably being greedy—a place where this crack sickness will often take you—and was out to get more. I knew the drug dealer I was about ready to go down on, which somehow distinguished my behavior from prostitution, at least in my mind, and thankfully, in the more fine print letters of the state law. In addition to the two vials of crack that I had in my pants' pocket, the dealer whose dick I was about ready to suck stuffed a couple more bags into my panties from underneath just as the police shone their annoying lights into his car. He walked and I was remanded to The Women's House of Detention at Riker's Island. It was there during that summer period that Bruny's song lifted my spirit to levels that it did not ascend to on its own.

We were in one of the dormitories in regular population. I had arrived first, having no idea that Bruny would follow weeks later. With the exception of the horrific heat, things were running pretty much status quo. I was "fiending" for a hit on the pipe, but as was mostly everyone else, was at least partially contented with the marijuana that I was able to get my hands on with acceptable regularity. Unlike many of my fellow sisters, my body had not as yet deteriorated to the point of no return. I still had pretty good weight on me, all of my teeth, and no visible signs of physical enervation. Hence, unlike my more unfortunate sisters, I wasn't either in bed or on the sick call line. Instead, I was mingling, spreading out the communication signals to those I knew on the other blocks about my recent arrival, and relying upon my more primitive survival senses to safely locate my drug of choice and harmoniously coexist amongst my peers. From both a hereditary and environmental point of view, I was well-prepared to negotiate all tasks quite competently.

As a result of wracking the part of my brain that hosts my memory and other executive functions, I've recalled more and more about the identities of my peers at the time. There was Loretta. Loretta was a large, loud, and lazy sister from Queens. Loretta's man sold drugs out of her apartment. This was the second time that she'd been to jail because of her man's illegal business operations. I guess there was something holding her back from learning the lesson that was obviously there for her to learn. Trish was another of my peers. Trish was a crazy basehead from Brooklyn. She was genuinely crazy. I'm not sure if she was a crazy person who started using drugs because she was crazy, or whether the drugs themselves had made her crazy. By the time we became dorm mates, however, it was evident to all of those with whom she shared any space that her elevator did not go all the way up. Trish belonged in a MICA program—a program for mentally ill, chemically addicted populations. The NYC criminal justice system just hadn't figured it out yet. Also in our midst at the time, there was the Jamaica princess from Crown Heights, Brooklyn. Like me, Princess sold and used drugs. A dangerous and very bad combination, especially if one desired to stay alive and out of jail. Princess was murdered two years later by a dealer who had given her one too many warnings about dipping and dabbing into his shit. Then there was an older sister who we called Mrs. M who had killed her preacher-husband when she observed him fondling their eight-year-old daughter. Mrs. M received three cheers from all of us for her seemingly justified heroic act. We had all heard too many stories about preachers' wives siding against their daughters after they complained about incestuous acts committed against them by their fathers. Mrs. M was definitely one of the good ones. There was also another sister. Crazy Chrissy. Crazy Chrissy wasn't really crazy. She just acted crazy. She committed armed robberies, and due to an infinite amount of apparent repressed anger and pain, behaved in a cruel, aggressive fashion toward others on a fairly regular basis. Crazy Chrissy was violent, mean, and menacing. She was the perfect television caricature of the typical female inmate. The fact that she was aware of the societal role she played only served to further entrench her negative attitude and behavior. There was also Jazzie who was from the Bronx. I had remembered Jazzie from my childhood days of living with Mama in the same building as Ms. Cathy. We shared stories from our memories about the Stinkdog and our days on the streets in the Bronx. Jazzie was a bully back then. She still was. Nothing had changed. In addition to the fact that Jazzie had developed herself quite an unsettling addiction to heroin, she still loved to get into fights. She was attracted to them and sniffed them out the way cats find mice. Quietly and efficiently. Jazzie was in jail for breaking up "a bitch's car and jaw." She couldn't remember which act she had committed first. There were at least ten other sisters in our dorm, most of whom were on the inside because of crimes related to their own use of drugs, whose faces and lives remain a blurred vision in my mind. They came and went. They are still coming.

Back in the summer of 1992 or '93, there were at least four Spanish sisters in our dorm as well. I remember them all. Just like it was yesterday. I remember two of their names. Linda was a beautiful, young Spanish sister with a crown of hair that dusted her waistline every time she as much as even slightly shifted sideward. She was sexy, with a foreign mysterious quality that haunted her about the eyes. Linda was being charged with beating her own two-year-old daughter to death. Nobody made any moves to become too chummy with Linda for a very long time. It was as if, on some maternal instinctual level, we all understood that she was guilty and sided with her deceased young. There was another Spanish sister named Melanie who, when she had learned about her husband's infidelity with her sister, had attempted to set her sister's apartment on fire with both her husband and sister in it to scorch their passionate affair for one final time at the stake. However, since Melanie's sister's apartment was not an island on to itself, and was instead housed in a building complex that contained nineteen additional apartments, and was attached to two other identical buildings on both sides, had Melanie's fire been a success, she would have been responsible for a genocide of approximately three hundred deaths. As is turned out, the fire department extinguished the fire before it had the opportunity to spread to more than three apartments. Two dogs died and two elderly people were injured. Melanie was still in one hell of a lot of trouble. We all told her that she should have shot the motherfucker in the head. There were other Spanish inmates sharing the dorm space with me that summer as well. One was an older, grandmother-age crackhead who, like me, had been brought in on "possession" charges. The other Spanish sister, the younger one, had been present when her boyfriend pulled out a gun and shot the owner of a bodega for all of the money that was in the cash register. She was Dominican and she only spoke Spanish. Nobody paid her much mind.

Finally, there were two white chicks doing time with us during that suffocating hot summer. One was middle-aged and rather slovenly in appearance. Her name was Helen. She had accidentally killed a neighbor's child when she was driving home drunk from work at about four o'clock in the afternoon. The bad news for Helen was that her license had already been revoked due to previous DWI offenses. There was also a younger and rather hip white girl named Donna who, like us, liked her drugs. She had been found with a hell of a lot of heroin and cocaine on her person, one too many times.

The above described motley of inmates periodically varied, depending upon who went to court, who went up north, and who went home. However, it was this group of women who became lodged in my memory in association with the event that occurred during the summer of 1992 or '93. In the early nineties there were many male correction officers who were assigned to work with us women. Too many. Although the NYC Department of Corrections attempted to assign a disproportionate amount of female officers to the Women's House, quite a large percentage of male officers continued to work along with the women on a regular basis. From what I heard, women had complained of being sexually molested by male correction officers for many years. Their complaints typically fell upon the deaf ears of administrative employees who, to give some of them the benefit of the doubt, were probably in denial of the fact that such events ever occurred. When reports of female inmates who had never had any visitors and had been incarcerated for several months disclosed multiple cases of first trimester pregnancies, even those administrators who preferred to remain in their typical ostrich stance with their heads buried deeply in the ground could no longer do so without repercussions of public outcry. Then, of course, there were those hundreds of sensual women who were willing sexual partners to the ethically sworn-in officers. Willing and able, to say the least. A true legacy who was housed in the Women's House at Riker's Island was "Dick 'em down Brown." Dick 'em down Brown, otherwise employed under the name of Officer Brown, was truly renowned for the amount of female inmates who he had fucked. It was estimated that he sometimes fucked at least two or three on his tour. I wonder what ever happened to Dick 'em down Brown. He is part of one of many elusive memories from my past. The fact of whether he played any critical part in my growth, was part of any grand schemes to prod me along in my evolving maturity into quasi-adulthood, still remains a question mark.

Sexual behavior in jail runs rampant—its presence so thick that its essence can be carved with a knife, albeit not so neatly and precisely. It occurs between officers and officers, officers and inmates, and inmates and inmates. It's one of those things that just is. Whether it's to our benefit or our loss, I am ill-equip to determine. It just is.

During the summer of 1992 or '93, there were at least four or five male officers who were regularly scheduled for tours on our block. If my memory serves me correctly, I was in dorm 9 at the time. The rest of the officers were women. The ethnic distribution of these employees was not so very much different from the previously described ethnic distribution of the inmates. The only difference was that whereas the captains and sergeants were typically Caucasian, the officers who manned our blocks and dormitories were almost always people of color, primarily black.

For whatever the reason that circumstances occur as they do, the time for racial tension was ripe in my dorm during that particular summer. Looking back now, I don't believe we brought this tension upon ourselves. Quite contrarily, I believe it was the correction officers who subconsciously brought it to the table and stood by with consciences with Cheshire cat smiles, as well as began to act out their more negative energies. Racial slurs began to be thrown around a hell of a lot more, particularly after we all recognized the undeniable fact that the two white women who were doing time with us were receiving preferential treatment. Although the preferential treatment doled out to them was made quite overt by the white officers, subtle traces of bias could similarly be detected with the black officers as well. More specifically, the two white girls seemed to have less pressure on them concerning what "decorations" they could append to their cubicle walls. They were also, on more than one occasion, rewarded with special "choice foods" that were brought over from the employees' kitchen. The fact that they delightfully and without hesitation shared their special foods with us was irrelevant. The tension, you see, had absolutely nothing to do with the characters of the two white women. It did, however, have everything to do with the color of their skin.

As time progressed, so did the visibility and seeming severity of the situation. One day, both Donna and Jazzie were coming off of a visit. For reasons unknown, the one who had been passed balloons of heroin must have gotten nervous toward the end of the visit and carelessly allowed one of the balloons to slip on to the floor before she reached the area in which every inch of her body would be searched and scrutinized. Another guess of mine is that whoever had sneaked in the contraband had done such a masterful job with stuffing so many plastic bags of heroin into the orifices of her body, she had dropped one extra bag on the floor due to the lack of available safe stashing space inside of her. Jazzie and Donna, apparently neither having been questioned by the police at an earlier hour, were both seriously nodding in the mess hall that night, seated at opposite ends of the large room outfitted with brightly colored plastic furniture and neon lights. It was not until shortly before the lock-in bell that Jazzie's cell was mercilessly torn apart by a substitute captain and his uniformed pawns. She was also later given a discipline ticket and moved off the block for having been identified as the obvious source of the transportation of contraband into the prison. It was later learned that two female officers, one Latina and one Caucasian, signed statements that they had witnessed Jazzie kick the balloon of drugs away from her as she was coming off of her visit. Lies were a large part of all of our lives. There was also not one among us who believed that the police were not telling lies that were as monumental as ours. What did, however, somewhat surprise us, myself included, was the institutional acceptance of the obvious transparency of the lie. Even though you know better, sometimes you just hope things are getting better—that the world is becoming a better place. When the folly behind your hopes slaps you in the face once again, you feel somewhat surprised, amongst other things. It is then that some of us stop hoping.

Needless to say that had either one of the lying officers seen Jazzie kick a small plastic item resembling a balloon immediately following her visit in actuality, they would have addressed the issue right on the spot. The fact that she had been left alone until hours later proved that their written statements were an exercise in collusion and prevarication. Additional lingering evidence involved the small detail that there were at least four other inmates present in the search area at the time, inmates of various ethnic shadings, who failed to see anything even remote to what had been described by the blatantly lying officers. I do not believe that anybody was averse to the Department of Corrections taking a stand because they had indeed slipped up on detecting either Jazzie or Donna transporting drugs during their morning visit. Hostile feelings rose amongst us because the Department of Corrections unanimously and without equivocation pointed the finger of blame directly into Jazzie's black face. As things typically work out, Jazzie was returned to our dorm a few days later. Somebody in a corrections uniform had reportedly made an error and sent her back to dorm 9 instead of to another dorm when she ran into a little social problem with the girls from dorm 7. As a result, Jazzie returned to our dorm one Friday before chow time with major attitude. Glad to see most of us, she stood in line ranting and raving about things like Jim Crow, twenty acres and a mule, and lynch mobs. Things that she really didn't know anything about, but at the same time, knew everything about.

She started referring to Donna as that washed-up, white dope fiend, more for the benefit of the officers than Donna. I still maintain that, at this point, Jazzie's anger was of a diffused and generalized quality, having virtually nothing to do with Donna personally. Her display of anger, however, persisted throughout the evening, into Saturday, and until Sunday morning when, Donna, feeling intensely dope sick from not having had even a one-on-one hit of dope for two or three days, finally staggered over to Jazzie's cubicle during one of her verbal ranting episodes, looked her directly into the face, and told her to shut the fuck up already. As such, the line of personalized anger had finally been crossed. Jazzie hollered something back to the effect that she was going to kill her fucking white ass, and then simply hauled off and punched her directly above her left ear on the side of her head. Enervated from being dope sick for so long, Jazzie's punch knocked Donna down at a sideward sprawling angle, way into the next cubicle. Before four police could wrench her off of Donna's back, her nose, ribs, and ear drum had been broken. The soul that was already lost inside the marble receptacle of addicts received but just one more injury. A mild concussion of sorts. One that never kills—just adds in pain and confusion. As a result of the one-sided brawl, Donna was placed into the infirmary and Jazzie was given but yet another ticket. Donna did not fare too poorly in the end. Being in the infirmary had its advantages. Namely, it expedited the process by which the institution played the let's-connect-the-correct-government-agencies dot game to ascertain that Donna was indeed an active client in one of New York City's Methadone Maintenance Programs and is therefore legally entitled to methadone. Since it is consistently said that being dope sick is one of the world's worst feelings, I imagine that the reward of receiving a daily methadone dosage was well worth the pain of a few broken and bruised body parts. As far as I know about what happened to Jazzie, she caught a couple more tickets and then went home. If one believes I am making light of the impact of the incident that occurred between Jazzie and Donna, I am not. I'm simply stating all of the facts for practical purposes. The fact that fragile egos chip away to nothing every time we act out other people's anger, other people's racist hostility and biases, was also a viable fact—but one that was unfortunately, for all intents and purposes, beside the point.

All hell broke loose in dorm 9 after Jazzie's assault on Donna. We started forming cliques, predominantly according to skin color. As if it was an unspoken rule, newcomers who subsequently came to dorm 9 unquestionably gravitated toward their "own kind of people," as if doing anything else would be unseemly and unnatural. The officers, without ever having to say a word, reinforced this silently accepted policy with just as much consistency as us inmates, for it was from them that the illogical concept of racism amongst us incarcerated female felons sprouted in the first place. Whether it was reality-based or fantasy-born, everybody in dorm 9 started to perceive the white and lighter-skinned Latina women as having more and better privileges and less daily harassments. Officers particularly picked on those who they believed had formed alliances with Jazzie— as if this signified any great insight into our own biased and noisome thinking. The fact that she and I had been acquaintances from way back placed me in a most unfavorable position. The fact that I was generally successful at ignoring the bullshit was, on the other hand, definitely an important strike in my favor.

In addition to our newly segregated dining and social experiences, many fights began to break out across our dorm. Fights that always involved people of differing shades of skin color. Fights that had previously been avoided. Unlike the original fight that involved Donna and Jazzie, most of the subsequent physical altercations were never observed by officers. Little battles quietly swept across every area of our incarcerated lives. Battles that sometimes completely lost sight of the greater and more significant war on hand. Battles that resembled those being fought in our greater and larger society on the outside. Crazy Chrissy went off on one of the new jack Latina girls, blackened both of her eyes and broke at least two of her teeth. Then, as if she couldn't rest with a job half done, Crazy Chrissy crawled into her area later that night and set her hair on fire. This was all because the Latina had supposedly looked at her wrong. This was all because our thinking had been seriously contaminated. Then about a day later, during one of the infamous riot squad sieges, the police lingered in Princess' area way too long for anybody's good, leaving Princess badly beaten and traumatized. This continued on and on. It affected every last one of us in a sentient, although tangential manner. Even I, the expert on wearing granite blankets over my feelings, understood just how insidiously I was being affected. Tainted by additional external sources of hate, if you will.

I finally flipped on the very same morning that Bruny was brought over to the Women's House from Central Booking. The cards, of course, were stacked in such an order that she was miraculously placed in my dorm. Dorm 9. Bruny was quite nasty looking by then. Obscenely distasteful to the visual senses. She was gaunt, shriveled, hair thinning in some places, and seemed to be partially hunched over in her posture. It was as if she had been hunched over one too many crack pipes or dicks in her lifetime and was now paying the price. Consistent with my treatment of her for the past couple of years, and rarefied by the recent reinforcement of the hate lessons that I learned in jail, I initially disregarded Bruny when I saw her huddled over her allotment of jailhouse hygiene products in the waiting area. I walked by without doing much more than slightly nod my head, as if I had casually passed a familiar passerby in the street. Her eyes momentarily lit up when they focused on my approach. As I passed her by and their momentary glimmer dimmed, so did the quickening of my repressed thudding heart.

    I had my first racially spurred fight that afternoon over phone slot time. The truth was that I had nobody to call. Especially nobody who would even consider accepting a collect call from me from jail. Picture that. However, there was this new, real light-skinned Puerto Rican chick that had recently been transferred over from another dorm with whom I was becoming increasingly pissed off with. She was one of those big-mouth princess types, well-manicured, no substance. All bullshit. She lived in Long Island, apparently with a family who was all about the drug money, and was arrested in the Bronx when she was found to be in the passenger seat of a car with enough cocaine to keep the entire South Bronx feeling nice. Despite the severity of the charges against her, the elite one, Jovanna, was confident that her hundred thousand dollar bail would be raised by her family by the end of the week, if not sooner, if she lived that long. Although the dorms typically housed sentenced inmates, Jovanna and I were both placed in dorm 9 while we were still fighting our cases. I never understood why. All I'm telling you is that I couldn't stand the bitch. She was conceited, fake, and weak. A punk bitch, if I ever saw one, perpetrating to be what she wasn't, what she could never be. Associating only with a few select Latina inmates and hip Latina officers, she generally disregarded the rest of the population, treating us with a subtle air of disdain when forced into some fleeting, meaningless exchange. Her major mistake was to believe that she could take over the phone. Once Jovanna arrived, there was no more slot time in our dorm, only Jovanna time. Like I said, me personally, I had nobody to call. I simply used slot time as an excuse to get to the greater issue on hand—my strong dislike for the new bitch in our dorm. Used what was really a mole for me, and consciously made it into a mountain. Every time that bitch was on the phone, I started to hang around her, voicing loud complaints about her abuse of slot time, about the officers' preferential treatment toward her. With each passing phone conversation, Jovanna was becoming more and more heated. I had to play my psychological warfare game correctly though. Imagine what could have happened if, out of fear or frustration, Jovanna had rushed off of the phone and handed it over in defeat. Given the truthful fact that I had nobody to call, unless I fronted that the person who I was calling was not at home, the situation could have ended up quite embarrassing for me. No, I needed to manipulate Jovanna's feelings, including her increasing contempt for me. Since the art of manipulation was one of the first lessons that I learned as a child, I successfully attained all of my goals quite well. On the same day that Bruny arrived, fortunately when there were no officers in our surrounding periphery, I got Jovanna to hiss at me through clenched teeth that I had better get the fuck out of her face. With a wide taunting grin overthrowing any other facial expressions, I looked to the left, looked to my right, and once secure that the police were otherwise occupied, grabbed the phone from her grasp and dealt her a forceful blow with it on the left side of her head. Her call was disconnected. At this point, the only thing that Jovanna could safely do to avoid a scene given that she was a punk and wouldn't think of fighting, was quietly retreat back to her cubicle area holding her head. She did. She didn't, however, forget. I knew that and so did she. In fact, all of dorm 9 did. It was only a matter of time.

Exactly how Bruny learned that Jovanna was planning on impaling my face with a homemade weapon that crudely resembled an ice pick, I'll never know. I surmise it was because Jovanna informed one of the Latina elite about her plans, who then passed the news down to one of the Latina nobodys. Bruny must have heard it from one of the nobodys. That's when Bruny looked past the limited sights that stood visibly in front of her nose. That's when Bruny acted out of a personal knowledge that there was a great forest that existed beyond the trees. That's when Bruny simply overlooked my character defects, glaring as they might have been, and exhibited a level of decency that was foreign in our surroundings. Bruny must have sneaked in a little personal goody bag of her favorite get-high when she first arrived. I knew that any drugs that she had in her possession could not have been delivered during a visit since she didn't have any. I also knew that despite her fellatio reputation on the streets, Bruny was no commissary hoe. I knew she hadn't been sucking on anybody's pussy for little goody bag rewards. Hence, I knew that it was Bruny who purposely set Jovanna up by placing her personal supply of drugs in a visible place in an area that was mutual, but was predominantly shared by Jovanna and two others. She knew that by doing this she would force the Department of Corrections to conduct a cubicle search. She also knew that this was the only way in which she, without owning any physical strength at the time, could prevent Jovanna from maiming me for life. Bruny, despite her shortcomings, always seemed to know a great deal, especially where the human heart was concerned. I often wonder if I'll ever come to know all that she knew as a strung-out crackhead in her twenties who had been dying a slow death since the day she was born.

Jovanna ended up being removed from our block that night after the search. The police found her weapon and ingeniously determined that trouble by the bucketfuls was brewing in our dorm. Jovanna was also bailed out as she had earlier expected by the week's end.

Bruny never spoke a word of the incident, nor did I ever catch her glancing at me ever so much even slightly askance. Yet, I know she was responsible for intervening on my behalf and for ultimately bringing serenity back to our discordant dorm. The reason why I was sure that it was Bruny who intervened was because there was nobody else present in our midst who would even momentarily consider sacrificing her own private drug stash in jail for another's benefit. Besides, on the very same evening that the police searched Jovanna's and her neighbors' cubicles, Bruny looked like she was feeling no pain. I guess she needed to make sure that she left no additional evidence around should her own space be searched in the process she had initiated. As sure as the tears that are welling up in my eyes, I was also certain that it was Bruny who set up Jovanna because I knew that she loved me. I may not have understood the complete definitive depth of the word, but I understood that it was from the qualities of this word that Bruny derived her strength and formulated many other ideas about people and life. Later on that night, about midnight, when the entire dorm was still feeling uneasy about the tone of their environment, she began to sing. She sung a song from the past. Our past. She sung the familiar Spanish song—the one that celebrated a love that was more spiritual than carnal. She sung the song that took us all to places we had never been, times we never knew, to a space not as yet traveled by our human hearts. Bruny, as she once did more than ten years before in a sleepaway camp for disadvantaged children, put her heart and soul into the words—the words from that sweet melody of rhapsody that tingled the senses, and with its gentle vibrations, massaged the soul. The one that, on an unconscious level, reminded us about the qualities of humanity that we shared, awakened us to the fact, that we were indeed all one people.

When Bruny's unsolicited performance ended, nothing but quiet sniffles could be heard down the long hallways. The officers did not breathe out even the slightest form of reprimand concerning her song. And then, from out of the silence, between muffled sniffles, whispers of prayer and praise could be heard pouring forth from what I figured must have been quite rusty lips. The Lord's named resounded across our dorm, as if a holy halo had been placed across it. There were sighs of relief, followed by the sounds of breathing that had been returned to more normal and peaceful levels. Then, as if preordained by a more divine presence, silence reigned forth across our small confined space again. Along time ago, Bruny told me that she could only sing when others listened with the ears of God. Once again, I saw that she knew what she was talking about.

Still, not having the nerve to utter one word in her direction, I managed to manipulate one of the kitchen staff to bring me two lollipops from the streets. I carefully wrapped them in toilet paper and placed them into her slippers at a very early hour the next morning when I was on my way to court. I wanted Bruny to know that I knew what she did for me and that I was thankful. I guess, in my own constricted way, I also wanted to show her that I loved her back. God let me know that she got my message. I was given two year's probation that day in court and never returned to the dormitory in which Bruny had played the role of celestial songbird the night before.

Shortly after my release from the Women's House, I supplemented my boosting income with money that I earned from selling drugs. I was not as yet thought of as a pathetic basehead as was so the case with many of my not so fortunate peers. This was especially true in the outskirts of the inner-city ghettos in which most occupants had not seen me at my worst. After playing around in Far Rockaway for a while, I played some of my old Bronx acquaintances and became more familiarized with circles from small-town ghettos directly above the Bronx. Ghettos that were smaller in size, but not too unlike their larger counterparts with which I was much more familiar. I swung a few quick episodes in New Rochelle and Mount Vernon, actually having grown quite sweet for the nigger I rolled with in New Rochelle, and then settled to work a comparatively small, high-rise set of projects in the southern part of Yonkers. Namely, the School Street projects—home of the infamous DMX. I opted to work out of School Street primarily because my own little crack habit was unknown in those parts. The facts that there were plenty of "fiending" addicts, the price of heroin $5 more than one would typically find within the five boroughs, and I had luckily chanced upon a brother that adored the shit out of me and trusted me with his merchandise, concretized my decision as well. At this point during my active addictive years, my brain had not as yet deteriorated to the extent that it could not recognize a ripe opportunity when it was staring me directly in the face. It similarly registered that an attempt to sell crack on my part would be the epitome of a travesty of errors. Hence, I stuck with the plan of selling heroin. It was a lot less of a temptation than having multiple bags of crack sitting inside of my pants' linings, absorbing the heat from my legs.

My routine was regular and simple. I spent the majority of my week sleeping in a crack house on the sixth floor of one of the project buildings on School Street. The apartment supposedly belonged to "a cousin" of the guy who adored the shit out of me. The guy who sent me downstairs at about seven thirty every morning, and would then re-up my pockets with drugs whenever the distribution of drugs and money became uneven in favor of the money. The guy who, despite his developing habit of the intranasal use of heroin, used to fuck my brains out every chance he got on his cousin's mattress that stood alone, an isolated form, in the back of his cousin's apartment. The guy who I can't seem to remember by name right now, though it's definitely going to come to me, I'm sure. When I tired of the routine and desired to go off on my own little private run, I told "what's his name" that I had to go spend some time with my dying mother and that I would definitely be back. Then I'd go to the Bronx, Manhattan, or Brooklyn, although it was usually the Bronx, and stay with "whoever" else. I'd get high as a motherfucker off some "crack," staying on the pipe with an unprecedented tenacity for at least two days. If I hadn't had enough yet, I might hit a department store and do "a little shopping," and then run back to wherever I was guaranteed the quickest hit.

At times, I would then stay on the pipe for at least another day straight. Somehow, I'd manage to get on the 6 train, take it to the last stop, wait for the bus to Getty Square, and trudge back all the way uphill to School Street. If I was lucky, "what's his name" would permit me to crash on the mattress undisturbed for about twelve hours before nudging me to either suck his dick or go on out and make some money downstairs. That twelve hours of sleep would sometimes be the only real sleep that I'd get all week. Don't ask me how I survived because I truly do not know. It's as if some presence has always been there to buffet my falls. All none withstanding, I've been very lucky.

I continued living in and out of this crazy life with "what's his name" for a while. One day, however, when I declared like usual that I was going to check on my sick and dying mother, but would definitely be back, I lied. I knew when I said it that I wasn't coming back. I knew I'd probably never see "what's his name" again. Of course, I'll never know exactly what he thought about my permanent disappearance. I'm uncertain whether he figured that my mother died and I decided to stay, that I died, that I ran off with another lover, or whether I was more of a sick and suffering addict than I had let on and I was merely behaving like one. At any rate, it was the latter line of reasoning that was correct. I simply wanted a change, had no emotional attachments to any human being, including myself, and had manipulated an even better living arrangement on the Lower East Side with these two Chinese guys who sold weed and cocaine, and a variety of different colored pills for the white people. I was to live there, use my smarts to help hold it down, help out with the business, and bring in a little extra cash every now and then from freelancing as a booster. Who was I to look a gift horse in the mouth? Especially two gift horses that were too stupid to know that my reeling habit left me no choice but to dip and dab into their products and profits quite frequently. No problem, man. This arrangement lasted for about four or five months. Then one day, as I was about to enter the corridor of the building, the apartment was raided. Despite the fact that the police knew that I was down with the chinks, I fortunately had nothing more than a tray bag of weed and an empty pipe in my pocket. I spent about three weeks back in the Women's House due to the fact that I had violated my probation, but was then released. While on the Rock, I never made it out of the receiving building—building 2. It felt like I had gone on vacation to rest up a bit with the ladies before I found myself back on the streets and running the same frantic race again. The race that I didn't ever even come close to winning. Propelled by the undulating effects of chemical substances and a lifetime of learned, self-destructive behaviors, I pushed on. A blind, but dutiful contestant.

Addicts win the prize for being incredibly compulsive people. We practically spend every waking hour obsessing about some aspect of some compulsive need, which more often than not, we contrived and reinforced on our own. At the time we cross that line within the disease of addictions—that windy insidious bridge that leads us into no man's land—we lose our will, our control over our compulsive behavior and thoughts, control over our own lives. This is what is referred to in the Anonymous Self-help Groups' First Step—"we admitted that we were powerless over . . ." Although I probably lost my ability to modulate my own behavior during my teens, the concept that I could not stop myself from what I was doing had never crossed my mind. Not even for a fraction of a moment. The idea that I was "an addict" was an even more foreign notion. I reserved such classifications for people like Mama, people like Bruny, people that slept in the street and begged for money, people that would fuck anybody or anything anyway for a teeny bag filled with their drug of choice, people that didn't look like me when I happened to look at my reflection in the mirror. I sold myself on the delusion that I did what I did because I wanted to, convinced myself that I stayed in the race because it was fun. Although that little part of us that absolutely refuses to buy into our tales of denial occasionally gnawed at my conscience with an annoying whispering voice of reason, I played deaf and continued to ride the merry-go-round of denial.

If anybody ever were to ask me to identify the very first time I had the smallest glimpse of insight into my own sick behavior, I'd have said that it occurred during the one-month period that I was placed back on probation and then mandated to attend out-patient treatment services again, directly after the police raided the chinks' apartment. After several years of resisting forming any sort of a meaningful relationship with a therapist since my experience back in the adolescent treatment facility, I actually found myself warming up to this older, gawky New Age brother to whom I had been assigned. He was as straight as a sewing needle, obviously skilled in his ability to cautiously pierce through my walls of defense and begin to weave a new tapestry of thoughts in my confused mind. As birdlike and strange as he was, Mr. Pat definitely could have been the father figure that I never had. The problem was that after having met with me on about eight different occasions, I resisted his verbal confrontations concerning my continued active use of drugs. Having never had practice with effectively coping with positive criticism from a loving authority figure, I did what most severely disturbed teens from dysfunctional homes do when limits are placed on their behavior. I fled. Ran away from home. Better to have fond memories of a loving dad than stick around to chance anger and rejection. As compared to "fight," the option of "flight" continued to be viewed by me as the preferential alternative. I said "fuck it" to treatment again, forgot about Mr. Pat, and choreographed yet another dance to entertain my addiction. I manipulated myself through an approximate two-year-long relationship with a man named Trevor. A man who I immediately inferred had ample money, sufficient security and stability in his life, and an unconscious need to hook up with somebody like me. Trevor, a man who I later understood, was probably just as sick as me. Water ascends to its own level. Many of us seek out people who will inevitably drown us. Trevor was one of these people.

CHAPTER SIXTEEN

*The trials of life are not to make us fail
But to see how far we can fly.*

—Unknown

SINCE STARTING MY recovery process, I've learned that I've played the role of Trevor in the lives of others on more than one occasion—the first time having been in my relationship with Mama, before I even understood that we had one. The blatantly obvious time, having been in my frenzied relationship with Johnny, after I misunderstood everything. At the time, you couldn't tell me that Trevor wasn't my complete opposite. Couldn't convince me that he wasn't a foreigner from some unidentified planet. A counterpole. As opposite as fire from water, as disparate as night from day. These were my erroneous beliefs, misconceptions all stemming from a lost soul who, had she had the courage to peer squarely at her own face in the mirror, would have noticed that her own character's shrouded reflection was one and the same with Trevor's, only inverted at the time being.

I met Trevor one night outside of a night club called Perks in Harlem. Johnny, who was supposed to have met me outside of the club at one in the morning, had stood me up. After futilely waiting up until about two, with a spurned rag doll's heart and a wilting magenta smile splashed across my face, I hoisted myself off of the car on which I had been leaning and began to inconspicuously check out my appearance in the car window's shadowy charcoal reflection. In reality, I was merely buying time to figure out where, and from who, I could get my next quickest high. And then, as if he appeared from the mist of a crackhead's most savory dream, up stepped Trevor. His reflection became visible behind mine in the car's tinted window, obscured and elongated by the scientific phenomenon of refraction and the streets' glittering lights. Bingo, I had hit the jackpot.

"I've been watching you."

I turned around. "Oh."

"Yes. I've been waiting on a parking spot for about twenty minutes and every time I'd circle the block, there you'd be, just as pretty and statuesque as the time before." He smiled.

Not knowing the definition of statuesque, I quietly thought he was trying to be smart or something and was calling me a statue. When I opened my mouth to start to tell him something about himself, his smile and my resourceful intuition intervened and closed it for me.

"Well, thank you." I thought hard, but quickly. Think long, think wrong. "That was very kind of you." Go Victoria, I was just too proud of myself. "Uh, did you find a good parking spot?"

"I sure did." He smiled again and pointed across the street. A black new and shiny Acura. You go girl.

"Would you mind my asking what such a lovely young lady is doing outside on the street so long at this late hour?" Oh brother, if he thinks this is long and late, he ain't seen nothing yet.

Meanwhile, I started peeping the threads. Chic. Classy. Cream-colored Italian linen. Designer shoes. Well, all right.

"My girlfriend Flo seems to have stood me up. Her son, he's three you know and suffers from asthma. Probably got worse." Did I say that correctly? Grammatically, I mean. Easy Vic, easy. Cross 'dem t's and dot 'dem i's.

"Oh, that's terrible. It's so sad when little children suffer. Such a shame. Have you called? How is he now?"

Shit. "Uh, now . . . Oh, I don't know. Nobody home, you know, light's out kind of thing." Boy, was I sounding dumb? "Probably in the emergency room. In the emergency room at the hospital." As if there was another. Breathe.

"Of course."

"Yes, of course." Breathe again.

"Well, uh, if things appear to be under control with your friend's son and you'd like some company and a drink, I'd love for you to be my date tonight."

Eyebrows raise, jaw drops. Then I catch myself.

"My date?" quizzically and lacking in desired finesse.

"Sure, my date. Is there a problem? Are you married or otherwise seriously involved?" He smiled with a smile that was as smooth as butter, or at least he thought he did.

"Oh, no." Nervous laughter. "No serious involvements." I tried to pitch him a demure smile as I internally bemused whether Johnny and myself qualified as an otherwise serious relationship. He caught it.

"Well then." The man, who within the next few moments politely introduced himself as Trevor—Mr. Trevor Clark, offered me his arm and led me into Perks. And they say miracles only happened on Thirty-fourth Street. The stage was set.

All the props were present. One can always find an available audience. The only thing left was for the characters to act. And act they did. Why not? They had rehearsed the script throughout their lives.

By the evening's end, I surreptitiously learned that Mr. Trevor Clark, who was twenty-six, came from a middle class home in White Plains, New York, graduated at the top of his New York University class, and was currently attending Columbia University Law School. He had a special interest in labor law. In addition to the obvious fact that he came from a wealthy family, Trevor worked part-time in a moderately sized law firm in downtown Manhattan. He lived in a nice, quaint section of Gramercy Park as well. What he failed to tell me was that his mother had died of cirrhosis of the liver when he was ten. He similarly did not tell me that the woman with whom he had been raised, the one who was universally referred to as "mom" by Trevor and all of his siblings, was really his stepmother. I found out anyway. His behaviors screamed the truth, and my dysfunctional character accurately interpreted the screams.

Being in a topsy-turvy relationship with Trevor made me question the concept of love. Aside from Ms. Cathy's and Jose "el salvaje's" torrid love affair, and what I had seen on television, I knew nothing about love between a man and a woman at all. At least I knew enough to know that. The intensity, the drama, the passion, the laughter, and the tears. Surely love was the title of our story, our bond's crowning glory, our purpose and our essence. Surely what Trevor and I shared was true love. Or so this is what I thought so very long ago. Today, I'd be quite hesitant to make such a sure statement. Today, I'd have to think again.

Trevor didn't know that I was a sick and suffering addict when he first met me. I hid it well. He learned about my sickness first hand across the time period of the first six months of our relationship. Then he just wallowed in it. For the first three months, I managed to keep everything but my alcohol consumption a secret from him. He'd been around me plenty when I was under the influence of other chemicals including the Big "C." He just never noticed. Didn't want to, maybe couldn't. After the passing of an entire season when I just couldn't help myself anymore, knowing full well also that the coast was actually quite clear, I nonchalantly laid out a line of cocaine across Trevor's lacquered living-room coffee table one Saturday evening and put my nose to the straw. Initially, Trevor was mortified.

"What the hell is that? Victoria, what in God's name are you doing?"

I looked up at Trevor, looked at my cut straw, looked at the white powdery line of cocaine on his table, and looked at Trevor once more, although slightly askance with a cocked eye this second time. In a rather sarcastic tone, I responded, "God has absolutely nothing to do with it. What do you think I'm doing? I'm doing what it looks like I'm doing. Now it looks like I'm doing a line of cocaine, doesn't it?" I was being abusive and hurtful and intimidating and I knew it.

"But. But why?"

"Oh, I don't know. Why not? Want some?"

An instantaneous rapid negative shaking of the head.

"Trevor, baby, I love you, and you know that. Look, if it bothers you, I could leave early tonight and come back tomorrow. Would that be better for you?"

Still mortified. More so now, at least this is what I thought. Trevor was also scared. Scared with that raw, gut-level type of fear of abandonment that immobilizes the heart and sucks out the air from inside you. A gut level fear that desperate lovers share many stories about.

"No, no, stay. At least I can make sure that you don't suffer from any bad trips or physical reactions to that stuff. God, Victoria." An exasperated sigh.

I completed my two lines of cocaine, allowed the effects to slip over me as easily as a silk night gown and encouraged Trevor to make wild, unharnessed love to me all night long. I stood smug in my confidence that I had won the first battle. Only at this point, I had no idea what the war was about, or who or what I was fighting for. Truthfully, I still don't. Not completely. I do know that about one month after the living room cocaine incident, Trevor caught me on the pipe in his bathroom at about five in the morning. Two robberies, several awkward and embarrassing moments, one arrest, and dozens of visible crack vials later, Trevor realized that I was in trouble. That I might actually be suffering from a drug addiction. Abstemious with life's truths to the end.

I often wondered why Trevor stayed with me, why he put up with all of my shit. He was smart, handsome, financially secure, socially popular, and on his way to becoming a lawyer. A successful one. At least he had all of these things going for him before he met me. He could have had any number of women, beautiful, educated, or otherwise desirable, but instead he stayed with the likes of me. Not only in the beginning of our dance together when the going was good and we were both basically dancing to similar beats, but also when the shit hit the fan and we slam-danced and spun on our heads in different directions as well. At first I was careful. Tried to mask as much of the madness as I could. Then one day, without realizing that we both were equally responsible for the choreography of a dance that had already been set into motion, I started not to care. Slipped into an apathetic mode and developed a real serious case of the "fuck-its." At this juncture, I didn't care about what Trevor knew, didn't know, or found out about me. I didn't give a fuck about my guilt with the downs in our relationship, his demeanor, or his life. Regardless of what empty threats he occasionally shot in my direction, I could tell that Trevor was along for the ride, the deeper haul. To put it simply, Trevor seemed to "fiend" me almost as much as I "fiended" the pipe. Maybe more. He was strung out to say the least. I had found a hope fiend, not understanding that I had been in the market for one all along.

The first thing that Trevor did when he learned about my relationship with cocaine, and later crack, was minimize it. Since he wasn't crazy and one couldn't totally deny another's use of drugs when they did them right in front of them, he simply downplayed my use, neatly categorizing it as "experimental." I believe his defense mechanism of denial wore thin around the same time period that he happened to be missing fairly large sums of money from his wallet, twice in a row. It was then that Trevor allowed himself to concede that I, at times, somewhat overindulged in the use of drugs for "recreational purposes." I, who on one level, similarly denied the intensity of my relationship with drugs, was quite pleased to minimize its existence. Trevor just helped me do that which I had begun to have a difficult time doing for myself.

Crazy as it may seem, Trevor didn't acknowledge that I was suffering from an uncompromising addiction to crack until I told him I was, from Manhattan Central booking when I called him collect to implore that he hire me a lawyer, bail me out after I was indicted on the following day, and humbly apologize for taking $50 out of his wallet before sneaking out of his bed and his apartment in the middle of the night the day before. If my memory serves me correctly, this time around I had been arrested on "petty larceny" and "drug possession" charges. Although still not believing them myself, once I coined the terms "drug addiction" and "disease" with Trevor, they became the mantra of his new mission. His mission to get me clean off of drugs. His mission to make me sane. Fix me. Constantly lying through my teeth and repeating quite the contrary, I was no way willing to be fixed. Especially then, when Trevor answered my every beck and call, and buffeted my falls.

Trevor tapped into unchartered reservoirs of emotional energy, and seemingly with little effort, dusted off a second-hand super hero cape and rose to the occasion to play the role of my personal savior. He had so many consultations with drug-related emergency room hotlines and treatment programs that I believe he was on a first-name basis with most of the counselors. The crucial point is that he had significantly more than I, which was no wondrous accomplishment considering that I had had none.

Directly after Trevor bailed me out of jail and arranged for a private lawyer, my desire to enter a long-term treatment program miraculously lost its initial fervor. Trevor and I, we went on many merry-go-rounds. The first was "It's not that bad and I can really do this by myself." By the way, I believed that at the time. That was probably one of the few statements that I wasn't lying about. Secondly, I began to make false promises about when I would be starting the treatment programs. After Christmas. After Valentine's Day. After my birthday. When hell freezes over. Looking back now, I don't know if I believed my own lies and false promises or not. Finally, when Trevor had my back up against the wall because I had committed some major transgression (i.e., being arrested again, robbing him, etc.), I actually allowed myself to be led by the hand and signed into some of his well-researched programs. I believed the longest I ever managed to stay in one was for about three days. Things got kind of hectic after that. It goes without saying that I uncovered each and every one of the programs' flaws. Flaws that Trevor hadn't detected, or hadn't considered to be flaws, while so diligently researching the programs that he later led me to by the hand. Once I uncovered flaws, I bellowed and whined, manipulating Trevor to simultaneously suffer for each of the program's flaws that he had so absentmindedly failed to detect. Flaws like the unpalatable food. The low lives with whom I had to share intimate space. The rigidity of the rules. The lack of phone privileges. The list went on and on. In the end, I usually had Trevor apologizing to me for his oversights. Once I was released on bail this time, while I knew that he went secretly off on another mission to locate the ideal program for me, I managed to keep him and his programs at bay for at least a couple of weeks.

Trevor loved me. He told me so. He told me directly and definitively, as well as in so many words. He told me in soft pleading hushes. I believed Trevor. Why shouldn't I have? Nobody had ever stuck by me like he did. Nobody had ever tolerated so much. Nobody ever put me before their own selves. Why shouldn't I have believed Trevor? He was my gallant knight in shining armor. My gallant knight who had come to rescue me from my own hand-made torturous castle while his coward spirit raged on battling internal wars.

I had no reason not to believe in Trevor's love, except one. One lonesome clue that defied a genuine loving essence. One night, after a one-month period in which I had been honestly attempting to temper my indulgence with all drugs, Trevor and I had a silly argument. A meaningless lover's quarrel, as most normal couples typically do. I, however, not being normal and having no drugs in my system to quell my undulating pangs of pain, became fixated on a childhood memory involving the color blue. I asked Trevor to tell me what color of the chromatic spectrum best represented the substance of his love for me. Believing that I was being silly, he waved off my request with as much interest as a person does to a nagging fly. When I asked again, this time that much more intensely and urgently, he failed to attend to any of my emotional cues and stubbornly, if not rudely, refused. A flashing glimpse of the color blue entered my memory's panorama. This is when something deep inside caused me to doubt the veracity of Trevor's declared love. I snuck out of his apartment that night, his lap top computer cradled under my arm, in search of the closest obliging dealer.

When I think back on the times that I spent with Trevor, I think about the passing time as lunacy evolving. It was as if on a psychiatric scale, our relationship's neurosis had developed into a full-blown psychosis. The sicker it got, the tighter Trevor dug his heels in and hung on, the more afraid he became of standing up for what I thought he once believed in. Floating with the current of fury, Trevor was going down with the ship in slow motion.

Backing up just a bit, I don't want to minimize the initial effects that my blatantly unconcealed use of drugs had on Trevor's serenity. He was crazed. While he attempted to deny and minimize the existence of the problem, Trevor was simultaneously driven to constricted fits of hysteria. He became worried, suffered from insomnia, and became jumpy and thinner, with a visible occasional twitch near the right side of his neck. Whether this took a toll on his work or school performance, I don't know. Aside from indulging in complaint binges on occasion, Trevor never discussed his weaknesses, not with me anyway. Things became the most visibly hectic after he acknowledged that there actually was an active disease that spurred most of my insane behavior. He took full responsibility for its cure, leaving me completely off the hook. If the stark exposure of my drug use contributed to a detectable slight nervous condition, my penchant for stealing put Trevor right over the edge. For reasons that I am still completely unaware, I used to steal, frequently and unabashed, every chance I got, including when I was in Trevor's presence. Poor Trevor and I would return from the local supermarket, my purse and wide pants' pockets full of unnecessary comestibles that I had stolen for "who knows what reason." Trevor would have bought me any food that my little heart desired, but instead I stole whenever I could get away with it on principle alone. This drove Trevor, the aspiring lawyer, mad—a point which he excitedly reiterated and droned on about time after time after time. Trevor was most afraid of my being caught in his presence—a shameful situation for any law-abiding citizen. Imagine my handsome Mr. Clark from the firm being accused of being an accomplice in a tuna fish robbery from the local supermarket, or perhaps, an accomplice in the theft of Tylenol from CVS. Indeed, Trevor had a great deal to be concerned about.

I believe that I, "fiending" for a quick fix on the pipe one day, misjudged Trevor's patience and tolerance threshold, and in doing so, almost got myself booted out the door of his previously welcoming abode. As calculating and experienced as I had become, this incident pushed him too abruptly and violently over the edge. We had been together for about eight months by then. Trevor had already gotten wind of the fact that there might be a blast from my past—namely Johnny—making his way back on to the horizon. A seasoned predator once again in search of its vulnerable prey. Already disgruntled and bristling, Trevor began his all too familiar chant.

"I don't know why I take this shit. Now I have to accept your ex-boyfriend into this already horrible scene. I don't think so. You won't go into any treatment programs. I can't deal with this shit anymore, Victoria, I'm telling you, I just can't take it no more."

I looked at him curiously and askance.

"Oh, Victoria, please. Miss Perfect. OK, you won't stay in a treatment program. You won't listen to anybody—not to anybody who is trying to help you anyway. You take my money, take my things. I can't sleep anymore, worrying about you, worrying about my things. You're killing me Victoria, really killing me."

A wistful sigh.

"Are you listening? Are you all right, sweetheart? You're not thinking about leaving again, leaving to go get high or see that guy? Johnny what's his name? Victoria, baby, I know I've asked you before, but are you sure that you didn't get back with him, sleep with him or something?"

It went on and on, continuing until he wore himself out, I wore him out by initiating a fervent lovemaking session, or I left. The second option was the most viable if I was in need of anything, if I wanted anything from him. It was also the most unctuous. The third option was the easiest. Addicts are inclined to go with the most easy. If left with the alternatives of fight or flight, we run like hell. I misinterpreted where Trevor's head was on that particular night, just exactly how much pressure I could place on his shoulders, and skipped out. I didn't steal anything from him on this particular occasion. Trevor had taken to bringing his wallet into the bathroom with him when he showered. He had done so on this particular occasion. While this one desperate maneuver on his part didn't prevent me from robbing any other of his apartment valuables when he was in the shower, it did remind me that Trevor was on the defense, cautioning me to tread lightly for awhile. I obliged this flash of a premonition and left without stealing anything from him that night. However, as with most addicts, my thinking stopped short directly thereafter. As soon as I left Trevor's comfortable, warm abode, I put him and everything having to do with him out of my mind. I had to. I was on a copping mission and I had to keep the focus. I went uptown on the prowl, found Johnny, got high, and fucked him. It was then that I vaguely remembered that I had something important to do with Trevor on the following day. Oh shit. That was it. I had to go with him to his sister's house for a family dinner in honor of Trevor's father's birthday.

Trevor's sister, an elementary school teacher, lived with her blue-suit husband and two children in an upscale brownstone in Brooklyn Heights. A neighborhood that I previously hadn't known existed before we attended our first family gathering there together. While the kids, both cute and early elementary school age, were all right, Trevor's sister and brother-in-law were both snobs. His brother-in-law related to most as if he had a stick permanently lodged up his ass, while his sister made the pejorative term "Oreo cookie" assume deeper layers of significance. His father and stepmother, while seemingly slightly overprotective and meddlesome, were basically wholesome, decent people. As for the additional visiting masses that traversed through the door jambs of family functions, I didn't pay them too much mind. I already had way too much on my plate and was feeling quite overwhelmed.

Dinner was scheduled for four. I called Trevor collect at three thirty. I knew he would be waiting by the phone. Frantically, he asked me where I was. When I responded, he unleashed such a moan that I was certain I'd feel its vibrations from where I was standing in Harlem. I stopped breathing for a moment and waited for the counter plates to rattle from within the luncheonette that I was standing in front of.

"Trevor, Trevor, please baby. Yes I know, please baby listen, you right, you right, you got that, but just listen, I love you. I'll be there. It doesn't take that long to travel from the Bronx to Brooklyn. I'm right in front of the 6 train now. Baby, if you'd just let me get off this phone, I could meet you there by five."

More expatiation. Less moans.

"Yes, I know the address. Baby. Baby, I've been there before. Remember? I won't screw up again. Just give me another chance, okay? Trevor, I love you, just one more chance."

More whining. Deep exhales of breath, identifying the unquestionable presence of an underlying exasperation.

"I swear, baby. You know I love you. Besides, I wouldn't miss your father's birthday for the world. No, no, I wasn't with Johnny last night. I was with Bruny in the Bronx. Yes, I swear. I swear on my dead mother. Can I go now?"

A final display of distress.

"Yes, Trevor, I know. Yes, I'll be safe. No, I'm not high. Trevor, believe me, I'm not hurt or sick. I'II see you at five. I'm leaving now. Love ya' baby, bye."

The simultaneous clicks of telephone receivers from opposite sides of New York City. I was high as hell.

I arrived at Trevor's sister's house at seven o'clock. I had several more hits on the stem that I wanted to take advantage of before embarking on my southern journey on the iron horse. I was wearing the same clothes that I had left out of Trevor's crib with the evening before. My hair was unruly and unkempt. I wonder if I had also smelled. Not having any idea which brownstone Trevor's sister lived in exactly, I had to beep him about five different times to get descriptive directions. In addition to the fact that I was so high that I accidentally kept putting in the wrong phone numbers, I was so high that I forgot the directions he had just provided me with moments before.

Trevor wore his thinning patience on his sleeve—the one that I could only imagine through the phone, the one that was evident despite the clamor of his sister's guests in the background. I was sure he was going to reach his hand through his sleeve through the phone to strangle me when I ran out of quarters and called his sister's house collect. My luck, Trevor's seven-year-old niece picked up the phone and beckoned her mother, "Mommy, the operator lady wants to know if you want to talk to Victoria. She says it's a collect call from Victoria. Mommy, who's Victoria?"

Trevor later reaffirmed that the phone incident had qualified as one of the most embarrassing moments in his life. He said it so flatly that I don't believe he fabricated any part of the story about how the entire room of people turned around to look at him all at once. I hadn't done it on purpose you know, but then again, I never did.

The madness didn't stop when I arrived at what appeared to be quite a pleasant family gathering. Trevor looked as nervous as hell. More nervous than an expectant father. Had he been wearing boots, he would have been shaking in them. While being taken by the arm and politely introduced to unfamiliar faces, at every available moment, Trevor leaned into my ear and hissed "Why don't you excuse yourself to go to the bathroom and fix your hair? I'm going to kill you, Victoria. This time I'm really pissed."

More smiles and stares.

With the exception of my rambunctious rough housing with Trevor's sister's children, he didn't verbally chastise me at any other point during the actual gathering. I tried to make myself scarce when I had the chance. At first I went to the bathroom to hide out for a while. Then I started searching for tucked away chemical pleasures in the medicine cabinet. Then I deduced that I could steal myself away from the action of the party in the part of the house where it was less populated without anybody noticing my absence. I really liked the fried chicken that Trevor's sister had set out buffet style in the living room. When the masses all temporarily moved in the direction of his sister's room to admire her ballet recital trophies, I made a mad dash for the meat trays and, as quickly as I could, stashed chicken wings and beef tips into my pocketbook after carelessly wrapping them in napkins. Trevor caught me after I had already managed to pilfer at least two pounds of cooked meat, startling me so that he caused me to drop a greasy barbecued rib on his sister's cream-colored plush carpet.

More wondrous stares and additional shameful moments. To this day, I possess a vivid visual image of Trevor sucking in air and brandishing pork rib tips in the air when he discovered my compact butcher shop once we got back to his apartment. I believe the worst, however, was when Trevor received that expected phone call the next day. The last one in a series that started out from his sister's house and went back and forth to all of his family members before stopping at his home. Much familial discussion concerning diplomacy and propriety had gone into this phone call. In the end it was decided that Trevor's stepmother would be the one to query ever so politely whether there was any small remote possibility that his girlfriend could have had his sister's pearl necklace accidentally slip into her pocketbook. That's when Trevor blew up, told me to leave, and would not speak to me for an entire two days. That is, until I called him collect three times in a row, a small tiny voice partially drowned out by the operator's, begging to have my call accepted.

Things stayed hectic in my life during that time period, albeit softened slightly by the presence of my imitation guardian angel—Trevor. He continued to function on the outside, meeting the minimal standards set for public consumption. At the same time, Trevor was socially isolating, depressed, and your basic nervous wreck. Having me for a girlfriend, Trevor was lucky if he was able to catch three hours of sleep a day. I continued to function like a crazy person, growing more and more foolish by the day. Increasingly self-centered by the second. I engaged in so much unacceptable, deranged behavior that I can't even remember it all. Probably don't want to. But, just to provide my avid reader with a taste of life with Victoria, the high-maintenance, active addict, I'll try to construe a list that vaguely matches the correct sequence of events.

I robbed Trevor's sister's pearl necklace on the day of his father's birthday party. I also robbed about $15 out of two women's purses that they had placed in trust in Trevor's sister's bedroom. We never received any complaints about these two minor thefts. No phone calls from anxious relatives in the middle of the night. Maybe they hadn't noticed or didn't want to make an embarrassing situation more embarrassing. Trevor made sure that I did not contribute to any more faux pas within his immediate family circle. I was, instantaneously and permanently, banned from all additional family functions. Big deal. If this exemplified the severity of punishments that he'd dole out for my poor social conduct, I'd gladly take the heat.

I somehow managed to exhibit about one week of fairly decent behavior after Trevor graciously accepted me back into his life. Then I got arrested for assaulting two dickhead, drunk yuppies in midtown Manhattan when they attempted to pick me up. As soon as I was released, I really pulled a fast one. Moments after I was released on $5,000 bail, I excused myself for a moment and ducked into a luncheonette to supposedly use the bathroom. When I was certain that his breathing had relaxed some, and was not focusing on any possible premeditated "escapes" at the moment, I ran through the restaurant's small cooking quarters and flew out the back door. Bifurcated freedom. I ran to the nearest train station, jumped the turn style, and headed uptown to get high.

Two days later at about one o'clock in the morning, I slowly made my way back downtown. Although I can't tell you why exactly, I ended up prowling through Stuyvesant Park in Manhattan's lower end. I came upon a dope fiend. He was male, I believe. He was seated on a park bench beneath a tree's transient shadows, appearing almost comatose and in a very serious nod. One of those nods from which some drift off into eternal slumber. I quickly shook off thoughts of Mama, as abruptly as another might blink an eye, and dug his pockets. He had one discolored, linty lifesaver, a flyer announcing the location of sexy Sally, and thirty-four cents. I kept the mint and the money. A thought surfaced as I walked away from the shapeless figure that could have most certainly been dangling before death's door. I stepped back, bent down to the level of his ear, and yelled "Stay away from the light." Then I stepped away, never knowing if he did. Beveled warnings.

After about two weeks of the typical ups and downs that characterized our existence together, the fury of mad winds rushed beneath my wings once more and swept me off headlong into another series of insensible, insane events. It all started out with me boasting and bragging with my get-high crew during one of my multiple quick departures to the Bronx. There were a group of us who used to get high together: Denice, Debbie, and Bianca. Bruny joined us on occasion as well. She looked real bad by then. For whatever reason, I made a conscious effort to stay away from her as often as possible. There was no denying, however, that she was one of us. At this point, only mildly different from any one of us, myself included. It feels so alien to have such vivid images of my old get-high crew sprout from my memory's pores. Denice, more affectionately known as Niecy, was only seventeen years old. God, I loved her. She was so much fun, so loud, so crazy. Niecy was a stoned crackhead. Don't let her age fool you. She'd seen more, and been around as many blocks, as most of us. Poor Niecy. A year later, she took a stab at trying to clean herself up, did good for about six months, and then had a tussle with a gun with her boyfriend when he tried to kill her in a club. The gun went off and killed him instead. She got twenty-five to life. Bianca was about thirty and basically homeless. She lived in and out of an apartment whose primary tenant sublet space to undomiciled crackheads. In these situations, sometimes the old-timers who lived in the apartment would attempt to intimidate the newcomers into paying them "rent" as well. Bianca wasn't having any of that. She was a seasoned hooker who had a pretty thriving business on Thirty-first Street in Manhattan on the far West Side. Debbie was just a nut. Pure and simple. I later heard that in the midst of robbing a guy for crack, she strangled him to death. I assume she's still her same insane self up North. I spent the most time with Debbie. I liked to run, and Debbie ran all the time. Ran the streets like a pro, from one agitated situation to another. We shot forth like skinny rockets propelled by our addictions at similar speeds. As for Bruny, well, let's just say you already know mostly everything about her. Just double it.

When I was off on my adventures away from Trevor and not with Johnny, I was running the streets and getting high with my home girls. In those days, this qualified as what I would consider "mad fun." We used to go into the many Bronx and Harlem projects and rob drug dealers of their stashed goods. I had learned that many street pharmacists used to stash their shit in hallways, sometimes behind poles, sometimes in project stairwells, and sometimes wrapped up tightly in squashed-up, seemingly discarded paper bags. The reasons for this were twofold. Firstly, they didn't have to go back upstairs to the headquarters apartment every time they had a sale. Keeping one's drugs on one's person was risky behavior in "hot" areas. Keeping too many drugs in one's apartment was even riskier. A considerable amount of these dealers lived at home with their parents. Besides, constant traffic to and from one's own apartment made you look quite suspicious when you lived in the projects. When one looked too suspicious, one set oneself up for a police raid. The girls and I used to hide behind walls in the urine-stained shadows, trying to peep the different stashes. Sometimes we silently scurried behind them when they entered a stairwell, listening out for clues about how far up lay their stashed little treasures. The girls and I procured bounties in amounts far exceeding hundreds of dollars in this manner. Our list of enemies on the streets was also multiplying rapidly.

In addition to our varied moneymaking pursuits, the girls and I frequented the crackhead classroom up on 135th Street. Believe it or not, the 135th Street crackhead classroom was an apartment that was set up like a classroom, equipped with numerous desks and chairs. For a small fee, you'd enter, be assigned a seat, and be provided with a place to suck on your stem with no interruptions. This was one school that we all attended regularly and faithfully.

On one particular day after obtaining mad loot and getting quite fucked up, Debbie and I began "shooting the dozens" with one another. You know, 'dissing each other. Somehow, this led into my bragging about my rich living accommodations with Trevor, the size of his monster dick, and all of the comforts of living I could have enjoyed. That is, if I would only keep my stupid ass home. When Debbie pushed further, forcing me to give her "real proof," I gave her Trevor's phone number, intonating that it was my phone for my own private use. At the time, I wasn't thinking one way or the other about the possibility of Debbie actually calling the number, or the possible repercussions of what would happen if she did. As usual, I didn't think at all.

About three days later, Debbie called the number and left a message. I had returned to the comforts of living in Trevor's secure home two days prior to sleep off my exhaustion from my extended run. Hence, I didn't hear the phone when it rang, nor the answering machine when it clicked on to do its operable functions.

Later on when I awakened, I pressed down the machine's play button to see if Trevor had phoned during my bear-like sleep. I was trying to get back on his good side since I was fixing to ask him for a "small loan." I heard Debbie's message and I was aghast. Thank God I was clever enough to check the messages before Trevor got back home. He'd be furious if he heard Debbie's intoxicated vulgar words. I just knew I was too smart that time. Too smart. The only problem is that when you are too smart, you're typically compensating for not being smart enough. The saga continued.

Maybe one-half hour before Trevor was expected home from work, I called Johnny on his cell phone. I hadn't seen Johnny in about a week and I was concerned. Concerned about whether he was holed up with another bitch. I started to dial Johnny's number in the process of halfway completing a rice-and-fried-chicken dinner for Trevor. He picked up on the third ring. The problem was that I heard another female's bedroom voice loud and clear, rising and falling in the background in my ear. A lonesome member of Johnny's harem, I went berserk. I was probably craving the pipe. I grabbed a few of my things, searched for some pocket change under the couch cushions, and bolted toward the front door. In the process, I tripped over the living room phone wire and knocked the entire answering machine on the floor. Exasperated, I looked down and saw that both tape reels had sprawled across the floor in different directions. I quickly put them back into the machine, set it up back on the counter, and pressed the "on" button. Trevor deserved that much. Then, I quickly dove out of the apartment, knowing full well that if I was lucky, I'd only miss crossing paths with him by minutes. I was lucky.

As for myself, I could not locate Johnny that night and he stopped answering his phone. I headed up further north, puffed on the pipe a little with Niecy, who was the only member of our crew that I could find, and started off back home at about five in the morning.

As for Trevor, upon being livid at yet another one of my abrupt disappearing acts, he cleaned up the pot and frying pan that contained charcoaled food since I had carelessly forgotten to turn the stove off before I left, and went out for a few drinks with a couple who invited him out from across the hall. As per the diatribe he unleashed later, he had returned to his empty apartment at about eleven o' clock at night. That was when he realized that something bizarre was going on with his phone. The caller ID read that he had received twenty-two calls that night, but yet only two people had actually left messages. Weird ones. The messages had been left by two very different people, his boss from the law firm and his stepmother, but yet they virtually communicated identical sentiments. A long period of silence, followed by "uh, Trevor, are you all right? Call me." No names, no numbers. Also to his surprise was the fact that he recognized at least six other numbers from the caller ID, numbers of people who never rudely hung up without leaving some sort of a message before they did. Numbers of people who had obviously called on more than one occasion throughout the evening. Trevor played his two short and sweet messages again, decided it must have been a fluke and that it was too late to return any calls anyway, shrugged his shoulders, and went to bed. He spent the next two sleepless hours wondering and praying if I'd call.

I arrived at Trevor's apartment moments before he was about to walk out the door. Appearing to be in a place that went far beyond exhaustion, Trevor railed at me for about fifteen minutes, switched gears, made me repeatedly promise that I'd stay home and not do anything crazy until he returned, and hurriedly left me in his apartment's sanitized vestibule. Out of all days, why oh why did I keep my promise and stay put until he got home? Why?

The door flung open at six-thirty on the dot with a loud whump, startling me out of a comfortable sleep. Glints of fiery light flashed from his eyes, pellets of anger shooting forth from his mouth. Nostrils flared, bellicose-like. At first I believed that he had finally lost his mind, crawled over the edge. He appeared to be violently berating me because I didn't pick up the phone that day. I hardly ever did. What was the big fucking deal? The fucking big deal was that the phone calls were from Trevor himself trying to tell me to turn off the goddamned answering machine since somehow the voice of one of my godforsaken junkie friends had managed to be on the receiving end of his phone spewing out vulgarity. Shit. I must have accidentally put the incoming into the outgoing tape cassette's place and vice versa when the machine fell. Shit. Practically every member of Trevor's family, his boss, his three friends, one life insurance salesman, and two of his professors from Columbia Law School had heard the tape. They had listened to Denise getting her wreck off on the phone. During that approximate twenty-four hour period, when anybody had phoned Trevor's house, they heard a scratchy bellowing voice that greeted one like this:

"I know you and what you're fucking doing right now, you stupid fucking bitch. You're sucking somebody's dick. I bet you're sucking on that big horse dick right now. What's his fucking name? Oh yeah, Mr. Rogers. Am I right? Hee, hee, hee. So what's the deal bitch? Same old, same old? Dicks and stems, they all the same. Hee, hee. I know you think you're better than me, but you ain't. You ain't shit, so you and your dick-sucking self can go straight to hell. Hee. You fucking bitch. I'm coming for you. I know where you at. I'll be checking your fucking ass out later." Click.

How in God's name Debbie got Trevor's name confused with Mr. Rogers I'll never know. Unfortunately, that little mix-up placed Trevor's once-upon-a-time secure and stable world into jeopardy. His family started to question him about his own drug use and his boss made more than one inquiry concerning his peer associations and sexual practices. I was evicted from his home for a whole week. Once allowed back in, I was no longer permitted to have any phone privileges.

During the week that I was on a long run in the streets there was a big snow storm. I was desperate for money, so I let this goofy guy pick me up in a hole in the wall bar in Hollis, Queens. Don't ask. I have no idea what the hell I was doing in Queens, or with whom I was doing it with. Anyway, the guy took me back to his apartment and, yes, believe it or not, paid me $10 to eat out my pussy. No problem, man. He gave me a $10 bill that was behind some magnet on the fridge as he quickly ushered me out the door. About four yards away from the guy's apartment, I saw a wallet lying boldly on top of a mound of snow. Bingo. The wallet had $30 in it. I went into an adjacent building, got myself feeling nice, and began to feel my brain's deformed wheels churning up crazy ideas in my head. The wallet had also contained an ID. Everybody wants their ID back. I'd go to the owner of the wallet's house, the person who was named on the ID, and try to strike a deal wherein he would have to pay me in order to get his ID returned with no formal agency involvements. Twenty dollars seemed like a fair sum for such door-to-door service. Crack gave you balls, but not as many as I'd need when I realized that the wallet belonged to the guy who had sucked on my clit the night before. It got better. He didn't answer his door when I persistently rang the bell the next morning. A woman did. His wife.

"What do you mean you'll sell me my own husband's ID? He said that there was thirty-five dollars in it when he lost it."

Liar.

"Look lady, I ain't gonna stand here and argue with you. Either you give me twenty dollars or knock yourself out downtown at the Motor Vehicle."

Grumbles. Dirty hard stares. "Okay, okay. What you asking for?"

She went back into the house, came back, and thrust a $20 bill into my outstretched palm. Then she glared at me again. I retrieved her husband's folded and slightly soiled ID from my pocket, shoved it into her hand, and defiantly stared back. I was two seconds short of telling her about her husband's pussy-eating skills. My better judgment prevailed and I decided otherwise. Better to leave some things alone and unsaid.

I ended up in the Women's House shortly after Christmas. Even though I was in on minor charges, petite larceny, Trevor couldn't bail me out no matter how much he wanted to because I had jumped bail the last time. In addition to everything else, I lost Trevor's $5,000. I guess neither he nor I learned our lessons yet. Before I was released from Riker's three months later, I called him to ask him if he could do me the favor of taking the ten-carat gold bracelet that I had bought him for Christmas with my boosting profits out of the pawnshop. He did. His 1994 Christmas present cost him $50. I stole it back and pawned it again two weeks after I was released.

While I managed to remain inert with my head stuck in the ground ostrich style with regard to the existence of my disease and the hypocrisy of this thing that I called a loving relationship with me and Trevor, some power greater than myself arranged to have the reality of my childhood friend's pending death slap me in the face with the piercing sharpness of a cracking whip. Call it the one hundred and first coincidental event in my lifetime, but Bruny was arrested and remanded to jail about four days after me. We didn't cross each others' paths in the receiving room. This is the first processing area of Riker's Island where your money and property are removed from your person, often never to be seen again, you are bathed, anointed with lice shampoo, and evaluated medically and psychologically. Bruny must have somehow fallen through the cracks, or in other words, through the careless fingers of some corrections civil servant, because the gravity of her medical condition was not detected. This is how she ended up in building 2 along with the rest of us newcomers who were awaiting sentencing. Bruny's immune system was visibly deteriorating more and more. In fact, it appeared as if it was doing so on a minute-to-minute basis. Due to her weak condition, Bruny went to lie down as soon as she was brought into our area. As a result, I didn't even know she was there. Not yet anyway.

It must have happened about two hours after her arrival. Chow time hadn't been called as yet. From out of the normal jail din emerged an uproarious commotion, startling me out of a lazy reverie. The noise's source appeared to stem from the shower area. As I shuffled over, my tread picking up speed with every swell of the rising clamor, I quickly identified the event to be a fight. A circle of inmates had gathered around quickly, drawn as magnetically as bees are to honey, to view what I gathered was a one-sided fight. Peering between my cheering peers, I saw that a somewhat familiar jail acquaintance of mine, Latoya, was beating the shit out of some skinny Spanish chick. When she heaved her off the ground to get better leverage with which to punch her on the other side of the face, my heart stopped, and for at least one second, I lived in a timeless world where thoughts and images merged as one. It was Bruny who lay as a helpless rag doll on the floor, face pummeled, spirit crushed. I pushed some cheering fat white lady out of my way, and before anyone had the time to draw another breath, I was on top of that bitch Latoya like white on rice.

"Get your fucking hands off her bitch." I picked her up from on top of Bruny and hurled her across the small space.

"What the fuck you think you doing?" Whack. One punch to the left side of her face right above her ear. Whack, whack. Again.

Somebody grabbed me from behind. I blinked, clearing my vision and mind long enough to register that I was in the middle of an assault, that I was assaulting someone because I was defending Bruny. Approximately two yards away, a shocked and fuming Latoya looked across at me wide-eyed trying to catch her breath. A surge of unrequited rage shot forth from a place inside that I forgot existed.

"Latoya, what the fuck you doing?" I jerked my shoulders, jockeying for some freedom from the confining hands that were grasping my shoulders.

"What the hell is it to you? Huh? What the fuck you think you're doing?"

"I'll tell you what the fuck I'm doing." A deeper breath. "I'm looking out for my girl here. Ain't nobody gonna fuck with her in front of me—not in this motherfucker."

"Victoria, don't fuck with me. I know this low life piece of Puerto Rican shit ain't your girl. She done sucked every nigger's dick in the fucking city, man. I heard she went after my man. Gonna show that hoe to stay the fuck away from my man's dick."

"Bitch." A look of surprise on Latoya's previously relaxing face.

"Bitch, let me tell you something. Your man's the biggest hoe I fucking know. He got mad bitches sucking his dick when you ain't around. What d'ya think, he's sitting around waiting on you? But fuck all that now. I don't give a fuck 'bout none of that shit. Even if my girl here was on your man's dick in front of your dumb-ass face, I still got her back. You feeling me?"

"Victoria." Somebody else nudged me on the shoulder. "Vic man," a voice, a sister's voice, shot through the sweaty shifting female bodies, "She's not one of us. She ain't a sister. She's one of them."

Everybody heard. With the exception of Bruny's heavy breaths and stirring body from down on the floor, a calming stillness passed over our heads. A decision was about to be made, a lesson learned. An important one.

I breathed more deeply, looking to the side, remembering.

"You know what Latoya, fuck that shit too. Bruny's my girl. And you know what the fuck else, she is one of us. Whether you fucking like it or not, we're one people."

Dead silence. An officious angel descended and gently sanded the rust off from our hearts. Fingers released their grasp on my shoulders. The angel softly pulled back on old childlike chords of innocence, fingers delicately strumming on harps of musical memories, kind and chaste.

Latoya, perpetrating a look of confusion to save face as she rocked her head from side to side.

"Victoria, you crazy. I don't know nothing about this philosophizing that you're doing, but we go a long way back. If Bruny's your girl. She's your girl. What the fuck can I say? Just tell her to be careful with whose dick she's sucking is all. All right?"

I simply stared. Latoya and everybody else knew it was all right when the angel had first descended.

I picked up Bruny and carried her to her yellowed, somewhat smaller than twin-size bed. Without snitching about what had occurred, I asked the police for the medical staff, informing them that Bruny had bruised her face as a result of slipping in the shower. Any employee who has ever worked on the Rock for more than one week knows better than to try to squeeze the truth about a fight out of any inmate. Only stupid suicidal birds sing the truth in jail. Anyway, medical staff treated Bruny's face with ice packs, rubbed some ointment into open skin abrasions, and left her exhausted and languished, huddled under the thin sheet on top of her bed. I left her alone to sleep for a while.

I couldn't sleep that night. Slumber simply evaded me. About two in the morning I understood why. I heard stifled sniffles from the other side of the dorm. I rose out of my bed and carefully weaved myself around the sea of beds in the direction of Bruny. Before the officious angel bid farewell to our building that night, it relayed one additional message. It let me know that my friend needed me.

I found her curled up into a fetus position whimpering into her pillow. I climbed into her bed and took her into my arms and held her, silently and with love. I held on to her until the sun stuck its forehead out from beyond the horizon in the early morning. Her tears had dried about a half hour before.

"Bruny," I whispered into the darkness, "can I ask you something?"

She nestled cozily into my chest.

"Huh?"

"Something I asked you a long time ago back when we were kids. You never answered me and I'd really like to know."

Her body stiffened slightly in my embrace.

"Ask Victoria. Right now, I'll tell you anything you want to know."

I breathed an endlessly long deep breath.

"The lollipops, Bruny. What's the story behind the lollipops? When did you start this thing with the lollipops?"

She became still and stiff as if in a trance, remaining that way for a long time. The sun was slowly making its ascent on to the day. I gave her the time that I knew she needed.

"When I was three."

"Why, Bruny, why? Can you tell me what it was with you and those stupid lollipops all your life? I've always wanted to know."

A weak sigh. The smallest, most grievous pair of eyes I had ever seen looked up to meet mine.

"My father did it." Strangled images. Fettered visions.

I knew she was sorry I asked before she completely answered.

"My father did it, Vic."

Her gaze became more focused. She looked intently in my direction.

"My father gave me my first lollipop—a red one, I think—on my third birthday. After teaching me how to suck on them real good, he made me suck on his dick."

I guess she read my mind and continued, "my mother was right there."

I knew better than to speak. This time, it was all about Bruny.

She sighed. "I always had a lollipop in my mouth, Victoria, because my father told me to keep practicing."

Curiosity momentarily got the better of me. "But . . ."

Her deepest sigh of the night. "Because if I didn't and didn't suck his dick right, he'd stick it up my ass."

A memory of a photograph flashed into my mind with the speed of nervous laughter. An image of a tiny, vulnerable Bruny with frightened eyes, looking up toward the monstrous shadow of her father. Lurid secrets caught on Polaroid.

Bruny and I were inseparable for the two weeks that it took the Department of Corrections to transfer me back to dorm 9 for sentenced inmates. We were almost as inseparable as when we were children, except that she required extended periods of rest. I comforted her around the clock for those two weeks the best I could. I don't know what happened to Bruny, where she was transferred to, or in exactly what time frame it occurred. I assume that since her charges were of a pretty unserious nature, she had been released back to the streets much quicker than me. Up until the point I visited her about a year later when she was on her death bed, I had little contact with her. We might have gotten high together in our usual form in our little girls' group once or twice, and I might have knowingly or unknowingly passed her by on the street, but my friendship with Bruny had once again taken a backseat in my list of priorities as soon as I was released and tasted what I thought was real freedom.

My three month incarceration at the Women's House was unquestionably my easiest bid. Of course, it goes without saying that, as a result, Trevor was the recipient of my sincerest thanks. I had somebody to call, constantly. I had somebody to write to and write me back, quite often. I had somebody to visit me, frequently. And I had somebody to look out for my commissary, consistently and maximally. While I refused to agree with Trevor's pleas to become involved with the Riker's Island Women's Substance Abuse Treatment Program, approximately one month into my stay in dorm 9, I conceded to attend classes for my GED. By the time I was ready to be released, my teachers stated that I was ready to take the test. I lied to Trevor and told him I did. I didn't though. I just didn't feel like it that day.

I was released in the early part of the summer and hit the streets immediately. Trevor was lucky if I gave him thirty solid hours of my time. After I accomplished my initial objective of getting high, I tracked down Johnny. I don't know why exactly. At the time, I didn't need to entreat him about him giving me any of his drugs, and within the thirty-hour period that I had been with Trevor, I surely had had enough dick. Maybe it was just a personal example of water rising to its own level.

Johnny and I swung another episode together. An episode that endured about two months. I was more than surprised when he quickly moved me back into the apartment. At the time, he was sharing it with his brother and uncle. Maricella had gotten involved in some legal trouble and the family had sent her back to Santo Domingo. I can't say I was contented during the two-month time period that I lived and worked with Johnny again, nor can I say that I was discontented. In fact, I don't remember feeling much of anything at all. Drugs and denial and forgetfulness took care of that. With one exception, when I was feeling lower than the curb on which I was standing on about three-thirty in the morning because I had forgotten to call Trevor for the entire two months that I lived with Johnny.

The gods of the universe sent down a warning on day 65 after my release. They ignited fire under my feet and placed rolling thunder above my head. Whether I was sent warnings in the past, I couldn't say. This was the first one that I noticed, the first one that made its mark.

Johnny, his brother, and uncle were still supplying a good portion of the northern part of the city with cocaine and heroin. Business was booming. They stepped on many toes. Important ones. They were becoming richer. They had many enemies. Invisible and visible ones. I knew about the superficial stuff. Johnny, as in the past, kept the finer, more intricate threads of his business a secret. Unlike Trevor, Johnny knew better than to trust an addict.

It happened on a Sunday. The Lord's day of rest and rejuvenation. We had just returned from a small Dominican-run after-hours joint uptown. It was about 5 AM. We were both high, feeling good, and preparing to fuck. Johnny's uncle lay prostrate, asleep on the living-room sofa, the television's luminescence casting soft pastel shadows across his face. Johnny's brother was in his own bedroom fucking. Muffle groans of pleasure escaped from inside the room. Johnny went to the bathroom to pee. He had already tossed off his shoes and designer shirt on the bedroom floor. A small hill of crumpled expensive attire. I had already removed my high-heeled shoes and silk blouse when they kicked the door in. I don't know how many of them there were. Lots. All with guns. All with hatred running through their veins. All with the intent purpose of killing us all. I dove under the bed as I heard the approaching shouts and running footsteps. My body weight pulled the sheet down off of the messy unmade bed as I dove so that it covered the space from the bed to the floor. I slithered under the bed across the floor, so that my back laid flat up against the wall, fearfully peering out at the gauzy shadowy whiteness.

Johnny's uncle must have died in his sleep. It all happened so quickly. The first five or six shots banged out so fast after the door had been kicked in, I couldn't discriminate between the sounds. Johnny's brother must have been positioned on top during his last sex act because his girl for the night had the opportunity to let out one scream before she was killed. Through all the ruckus, I never heard any blood-curling yells from Johnny's brother. I assumed he was shot in the back.

Being in a more favorable position, Johnny had enough time to run to the entrance of his bedroom before he was fatally wounded. The gunmen fired so many shots that Johnny must have been lifted up off the floor and cast on the bed, blood gushing from his almost every pore. He had so much cocaine in his system that he must have stayed conscious long enough to see the multiple holes in his body. He must have stayed alive long enough to watch himself die.

Once the gunmen were satisfied that Johnny was dead, I heard them quickly rummage through the apartment. Closet doors flung open. Shouts were tossed about. I think they were looking for more people. These were hired killers, not your typical robbers. Blood darkened the sheet that was draped over the bed that Johnny laid dead on. The same one that I was hiding behind. His blood trickled down the walls behind me. It surrounded me. I could taste it. The sound of footsteps vibrated across the floor, coming closer in my direction. I said a prayer, an earnest one, for the first time in my life.

I survived. The approaching footsteps didn't result in my death. Instead, they fell about three yards short in front of me. A pair of feet shifted to the right, to the left, turned on their heels, and went out the door. Once the footsteps' vibrations could be heard in the further distance, I rolled quickly from under the bed, pushed the crimson-stained sheets and Johnny's limbs out of my way, sprung up off of the floor, opened the window, and leapt out on to the rickety fire escape. I scrambled down the steps, and ran for blocks and blocks, numbly and blindly. My blouse, shoes, and heart were left behind in Johnny's blood bath of an apartment. Someone had heard my prayer.

CHAPTER SEVENTEEN

But if I am to heal,
I must first learn to feel.
—From the song "Ruins"
by Cat Stevens

AS MY LIFE'S story unfolds on a trail of print before my eyes, my memories of people and times long forgotten are becoming that much more vivid. Poignantly so, at times. While writing down the details of my past, I relived the experience of having Johnny's blood saturate my senses, and Bruny's pained eyes, impale the core of my soul. The most amazing aspect of this autobiographic writing assignment thus far has been that I haven't picked up, although I'd be a liar if I told you that I didn't think about it more than once.

I must have embarked upon this self-help literary journey about five months ago. I'm still attending NA, regularly and consistently. I've been promoted to assistant manager in the store in which I am employed. Last month, I applied to some four-year colleges that I'm considering attending. For about the past half a year, I've been seriously contemplating the idea of pursuing a career in social work, with an emphasis in child welfare, believe it or not. And since I eventually tired of hearing my sponsor nag me about dealing with some of my issues of past sexual abuse on a more professional level, I recently registered for a weekly "Adult Women Victims of Sexual Abuse" group at one of the local community mental health centers. Aside from my day-to-day struggle with maintaining my sobriety, the biggest stress in my life lately has been my relationship with Thomas. I almost just wrote that my biggest stress was Thomas, but that's not accurate. It is merely a classic example exemplifying how we addicts prefer to place the blame for our problems on others. Thomas, in actuality, has not done anything but be Thomas. He's been honest, friendly, and supportive from the onset. But, you see, it's hard for us addicts to cope with honest, friendly, and supportive at times. We prefer sicker styles of communicating and relating. My chief complaint with Thomas is that he just won't commit to me on the level that I want him to. I know he likes me. In fact, I know he likes me a lot. Not only does his sister tease me about this constantly, but I can also pick up on this on my own. Women's intuition. I also know that Thomas is sexually attracted to me. He even slipped twice this very month with regard to his "No Sex Yet" campaign. We all have our weaknesses, I guess. The problem is that I'm really feeling him, really feeling him. Okay, I'll admit it, my ego is on the line here and right now it feels so soggy and used that I might as well just hang it out on the line to dry. I was feeling particularly low yesterday. It was Saturday and Thomas had not made one move to ask me out. My big excitement for the night was an 8 PM anniversary NA meeting in South Brooklyn. By Sunday, I was fuming. There was smoke visibly exiting from my ears. I called Thomas and invited myself to his apartment under the guise of needing some help with a college financial aid application. (An old Trevor move.) My lack of interest in completing the financial aid form became apparent about ten minutes after I had walked through his apartment door. An argument ensued about five minutes afterwards. As most arguments go, I don't remember how it started or what small trivial topic we were arguing about. I quickly bypassed all of the superficiality and got right to the point. Bulls eye.

"Thomas, why don't you cut the bullshit, you don't really want a relationship with me. You believe you're better than me and you're afraid to tell me the truth."

"That's not true, Victoria. I don't lie to you. You just don't accept my truths and I'm not a . . ."

I cut him off, "What truths? What truths are those, Thomas?"

"Well, first and foremost I think, no, in fact I know, you're doing wonderful recovery work. But I don't believe you're ready for a relationship yet, Victoria. Not the kind of relationship that we're talking about here anyway."

"Who the fuck . . ."

This time he cut me off. "Victoria, let's not go there. I'm just exercising my right to take care of myself right now and I just don't think you're ready."

I fumed once again, causing more smoke to exude from my upper auditory orifices. "And who died and left you to be the fucking king? Who are you to judge me?"

"Victoria, I'm not judging you. I'm . . ."

"Yeah right. To hell you ain't. Instead of judging me, what you need to do is keep the focus on yourself."

I picked up my jacket and paperwork and angrily marched toward the front door. When my hand reached the knob, I heard his voice from about two yards behind me, "That's what I thought I was doing, Victoria. That's what I'm trying to do."

A moment of silence hung between us like a dank curtain. I had to think about that, process it. I turned the knob, opened the door, and righteously walked out. A confused and wounded young girl in the beginning stages of recovery.

After witnessing the massacre of Johnny and family, it was to Trevor's apartment that I later returned, of course. That is, after I ran until I couldn't run anymore. When I collapsed on the pavement, sheer physical exhaustion the provocateur of my fall, I remained there leaned up against a trash can, thoughts buzzing in my head like incited bees. I don't know how long I sat there until it dawned on me that I wasn't wearing any shirt over my bra. This realization preceded my flitting recognition of the fact that I was covered with Johnny's blood. It was an early morning hour. Seven o'clock perhaps. Light had already drawn back the curtains from the previous night. There were signs of life on the street. Small stirrings inside of the ghetto. Cars and people. All with a purpose. All with a mission. I quickly rummaged through a garbage bag that I saw in the near distance that was overflowing with some family's old clothing. I yanked out a worn holey blouse by the sleeve, put it on and adjusted it, and headed for the nearest train station. I washed as much blood off as I could in the dirty bathroom of the station and literally jumped through the doors of the arriving train. I was worried about the police catching on to the fact that I was the closest witness that they had to a near massacre. My head pounded. My body felt filthy with the residual taste of Johnny's blood in my mouth. Metallic and sweet. Nauseating. I needed to rest. Rest my body and my thoughts. I believe it was the first time I truly knew what it was like to be tired of being tired. With these thoughts grappling to root firmly in my mind, I made the conscious decision to go to Trevor's house and get myself cleaned up. My good intentions lasted about as long as it took Trevor to scrub Johnny's blood from my pores.

Trevor barraged me with a thousand and one questions when I arrived, all to which I responded with a thousand and one lies. To this day, I believe he believes that Johnny is among the living somewhere. His death must have not received too much attention from the media. I just couldn't endure the onslaught of inquiries that would ensue if I told Trevor the truth about with whom I had been living and about what happened to him. My thinking was definitely still scoring high on the self-centered charts. So, I avoided any probable negative repercussions, told Trevor a brief bogus story about trying to get myself clean through some New Jersey church that I had forgotten the name of, how the program had failed me and caused me to relapse, and how I had recently escaped after witnessing my friend's harrowing rape and murder. Very partial truths. Of course, Trevor was so concerned about my well-being that he gulped down my story with a funny face as if its sour taste had made it somewhat hard to swallow.

After he practically dragged me to the doctor to double check if I "really was all right," he allowed me to rest, undisturbed and in peace. If I am recalling this portion of my life accurately, I believe that when I finally hit that bed, I slept for three days straight. I awakened midweek mid-afternoon one day after Trevor had already left for work. I stuffed a change of clothing into a plastic bag and found a pair of gold cufflinks hidden in a pair of dress socks in a shoe box in his room. I stole them and made tracks out the door. At the moment, I had no idea where I was heading. In spite of this, I knew I'd be back. I also knew that I'd be let back in. Trevor always let me back in. By then I believe that he was so codependent that he would have probably shown my baby pictures around at an Al-Anon meeting if he had been smart enough to go to one.

Things got worse. Much worse, with no promise of ever getting better. My three days worth of sleep was the quiet before the storm. I boosted. I got high. I pulled scams on people. I got high. I sucked on a few dicks. I got high. In fact, I was high so often that I forgot what it was like not to be high. Sobriety was a long forgotten concept from the past.

This was the period of time in which I spent a great deal of time sleeping and getting high in parks, abandoned buildings, department stores' dressing rooms, and when I could, in the crowded rooms of distant acquaintances who were fortunate enough to always have a roof over their heads at various welfare hotels. I was spending much more of my time in Brooklyn and midtown Manhattan, probably because I thought the cops were looking for me further uptown. The Prince George and Martinique Hotels were becoming my regular hangouts. One incident at the Prince George stands out above the rest in my head.

I was "tight," at least as tight as an addict could be with other drug people, with two different families who were involved in selling drugs out of the Prince George Hotel. One family, the Bridges family, was comprised of two brothers, both of whom did not get high. The other family, the Harrisons, was also comprised of two brothers. Although both of the Harrison boys used to use, one of them, Joey Harrison, cleaned himself up. Not knowing any better, Joey used to continue feeding his younger brother's habit by giving him drugs whenever he hollered loud enough. The younger Harrison, Bobby, was the more personable of the two. In spite of his habit, he was always jovial and jocular. He always tried to find the best in people. Everybody liked Bobby for this reason. I was tight with both families. Both of which were beginning to become too greedy and nearsighted. Disagreements broke out between the Harrisons and the Bridgeses over turf issues, particular the turf involving the Prince George. The fighting worsened and an ongoing feud developed, one that became increasingly nasty and shortsighted. I was in the middle. Personally, I didn't give a shit who took over the Prince George just as long as I continued to have a steady flowing supply of drugs available. Occasionally, both the Bridges and the Harrison boys would cut me a good deal—a wonderful discount on crack. On rare occasions, I thanked them with small sexual favors performed on the hotel elevator. This little cozy scene perpetuated for about six weeks before it erupted in my face. The Bridges used me to set up the Harrisons. The Queen of the Dupers—the Dupess—got duped.

One day, the younger of the Bridges gave me a couple of vials of crack suggesting that I share them with Bobby. As was their plan, he was waiting for me in the stairwell of the Prince George. We smoked together and then I obeyed Ace Bridges' order to come back once I finished smoking with him. It must have been directly afterwards that the Bridges brothers found him alone on the stairwell and shot him to death. The way the story was told, Bobby caught at least eight shots, four of which were distributed between his head and chest region. The Bridges won the feud. Joey Harrison was so devastated about his brother's murder that he got his savings together, packed up his shit, and moved down south. I heard that he moved somewhere in the quieter neck of the woods where there wouldn't be any reminders of drugs, guns, and murdered brothers. The fact that I had been used, had actually been instrumental in Bobby's death, unhinged me. I responded by fleeing the welfare hotel scene and the borough of Brooklyn for a long while. I said fuck it and headed back uptown toward my old stomping grounds in the South Bronx. I still had some old drug ties there. Addict acquaintances who wouldn't ask any questions and would allow me to crash in their cribs on the strength of my good reputation for bringing in money. One of my latest tricks to make quick money was to quickly locate addicts with whom I was not familiar who had been on the run for several days. I had a keen eye for them. I'd wait for them to completely crash out somewhere like in an alley, park, or abandoned building. Then, I'd slice their pockets and be gone.

During my days of transience and itinerancy, I saw many things—some of which made me question the point of the race I had willingly joined. I believe that one of the most disturbing things I ever saw was a young, laughing drug dealer convince a strung-out addict, who was obviously in pain, to fuck his dog in front of his boys in exchange for one free hit on the stem. I've seen so much, but that one memory seems to have fossilized in my memoirs. The other most disturbing thing I ever saw was basehead hookers sell their own children for drugs. One case in particular stands out.

Approximately three months after Johnny's death, I started staying with a "polydrug" user named Martha. Martha had an alcohol, heroin, and crack habit. She was doing pretty badly. Martha also had three kids. She had one son, Reggie, who was eight, and two daughters. Her oldest daughter, Monaya, was six. The youngest, Star, was two. Martha, Reggie, Monaya, and Star all lived together in a two-room apartment that often failed to produce adequate heat and hot water. The apartment was small, dank, and dirty. Vermin and rodents reigned. The children were often neglected, unsupervised, and deplorably filthy. The two oldest hardly ever attended school. After about two days of staying in their apartment, I observed Martha having one or two unfamiliar visitors who arrived at her door unannounced. They would inevitably disappear behind the closed door into the other room with one of the children. As soon as my mind registered that something was dreadfully wrong, I followed one of the strange men into the room after he and Reggie had been inside for approximately five minutes. The vision I saw wounded me for life. I saw a grown man with his dick plunged down Reggie's little throat. Little brown eyes, glazed and expressionless, stared back across the room at me. I screeched, ranting and raving like a hurt and frightened animal. This caused not only the strange man, but also Martha and her kids, to flee from the apartment. When my brain started to function again, I realized that Martha had fled the apartment with her kids to avoid the ACS from removing her star employees from her home. I hurled a few glasses after her and left. About two hours later when it dawned on me that I'd have to find warm and dry lodging for the night, I remembered previously seeing Martha's little toddler being carried into the room by another strange man the day before. I threw up everything I had eaten that day and fell asleep on a park bench. This became my home for the better part of the week. I might have showered once at a friend's apartment during the entire time period that I resided on that park bench. I was not doing very good.

After I was clean for about six months, a beginner at NA questioned me about how I knew my last attempt to stay clean would in fact be the one that worked. I thought about the question deeply. After pondering over my initial struggle with sobriety for several minutes, I had to admit that I was unable to accurately identify the differences between my last few attempts to get sober, nor the exact steps in the processes I experienced. One thing I knew was that I had genuinely become tired of being tired. I also knew that I had finally stopped giving only lip service to the fact that I had a drug problem. Finally, I believe I started to become saturated with confident feelings about being able to lick this problem if I wanted to badly enough. That is, if I truly possessed a burning desire. I don't know how much more I knew. Interestingly enough though, when that same person asked what were the three events in my life that were most critical in propelling me toward recovery, toward that point in which I truly became tired of being tired, I said that Johnny's murder and Bruny's death accounted for two out of the three. I was so caught up in the insanity of being insane that I dismissed Bruny's rapidly deteriorating physical condition and, as usual, did not pay much mind to her whenever I happened to see her shuffling down the street. Once, I thought I saw her mumbling to herself while she was walking. I got scared. My fear caused me to keep myself at an even greater distance from her than I had done before. After making the city park my residence for almost one week, I became quite sick with a serious case of bronchitis. When my fever reached such a high level that I lacked the strength to fend for myself and cop the drug that drove me to go to sleep on park benches in the first place, I put an invisible tail between my legs and went back to Trevor. He slowly nursed me back to health. It was at this point that I absconded from his watchful eyes again, this time when he was in the shower. With much more lucidity than I had enjoyed over the past couple of months, I decided to cop and then go check out one of my newest favorite boosting partners, Papo. Papo was a fine, about forty-five-year-old Puerto Rican brother who lived in the Farragut House projects directly in front of the Brooklyn Navy Yard. He had a wife and two kids and a serious addiction to heroin. In addition to his attractive appearance, Papo had magnificent boosting skills. We worked well together. With the exception of when he signed himself into one of the local hospital's detox wards for a week's rest, our relationship was never a sexual one. But, I could never resist the "dope dick" that Papo had without fail every time he completed a detox program, failed to follow through with any discharge follow-up services, and sniffed up a bag of dope hours following his discharge. Papo loved detox. He carried his Medicaid card around like a cherished badge. I have fond memories of hearing Papo joke around and say, "Medicaid, don't leave home without it." "Smart" heroin addicts have a revolving-door policy with their local hospitals' detox wards. Here's the deal. Their tolerance for heroin after a while starts to reach sky high levels. For some, that means that they don't feel the drug's effects at all unless they use three or more bags at a time. This translates into anything from a ten- to-fifteen bag a day habit. Too expensive and unpractical for most. It is virtually impossible to keep up with all of the legwork involved in supporting that kind of habit unless one is independently wealthy and has an abundance of connections. To combat this inevitable problem, addicts voluntarily enter detox programs. By doing so, they enjoy decent food, rest, medical care, and tapering dosages of methadone to maintain them for up to one week. At the week's end, the addict is physically stronger and is thus more adequately equip to sustain the addict street lifestyle. More importantly, their tolerance levels have been significantly lowered. This means that an addict who previously had a hundred-dollar a day habit could get high off $10 worth of dope. Habits always build back up again. In the meantime, however, detox is a heroin addict's best friend. It's also the heroin addict's friend's best friend. The fringe benefit of being the "friend" of a heroin addict who periodically signs himself into detox is the dope dick. "Dope dick" is the coined term for the temporary return of the male heroin addict's sex drive after the first hit of dope that he takes following a long detox period. Their dicks have never been harder or more erect. That first sexual contact after detox is powerful and seemingly never ending. That's about one of the only good things for the wives of male heroin addicts. And I repeat, about one of the only good things because of all of the negatives, i.e. possible exposure to HIV, infidelity, stealing, lying, etc. Unfortunately for the typical heroin addict, after about the second or third day of consistently getting high again, they can't do a damned thing else with their little limp dicks in the bedroom.

It was Papo, my very rare dope dick partner and friend, who informed me that he had heard that Bruny was on her death bed at Kings County Hospital. It seems that she was in Brooklyn when she finally collapsed on the floor, being unable to take one more shuffling step. Papo believed she was in Brooklyn at the time because she had gone to the apartment of one of her incarcerated brothers' wives to beg her to give her a small space on her living room floor so that she could rest herself for a while. Bruny's sister-in-law refused her request and sent her skeleton of a relative back out into the streets. About two hours later, she collapsed on Fulton Street in front of Macys. After being stepped around and over for several minutes, Macys' security guard notified the police that somebody had fainted or died in front of the store. Bruny was first transported to Brooklyn Hospital by ambulance. The medical staff at Brooklyn Hospital quickly determined that Bruny was in the final stages of full-blown AIDS. Her T-cell count was way below two hundred and her failing immune system was unable to successfully fend off yet another acute case of AIDS-related pneumonia. When the social work and billing department staff assessed that Bruny did not have an active Medicaid account, nor any positive identification with which to apply for one, she was transported to Kings County Hospital and placed into an AIDS ward to die. Her condition worsened during the one-week period that she was hospitalized, necessitating that Bruny frequently be placed on an oxygen machine. Upon her initial admittance, she was provided with nutrients and medication intravenously.

I smoked a little with Papo, much less than usual, asked him for a token, and traveled across Brooklyn to see my dying friend.

When I saw Bruny under the hospital's florescent lights, I understood that AIDS' hand of death had been kind and generous with Mama. Bruny was always slight and petite, but the figure lying across that bed was not the friend I remembered. I barely recognized her. On her death bed, Bruny was the size of a small, nine-year-old child, about seventy-five pounds, virtually bald, rashes and sores splotched across her skin, blisters oozing from her lips. There was no drug available in the world that could soften the truth that the wretched, pathetic near-corpse before me was dying. This reality struck me with the same certainty as the fact that I was standing in front of my home girl Bruny in a hospital. I was sure that if I squinted hard enough, I could probably see the hands of death tugging on her shoulders. Bruny stirred when she sensed my presence, shifted slightly, and opened her eyes. She seemed exhausted from this minimal effort. Fortunately, she was not in need of the oxygen tank at the time of my visit. This meant that Bruny could communicate with me through parched whispers.

"Hi." Surprisingly, her eyes were still the same. Haunting hollow entities that quickly carried my sentiments across several passages of time.

"Hey Bruny. What's up, girl? Are you, uh, all right?"

Talking about being at a loss for words.

She smiled weakly. "No, Vic, I ain't doing too good. Not good at all. But how are you, girl? You look good. Staying out of trouble I hope." This came out more like a statement than a question. Had it been a question, I think she would've already known the answer. "Are you clean?"

"I'm good Bruny. You know maintaining."

She interrupted me. "Yeah, yeah, but are you clean? I know you've tried and ain't that pretty boy boyfriend of yours supposed to be helping ya' out with that?"

"Uh, nah, I ain't gonna lie. I'm still getting high."

A mild look of disappointment swam across her dying eyes.

"I know."

"So, when do the doctors say you'll be getting up and out of here? When do they think you'll get better?" I don't believe I had ever suffered from such a severe case of social retardation before in my life, at least none as severe as I experienced during the first segment of my visit with Bruny.

"Vic, Vic, my girl, I'm dying." An intense questioning stare. "Don't you know that?" "Hello! Is there anybody home in that drugged-out brain of yours?"

Silence pervaded.

"Vic, really girl, can't you tell? Can't you see? I'm dying, girlfriend. Dying."

Bruny was always good at forcing answers out of me.

"Well, I don't know 'bout all that. I mean ya' look bad and all, but people get better you know. People are always getting better nowadays, even when they is real sick. Ya' got a good doctor? What'd he say?"

"Vic, stop. Please stop. I ain't gonna get no better, not in this life anyhow. The truth is that I'm dying. I want you to understand that, okay?"

More silence. You could carve it with a knife.

"Feels like I'm dead now."

I wanted to tell her that she was wrong, that she should stop talking like that, but I stopped myself this time. The tragic reality of the situation bit down hard on my tongue. I stared at her long and hard. Teaspoons of tears welled up in my eyes. I inched forward and reached out to touch her hand, ever so gingerly, ever so lovingly.

"Bruny, I'm so sorry. I'm sorry for everything." The tears pouring down my face were now coming in buckets. A dam had been opened.

"Bruny, you my girl, you my girl, you my girl," I sobbed. "Ya' can't die. I still need you. Damn, I always needed you. Shit." I was choking.

"Bruny." I looked into her eyes, my face a messy patchwork of tears and mucous. "I love you, you know that, don't you?"

She slowly nodded her head up and down in a knowing and comforting way.

"I've always loved you, from the beginning, even when we were kids. Ya' do know that, don't ya'?"

A gentle nod. "Yeah Vic, I know. It's all right, I know girl. Listen, Vic, pretty soon I'm gonna get too tired to talk, so let me ask ya' something, okay?" I nodded in-between sniffles.

"Vic, ya' remember when we were real little, right? We were crazy little girls, weren't we?"

This time it was my turn to silently nod my head in agreement.

"Member I told ya' that you could be and do anything ya' wanted to? Remember I told you how you were special?"

Bruny seemed to be pleading with me now, her energy waning with every breath she took.

"Yeah, yeah, Bruny. I remember. We were at summer camp. Why?"

"'Cause ya' act like ya' don't. That's why. I spent a whole life time watching you act like ya' didn't hear me."

She was beyond the point of exhaustion now. Her whispers, barely audible.

"Well, hear me now, girl. Victoria, you're special and you could do any thing you want."

My eyes, still overflowing with salty tears, communicated my gracious sentiments. Then, as if I wasn't in the room and we hadn't been having the deepest conversation in our lives, she fell asleep. I sat and looked at my friend for a long time, remembering. Graphic memories moved slowly across the floor of my mind's stage. A half a teaspoon of tears lingered inside of each eye. When I reached the point when I could no longer stand to look at her, I stood up to leave. Bruny opened her eyes halfway as if she sensed my pending departure. And then, as if sharing in my reveries from the past, softly said, "Hey, I heard your name's Victoria. I'm Bruny. Ya' wanna lollipop?"

I was crying profusely and uncontrollably now, looking in the other direction, trying to hide my blubbering face. I swallowed as many sobs as I could.

"Nah, that's all right."

"Yeah, whatever. Maybe later you'll change your mind."

Her eyes focused on me and she let out one last sigh in my presence.

"Well, what can I say?"

"Nothing that I don't already know."
We looked at one another. My sobs subsided.
"Bruny, I'll see you around."
"Yeah, I know."

I turned on my heels and walked out, briskly and freely, away from a friend who only had a few more breaths left inside of her. I walked out and never returned. I know that Bruny knew I wouldn't.

Directly afterwards, I did what any other sick and suffering addict would do under the same circumstances. I got high and I stayed high. During the violent throes of this period of insanity, I robbed a woman's purse from beneath a bathroom stall in Macys. She must have been sorry because I got away with a whole $500. Then, I went back to Trevor to manipulate him by singing the blues better than any jazz musician ever did. This time, however, with the crystal clear intention of robbing his credit cards. Since I couldn't find the pin number of Trevor's MasterCard and Visa cards, I settled for having one of my male hustler friends buy $1,000 worth of merchandise and then help me sell it on the streets directly afterward. We split the profits, each earning about $300 a piece. I don't recall what I did with Trevor's credit cards after we bought the clothes out of Macys. Probably lost them.

It was with the combination of this luck, stealth, and inhumanity that I managed to stay high for the better part of the next two weeks. When I finally allowed myself to crash for about a day and a half, I spent half of the time sleeping in the park, and the other half in an abandoned building. When I awakened from my twilight sleep, I ambled back over in the direction of Papo's projects and learned that Bruny had died two days before. We had both laid ourselves down to rest at the same time. The only difference was that she would never wake up again.

I allowed my friend to die alone, without a caring soul nearby to hold her hand or whisper comforting words into her ears. The pain of not having been there pierced through my concrete wall of defenses into a tumultuous sea of inner turmoil, passed over me like a tidal wave, and left me shipwrecked with a broken heart. I started off to make some reparations.

It was a few days later, around sunset, when I arrived. The air was balmy and vibrant. The ambiance, serene. It was too late to enter by means of legal entry, so I ignited the coals beneath a few of my cerebral neurons, and started to devise a plan about how I could get over illegally. I was on City Island. I had taken a bus over after learning that Bruny was buried in Potter's Field over on Hart's Island in the Long Island Sound. Once I arrived I was told, believe it or not, that trustees from Riker's Island were ferried over and paid about thirty-five cents an hour to inter persons who died indigent or whose bodies were unclaimed. Bruny easily fit into both of these categories. It was ironical that in the end, it was

Bruny's peers, probably men with whom she had gotten high and had performed fellatio on, who ended up being responsible for the burial of her body. The main problem on hand for me, however, was the fact that Hart's Island was not open to the public. I was left with no options. I had to steal a boat. The only way I could do so was to hunt down another addict, one who was also desperate at the moment. I found one about forty-five minutes later. An older white, probably Irish, male alcoholic named Larry, who was willing to exchange his seafaring expertise for $25 for booze. We "borrowed" a small motor boat from a derelict dock and cut across the aquamarine rolling carpet in the direction of Hart's Island. I had never been on a boat before in my life, but I didn't have time to think about that at the moment. Clutching a huge plastic bag full of brightly-colored lollipops to my chest, I kept my gaze steady and focused, converging on a small dot of an island that lay beyond the soft frothing turquoise waters. I was not high at the time, only electrically determined.

Larry and I agreed that he would wait for me in the boat at the dock to avoid having both of us get into trouble if we were caught. I knew he'd wait for me. I hadn't paid him his $25 yet.

I climbed over three gates and cowered in the shadows. I was sure that some form of security was manning the island of poor, dead, buried corpses. In Potter's Field, there is no visible indication of who or where one is buried. Instead, there's just stretches of land with hundreds of nameless adults and children buried beneath. I walked until I reached a place where my heart spoke to me. A place that caused my heart to tingle. I knew that it was Bruny's soundless lamentable song that was causing my heart to tingle and that I was very close to her burial ground. I stopped, put the plastic bag down on the floor, and sighed deeply.

I stayed for about one hour, the first half of which was spent sticking hundreds of freshly stolen lollipops in the surrounding terrain. I spent the latter portion sitting still in the invisible company of my beloved childhood friend. When I was finished making what I later learned was called "amends," I turned to go, feeling lighter and less troubled. It was as if the lion had finally laid down with the lamb. I walked a few feet down the winded path that would take me back to a stranger I had just met—a stranger named Larry. When I turned for the final time to view the totality of my efforts, I felt pleased and proud. I knew that Bruny lay somewhere beneath the soil I was standing on, surrounded by a garden of many colors—a rainbow of indelible bright colors created from lollipops of every flavor imaginable. I knew that their shadows would keep her feeling safe during the twilight hours. I also knew that Bruny would feel warm and hopeful when the sun shone iridescent specks of colorful light across her grave. It was with these museful thoughts that I said my final good-byes to my friend and left.

Something about my having to say my final good-byes to Bruny triggered a mysterious internal need to say good-bye to Trevor. Or at least, farewell. I believe that "something" was connected to the incision that was made through the wall of my defenses. Particularly the one that, at least for a few days, forced me to get in touch with feelings of pain. I believe this experience triggered a need to put some real distance between Trevor and me—enough distance to ensure that I would no longer be the knave of his suffering. Approximately two days after my visit to Potter's Field, I showed up at Trevor's house at about two in the morning. I knew he had to go to work in the morning and couldn't stay up with me all night talking. As it was, he preached a story about credit card fraud to me, federal prison, and his heart's suffering for at least two hours. When I was secure that he was fast asleep, I slid out of bed from beside him and went into the kitchen. By candlelight, I wrote him the following note:

My Dearest Trevor,

> When I was walking down the street the other day, I passed by a store with posters in the window. This is what one of the posters said, "If you love something, set it free. If it comes back to you, it is yours. If it does not, it was never meant to be." This is my message to you. I'm sorry for everything, all of the trouble, all of the pain. I love you, and because of that love, I'm setting you free.
>
> With love always,
> Victoria

I placed the note under a paper weight on top of his kitchen table and quietly slipped out the door. I never turned around and I never went back. I guess Trevor and I were not meant to be.

Although I firmly believe that Johnny's murder and Bruny's death were two giant seeds from which my desire to seek recovery later grew, they didn't immediately take root. As with most growth processes, additional seeds and a great deal of water and sunshine were also required. I didn't find any of those additional supports until I was incarcerated and subsequently released. I didn't find any of those supports probably because I wasn't looking for them.

Although I attempted to remain fairly levelheaded after leaving Trevor's apartment for the final time, I returned to my own ways within a matter of days. I initially begged a couple of acquaintances, Jerry and Trish, if I could crash at their crib until I "got myself together." At the time, I had no concept about the true significance of that term, believing that I could accomplish the recovery objective by myself and within about one week's time. Jerry and Trish were a young couple with two children who lived in the Marcy projects in Brooklyn. I knew them because of Trish who I initially met at one of my mandated treatment programs. I ran into her again later during one of my brief vacations at Riker's Island. When she had beef with one of the bully "dykish" inmates, I looked out for her by placing her under my watchful eye and wing. My reward was a few commissary items and an open invitation to come and visit her and her husband after her release. I liked Trish, so I took advantage of her offer from time to time. Trish's common-law husband, Jerry, had a job laying carpet. He drank and smoked weed regularly. Trish was the one who had gotten in trouble with crack. Although she still smoked from time to time, she typically made a genuine effort to do so on very rare occasions since she didn't want ACS placing her two young children into foster homes again. I figured this would be a good environment to chill out in for a while. I was wrong.

I was satisfied with just smoking weed and drinking a few beers for about two days. On the third day, I convinced Trish to take a few hits on the stem with me. I disappeared from their house on the fourth day, remained one more day, and left for good on the sixth. I was back to the races.

I ran the streets for a little over a month with few obstructive forces working against me. I lucked out and found different friends who were willing to take me in for a night or two. I was doing so well, boosting and pulling off trivial robberies on other addicts, primarily dope fiends, ever so often, that I was seriously considering making an offer to one of my street cohorts. I literally thought about asking Stacey whether I could become her roommate if I picked up on half of the apartment expenses. I guess I hadn't completely learned about the cycle of addiction as yet. Once again, I was becoming too cocky, forgetting about my humble origins and the places I'd been. This was when I executed extremely poor judgment and got myself into a situation that I couldn't easily get out of, not for the next two years anyway.

I got greedy. I was high one day and foolishly agreed to be the lookout for two brothers who asked me to help them rob a house in the Canarsie section of Brooklyn. One of the guys, Boo, said that the neighbors told him that the owners of the house were away on an extended trip to Disneyland. He was also told that they owned a business and were fairly well-to-do. Supposedly, their home was lavishly furnished and contained several different items that would be of major interest to petty thieves like us. I was sold when Boo informed me that the family had a new computer that they had not even taken out of the original carton as of yet. The other guy, Pino, borrowed an old car from his brother and drove us to the house. My job, for a quarter of the profits, was to nonchalantly stand around outside of the house to alert Boo and Pino if there was any trouble coming their way. The bottom line is that I did my job well. I alerted Boo, who was in the front part of the house, that I had just observed Five-0 on the corner. We simply didn't have enough time to make tracks. The police came out of nowhere from both directions. When you are in a strange neighborhood and have about five policemen with their guns drawn on you, you listen to what they are telling you to do. You listen if you want to live. The three of us wanted to live, so we put our hands behind our backs, and laid down on the floor. I stood anchored in place and quiescent as two male cops roughly searched me, carelessly read me my rights, and threw me into the Sixty-ninth Precinct's squad car. I put my head down between my legs to avoid all of the curious onlookers from the passing streets. The jig was once again up and I was going back to jail. This time, I supposed, for quite a long time.

I was charged with "Trespassing," "Accessory to a Burglary," and "Criminal Possession of a Controlled Substance." Stupid me had two vials of crack in my pocket. Had I not violated so many of my previous probation and parole sentences in my recent past, I probably would have been in much better shape. As it was, however, the tired judge who heard my case was apparently exasperated with my recidivist behavior. I was sentenced to two and a half to five years. In total, I spent about two years behind bars for this bid. I spent the first six months at Riker's Island when the courts were hearing my sad case. Due to my realization about all of the time I would have to spend in jail, the months spent at Riker's flew by as if on a bird's wings. I was so exhausted from running and a serious case of malnutrition, I viewed the first two to three months that I spent on the Rock as R & R. The rest of the time passed by my attending GED classes again, working a small job in the mess hall, and bullshitting with the girls. Aside from all of the he-said/she-said usual talk, the latest topic of interest revolved around the ghosts with whom we were confined in jail. According to the lore, there were two ghosts taking up residence with us at Riker's Island. One in dorm 9 and the other in C 73. As the story went, a man had been murdered in the last shower stall when dorm 9 was still used for male inmates. Due to the fact that too many mysterious, and at times, dangerous things happened to men who subsequently showered there, it was boarded up. This did not stop future inmates who frequented the shower stalls in dorm 9 from feeling its presence. The girls and I spent many hours sharing stories about the eerie laughter that was occasionally heard from that area very late at night. One of the inmates, Ellen, swore on ten stacks of Bibles that she once saw a vision of an estranged head bobbing up and down on invisible waves in the darkness. I never saw or heard such things, but I believed in what the others were telling me. The time passed and then I was sent up north.

I spent a little less than a month in Reception at Bedford Hills. I was then transported to Albion Medium Correctional Facility for women. I don't remember feeling anything during this process. I was like a mummy, simply going through the motions. If I did ever feel any fear or anxiety, it must have been quickly arrested. Jail is jail. Once you've seen one, you've seen them all.

One of the first things that I remember doing at Albion was sitting for my GED. I passed with flying colors. The second thing I remember was having a one-on-one fight with this bitch named Sunny who was from Peekskill and literally believed that the sun always shined on her big fat ass. We shared the same block. Sunny zeroed in on me the first second I stepped foot on the block. Then she agitated and agitated me until, after three days time, she left me with no choice but to go buck wild on her. So I did. Sunny never so much as looked at me cross-eyed ever again.

The only other physical confrontation I had while at Albion was when I was once jumped on my way to sick call. I had a severe migraine headache and wanted to get myself checked out. A crazed sister jumped out of nowhere and pulled me into a somewhat secluded area. She had a kerchief covering most of her face and a homemade ice pick pressed up against my neck. The crazed female was hissing out gibberish that I didn't understand. I believe she must have had me mistaken for somebody else because I believe I didn't know the bitch from atom. But since my life was on the line, there was no time for logical reasoning. My sense of self-preservation surged forth and I managed to divert her attention to the doorway for a minute. Then I overpowered her by sticking my strongest finger, the second one on my right hand, directly into her eye. When I withdrew my finger, it was covered with mucous and blood. I hauled ass out of there and never spoke about what happened with anybody. This is the first time. It will probably be my last.

My time in Albion generally passed uneventfully. I smoked a little weed, took a few pulls on a stem when I could successfully locate one, pursued my education, and worked in the laundry room. I still refused to attend any in-house rehab programs. I developed a close tie with a woman named Ruth. Ruth was a big-boned, heavyset woman who was originally from Alabama. She had been sentenced to three and a half years for beating a man to a pulp. The man had sexually abused her five-year-old daughter the year before. It had taken Ruth almost a whole year to find him. If the police hadn't found Ruth bludgeoning the man with a bat on time, she wouldn't have been placed together with me in Albion. Instead, she would have been serving a life sentence for murder at Bedford Hills.

Ruth and I chilled out together on a regular basis. Once we met each other, Ruth and I would often smoke weed together and talk for hours. She never smoked any crack. But as far as I was concerned, Ruth was all right by me.

About eight months after we met, our relationship shifted. It took on a subtle unsettling dynamic. Ruth became zealously involved with the Bible. This was a commonplace occurrence in jail. The worst of our nation's murderers, thieves, and sex offenders find God in jail. Ninety-five percent of them lose him as soon as they step foot out of the prison's gates. In addition to regularly attending the prison chapel, Ruth started reading the Bible every chance she got. What made things worse was that she got a little bit too "preachy" for my liking, causing a rift to surface in our friendship. I had never fared well with pressure. Ruth started singing the same song about church to me every day.

"Victoria, why don't you come on and come to the chapel service with me? It will help you, you know?"

"No, it won't, Ruth. I don't believe in God."

"But God is real, baby. God is real. Why don't you give him a try?"

"Because I don't believe in him and I don't want to. Ruth, why don't you just get off my back? Why don't you?"

She would never look injured, although she would usually leave me alone once I told her to do so. This circular exchange of words between Ruth and I characterized our communication for about the next eight months. I still liked Ruth. I just spent a lot less time with her.

About three weeks before I was scheduled to be released from Albion, Ruth turned the pressure valve all the way up. It almost seemed as if she presumed that her main spiritual calling in life was to convert me into a believer. I was not in agreement with her presumptuous thinking and fought her all the way. I moved away from her, avoided her, ignored her, gave her the cold shoulder, made argumentative retorts, and when completely overwhelmed by rising sensations of exasperation, cursed her out. Nothing worked. She kept coming back for more. I was deathly afraid that I'd eventually just have to jump up and hurt her. I didn't want to do this. I had just cleared the board and wanted to go home without any distracting problems. Plus, I liked Ruth and genuinely didn't want to see her body sprawled across the prison floor due to my own doing. Our cyclic interaction repeated itself again and again.

One Saturday night she got me. I was menstruating, weak, and tired of arguing. I also knew that I'd be leaving soon. Ruth still had at least one more year left to do. I think she was more surprised than I was when I turned away from the bolted-down prison television just long enough to say, "Okay, okay already. You win. What time do I have to be ready tomorrow, ten?"

A profound sense of accomplishment registered on her face as she gently touched my shoulder.

"Uh, huh. Ten is good, Victoria. Ten o'clock tomorrow morning. Oh, God is good. Thank you, Jesus."

I was grateful that she quickly started to move away from me. If I had to hear one more of her "'thank you Jesus'," I'd have changed my mind about going. As it was, Ruth's mumbles became increasingly less audible as she neared her cell.

I was bored the majority of the time that I spent seated next to Ruth in the prison chapel on the following morning. Bored, hungry, and extremely sorry that I had given in to her incessant request. Toward the very end of the sermon, I briefly glanced at a pamphlet that was resting on the chair beside me. I read the words in bold print, "Though I may walk through the shadow of death . . ." I felt an almost imperceptible quiver cross over me and quickly turned away from the pamphlet I had been reading. I had enough. No more of this church business for me. I was through with it.

About eleven hours later when I went to bed that night, I momentarily entertained the possibility that this was just not so. I might have been through with it, but it wasn't through with me. A voiceless nagging gnawed at my heart. When I couldn't stand it any longer, I proclaimed aloud and sincerely into the darkness, "All right already, enough. If you are in fact real God, prove it to me. I'll give you three days. If you don't prove yourself to me in three days, leave me the hell alone forever." Talk about making vacant ultimatums. When I was through intimidating God, I felt restful and relieved, almost as if all of my mounting anxiety had effortlessly been sucked out of me through a straw. I fell asleep that night without any trouble.

That night, however, I had a strange dream. I dreamt that I saw Mama in a flowing white robe, a youthful and pretty Mama, holding out an electric drill in outstretched hands. Although her lips appeared to be moving, I couldn't hear any sounds coming from them. Her facial expression looked like she was pleading with me. I couldn't see myself in the dream. Yet, I knew that I was there.

I awakened the next morning in a cold sweat, unhinged from having seen Mama in my dream the night before. As far as I could remember, I hadn't seen Mama in any of my dreams since she died. I sat up in bed that morning puzzled about what it all meant. When I couldn't figure it out in about a half an hour's time, I shrugged the dream off and proceeded on with my day as usual.

On the second night, I dreamt the same dream again, only this time more vividly. Mama's eyes were imploring me during this second night's dream. I sat up in bed again the next morning. What the hell did the dream mean? What was Mama trying to tell me and why did she have an electric drill in her hands? My head pounded. I shrugged the dream off once again and tried to let it go, although this time not quite as successfully. Throughout the day, my soul felt an internal tug ever so lightly as if by a string that was as fine as silken thread. An invisible string of urgency that was tied to my past.

On the third night, I dreamt the dream one last time. Toward the dream's concluding moments, Mama's pleas seemed to be finally heard. I woke up just in time to see her passing the electric drill into my hands, while a look of relief and peace washed across her face. On that third morning I was also not so coincidentally awakened to the sound of construction workers beginning to do repair work in the cell that was across from me. The sliding gate door had come off of its track and prevented the cell door from closing efficiently. One of the workers had begun to drill into the resistant iron bars with an electric drill. With an electric drill. He began to drill into the iron gate with an electric drill. I was soaked all over. I began to tremble and cry, remembering.

"Because I'm trapped behind a curtain of dread."

A child's voice. "But Mama, curtains can be moved or pushed aside."

"Not when your curtain of dread is made of iron."

The wee voice with the message at the end of the string was actually my own. "But, there's always electric drills."

"Oh shit." I jumped up and down and started to shout at the top of my lungs. "Oh shit. There are always electric drills." I banged fiercely on the bars, screaming like a lunatic. "There's always electric drills. Do you hear me?" I said, "Do you fucking hear me? There's always electric drills." I sat down on my bed and laughed hysterically. Fat tears dripped off my face. If you drill deep enough, you'll eventually strike gold.

The correction officers on duty that morning thought that I had lost my mind. They also temporarily considered that I had a crazy impulse to break out of jail with an electric drill right at that moment. I had no intentions of doing so. The dream had drilled a hole through the first and most durable wall of dread that surrounded me. Now I was ready to fight, because even when you are surrounded by a curtain of dread and your curtain of dread is made of iron, there are always electric drills. The prison psychologist felt that in spite of my one brief isolated outburst, the plans for my pending release should proceed as normal. That night, when I laid myself down to sleep, I thanked Mama and the mysterious forces behind her appearance. I laid still and ponderous. Just as I was on the brink of drifting off to sleep, hope crept into my cell on a cat's padded paws and purred the whole night through.

CHAPTER EIGHTEEN

The searching heart finds hope in unexpected places.
—Anonymous

I WAS RELEASED from the Albion State Correctional Facility for Women six days later. Due to the fact that I still owed the state about twenty months, I was placed on parole. For reasons of convenience and simplicity and nothing else, I contacted Ms. Cathy prior to going before the board. With the exception of Trevor with whom I had ceased all contact, Ms. Cathy was the only functional decent citizen I knew. She seemed to believe that I honestly wanted to do the right thing this time and agreed to have me use her residence as the address that would be on file with parole. At the time I made this agreement with Ms. Cathy, I had already made up my mind that I was not going to go near the old neighborhood. Too many memories. In drug rehab, they refer to these kinds of memories as triggers. People, places, and things. I didn't want anything or anybody interfering with my staying clean, so I desired to keep possible "triggers" at a safe distance. I was released from Albion on June 29, 1997. The last time I did drugs was on June 20, 1997. This is when I had gotten my hands on a sizable amount of marijuana in jail and called myself having a belated solitary birthday party. Mama visited me in my dream holding the electric drill for the first time in the middle of the following night. Legally speaking, June 21 of last year marked my first anniversary for sobriety. It's April of 2000 now and I'm coming up on my second year clean. Believe it or not, it has taken me almost an entire year to write my life story. In fact, I might as well say that it took me a year since I'm not done writing it yet. I believe I left off at the part when I walked through Albion's metal gates into freedom after slightly more than two years of confinement.

After my day of enlightenment about the significance behind the recurring presence of electric drills in my dreams, I made up my mind that I was going to fight for my life, or in other words, fight for my recovery. I wasn't exactly sure what I had to do to fight, although I was certain that I'd have to fight with all of my might. It was during the last three days of my incarceration at Albion when it finally struck me that I needed support from some form of a structured rehab program in order to stay clean. I knew that if I didn't receive this help it would only be a matter of time before I fell back into the races. I also knew enough about the way I functioned to understand that the most important thing I could do was stay away from all reminders of my past life. Despite my capricious treatment history, I was acutely aware of the majority of my true triggers. It was for all of the above reasons that I decided to sign myself into a short-term inpatient drug treatment program on the same day that I was released. It was on this same day that I learned a very important lesson—just because one decides to do right does not mean that everything is going to work out right. For the first time in my life, I met trials and tribulations head on. In other words, I decided to give more than just lip service to the concept of facing life on life's terms.

During the entire ride back to New York City on the greyhound bus, I thought about getting high. I tried as hard as I could to force this thought out of my head, squeeze it out of the core of my being into another dimension of the universe. Nothing I did worked. I ended up having these toxic thoughts hover about the whole ride home. It seemed as if I wore them loosely like a worn familiar hat. When my bus pulled into the port authority in Manhattan, my hat and I headed out to one of the detox programs with which I was familiar. This was when the problems started.

Since I had never possessed any earnest desire to change my ways, I never knew how difficult it was to deal with the formal administrative aspects of entering a recovery program. With the exception of my release papers from jail, I had no personal identification at the time I was released from Albion. Street addicts are known for losing everything. I was no exception to the rule. Why the hell would I have ever worried about having a birth certificate or library card? When I was in jail and somewhat more lucid in my thinking, it never occurred to me just how important it was to apply for different sources of identification. I never thought about it and nobody told me otherwise. One of the first messages I received about "the system" was, just like everything else, drug rehab was a business and all about the money. I didn't have any health insurance, meaning that no agency could be paid for providing me with services. When agencies know they won't be paid for helping you, they don't help you. I couldn't apply for emergency Medicaid because I wasn't suffering from any ailment that the hospital's detox program could pigeonhole into a medical emergency category. I was also informed that people didn't have to medically detox off of crack. Even if I had been using crack up until the day I sought out treatment, I would have had to claim that I was physically withdrawing from alcohol or heroin to be admitted into an in-patient hospital program. The other crazy fact that I learned was that in order for me to be admitted into a detox program, alcohol and/or some other drug would still have to be detected in my system. The receptionist at the second hospital I visited actually made the subtle comment that "some people in this same situation get high one last time" just to make sure that there would be enough drugs in their system to make them Medicaid eligible. I wondered if the receptionist actually believed that this comment was supportive.

I went to four hospital detox programs within a three-hour time period on my first day out of prison. Rejection and disappointment met me at every door. I pleaded and I begged to be admitted. I even cried at the fourth hospital. The problem was that I couldn't be easily admitted into a thirty-day in-patient treatment program, which typically preceded acceptance into a long-term treatment program, if I wasn't referred by a seasoned social worker from detox. At the fourth hospital, I met an angel in a social worker's suit. He took pity on me and led me into his office when he recognized how distraught I had become. He subsequently explained the intricate details involved in applying for Medicaid and emergency Medicaid in as kind and patient a voice as possible. After a five-minute conversation with him I determined that it would be a waste of time for me to go to any more detox programs to seek treatment. I wondered why none of the previous workers had bothered to take the five minutes to explain the Medicaid application process. This would have saved me considerable time, energy, and carfare—three things that I could not afford to lose at the time. During my half-hour wait at the third hospital, I heard a receptionist scream at two obviously very sick heroin addicts because they decided to go to "her hospital" instead of the one in their "catch mit" area. After she finished taking out all of her pent-up anger on them, she told the pathetic-looking couple that it was too late to be admitted anywhere anyway and that they should seek detox on the following Monday morning. Meanwhile, she practically conducted the next perspective client's social history through a thick glass window with the aid of a microphone to hear the client's responses above the din of the waiting room. Everyone in the room was apprised of the sordid details of this client's personal life, including his past legal history and HIV status. I believe the most ludicrous, yet disheartening dialogue I overheard on my first day out of prison was between an intake worker and a middle-aged heroin addict. The addict had just informed the worker that she had used her last token to travel the distance from her home to the hospital. The worker, pretending not to hear a word that the perspective client was saying, insisted that this individual purchase a $15 photo ID from one of the Chinese rinky-dink photo centers as well as travel to the Department of Labor to pick up a form that verifies that she did not work at all during the past year. Exasperated, the addict sighed and told the worker, "Lady, I just told you I ain't got no money. And don't you know that if I did, I'd spend it on dope. I'm an addict. That's why I'm here in the first place." I no longer wondered why so many of us addicts don't choose formal treatment centers as the means by which we combat our addictions.

My angel in a social worker's suit referred me to an out-patient program, explaining that they should be able to accept me into their program and then walk me through the steps of obtaining Medicaid health insurance. He was wrong. Dead wrong. The rude clerk at the out-patient clinic, who sat like a peacock perched at the edge of her chair, told me that my problems were "too extensive" and "out of their jurisdiction." It was five o' clock by then. I had no safe place to spend the night and hardly any money left inside of my pocket. I was scared and frustrated and felt like saying "fuck it" and getting high. Instead, I sarcastically whispered "thanks" to the brusque clerk and went out into the hallway, leaned against the wall, and cried. This was when I met my second angel for the day, a male one in a security guard's suit. I told him about my unfortunate circumstances. In response, he suggested that I attend a self-help "Narcotics Anonymous" meeting that was scheduled to take place in two hours in the basement of a church that was located around the corner. Through my choking sobs, I reminded this second angel that I not only needed rehab assistance, but also a roof over my head. He acknowledged the precarious nature of my plight, but insisted that I should attend the meeting anyway. His parting words were "you never know." You never know, umph, that's for sure. In spite of my conflicted feelings, I took his advice and went to the meeting. I sat in the back, scared and desperate in a wobbly folding chair.

At my first NA meeting, I heard the Twelve Steps and Twelve Traditions and wondered what I was doing there. Afterwards, I heard people share from the floor their goals, sorrow and pain, and joy and accomplishments. Then, I had a vague idea about what I was doing there. Nonetheless, my anxiety level heightened as the meeting neared to a close. I couldn't think anymore. I stopped hearing what people were saying. My thoughts revolved around one issue only—the issue of where I'd be sleeping that night. Approximately five minutes before the meeting formally concluded, the elected "leader" announced the time and inquired as to whether there was anybody present who had a burning desire to share before the meeting's time was over. I had no idea what I was doing, but I stood up.

I stood up, stated that my name was Victoria, admitted that I was an addict, and told anybody and everybody who was listening everything. When I finished I sat back down on the wobbly chair, feeling mildly light-headed, although somewhat relieved. I put my head down on the table in front of me and wept, legions of unrestrained tears.

The feel of a reassuring pat on my shoulder carried me back through my tunnel of self-pity into the present. I slowly looked up, trying to simultaneously wipe the wetness from my eyes with my shirt's sleeve, and looked into the smiling face of the third angel that I was destined to meet that day. An angel named Opal. Thomas' sister.

Thomas' sister Opal, much like myself, had suffered from a serious addiction to crack. Not being different from the rest of us, crack brought the worst out in Opal. She suffered from an active addiction for more than twelve years, and like me, paid a high price for living the low life of a street addict. Opal was the second of four children born to her alcoholic unmarried mother. While she and her older brother both suffered from active addictions to drugs and alcohol, her two younger siblings, Thomas and Sheila, seemingly escaped the burden of being chemically dependent. But, as I was yet to learn along my own personal recovery journey, they did not escape entirely unscathed. Opal used drugs such as marijuana and alcohol throughout her teens. She took her first hit from the pipe when she was eighteen. She jetted off to the races directly afterwards, not bothering to bring her head up above troubled waters for the next twelve years until one day, while peering at the frightful forbidding countenance that stared out at her from the faded cracked mirror that hung crookedly on her mother's wall, Opal decided that she had had enough. She knew that there was another person buried beneath the horrid reflection of a scarecrow that looked out at her from the mirror. Her recovery mission was to find that person. She spent the next three years searching. At her recent fifth NA anniversary, Opal stated that she believes that she finally found the person. It was a young woman who she had long since forgotten, denied and rejected. Herself.

After gently stroking my shoulder and looking into the pith of my soul for about two minutes after I had shared my burning desire at my first NA meeting, Opal asked me if I genuinely wanted to stay clean and whether I'd accept help. When I responded that not only did I want to stay clean, but was also worn-out from my day's futile desperate search for assistance from drug rehab programs, Opal smiled empathetically and reassured me that I had come to the right place. I dried my tears, threw some water on my face in the women's bathroom, and crossed the meeting floor to meet another young woman who was in her second year of recovery from both heroin and crack. Her name was Mary. Mary had a job at a local supermarket as a cashier and was looking for a roommate to share the costs of her apartment. Her previous roommate, Theresa, who she had also met in the rooms of recovery, had relapsed and gone back to a life on the streets. For the next three days, I slept on the living room couch at Opal's house. Opal lived in a one-bedroom apartment with her boyfriend. Her boyfriend, Alex, was a recovering alcoholic. During my stay with Opal and Alex, they introduced me to the underlying principles and doctrines of NA. Opal took me to the out-patient treatment program from which she had successfully graduated that was located on the opposite side of Brooklyn. A deal was struck wherein I would be admitted into the program, with a Medicaid pending status. On the second day that I spent with Opal, she accompanied me to reapply for such vital personal documents as my birth certificate and social security card. Based on the fact that the treatment facility had supplied me with a letter of introduction for my application for Medicaid, the Medicaid application process was expedited. On the third day, Opal's boyfriend talked to someone he knew in order to get me my current job in the small department store in which I am still employed. As soon as it was ascertained that I would begin receiving a regular paycheck in two weeks, I moved in with Mary and we formally became roommates. July of 1997 marked the first time in my life that I had a job and my own apartment. At this juncture, I had a few days more than two weeks clean from drugs. But, as they say in NA, I kept going back.

Although I lived with Mary, Opal and Alex continued to keep me under their protective wings. I accompanied them to different NA and AA meetings practically every night. I began to feel part of something, something positive. About six weeks after I'd been attending meetings on a regular daily basis, I attended a meeting in South Brooklyn that played a large part in changing my life. I met another angel. An angel who was also an addict in recovery and sharing her story. I related to everything she said. Her story touched my heart and left me feeling open and desirous for more. At the close of the meeting, I humbly approached the angel who was the meeting's speaker for the night, shared my feelings that nobody's words had ever touched me like hers, and asked whether she minded being my sponsor. I couldn't think of any better way of asking the question. She looked at me knowingly, as if remembering something crucial from way back, searched my eyes as if trying to validate my true intent, and graciously agreed. I am certain that I lucked out that night. I chose the best sponsor in the whole world. A better one does not exist.

Over the last year and a half, my recovery process has taken many twists and turns. Its progress has never, not even for one day, followed a linear or constant course. I have good days and bad ones. I've also had excellent days and extremely horrid ones. Fortunately, the horrid ones have been far and few between. Thus far, I've had the most trouble controlling my anger. My anger, much like my active addiction, seems to have a life all of its own. Much to my dismay, it typically does its own thing as it chooses. I don't remember being this angry when I was still getting high. But then, on the other hand, I don't remember feeling much of anything at all during those days. The experience of having feelings has been very much like an adventure into new and unexplored frontiers. My weekly therapy prepares me for these excursions by drawing me maps, warning me about the mountainous regions, and providing me with insight into my own strengths and weaknesses. Concepts that I spent minimal time considering before.

My sponsor, on the other hand, is as the song says, "the wind beneath my wings." One day at a time, I fly on.

I've been involved in both group and individual therapy for over one year. During the course of this year, I've learned many things. One of them is that Mama is my one sensitive topic, my sore spot so to speak. My personal insight about my heightened sensitivity in this area falls short of understanding my apparent conflicted feelings toward this familiar, beloved relative. Particularly in my group work, I've encountered many a recovering addict whose parent was purposefully cruel, abusive, or overtly selfish and uncaring. Mama was never any of these things. She was just Mama, trying to do the best she could under the circumstances. I never had a negative thing to say about her in any of my groups. Contrarily, I generally applauded her efforts. This strategy had been effective over the years with every other form of treatment that had been jammed down my unwilling throat. I initially believed it was effective now as well. That was until I realized that my group leader was not only compassionate and sensitive, but also artfully perceptive. Without my being able to pinpoint her clever strategy, she would occasionally pull back the layers of denial and intellectualization from my sanitized statements and momentarily leave me facing the bare bones truth. I never did do well with skeletons. They left me feeling frightened and unnerved. The feeling of one huge knot twisting in the pit of my stomach. A primal fear, stretching within the vulnerable and hollow regions of my ego. Once my individual therapist exhausted himself from pushing me deeper and deeper into the frosty caverns of my childhood's affective memories, and then finally let the topic of Mama go, concluding that I "wasn't ready to go there yet," I was grateful that such therapeutic conclusions had been reached. The problem was that my heart was not as yet convinced. As if it were a small omnipresent organ with a natural function, the knot that I frequently felt twisting in my stomach remained, seemingly undaunted by my therapist's conclusions. A process had already begun.

CHAPTER NINETEEN

A man's heart deviseth his way: but the Lord directeth his steps.
—Proverbs 16:9

IT IS APRIL of 2000 and I feel like I'm losing my mind. I don't know what's gotten into me lately, but I've surely taken a turn for the worse. If I had to affix a marker to identify the beginning of my decline, I'd say that it began shortly after the clock struck midnight on New Year's Eve. I recall starting to have a real hard time of it almost directly afterwards. The question on the table is why. Why? I still attend meetings, although not with the identical ardor and consistency as before. I still see my individual therapist on an every other week basis. For whatever it was worth, I supposedly successfully completed group therapy. As I believe I already mentioned, I also attended a closed group for Adult Survivors of Sexual Abuse for three months. I completed this group in mid-February with an unblemished attendance record. While I've made evident my increasing low tolerance for frustration and waning patience at work on more than one occasion in the recent past, I am fortunately still employed. Although Mary and I never became the best of friends, in my opinion, we enjoy a perfect roommate arrangement. We respect one another, maintain healthy boundaries, make regular, helpful and supportive gestures, and about once a week, plop down on our old, tattered sofa to drink coffee and do "girl talk." A better roommate situation does not exist.

I have friends. Although I haven't met anybody quite as special as Bruny, the many men and women from the rooms with whom I currently socialize are all right by me. It is for this reason that I am at a loss for explaining why I feel such a gnawing sense of boredom and emptiness all of the time. I am a very busy woman, very busy.

At present, due to our ongoing "differences of opinion," and obviously disparate goals and needs, Thomas and I do not see each other as regularly as before. I guess you could say that we've made up since our last door slamming argument. We talk often, at least every other day, albeit with a definite element of detachment and reservation. Deep, deep down I know that Thomas loves me. Not just in that benevolent manner that people love other people, but in that special way that a man loves a woman, intimately, with a quicksilver strength. In spite of all of my own dysfunction and craziness, I feel his love. Intuitively, with a feminine acuity. I also know that I love him back. Yet, in spite of these mutual feelings of romance, some unidentified presence continues to prevent us from tying our passionate love knot together. Something gets in the way of the business of our loving. If it wasn't for the virtue of patience, Thomas and I would be apart. Presently, it is the only predilection that keeps us bound together. Graciously, functioning much like crazy glue.

I have not stepped foot into any of my past deceptive dungeons wherein I was always tempted to get high. I've kept myself away from clubs, bars, all of the peers from my past with whom I used to run the streets with and get high, and from Ms. Cathy. In keeping my distance from Ms. Cathy, I've kept all of the memories that lie dormant in the old neighborhood at bay—the old neighborhood in which I spent a large part of my childhood. Probably, the one of the few neighborhoods of which I am inclined to call my own. I miss the streets. I miss the excitement. And, don't let anybody tell you otherwise, I miss getting high. Hardly a day goes by without me thinking about getting high and missing it. It's only a question of to what degree. Interestingly enough, I missed getting high less during the first few months of my recovery walk. I guess I had so much else to worry about at the time in terms of my own day-to-day survival that I could not afford to allow thoughts of getting high rent any space in my head. I've survived sober and independently for more than a year now. I guess I didn't notice when the "For Rent" sign recently went up in my head.

For the last couple of months, memories and thoughts about getting high have overwhelmed me. Their strength has been such that they have successfully pushed aside other more pure and positive thoughts, and have then stood, proud and haughtily, in their place. I have drug dreams constantly. Dreams in which I am vividly portrayed combing every nook of my surroundings for an accidentally discarded vial of crack. Dreams in which I am high, soaring and powerful, dwelling contently in my own skin. Dreams in which my trembling hands raise the long sought after pipe to quivering, chafed lips. The sounds of desperate sucking. Gurps. Dreams in which I, without fail, awaken drenched in my own perspiration, wide-eyed and frightened, with the faint, bitter taste of the crack pipe lingering on my tongue. After the incident with the electric drill in jail, Mama stopped visiting me in my dreams. I am angry about that. Angry at her and angry at the executive coordinator of all dreams. Just plain angry.

I don't know what I'm going to do anymore. I know without question that I am at the end of my rope, standing out on a limb, teetering over the edge, counting my days. One minute at a time. If something doesn't give soon, I know I'm going to give up. Give up everything I've worked for, strived for during these past many months of sobriety. The pain and frustration of it all is so deep, so cutting. It mangles the heart. I have no idea what is at its core, or even why it presented itself when it did. It is like a cruel uninvited guest, torturing me with each passing day that it remains in my presence. My head pounds. My heart races. Flutters, at times. Tears escape from my eyes in buckets. I have no idea why. Recovery was supposed to make it all better. It's not better at all. I feel now and it hurts.

My sponsor urges me to hang in there. Write more, go into further detail. Reach out and call her more. Go to meetings. Keep coming back. It works if you work it. So work it, you're worth it. I don't want to work it anymore. I'm an NA failure. Maybe, just maybe, I'm really not worth it.

Last night, I woke my sponsor up at two in the morning. She heard the ring of sheer despair in my voice tone and told me to hurry over. I ran all the way there. More than twenty blocks. I collapsed into her arms and sobbed dry tears. I passed through the night without having to pick up, without having to get high. I slept in my sponsor's living room on her couch. She stood over me in the morning, her body blocking the sun from spilling its rays into my eyes, and gently shook me awake. She told me that a new idea had occurred to her very early on that morning. I couldn't imagine it being any earlier than it was at that very moment. My sponsor suggested that since Mama had stopped visiting me, it was high time that I went to go and visit Mama. I told you a long time ago that I think that my sponsor is crazy. I currently possess the same belief. However, when I looked toward the right of me at my crumpled clothing strewn across her living room furniture, I passively agreed. My sponsor might, in fact, really be crazy. But, on the other hand, I know that I'm crazy, so what have I got to lose by giving it a try? I'll go on one of my days off from work. That is, if I haven't relapsed yet.

April 15, 2000

I visited Mama yesterday, two days after I agreed I would. I probably still would not have gone had my sponsor not repeatedly called me to remind me of the passive promise I had made a couple of days before in her living room at dawn. I guess there was a large part of me that didn't want to go. Now I know why.

I arrived at the cemetery shortly before sunset, probably fifteen minutes before I wouldn't have been allowed legal entry anymore due to the lateness of the hour. Fate was testing my graveyard trespassing inclinations quite a bit lately. With a bowed head and eyes that searched the pavement for unknown entities, I scurried between the parked cars in the parking lot and slipped in through the front gate. Undetected, I hoped. Although I had reached a point in my life where I no longer had to slither and hide, on this particular day, I preferred to remain invisible. Out of habit, perhaps.

I weaved my way around the small islands of the dead, taking brisk steps in the direction of where I remembered Mama's corpse lay. I located the tiny stone slate that marked her plot within a matter of ten minutes. It was positioned in the center of a row of plots, all with equally small head stones and lacking in garishness. The moment I permitted my eyes to settle on her name, Anita Rosa Gonzalez, chills climbed up my spine, as if scrambling up the steps of a ladder, one vertebra at a time. I wasn't spooked, just acutely aware that her spirit had been waiting for my visit. Within seconds, my mind dashed past the flashing scenes of my childhood days spent with Mama. Mama and I crouching down low in dark and scary ghetto alleys. My early school-age self leading Mama out of playgrounds by the hand when her nods were so intense that she almost tumbled off of the park benches. Mama taking me to school, often three or four days after it had already started. Mama and I sitting up late at night in front of rusty, poorly functioning televisions, both of us having an equally hard time keeping our eyes open and focused on the screen's achromatic images. Standing there in front of her burial plot, I envisioned the times when Mama had accidentally overdosed. I revisited the sensation of my thundering heart. My skin felt the clammy touch of the greasy vagabond men who Mama often allowed into our apartments. Wandering, invading hands on naive, satiny smooth little girl skin. Mama, oblivious, basking in the pleasure of insentience, my wounded child lying equally as still and lifeless, terrified in a corner of the same room. Only feet away from her reach, but light years away from her protective reaction. I saw us sitting up in Family Court again and again and again. Foster care, emergency rooms, methadone clinics, and victims' service offices, welfare. Two pathetic, vulnerable souls joined together by similar genetic structures and the substance of the heart.

I fell down on my knees in front of Mama's tomb and howled, toddler-style. I bellowed and I shrieked, daring both the living and the dead to stop me. I cried from the belly of the wounded child that lied within.

"Mama, why, why, why did you do this? How could you let it happen? I hate you." I hollered up toward the heavens, raking the ground with dirt-stained fingernails. I beat at the dusty air with clenched fists.

"I hate you. I hate you for what you did. Look at what you did to me. Mama, look at what you fucking did. I'm no damn good Mama, and it's all your fault." I fell down on the ground and found myself rolling over into a fetus position. I choked on my own tears.

"Mama, those men. You never stopped them, never told them to leave me alone. You didn't fucking care. I needed you, Mama. I needed you at home. You were never fucking there. Never. I hate you, you stupid fucking bitch." I heaved myself back up and on to my knees.

"It's all your fault. All of it. I needed a fucking mother and instead I got you. Why did you ever have me? I'll always hate you Mama, and I'll never forgive you for what you've done. Never."

Although I can't remember the specifics now, I believe I kneeled there on top of Mama's grave, sobbing and repeating phrases full of pain and hatred until my mind and body went completely numb. When my eyes and lips were dry, my head and heart seemingly empty, I lifted myself up from the ground, wiped my nose with my jacket's sleeve, and slowly walked away. I did not say goodbye.

May 15, 2000

After purging just about every pent-up feeling of pain and anger that I ever possessed at Mama's graveside the other day, nothing major occurred in my life. It was for a lack of better words, anti-climatic. I continued with therapy and my meetings. I worked. I socialized with my NA friends on occasion and I had hour long conversations with my sponsor, seemingly all to no avail. I still felt like shit. While my anger was no longer spilling over the rim, my feelings of emptiness, hopelessness, and confusion prevailed. "Lost" would probably be the most accurate term to describe my daily experience. In actuality, I had probably been lost throughout my life. I was just that much more aware of it now. Like an automaton, I persevered. One day at a time. I also never picked up.

May 29, 2000

My mood and attitude are making a change for the worse again. I feel as if I've jumped off of a diving board, descending in slow motion into the dark, murky waters of despair. I don't want to sink to the bottom again, neither figuratively or literally. I need to find a life vest, something, somebody, to help keep me afloat, prevent me from going under. I went to my sponsor's apartment for the thousandth time after work today to tell her about my deteriorating status. She suggested that I pray. I was desperate, so I did.

"God, I don't really believe in you. No offense, but you just haven't played that big of a part in my life before. But, right now, I'm desperate and need help. So, if you are there like so many others seem to believe, if you do exist and are really out there listening to me, hear my prayer. Help."

June 14, 2000

Since the night that I prayed to God, I've seen Mama and Ms. Cathy in my dreams. Together the two of them come and visit me every night. It doesn't seem as if they are trying to relate any urgent pressing messages. They're just there, together in my dreams, visibly content and happy. Both are smiling and wearing blue.

This is driving me crazy. I still feel wretchedly heavy with affliction. Yet, I don't know why. I sense that there's something out there waiting. A vital message perhaps. One of life's lessons. An aura of expectancy permeates the air that I breathe. I'm less than a week away from my second anniversary. How the hell can I speak in front of anybody feeling like this? I'm choking on the expectancy.

June 17, 2000

My suffering became so intolerable, my burden so heavy, that after pacing back and forth in the darkness of my room for an hour, my heart finally exploded as if it endured the most unkindest laceration of all. I streaked out the front door in search of relief. It was about three o'clock in the morning. I went to the nearest station, climbed on the train, and headed uptown to the Bronx. I just couldn't take it anymore. I had given up. A crooning voice was pestering me. It was telling me that there was something in the Bronx that could make me feel better. A remedy to help allay my throbbing mental aches. A panacea. I thought the voice was talking about crack. Last night I head uptown with the conscious intention of getting high. Fortunately, it never happened. I found my medicine and it didn't take the form of crack-cocaine.

When I disembarked off the train in the Bronx, the brightly lit station was full of people. More specifically, people in blue police uniforms. Somebody had apparently just been stabbed and robbed on the station and the police were everywhere. There was something about the scene, seeing all of those official uniforms that made me slow down. Their formal, authoritative look laded my step when I left the station and stepped out on to the Bronx pavement.

When I finally arrived at the closest cop spot, a building that was located about two blocks from the building in which Bruny had once lived, I took a deep breath and looked around before I stepped inside. There were foul-smelling overflowing trash cans littering the sidewalk. Broken beer bottles and crack vials were strewn about openly on the floor. Mangy stray cats in pursuit of scurrying rats. Filth and depression and waste. I shook these thoughts loose from my head and entered the building anyway. As soon as I stepped inside, I saw that over in the dimly lit building's vestibule lay a figure huddled in the corner. A human figure, female. Cautiously, I walked over. Standing above, I still couldn't get a good look at her face. A part of me said "fuck it," telling me to mind my own business and keep looking for what I came for. Another part, the more human part that had been nurtured and cultivated over the past two years, kept me with my feet planted on the ground in front of the lifeless female figure, curious and concerned.

"Hello, uh, hello, are you all right?"

No response.

"Yo, uh, wake up. Are you all right?"

Dead silence. A car honked his horn three times somewhere in the smoldering dark in the distance.

"Hello." I took hold of one of her shoulders and shook it gently. Nothing. She lay as still as a stone. Out of frustration, I knocked the woman's shoulder up against the wall, knowing that her head would have to roll up along with it. It did. It was then that I figured out that she was dead. I stared into a pair of moist eyes that were rolled up into the back of a black woman's head. Her mouth was open and it was apparent that she had taken her last breath some time ago. I stared into the white moons of the stranger's eyes for what seemed to be forever. In reality, it must have been for less than thirty seconds. I saw the reflections of Mama and Bruny and then me in those glazed rolled up eyes. It was then that I understood that it was here, in this strange woman's eyes, where the message that I was propelled to go seek lay. Simple and clear. I left out the building, went to a corner pay phone and reported the corpse's whereabouts to the police. I never once considered digging the strange woman's pockets. I was overcome by feelings of sentimentality and neediness. Under the circumstances, I could think of no better place to go than to Ms. Cathy—the character from my recent dreams who I had not seen in real life for about ten years.

I headed off on foot in the direction of her apartment. I never did cop that night. Amongst others, the lesson that lied within the eyes of the corpse was "Don't pick up."

It must have been about six in the morning when I arrived at Ms. Cathy's apartment. Lately, I seemed to have a thing with having deep encounters at the strike of dawn. As usual, somebody had broken the lock and buzzer system on her building's front door, making my quick entrance a smooth and easy task. I knocked firmly and purposefully on her door one minute later, with memories of running through the same building's hallways as a child starting to assemble in my mind. I knocked to the staccato beat of three, waited for a few moments, and put my knuckles to her wooden door with the same rhythm once again. One, two, three. An older, more worn version of Ms. Cathy opened the door, stepped aside while rubbing the sleep from her eyes with the back of one slightly liverish blemished hand, and hoarsely beckoned me to come in. She never questioned my identity from behind the other side of the closed door. Eerily, it appeared as if she was expecting my visit.

Ms. Cathy led me inside by my elbow. Nothing had changed. Her apartment was the same as I last saw it one decade ago. It was redolent of a lemon fresh mahogany scent, furniture neat and tidily positioned on sanitized shiny floors. A might experience of deja vu filtered through my senses. Once again, I was overcome with sentimentality, albeit this time within the context of familiar homey surroundings. For a lack of a better description of the feeling, I had finally come home. I looked up, and there in Ms. Cathy's teary blue eyes stood layers of evidence of compassion, kindness, and love. For the first time in my life I understood the significance behind the hackneyed phrase "There's no place like home."

As if she could read my mind, Ms. Cathy slowly guided me through her apartment, permitting me ample time to absorb and process and feel. Although everything that I remembered from my childhood was just the way I had left it, when we entered Ms. Cathy's bedroom, I noticed one change. There was one difference in the overall decorum from how I remembered the way things used to be. There was an eight by twelve inch glossy, finished photo of Jose "el salvaje" next to her bed. It was to the right of her Bible, placed neatly beneath the lamp on her nightstand. My eyes quickly turned to her questioningly. Before I could verbalize my curiosity, she softly explained that an old wallet-size picture of Jose had mysteriously turned up one morning when she was sweeping the floor. As soon as the local photo store opened that day, Ms. Cathy had brought it in to make copies and have it enlarged. I didn't have to ask any more questions.

When my tour was completed, Ms. Cathy led me back into the living room, placed a cup of hot coffee in front of me and began to search my eyes.

"You're okay now, child, aren't you?" My upper lip started to tremble. I nodded anyway.

"Yeah, I mean yes. Yes, Ms. Cathy, I'm okay."

She looked at me inquisitively, as if she couldn't quite put her finger on something that she knew was there. I sighed deeply.

"If you meant whether I'm off of drugs, yes I am. It's been almost two years now. I'm about to celebrate my two year anniversary in a couple of days."

"God bless you. I always knew you could do it. I believed in you, Victoria, always. You do know that, don't you?"

I started to cry. She inched over closer towards me on the couch, softly stroking my back with the palm of her hand.

"What is it? What is it? Victoria, why are you so sad?"

I leaned into her body and cried a lifetime of tears. She held me, rocking me ever so gently. Her touch, as mild as mother's milk. After I had shed every last tear that was left in my ducts, I pulled back and wiped my face with a napkin. Ms. Cathy never took her eyes off of my face.

"What is it, Victoria? Can you tell me now?"

Sniffles and sighs.

"Well, the truth is Ms. Cathy that I don't know. I just don't know. To the rest of the world, I'm doing just fine—to them it looks like I got my life back. But to me it feels like there's something missing. Something crucial, you know, something like . . .

I just . . ."

I sighed for a lack of appropriate words with which to continue. Descriptive words that could possible relate the gist of what I was trying to communicate, to process.

"I knew you'd be coming. I was expecting you."

I looked up at Ms. Cathy quickly, surprised, almost spooked. Goosebumps made a disorganized trail across my limbs.

"What did you say? Excuse me, but could you please repeat that?"

Ms. Cathy smiled.

"I said that I knew you were coming and that I was expecting you."

"Who, who . . . how?" I was stammering.

"Your mother told me you'd be coming."

Wide-eyed and aghast. "Huh, what the hell did you say? Mama, how?"

I got up from my seat and stood directly in front of her face, eye to eye.

"What are you trying to say Ms. Cathy? Don't play games with me now. Not now, please. I can't take it." And then, as if she didn't already know, "Mama's dead."

"Victoria, Victoria, calm down. You always were a jumpy one. Calm down. Of course, your mother's dead. I buried her myself. I'm not playing with you, child. Please, sit back down. If you give me a chance, a few minutes, I'll explain everything to you in one moment."

Still stunned and rather numb, I allowed myself to be led by the hand back to the living room sofa.

"I'll be right back." Ms. Cathy escaped through her bedroom door. I heard a closet door creak open slowly, the rustling of papery packages, and a quiet prayer. Whose?

She emerged from her room with a small old manila envelope. My name was written across its face in black magic marker in huge print. I recognized the handwriting as Ms. Cathy's. She approached me, wiped one lone tear off my cheek and explained how she knew I was coming. While doing so, she removed two items from the envelope, the gold chain I had given Mama as a present when I was fourteen years old and an audiotape. Ms. Cathy explained how Mama had given her the gold rope chain to hold just days after I had given it to her. Mama, she said, had known that she would sell it as soon as her "jones" came down on her. By giving it to Ms. Cathy to hold, she was guaranteed that the chain would be safe and protected from her own addictive behavior. I turned the chain over in my trembling fingers. It still bore the same inscription. "God Loves You, And So Do I, Victoria." I couldn't believe my eyes. Once again, tears were glistening in the corners of my eyes. The audiotape on the other hand, Ms. Cathy explained, had been given to her by Mama less than one week before she died. She shared how Mama had come to her early one morning, just as I had, to request that she give me this very same audiotape when I was ready. Mama briefly advised Ms. Cathy that I'd be seeking her out when the time was right. When Ms. Cathy queried her about how she would know when the time was right, how she would be able to tell, Mama looked her dead in her eyes and said, "You'll know. It's a divine appointment."

CHAPTER TWENTY

For with God all things are possible.
—Mark 10:27

MAMA HAD THOUGHT about me, considered me, left me something before she died. Why did Ms. Cathy hang on to such jewels for more than twelve years? I was furious, but I was more shocked. Feelings of shock washed over the anger, like varnish over wood. On the surface it appeared to erase it, as if deleting stray pen marks from a writing tablet. The ink color may have not been visible any longer, but the imprints were still there. I listened to Ms. Cathy provide a few more details about the night Mama had mysteriously arrived at her house with two treasures in hand and then I granted myself permission to bid her a quick "good-night." I'm not sure if Ms. Cathy discerned that I was angry at her. I'm similarly unsure if I invited her to my upcoming anniversary. I hurried out of her apartment in a flurry, as if her floors were paved with hot coals that were singing the soles of my feet. She didn't attempt to stop me.

    I spent the one and a half hour train ride back to Brooklyn with Mama's willed belongings clutched to my chest. When the train lurched to a stop at 125th Street in Harlem, an obviously "fiending" basehead stepped into my car and began to give me that familiar unctuous once over look—a quick scan of the exterior to determine what strengths and weaknesses lied within. I think I would have killed that motherfucker if he had made one iota of a contraindicated move in my direction. Nothing, and I meant nothing in the world was going to get in the way of my being able to hear the contents of Mama's audiotape as soon as I feasibly could. His radar must have been on target because the basehead quickly turned away and didn't come anywhere close to my direction. I don't remember any of the other specific thoughts that crossed my mind during my trip back home.

When at long last I arrived, I rushed into my apartment, practically knocking Mary over on her way out the door to work. She asked me what was wrong. I told her "nothing." Addicts have a sixth sense about when they shouldn't push you any further, when it would just be best to leave you the hell alone. Mary shrugged her shoulders and stepped forward to continue on with her day, obviously not unduly phased by my erratic behavior. Once I locked my bedroom door behind me, turned off the lights, and adjusted the shades so that most of the morning's sunlight was trapped on the other side of the curtains, an ethereal dim light was cast across my room. Like lacquer, it covered my furniture with an enamel of billowy swimming shadows. I slid the tape into my compact stereo system's cassette player and sat down on the edge of my bed with feet that were beginning to feel quite cold. I held my breath and pushed the play button. I'm not exactly sure when it was that I started to breathe again.

Mama's familiar throaty voice filled my room.

"Hi Victoria. I'm sure you never thought you'd be hearing from me again. I guess I always was full of surprises. I don't know when you'll get this tape and hear my message. But I'm sure that it will be at the right time. The time that you were supposed to hear it and take it all in.

In case you're wondering about when I did all of this, you're sixteen now, and me, I'm thirty-four. I just got out of Lincoln Hospital about five weeks ago and the truth is I ain't doing too good. I'm sorry 'bout all the coughing. I hope you can understand everything that I'm trying to say. I sure wouldn't want nothing to go wrong with my final message to my daughter. A daughter who I love very, very much.

Let me start at the beginning 'cause I'm picturing you sitting there, all pretty and all, wondering what the hell is going on. You probably still got your mouth open, don't ya'?

Well, Victoria, I ain't gotta go back too far. Unfortunately, you know it all. You know 'bout what happened to me when I was a kid. You know 'bout all of the drugs, 'bout the men, how I always had my ass out in the street. Like I said, ya' know it all, probably better then anybody else. You were there."

There was a momentary pause and a muffled sniffling sound.

"Sorry, but I'm trying real hard not to cry right now in the middle of explaining it all, but I started thinking 'bout how much you know about me being a bad mother. It was you who I treated bad."

Mama's sobs were interrupted by fits of coughing. Deep, phlegmy ones. Then she cleared her throat and there was silence. I felt scared, immediately stricken with fear that something had gone wrong with the tape, thinking that she wouldn't have the chance to finish now. As if she had a crystal ball in her hands and was able to read my future mind, my room was once again filled with her voice. Only this time, of a more hoarse quality.

"Sorry. Anyway, what you don't know, Victoria, is the fact that for the last few weeks that I spent on this earth, I didn't get high. I ain't used no drugs, not even meth. So everything I'm saying to you now, I'm saying with a clear head. Ain't that something? What happened was that after my meth was brought down to nothing after I was at Lincoln for about a week, I wanted to die. I didn't want to die because of the physical pain. And don't let nobody tell you no lies. AIDS hurts. I didn't want to die because I was dying anyway. I wanted to die because that morning when I woke up, I looked around 'dat hospital room and, for the first time, saw everything that I'd done. Seen it all, Victoria, right before my eyes. All the dumb shit I'd done to get in 'dat there hospital in the first place. What made it so bad was that I knew that there was nothing I could do about it. Nothing. That's when I thought about you and wanted to die.

Oh Victoria, I cried and I cried. I covered my face wid' 'dem ol' hospital pillows and I prayed to the God who I had always ignored before. I asked him to just kill me right there and then. There was no way I could think about you one second longer and not die of a broken heart. That's when the nurse came in. A big fat Jamaican one, I think. 'Dat nurse, she asked me what I was crying about. So, I told her. When I was through and told her that I didn't know what I was going to do anymore, that I wanted to die right there and then from all my pain, she asked me why I didn't stop trying so hard. Can you imagine? I thought she was the dumbest nurse in the whole world. Yeah right, stop trying so hard. I laughed. I laughed right there in that big dumb Jamaican nurse's face. I tol' her, 'Is you for real?' Stop trying so hard, 'dis here is where I got trying hard, where'd 'ya think I'd be if I stopped? I couldn't believe my ears, Victoria. Stop trying so hard. Yeah right. Then, as if that fat nurse knew what I was thinking about up inside my head, she laughed back at me, called me love and sweetheart and all, and told me that she hadn't meant it like that. That's when she held my hand and looked at me real hard. D'ya know what she said to me then, Victoria, d'ya know what 'dat big fat lady said to me then? She said, 'I mean why don't you stop trying so hard, and instead, let God do the trying for you. Let go and let God.' Something 'bout that moment, something about that moment and about what she said changed me, Victoria. Something happened inside me when 'dat fat nurse was talking to me and holding my hand. Don't think your mama gone and went crazy now, but all of a sudden I started to feel different laying up in 'dat there hospital room. Less stressed. If I didn't know nothing else, I knew that I was never gonna shoot no more drugs for as long as I lived."

Now it was my turn to press the pause button. I had to go to the bathroom, throw some cold water on my face, collect myself, and breathe. I returned to my original position, rigidly perched on the side of my bed. I pressed "play."

"Anyway, 'dat nurse gave me a whole bunch of information 'bout her church. She told me that it was real close and that I should come sometimes. She didn't have to tell me twice. 'Dat's why I left out of Lincoln so early 'dat day. I knew that you and Ms. Cathy would never believe me. Could ya' imagine me sitting there and telling y'all some mess 'bout me wanting to go to church? So, I didn't bother telling y'all nothing, but what I did do was sneak out of the hospital to go to an early prayer service. Y'all just knew 'dat I was off getting high. Since I had such a bad reputation with y'all, I didn't bother to tell you that that wasn't true. I just knew you'd never believe me. Why should ya' have? I almost didn't believe myself. Up until I couldn't walk no more from the AIDS, I went out to 'dat little church everyday. I even met a whole bunch of nice people there, Victoria. Good people. People who liked me and treated me nice. I told Ms. Cathy 'bout the church one or two times. I couldn't tell by her face if she believed me or not. You know how Ms. Cathy is.

For the first time in my life, Victoria. I felt good. Didn't have to use no drugs to feel good either. I was going to church, talking with my new friends, and praying up in the apartment at night. I don't know if you remember, but I even had me a little Bible. Now I know you know that I can't read, so I ain't gonna sit up here lying to you 'bout reading no Bible. I used to just like looking at it, touching it, ya' know. Pretending I was like everybody else when I prayed. I lived, Victoria, really lived, for the last few weeks before I died. So don't feel too bad, baby, at least I had a chance to do 'dat. I'm real grateful for it. There was only one problem and that problem was you. I was still suffering because of you.

I knew you'd already started messing around on the streets and all. I knew you wouldn't have believed nothing I had to say. And since you were already using yourself, I knew you couldn't hear me. I sure couldn't hear nobody when I was using. Not even you. I hope you believe that if I could have heard ya', if I could have heard just one word that you were trying to say to me Victoria, I would have listened. With both ears and my heart baby, with both ears and my heart.

So, I shut my big mouth and prayed. It almost killed me Victoria. I mean it almost killed me before I was ready to die naturally. The reason it almost killed me was because all the while I was forced to sit and watch my only child taking her first baby steps in my own rotten shoes. I had to sit back quietly and try to not do nothing to help. I had to continue listening to that lady's advice about not trying and letting God. And like I said, I had to suffer like this without having no drugs in my system. I prayed and I prayed, repeating the fat nurse's words over and over in my head 'let God.' I believed, but I ain't gonna lie Victoria. It's real hard to keep believing when the child you love is choosing the wrong path right there in front of you, especially when you know that it was your teachings and guidance that led her there. The worst part though, Victoria,

I mean the absolute worst, was that I had to believe enough that God could do it, would do it for me, knowing that I'd be dead and never have the chance to see for myself. Somebody in church tol' me that the words for that is 'blind faith.' Well, let me tell you something, having blind faith is one of the hardest things in life that you could ever do. At least it felt that way for me. Do ya' hear what I'm telling you child? Do ya' hear what I'm saying? Don't go and get yourself confused Victoria, not even for a minute. The only reason that I was able to do any of this was on the strength of my love for you."

There was a long period of silence. Just as I began to sense the taste of bile on my tongue, her voice came crackling back into my room again, stronger and more determined.

"Sorry, this is hard. Where was I? Oh yeah, blind faith. Well, what happened was that two nights ago, I thought I was finally going to die from too much suffering and too much worrying for sure. I got down on my knees, held that small old Bible real hard against my chest, and asked God to take just a little bit more pity on me. I didn't want to seem too greedy, ya' know. Anyway, I begged him to help me figure out a way that I could help you while I was still alive. I figured that if me and him put our heads together, we'd surely be able to think of something. He came to me in my dreams that night, put his hand on my shoulder and told me to leave you one final message on tape. This way you'd be able to hear it when you were ready. I guess God knew that I didn't know how to write. He told me to give the tape to Ms. Cathy and that he'd take care of the rest. It is only because of this dream that I know I will be able to die in peace."

There was some static and then silence. A second later, Mama's voice returned. Its soothing sound, filling the ears of her long-suffering child. A rose who had always been in aromatic pain.

"Victoria, what can I say? God, if it's the last thing I do in my life, please help me say the right thing to you now." Silence. A deep breath.

"Listen child, I'm your mother and I love you. I've always loved you. Oh, I know that you might find that hard to believe, probably even impossible, given the way I've been. But believe me, it's true. I swear it. Do you hear what I'm saying to you Victoria? You've got to hear every part. None of this was your fault. You did nothing wrong baby girl. Never. From the moment I laid eyes on you and named you, I knew that you were the sweetest, smartest, and most precious thing in the whole world. It's because I hated myself so much that I didn't know what to do about it, do about you. I had no idea how to be a good mother. I didn't know what being a good mother to you meant, and with 'dem drugs in me, I couldn't think. Not good thoughts anyway.

Listen and listen good Victoria, I wasted my life using drugs. All of it. There was something terribly wrong with me because that's a crazy thing to do. Now

I might have been crazy and that could explain a lot of things, but I was never so crazy that I stopped loving you. I always loved you, my little lady, always. It was the drugs that got in the way of my showing it. From where my head is at now, I want to tell you that all mothers love their children. All mothers, even drug addict ones. It's the drugs that make it seem like we've forgotten that. I know that I can't begin to ask you to forgive me. That would be asking way too much. Even I know that I don't deserve that. But what I am asking ya' for Victoria, the one last thing that your mama is begging ya' to do, is to remember your name. Remember who you are. Victoria, which stands for victory, strength, and power. Something inside me, maybe it's that thing they call mother's instinct, is telling me that you needing something real bad right now, baby girl. It's telling me that ya' need your mama real bad. Well, here I am baby. Here I am. And I'm here to tell you that I love you. I'm here to tell you to stop trying so hard sometimes. Don't follow behind in my old stupid stubborn footsteps. Pray. Let go, and let God. Listen to your old mama and let God. I'm here to tell you that you're special and you're gonna get through whatever it is that you're going through. My precious daughter, please, please don't ever forget to put yourself first. Remember the little baby girl who I once upon a time and long ago named Victoria. The one who is special. Daughter of Anita Rosa Gonzalez. Blessed child of God.

Go in peace and be happy baby. Your mama loves ya', always."

The tape ended and so did most of the madness inside my head.

CHAPTER TWENTY-ONE

God sometimes moves mountains one pebble at a time.
—Rebecca Barlow Jordan

I DON'T KNOW how long I stayed there sitting in the darkness of my room. It must have been for at least ten hours that I sat there, with the curtains drawn and my heart opening up little by little. I listened to Mama's tape, her "final message to her only daughter," until it was committed to memory. Then I listened to it again. By the seventh hour, I believe I got it, completely understood all that she was trying to tell me. Just to make certain, I sat there and pondered over her words for the next couple of hours and listened to the tape some more. By the time I emerged from my room, Mary had returned from work, eaten, and plopped down in front of our small television in the living room. It was already dark outside and, unlike most nights in the city, many of the stars were visible. I told Mary that I was going out to take a walk. At first she looked at me strangely, cocking her head to the side as if unsure about something. She approached me, stopping about six inches away and took me in her arms. Her hug was warm and generous and comforting. It was only then that I wondered whether she had heard Mama's voice repeating the same message over and over again from behind my closed door for the past several hours too. If she did or didn't, it didn't seem to matter. I smiled at her serenely when she released me and left out the door.

First, I walked to my sponsor's house. She must have been surprised to find me ringing her buzzer at such an appropriate hour. That must have been her first cue that something was terribly amiss, or at least, markedly different. When she opened the door and ushered me in, I spilled out all of the past day's events. Everything. Before I was able to share my feelings about how I believed the past several hours had changed me for life, I observed a radiant smile creeping across her face. It crept along with mincing steps with the joviality of a kitten pouncing on a piece of moving yarn. Her eyes were moist and beaming. Despite the fact that she already knew what I was about to tell her, she let me do it anyway. She permitted me the experience of giving utterance to the message from my own lips. At the end I thanked her, from the bottom of my heart. I told her that I understood now that it was always God who had carried me through the trials and tribulations of my life. My one and only remaining question was why she had never mentioned that he had also sent down one of his angels disguised as an NA sponsor to be my guiding light.

Once I left my sponsor's apartment, I headed on over to Thomas. We hadn't spoken for about five days and he was surprised to see me. Pleasantly so. I mentioned nothing to him about my impulsive dash to the Bronx or Mama's tape. I didn't tell him that things seemed clearer now. Better and more settled. I didn't tell him anything except that I loved him and how my love for him was like the color blue. That seemed to be enough. He smiled and embraced me in a way that told me that he understood everything. Even the things that I didn't say. I didn't sleep in my own bed again until three nights later.

I spent the last couple of days before my second NA anniversary celebration taking care of two very important items of business. The first was to invite all of my guests. People who played an important role in my life, now or in the past. People who I hoped would be a part of my future. The second thing I needed to do was pay Mama another visit and make amends.

I invited all of my NA peers with whom I had shared special moments, clients from the different clinics where I attended therapy, and several of the people who I trusted from my job. I invited Mary and Thomas and Opal and Alex. I trucked back on up to the Bronx to my old high school to invite the teachers who were still there who I believed had believed in me. I invited the ones who didn't as well. The fact that I had to admit my ultimate character defect to all of these people, that I was a drug addict, didn't bother me as it once would have in the past. I let the feelings go. My only regret—a major one—was that I could not find Ms. Cathy when I went back to her apartment to present her with my verbal invitation. Unable to accept the fact that I couldn't personally invite her, nor thank her for all that she had done, I stood outside her door, tapping a steady beat with my knuckles and calling out her name until a neighbor stuck her head out and told me that she wasn't home. She must have been a new tenant in the building because she didn't recognize me. Instead, Ms. Cathy's new neighbor looked at me nervously, clutching her door between tautly stretched fingers, clearly involved in a solitary silent contemplation over whether I was planning on robbing the apartment or not. When I asked her if she'd be kind enough to give Ms. Cathy my phone number, she told me to stick a note under the door before she hurriedly closed her own. Exasperated that I had left Ms. Cathy's invitation to the last minute, I reluctantly headed back to the train station that would eventually take me home to Brooklyn.

I had to make a meeting and then review the anniversary meeting's procedures with my sponsor for the next day's celebration. I also had one more very important order of business to take care of after work on the following day. I had to make my amends with Mama.

The next day, I left my job a few hours early and headed back uptown. This time, I felt whole and receptive, in absence of the rage and grief that I had carried with me before when I went to Mama's grave. This time I had a purpose, one that was sound and pure of heart.

I arrived about two hours before dusk. I walked straight through the cemetery's gates in an august manner, excited by the prospect of forgiveness. I nodded to passersby who were in different stages of mourning as they passed me by on the neatly paved cement street. I walked up to Mama's grave with a sense of purpose and a small plastic bag tucked under my arm. For the first ten or so minutes I just sat. I sat quietly and still, remembering the past, hearing her words, feeling her presence. It was only after I felt a spiritual connection with her that I spoke aloud.

"Mama, hello again. It's me, Victoria. Uh, I brought you something to make up for the way I acted the last time I was here. This way you'll also have a little something to remind you of me always." I took a six-inch round plaque out of the plastic bag. It was a mahogany colored plaque, about the size of a medium dinner plate. On its face was an inscription in gold block print letters. Its message was one and the same with the one on Mama's charm which I now wore around my neck. "God Loves You. And So Do I, Victoria." I placed Mama's gift up against the stone slate that marked her grave. I continued.

"Mama, I thank you. Despite everything that happened in our lives together, I now know that you did the best you could and I thank you for that. I thank you for teaching me about the gift of acceptance. Just as I know that I am with fault, I accept that you were not perfect either. I heard and believe every word that you said on the tape. You have no idea how much you've helped me. How much I needed to hear your voice. And most of all Mama, you don't know what it meant to me to hear you say that you loved me. Today, I believe that your message was truly facilitated by God. What was it that Ms. Cathy said you called it, oh yeah, a divine appointment. Your message was definitely a divine appointment, Mama. A divine appointment that saved my life.

Mama, oh Mama, how I used to love you so. You were my world, you know. My whole world. I'm so sorry that your star angels came when they did, so late, when your life was almost over. Yet, I heard the happiness in your voice and understand that I should feel gratitude about the fact that they came at all. That you were able to feel alive and free for a few weeks at the end is more than many can boast of, and much more than I ever imagined to have been true for you. I'm grateful, that at least at the end, you were able to enjoy the angels' gift.

Guess what, Mama? In just a few hours, I'll be celebrating my second anniversary. Two whole years clean. Ain't you proud? I want you to be there, Mama, looking down from the heavens smiling with them beautiful eyes of yours. I'm giving you a personal invitation now. Please come. Don't worry about me, Mama. I'll be all right. Recovery is a beautiful thing, you know. Before I say good-bye, I want you to know that your message filled a void in me. Without your help, I'd still have a big gaping hole right in the center of my heart. I'm more complete now, able to feel your love, Mama. Able to feel other people's love too. And do you know what else, now I feel God's love. For the first time in my life, I know that I have a higher power in my life who loves me, and who carries me when I'm too weak to go on by myself. Like you said, Mama. God's love is a wonderful feeling. A beautiful thing. A blessing.

I'll take your advice from now on and I'll try letting go sometimes. I'll try letting God. I'll try to live up to my name Mama, make you proud. I'll try to be the best I can be. You did good Mama, real good. God bless you and rest in peace. I'll always love you too."

With watery eyes, I made my way away from Mama's grave back to Brooklyn to celebrate my two years of sobriety.

The train broke down. Approximately fifteen minutes later a frustrated sounding conductor started making apology announcements about the projected one hour delay. My anniversary meeting was scheduled to begin at eight. I arrived a little after nine. This left me about fifteen minutes to speak. There were many in the rooms who believed I had relapsed into my recent deteriorated state of mind and wasn't coming. My sponsor wasn't one of them. Mary later told me how she had dismissed all doubt that might have been growing in the minds of some of my guests by telling them a small fib. She assured my audience that although a matter of urgent business was unexpectedly going to detain me for "just a bit," I'd be coming right along. Mary told me that she had laughed heartily to my audience, pronouncing that wild horses couldn't drag me away from this event. She was right. To accelerate my traveling speed, I jumped into a cab instead of taking the bus once I disembarked on the other side of Brooklyn from a train which had been forced to take an alternate route. From the backseat, I prayed to God that the driver would hurry the hell up. Addicts. I guess I still had a proclivity for drama as part of my repertoire of character defects. In the end my lateness to the meeting proved to be no big deal. The only thing that happened as a result was that the group leader shifted the order of speakers, leaving me for last. Once I arrived and saw the turn out of people who had come on my behalf, I quickly understood that while I might have been last, I was definitely not least.

My sponsor was waiting for me outside. I observed her as my cab rolled up in front of the back of the old church school building where my second anniversary was being held, pacing slightly and pulling deep drags off her cigarette. Her hands were already pulling at me as I bent back into the cab to pay the driver. I'm not sure that she understood one word that I was trying to tell her about visiting Mama and the train breaking down. To her, what mattered was that I had arrived for my second anniversary, clean and sober. Whatever circuitous route I needed to take to get me there, in her estimation, was all good and part of the plan. My divine plan.

The previous speaker was just ending as I entered the building. I sat in the back. The group leader quickly announced my arrival, making a small good-natured joke about my tardiness. Something to the effect that we addicts love making grand entrances. I smiled. If only he knew. I quickly walked to the front of the room. My heart raced. I turned around and saw a sea of friendly smiling faces. With few exceptions, they were all there. All of them. All the people from my past and present who I cherished. Held dear to my heart. They were all there smiling warm, beaming smiles, clapping, celebrating my recovery. My sponsor, Thomas. Mary, Opal and Alex were seated in the front. Thomas blew me kisses and looked as proud and happy as I had ever seen him. My NA peers were scattered around the room, some alone and others in small cliques. In the back sat a row of my fellow employees. My eyes pivoted around older versions of the faces of the two teaching staff from my high school days. I couldn't believe my eyes. I saw Ms. Rivera, looking like she had been crying but didn't want anybody to know. Next to her sat one of the staff who had not liked me back in those days, who I believed had been racist, who had gone against me. I guess I was not the only one who learned the lesson about the spirit of acceptance and forgiveness. Just as I was opening my mouth to speak, I saw her from the corner of my eye. Two wizened saucers of azure blue beneath a shroud of golden hair, peeking out at me from a chair on the far side of the room. Her expression, peaceful and contented, omniscient. Ms. Cathy had somehow gotten my message and come. Although I couldn't see her, I knew that Mama was also there. Her spirit, hovering about the room. I felt her presence. She was a part of me. I touched the gold chain from so long ago that I wore around my neck, looked up to the ceiling and prayed. Then I began.

"Hi, my name is Victoria and I'm a sick and suffering addict and . . ." A wave of sentimentality washed over me and I started to cry. I turned away. I couldn't go on, couldn't talk. Tears poured from my eyes while visions of my past danced around in my head. Visions of me as a little girl. A pure one. A wounded one. Visions of Bruny. I almost broke out into a fit of nervous laughter thinking about how Bruny would have cursed me out if she saw me standing up there crying in front of my two years of sobriety anniversary celebration. I had visions of colorful fields strewn with lollipops. Visions of me getting high, Trevor, jail, Smooth, and Johnny. I had images of a younger and prettier Ms. Cathy, Jose "el salvaje," and the infamous Stinkdog. I saw them all. Characters from the scenes of my life. Nostalgic memories that gushed forth from my heart, lolling along the salty ebb and flow of my tears. That's when I saw Mama. A tranquil, unalloyed Mama who found her bliss before she departed from this world. She was smiling in my vision, transported to an isle of serenity that I have yet to visit. I remembered her words, wiped the tears off my face with the back of my hand, and turned back to my guests, a refreshed woman who was two years into recovery. Curiosity, sympathy, and patience characterized the faces of my awaiting friends and adopted family. My voice boomed with newly found strength across the floor.

"Hi, my name is Victoria and I'm an addict and I got something to say to you." With the comforting hand of my higher power resting on my shoulder, I said it all.

EPILOGUE

June 30, 2003

THREE YEARS HAVE passed. I just completed my fifth year anniversary. Fewer guests attended this time. Yet, it was still a memorable, joyous occasion. One of the missing guests was Ms. Cathy. She died of a heart attack about three months after my second year anniversary. I have often sat back and marveled over how the timing of her death was so intricately woven into my divine plan. At the same time knowing that her ascension into heaven to finally join her beloved Jose was another divine appointment as well. Hers. I visit Ms. Cathy's grave twice a year. Once on her birthday, and once on the day before my own NA anniversary. She was an instrumental part of my recovery process. I'm in college now, slowly earning a degree in social work. I have a job in a group home working with disadvantaged youth. Problem children. Kids like me. Whenever my heart fills with pain after looking into the familiar eyes of a suffering child, I work as best as I can, do the best that I can do. Then I sit back, let go, and let God do the rest. We all have our celestial plans and divinely appointed times in which to complete them.

I still wear Mama's chain around my neck. I feel her fleeting presence from time to time. She's a part of me. Every once in a while when I get down and need a boost, I replay her tape and allow the message behind her words to sink in and comfort me. I understand now that Mama loved me and so does God.

I still attend meetings and I still talk with my sponsor, regularly. I will never forget the importance of it all, and so I "keep coming back."

Thomas asked me to marry him on the evening that I celebrated my third anniversary. I did. We have a good relationship. A solid marriage. One night after we had been married for over a year, I asked him what color would best describe his love for me and held my breath. He smiled, took me in his arms and said, "Every last color in the rainbow, baby." I was satisfied.

Six months ago, I had a baby boy. He was born in good health, with no complications, in a reputable hospital. After the delivery, when Thomas reached across my bed to take my hand in his and asked me what I'd like to name our son, I looked into my baby boy's big brown eyes, and without a second thought, said "Victor—for victory, strength, and power."

The End

BVG